PRAISE FOR BE

AUTHOR STELLA CAMERON AND HER NOVELS

"A BEAUTIFUL, EMOTIONAL BOOK WITH A HAUNTINGLY LYRICAL QUALITY."
—*Affaire de Coeur*

"A SENSUAL, ROLLICKING LOVE STORY ABOUT THE MISCHIEVOUS, MADCAP SIDE OF LOVE."
—*A Little Romance on Bride*

"CAMERON LEAVES YOU BREATHLESS, SATISFIED . . . AND HUNGRY FOR MORE."
—Elizabeth Lowell

"A MARVELOUSLY TALENTED HISTORICAL AUTHOR."
—*Romantic Times*

Also by Stella Cameron

Bride*
Breathless
Charmed
Fascination
His Magic Touch
Only by Your Touch
Pure Delights
Sheer Pleasures
True Bliss

*Available from
Warner Books

STELLA CAMERON

BELOVED

A Time Warner Company

For Maureen Walters

WARNER BOOKS EDITION

Cover design by Elaine Groh
Cover illustration by Bob Maguire

Warner Books, Inc.
1271 Avenue of the Americas
New York, NY 10020

A Time Warner Company

Visit our web site at
http://pathfinder.com/twep

Printed in the United States of America

First Printing: October, 1996

10 9 8 7 6 5 4 3 2 1

AUTHOR'S NOTE

Castle Kirkcaldy doesn't exist, but the village of Dunkeld is very real, as is Charlotte's Square in Edinburgh. The land of the Rossmaras is as beautiful in fact as it is in fiction, and I hope many of you will visit Scotland.

The Franchots are Cornish. Not far west of the charming gray-stone town of Fowey are the wild hills where I imagined Franchot Castle.

London was once my home. As with all other locations in FASCINATION, CHARMED, BRIDE, and BELOVED, I've walked every mile with the Rossmaras, the Franchots, and the Avenalls. London is an incredible city, unchanged in so many ways. If you stand on Bond Street today and pretend, you will swear you can see Ella, or Justine, or Pippa, or Grace, each carrying a hatbox, perhaps!

If you're ever in Maidenhead, in Berkshire, you may come upon a lovely tudor house called Beehive Manor. Beehive Manor was the Dog and Partridge Inn when Ella and Saber stayed there. You may stay at the Beehive Manor today, as I have.

Travel to the north Cotswolds, to Worcestershire, and the ancient village of Bretforten, and you'll find The Fleece, a National Trust inn dating from the sixteenth century. Bretforten Manor, owned by Queen Elizabeth I in 1576 (and another lovely place to spend a night or so if you're in the area), still looks very much as I have described it.

—Stella Cameron

Chapter One

London, 1828

Only madmen see Sibley's ghost.

"Your call, I believe, Avenall."

Saber, Earl of Avenall, heard his name and remembered to breathe again. "Sorry, Langley. I'll fold."

Mumbling into a glass of hock, Lord Langley squinted at his cards.

Only madmen see Sibley's ghost.

Probably true, Saber decided. After all, he'd doubted his own sanity for four years—ever since the first endless days and nights of half-life after he'd been left for dead by a hill tribe in India.

And now any doubt had been removed. He must be mad.

Dressed in a flowing gray gown, its head and shoulders draped about with a drifting gray veil, the ghost of Sibley's Club stood, quite still, upon a small raised platform at one end of the smoking room.

"Things aren't what they used to be, eh, Langley?" Sir

Arthur Best remarked querulously. Ropes of twisted blue veins showed in his thin, ancient hands. "Time was when there were five or six full tables in this room every night. Deep play in those days, too. When there wasn't a poetry reading or a damn good political wrangle in progress, eh?"

Langley inclined his head. Meager light glimmered on his mane of white hair. Coals burned low in a smoke-stained marble fireplace, as low as the candles guttering in sconces around mahogany-paneled walls.

Saber's skin prickled. He was grateful that his overlong hair served to shadow the pallor he felt upon his face.

"Thomas," Colonel Fowles, the fourth at the table, summoned a hovering steward. "The fire, man! And two more bottles."

"Make it three," Langley said.

They didn't see it.

Of course not. They were old, but not mad. He was a young man in an old men's club, and he was quite insane.

Saber rested his jaw on a fist and contrived to look toward the velvet-curtained dais without entirely turning his head.

The ghost revolved, its full silken robe billowing wide, only to wrap tightly about the form—or should that be lack of form?—as it reversed direction.

A female form. Oh, certainly. Very female.

Coals clattered in the grate.

The colonel coughed, his lungs rattling as if in an empty cavern. He cleared his throat. "Fine weather for March, hmm?"

"Should say so," Sir Arthur agreed. Purplish hammocks of skin hung beneath his eyes. "The gay young things will be showin' off their finery in the Park, no doubt."

"I'm feelin' good enough to chase a gay young thing or two meself," the colonel announced, guffawing, before another gale of coughing shook him.

Sir Arthur's pale eyes flickered to his companion. "I might

just keep you company, sir," he said, chuckling. "Never felt better meself, either."

The platform was intended for readings and the like. Heavy gold ropes looped back the deep-red, faintly dusty curtains at each side. The lady in gray hovered near one of those curtains.

Lady?

A ghost was a ghost. Plain and simple. A manifestation of who knew what?

Saber looked from one of his companions to another. They studied their cards, clearly oblivious to any apparition.

But they were not mad.

Thomas returned, passing within feet of . . . She danced! *Danced.* Twirling, her feet barely touched the boards. Ghosts' feet didn't have to touch anything, did they? Saber glared at Thomas. The man proceeded serenely past the dancing spirit, his face in its customary impassive folds.

Sibley's ghost was a joke! Tales of sightings were without foundation. The names of those who had supposedly seen the thing, and been borne away in restraining jackets, were unknown.

Saber closed his eyes tightly and opened them again.

Her ankles were slim. As she turned, a suggestion of shapely calf showed.

He became hot, then, just as quickly, deeply cold once more.

"Fill Avenall's glass," Langley bellowed. "The man looks positively peaked. The young aren't what they used t'be. What d'you say, Best?"

"Couldn't agree with you more," Sir Arthur said. "Fill 'em all around, Thomas."

Tall and slender. A slender waist and small but curvaceous hips.

Sweat broke on Saber's brow. He sat straighter, but bent his face over his drink and trained his eyes on his laced fingers.

Surely there was the faintest shuffling of . . . slippers on wood?

"Should think it's about time to replace those curtains," Langley announced loudly. "Old place is lookin' a bit frayed around the edges, wouldn't you say?"

Muttered assent followed.

The curtains?

Saber raised his gaze to Langley, who stared directly at the red velvet curtains . . . flanking the platform . . . where . . . "I rather like a nice patina of age on things," he ventured, all but swallowing his words. If he continued to sit mute someone might twig his discomfort.

"Patina?" Sir Arthur Best filled his sunken jowls with air, then pouted before shaking his head. He regarded the curtains in question. "Might be a good thing on fine silver, I suppose. Hmm. Patina, eh? Hardly think it applies to threadbare velvet. A coat of polish wouldn't hurt the floor, either. Now, that'd produce a little patina, what?" He laughed at his own weak humor.

Langley and Colonel Fowles slapped their knees and rocked in their chairs. "Floor polish," they sputtered in unison, pointing at each other. "Pa-patina!"

Saber slid his eyes toward the stage.

Long, elegant hands wove slowly upward to wrap at the wrist high above the veiled head. The body undulated.

There was a sound. The slippers did make a soft scuffing.

Silk clung to small, pointed breasts as if those breasts were concealed by nothing other than that silk, nothing other than thin, floating silk . . .

He shifted in his seat.

A spear of arousal hit with a force that was sweet agony.

Aroused by a ghost!

"I certainly do feel fit," Langley said. "And I do believe my wits grow sharper as I grow older."

Sir Arthur downed the contents of his glass and smacked his lips. He leaned back in his chair. "I was about to say the same thing myself. A regular game of cards, gettin' about a bit, and good company. That's what I put it all down to."

"A three-bottle man always has the edge, I say," Colonel Fowles roared, raising a glass in one hand, a bottle in the other. "When the wine's in, the wit's . . . the wit's in too, I say."

Saber frowned. The rising babble raked his nerves. He came here to St. James's Street from his rooms in Burlington Gardens to escape any possible visitors—and to find peace. He'd chosen membership in a club frequented by antiquarian gentlemen because no one from his former life would consider tolerating such dull company. No one except his determined friend, Devlin North, and even Devlin avoided the place unless he was too foxed to give a damn about his surroundings.

Burlington Gardens would have been a better choice tonight. Even the disapproving comments of his gentleman's gentleman, Bigun, would be preferable to this jabbering tribe—and the sensual ghost on the stage.

"D'you remember the old story about the ghost, Thomas?" Langley asked suddenly.

Saber jumped.

"Y'know the one, man?"

"My lord," Thomas said, making a valiant effort to straighten his permanently stooped shoulders. "Certainly do, my lord."

"D'you recall the name of the madman who last saw her?"

A crawling sensation attacked Saber's insides. He raised his glass to eye level and swirled the contents rapidly. From the corner of his eye he noted a slowing of the apparition's dance.

How long could a ghost's manifestation last?

Thomas scratched his head and bunched up his face. "Can't say as I do recall who it was, your lordship. Before my time. There was a mention of it in the book."

"Bring the book," Saber demanded abruptly. He'd forgotten the bloody book.

Sir Arthur poured more hock. "Good idea," he said. "Bring the book, Thomas."

"Can't do that, Sir Arthur," Thomas muttered. "That would have been the one before the one before the present book. Never did know where that one went."

Saber pounded the gaming table. "Find the thing anyway!"

"I say." Langley tapped Saber's arm. "Steady on, old chap."

If he didn't control himself, they'd realize he was unbalanced. Saber shrugged. "Thought it might be entertaining. Forget it, Thomas."

"Good thing madness doesn't run in families," Colonel Fowles noted.

Lord Langley arched his neck inside his stiff collar. "No madness in my family, I can tell you that."

"Nor mine," Sir Arthur said.

Shifting gray, with the floating quality of cobweb gossamer, wafted at the edge of Saber's vision. "Where's it written that madness doesn't run in families?" he asked, aware of the truculence in his voice.

Graceful hands lowered and rose again, taking the veil with them.

Saber's heart stopped beating.

The veil swirled in circles above sleek black hair.

He dared not look at her directly. Somehow he must get out of here, out and away before his condition was noted—before he said something that would brand him crazed.

Colonel Fowles said, "It's a scientific fact. About strong families having strong minds."

Saber's hands shook. He set down his glass.

"Never a whisper of that sort of thing in my bloodlines," Sir Arthur said.

Saber bowed his head and contrived to tilt his face just enough to see his ghostly nemesis more clearly. Straight and shimmering, the black hair fell well past her shoulders. Her brows winged gently upward over dark, almond-shaped eyes. Rather than waxen or transparent, her skin bore a golden sheen and a rosy tint colored a full mouth some might consider too large.

Her mouth was not too large.

Not too large for a ghost?

He was completely mad!

She smiled. She smiled and wiggled the fingers of her right hand enticingly. At him.

Saber's eyes swiveled to his companions. All three studied the yellowing molded ceiling.

He returned his attention to the stage and barely grabbed his glass before he would have knocked it to the floor.

"Probably time I got along home," Colonel Fowles announced.

"Probably," Saber said evenly. He did not add that the colonel should leave before he admitted he'd seen a ghost. And the colonel had definitely seen her.

Langley stirred and checked his fob watch. "Yes, indeed. Lady Langley worries if I'm too late."

Would that be the same Lady Langley who was supposedly in Northumberland to attend the birth of her daughter's latest child? Langley, too, must get away. He had also encountered an "apparition" and feared—despite his marvelously stable family—that he'd be branded a lunatic.

Damn, but she made a beautiful ghost. How long was it since he'd last seen her? Three years, of course. Three years while he'd ignored her letters, and refused to see her—as much as he'd longed to do so.

"I'll come out with you, then," Sir Arthur said, pushing back his chair. "Call my carriage, will you, Thomas?"

The steward retreated so quickly he all but fell into the echoing, stone-flagged vestibule.

Another man fearful for his sanity.

Saber rose with the others.

She had grown still. He felt her stillness, her will demanding that he remain where they would be alone—and he would be forced to confront her.

"You too, Avenall?" the colonel asked. "Calling it a night, are you?"

"A lady awaits me, also," he announced, loudly enough for anyone to hear.

Sir Arthur chuckled and slapped Saber's back. "The fair Countess Perruche? We've all heard about her, man. Exotic, eh? *Demanding?* From what they say, it's a marvel you can tear yourself away at all."

Saber looped an arm around Langley's shoulders and ambled toward the door. "A man has to get his strength back now and again," he told them.

They all laughed. Men together, they strolled from the room.

Saber knew that Best, Langley, and Fowles controlled their urges to run from the "ghost" each thought he, alone, saw.

How had she learned the legend of Sibley's Ghost?

How had she gained entrance to so male a sanctum?

How? Hah! By using the quicksilver mind that seemed to curl around his even now.

Without another glance, Saber did what he had to do. He walked past the only woman he would ever love, the woman he could never bear to burden with the dark, damaged thing he had become.

He walked past, and away, from the most beautiful, vibrant creature in the world—Ella Rossmara.

"Ella Rossmara!" Dressed in a peach-colored satin night robe, Lady Justine, Viscountess Hunsingore, rose from a chair by the window in Ella's bedchamber. "There you are at last. Close the door and present yourself at once. At once, do you hear? What have you done? Where have you been? Explain yourself. If your father awakens and misses me you will have more than my disapproval to deal with, miss. Out and about in the middle of the night wearing . . . wearing . . . Oh, sin's ears, this is the veriest muddle. Tell me—"

Ella interrupted her adoptive parent. "Please, Mama! How can I explain anything if you will not be quiet long enough for me to speak?" She closed the door and leaned against it.

With one long forefinger jabbing the air, Mama approached, her limp more pronounced than usual. "Do not take that tone with me, young lady. You have quite frightened me out of my wits. What is that thing you're wearing?"

"A ghost costume." *Oh, perish a foolish girl's careless mouth.*

Mama's mouth formed soundless words. Her lovely amber eyes grew quite round.

Without thinking Ella said, "Who is Countess Perruche?" *Oh, fie!*

"Ella!"

"Mama?"

"I shall rouse your papa at once."

"I shall cry if you do."

"No you won't. You never cry. Where have you been?"

Ella pressed her hands to her cheeks and willed herself to be calm and sensible. "To Sibley's Club in St. James Street."

Once more Mama's voice failed. She backed to the little pink damask chair and sat again—with an audible *bump*.

"I had to—"

Mama held up a silencing hand. "That is a gentlemen's club, Ella."

"Yes."

"You went *inside* this place?"

"Yes."

"You . . . How did you get there?"

"Potts—"

"Potts!" Mama closed her eyes for an instant. "Naturally. How can I even think of chiding the poor man? He is butter in your wheedling fingers."

"I seem to recall that he is also butter in your fingers, Mama." Potts had been a coachman in the employ of Mama's family for more years than he claimed to remember. After her marriage, Mama had persuaded him to work for the Rossmaras. "Papa has told me how you made some risky journeys in Potts's company." Potts invariably did his best to dissuade his employers from questionable excursions, but could always be relied upon to do as he was asked eventually—and to hold his tongue.

"We will not refer to those occasions. Why did you go to this club?"

"To make Saber see me."

Silence followed. Mama sat further back in the chair. Saber was her cousin, and she loved him dearly. She plucked at the ribbons on her robe and turned her face away.

"Saber belongs to Sibley's Club. He goes there frequently. I found out a legend about a ghost that only madmen see, and I pretended I was that ghost."

"Oh, Ella, how could you?"

"You know how I could! I love him and he loves me, yet he will not even *see* me."

"He will not see any of us. He has not seen any of us for years—not since, well, not for years."

"I love him," Ella repeated stubbornly.

"You think you love him. You're little more than a child."

Ella tossed the gray veil on top of her pink counterpane. "I am twenty. And, in case you have forgotten, I am in London at the urging of you and Papa because you want to get rid of me."

"Ella!"

"Well, anyway." Mama's stricken expression chastened Ella. "I'm sorry. You don't want to get rid of me, but you do want me to find a husband and marry. Children don't marry, or they shouldn't. So you must consider me a woman, mustn't you?"

The ribbons suffered considerable punishment. "You will always try to twist my words," Mama said.

"No. For three years you have urged me to make a Season. Surely that means I am all but an old maid by now."

Mama's chin rose. "Since there was a certain Lady Justine Girvin who did not marry until she was an ancient of five and thirty, I doubt if that same lady considers you an old maid."

Mama referred to herself. Hoping only to be near him, she had followed the man she loved to Scotland and become not only his good friend, but his wife. Struan, Viscount Hunsingore, had swept Justine away and refused to accept less than her hand in marriage.

Orphaned Ella and her younger brother, Max, had already had the great fortune to be rescued from dire circumstances by the viscount. After the marriage the couple had promptly adopted Ella and Max. That had been three years earlier and there were now two more small Rossmaras at home in Scotland. Edward was two and his sister, Sarah, just a year old.

"I asked about Countess Perruche," Ella persisted.

A flush rose on Mama's cheeks.

Ella tapped a toe impatiently. "What does it mean when a

lady is referred to as *demanding*? And when a gentleman says he needs time away from her to regain his strength?"

Mama closed her eyes and kept them closed.

"Is she a ladybird?"

"You know entirely too much, my girl." Mama rallied and sat quite straight. "These are not matters for an innocent like yourself to consider."

"Innocent?" Ella tossed her head. "I have seen things—"

"Do *not* mention that. You are an innocent. If your father and I could erase the memories, we would. We are grateful you were blindfolded through much of your time in that place. But regardless, what you were forced to witness did not touch your person, thank goodness. You are not only innocent, you are the dearest daughter any parent could have. I will not listen to you saying otherwise."

Unfamiliar tears sprang into Ella's eyes, and she turned quickly away. "I love you," she said softly.

She heard Mama sniff before she said, "Come here. We must talk about this situation. We should have talked about it a long time ago."

Ella went to her and sat on a plump tapestry stool near her feet. "He pretended he did not see me," she mumbled.

Mama stroked her hair and placed a kiss on her brow. "I know the legend. Surely no man would admit to seeing a ghost at Sibley's unless he was prepared to be considered insane."

"True. But I took off my veil and I *know* Saber recognized me—even though he never looked at me directly."

"Ella! What of the other gentlemen there?"

"All about two hundred years old and all pretending they saw nothing. They'll never mention the incident. Saber could have remained behind if he'd wanted to."

"That is an extraordinary gown," Mama said, perusing the gray silk more closely. "What exactly is beneath it?"

Ella hunched her shoulders. "Nothing."

"Nothing?"

"Nothing, Mama. It's supposed to appear ethereal. Undergarments might spoil the impression."

"The lack of undergarments presents far too *much* impression. Where did you acquire the . . . Where did you get that thing?"

"I cannot say," Ella told her. "Please do not ask again." Rose, a favorite maid, had been coerced into buying the garment from a woman who made theatrical costumes.

"If your papa learns of this we shall undoubtedly ask about the finer points again." A faraway expression entered Mama's eyes. "How did Saber appear? Is he completely recovered from his injuries, do you think?"

Ella's frustration resurfaced with fresh force. "His hair is long. It curls over his collar. I saw nothing more than his sideways glances while he pretended I was not there. But when he left he stood straight and walked well." She swallowed. Sad longing crept about her heart. "He is Saber and I love him. Why has he decided to ignore me?"

"Who told you this ghost story?"

"Do not change the subject," Ella said, changing the subject herself. "Tell me about Countess Perruche? Have you heard of her?"

"She is French," Mama said simply. "A toast with a great many vague rumors circulating about her. Some refer to her as a courtesan sought after by many men who want . . . I cannot imagine Saber having any connection to her."

"He said he would love me forever."

Mama's hand grew still in Ella's hair. "You never told me that."

"I was a child then. When Papa first brought Max and me to Cornwall and we all met you. Saber told me he would look after me forever—that I could always go to him. He helped me when I discovered my birth mother had died."

"Ah, yes."

"I have not forgotten even if he has," Ella said vehemently. "And if he has forgotten I shall find a way to remind him."

"Ella—"

"This French toast had best seek another admirer. Not that I believe for a moment that Saber would dally with such a person. I only agreed to this Season because I heard he was in London. He is trying to deny his natural desires, and it will not do. It will not do at all."

"Oh, Ella, please—"

"No! No, I shall not be diverted. Some might consider this evening's events a calamity. I see them in quite another light."

"You are so headstrong." Mama held Ella's face between her hands. "We will talk to your father, my poppet. I know he will consider your plea, but you cannot assume that his wishes and yours will be the same. And, in the end, we must abide by his decisions—even if we do not always fully appreciate his wisdom. Promise me you will go on no more wild excursions, and that you will allow us to deal with these matters for you."

"By all means deal with whatever you can, as long as it means Saber and I are together at last." She heard her own demanding tones but could not turn back. "If I made him uncomfortable tonight, just wait until I decide how to approach him next!"

"Sin's ears! I shall have to watch you every moment. We cannot have you running around in the night. You will be ruined. And, lest you forget the way of things entirely, we are in London to launch you. We shall do so admirably, I assure you. I, too, embrace the power of love, but there can be no question of any hasty decisions regarding your future."

Ella collected herself. She was being foolish. Under no circumstances must she risk her freedom. "I am being silly." She laughed lightly. "This has been too much. Too long a day and night after all the excitement of arriving in London. The modiste. The shopping. Getting ready for such lovely affairs. Don't worry for another instant."

Mama narrowed her eyes. "You change your tune too quickly, my girl. Don't think you can trick me so easily."

"I mean it." Lying was wrong, but her life was at stake—any chance she might have for happiness. "Isn't there a soiree the day after tomorrow?"

"Yes," Mama said slowly, still looking deeply suspicious. "The first major event of the Season. The Eagletons' soiree. It will be good to see James and Celine again. It's been too long."

"I'm so looking forward to that," Ella said. "I must decide what to wear." What she wore concerned her not one bit. She would direct a note to Saber at once, informing him that she would hope to see him at the Eagletons'. Not that he would respond—or appear—but meanwhile she would contemplate her next move.

"There was a particular reason for my visiting your rooms this evening," Mama said in a tone that assured Ella's complete attention. "Your papa had suggested we await further developments before mentioning the subject to you. I decided I would at least give you a hint that something momentous may be afoot. Men do not always understand the way a woman's mind works, do they?"

There was something indefinable, something ominous hidden in those words. "You are the expert on these things." Mama had written a book on the subject of relationships between men and women, a famous volume that Ella had yet to be allowed to read. "What exactly is this momentous something?"

With the rustle of sumptuous satin, Mama got to her feet

once more. "Nothing definite yet. Not until Struan has received them."

Ella wrinkled her brow and got up too. "Them? Until Papa receives whom? What can you mean?"

"I really mustn't go entirely against his wishes. You shall learn about it tomorrow if he decides there is something we should consider."

"Consider?" Ella all but squealed. "Consider *what?*"

"Ooh"—Mama waved a hand airily—"I do not know them personally. I'm not even entirely certain how well Struan is acquainted with them." She approached the door.

"I shall explode! You cannot leave me with such intriguing hints and nothing more."

"Tomorrow, Ella. You must be patient until tomorrow. But I will tell you that serious interest has been tendered. Interest in you. In your hand in marriage."

Chapter Two

Ella remembered the smells, the sights, the feel of London in the early hours of the morning. She remembered them too well.

Smoke and dust, and a suggestion of animal sweat and leather . . . and old fear. A bite to the air. And over and around it all, a faintly silvered mist unfurling beneath the blue-black sky.

Tonight the scent of fear was imagined, of course—a recollection of her wretched days in Whitechapel. There, in the eastern reaches of the city, the buildings crowded meanly together and most of those about at this time of night were about mean business. She was not in Whitechapel now. Between Hanover Square and her destination lay nothing but the fine homes of the wealthy. The wealthy who were all tucked into their sweetly scented sheets preparing for the next day of pampered appetites.

The wheels of the Rossmara town coach ground through the streets, echoed over the sounds of the horses' hoofs and creaking tack. Ella huddled in a corner and tried to feel nothing but the jarring sway of the carriage.

Not thinking about what she had set out to do was impossible. She was on a desperate mission. Nothing less would have sent her to awaken poor Potts and beg him to perform yet another service guaranteed to make him grumble fiercely, if quietly.

Desperate. Desperate. Desperate.

The word repeated with the turning of the great wheels.

She had no choice but to take desperate steps to avert a desperate situation.

Papa was to receive some people who would discuss the disposition of her person as if she were a body without a mind? Never. She would die before she would submit to such horror.

The coach slowed.

Perhaps she should just die anyway.

The coach crunched to a halt.

Ella covered her mouth. Her heart felt in danger of leaping away completely.

There was no expected sag of the springs under Potts's dismounting weight.

"You'll change your mind, Miss Ella," he said when she'd at last coaxed him into making the journey. "At least, I hopes t'Gawd you changes your mind."

Now he was waiting for her to do exactly that.

Beyond the windows lay the dark facade of a terrace of grand houses. Very dark. Barely a glimmer of light showed anywhere.

Ella reached up and rapped for Potts.

The trap slid open. "Miss?"

"Oh, Potts, don't be so difficult."

"Difficult? Me? Oh, no, I mustn't be difficult, must I? Drivin' around in the middle of the night. Runnin' the risk of 'is lordship 'avin me guts fer garters."

Despite her agitation, Ella grinned. Potts had never been

one to temper his language. "I shall pay my visit now, if you please."

His grumbling fell so low, she no longer heard the words.

When he handed her down, she requested, "Await me here, please, Potts. And do not concern yourself. I shall be quite safe." She did not tell him she'd come to the house in Burlington Gardens once before—when she'd been certain Saber would be out. On that occasion she'd found an unexpected accomplice in her cause, but "safe" hardly described the way he'd made her feel.

"It's almost three of a mornin', miss. What'll anyone think—?"

"Hush," she told him. "I am in no danger, I tell you. I have a message to deliver and then we'll return to Hanover Square at once."

"That's what you said when we went to that gentlemen's club last night. You was gone—"

"That was then. This is now." She left him, ran up a flight of stone steps to the front door, and pulled the bell before she could change her mind.

Somewhere inside the building a faint jangle sounded.

Ella waited. She felt Potts's eyes on her back but would not turn around.

She pulled the bell again.

Almost three in the morning. Mama and Papa were asleep. Ella had waited long enough to be certain of that. And she must return and be asleep before they awoke or her world would crack apart.

Her world was already threatening to crack apart.

Everyone was asleep here too.

A burst of jewel-toned glow through the fanlight above the door made her jump. The soft *swish, swish* of footsteps approached, and the door opened.

Ella looked directly into the face of the wiry little man who stood there. She whispered, "Good evening, Mr. Bigun."

"Bigun," he said shortly, scowling his annoyance at being disturbed. Worn over full, white trousers, his red brocade tunic was wrongly buttoned. "The evening is gone. The morning has come."

"Bigun," Ella amended hastily. "And it's not quite morning, although I do know it soon will be. That is why I'm so anxious to complete my business and leave you to resume your rest."

He inclined his head. "So you say." He wore a slightly askew gold turban, the same gold turban she'd seen on the occasion of her first visit. "Had you not disturbed my rest, it would not have to be resumed." His voice bore a mysteriously clipped foreign accent quite unfamiliar to Ella.

She smiled brilliantly at him. The effort was wasted. Haughty disapproval remained on his fine-boned, bronzed face. Ella continued to smile. "I wanted to thank you for telling me about Sibley's Ghost. And to report on my progress in the little matter we discussed."

His right hand shot out and he jerked her into a vestibule hung with lengths of silk that matched his tunic. "Do not speak loud," he said, bringing his large, dark eyes nearer to her face. He closed the door. "I told you. Nothing more. Nothing repeated. Now you go, miss."

But he had given her a weapon to make certain she did not have to go—not immediately, anyway. "You do not wish me to speak loudly?"

He shook his head.

"Then I won't. . . . But I do need to talk to you about Sibley's—"

Bigun's fingers closed on her wrist once more and he hauled her with him across tessellated black and white tiles.

Her kidskin half-boots made no more sound than the servant's soft, gold slippers.

The room into which he drew Ella completely stole her carefully prepared and persuasive speech.

Bigun closed them in and set about lighting too few of the candles held aloft by an extraordinary company. Ivory and jade figures, some more or less human, some reptilian or beastlike, offered up thin, white tapers in golden vessels. On her previous visit Ella and Bigun had conversed in the vestibule. She rather thought she might prefer to return there.

"I came to see Lord Avenall," she said shakily when her voice at last returned.

"You did not make progress at Sibley's." Bigun faced her. The scanty flickerings from the candles wove fingers of yellow through the shadowy crowd. "You failed. My decision was wrong. What occurred there troubled my master."

"How do you know?"

"Leave now."

Ella pressed her elbows to her sides. "I know he will want to see me."

Bigun shook his head. "I know he will not."

Ella gulped, and breathed through her mouth. "Ask him."

"No."

"He will be angry if he discovers I was here and you didn't tell him."

"He will not discover."

Nearby, jeweled eyes glinted in the two heads of a green jade creature. Ella stepped away—and bumped into an ivory dragon with a long, lolling gold tongue.

Candlelight gleamed on Bigun's gaunt features. "My master cannot receive you," he said. "Leave, please."

A subtle aroma reached her nose. Burning flowers? Her eyes stung. "You don't understand, Mr. Bigun. As I told you the other day, it is imperative that I see Saber."

"Bigun."

"Sorry. As I said the other—"

"I do not remember another day."

Ella opened her mouth—and promptly closed it again.

"Leave. If you please. Do not return. Do not trouble my master further."

She was not alone in feeling desperate tonight. "What's afoot here?" Beneath the servant's cold exterior Ella felt deep anxiety. "Is something wrong—with Saber?"

He didn't answer.

There *was* something wrong with him. "Tell me." Her chest grew tight. "He is ill. That's it, isn't it? He's ill and doesn't want me to know."

Bigun's face lost all expression.

"I want to go to him, please."

"That is not possible. Not wise. Out of the question. My master is quite himself. He will not see you."

Quite himself. He had not been himself since he'd left her in Cornwall four years earlier. She'd tried and tried to forget him, but then she'd discovered he was staying near her Scottish home at Castle Kirkcaldy—so near that he could have come to her within an hour.

He had not come, so she had gone to him.

On that occasion she'd managed to get into his presence, though only for a short time. He had sent her away. But he had been recovering from a battle injury and she'd been certain he did not want to burden her. She'd also been certain he would seek her out once he was whole again.

He was whole again. Ella had seen him at Sibley's. Still he had not come to her. He had walked away. She drew herself up and said, "Is he alone?" Or with the famous Countess Perruche?

Bigun's eyelids lowered briefly. His mouth drew straight. "I should not have spoken of my master's club to you."

"I thought you were worried about him. I felt that. You saw that I cared for him and you wanted me to see him, didn't you?"

"He is alone."

"You never answer my questions directly, Mr. Bigun."

"Bigun."

"Yes, as you say. I am in serious trouble. That is, I may be in serious trouble. And I am certain Saber would wish to know. He once promised me he would always come to my aid if I needed him. I need him now."

Bigun's brow furrowed.

Trembling, Ella struggled to open her reticule. Her fingers caught in the ribbon rosettes at the closure. By the time she tugged a folded piece of paper into view she was close to tears. "Please, Bigun," she implored. "If you doubt that Saber would come to my aid, take this to him. When he reads it, he will not turn me away."

With another of his unexpected grabs, Bigun snatched the note.

Ella took a step toward him. "You'll give it to him? Now?"

He turned away and opened the door. "My master sleeps."

"I beg you to do this. If you will not, I don't know what I shall do."

With his back to her and his head bowed, Bigun paused.

"Please will you . . . ?"

"Remain here."

He left, closing the door firmly behind him.

Relief and hope lightened Ella's head. She reached out to steady herself—and grasped the ivory elephant's cold, golden tongue.

Sunlight shot along curved blades.

His horse reared. All around him horses reared and screamed. And men screamed. He fought his mount. Down. Down. "Down. Get down! Everyone, retreat!"

Nigel Brannington's horse smashed into Saber's. "Hold on, Nigel. Hold—" Nigel didn't hear him, would never hear him again. His remaining blue eye saw nothing. The rest was blood.

Hot, so hot. Bound. Hot and bound. Twisting against his bonds. Sweat and blood. All, sweat and blood. He had to be free, to help them. His company. He must save them.

"Sir! Sir, help!" a soldier shouted to him, a soldier thrown from his horse.

"Mount and ride, boy, ride. Go! Go! Go!"

Little more than a child.

A blade sang overhead, swept this way and that, swept down toward the child soldier.

Saber ran through the next tribesman to come at him, withdrew his sword, and leaned to sweep up the boy. "Hold on. Keep your head down."

He rode with the boy, made it safely from the tangle of whooping men protecting their barren Indian hill, made it out of the sea of blood and flesh and terror.

The company was his. They had expected no trouble, simply a quiet reconnaissance of the area. He must go back for them. Not one more must be lost.

Nigel Brannington was already lost. Many were lost.

He must go back. Bound. Twisted in bonds and held down. Sweat. So hot. "Go back!"

Sweat ran over his horse's hide. Lather dripped from the mud-spattered animal—lather and mud, and blood. Foam flew from its mouth. The whites of great, frightened eyes rolled upward.

Saber spurred the beast on, away from the edges of the safe village where he'd quickly left the boy.

He had led his unsuspecting men toward death.

"Faster." He was strong. He would not die because he was strong, and he must save the rest.

Blowing hard, the horse crested a hill and Saber saw the fray again. "On. Faster!" The animal's hoofs drummed. They beat the sun-baked ground. They hammered. They pounded.

Bound by twisted bonds. Bonds that raked his damp skin. Holding him down. Stopping him from saving them. His men. "Silence! I've got to have silence! Stop! Stop, I tell you!"

Saber's own shout forced his eyes open.

Pounding, pounding. *The hoofs.*

He flung himself to the edge of his bed and thrust his feet to the bare wooden floor. It was always so. The sheets wound about his body, the screams—then his feet to the cold floor. No carpet, so that the floor would be cold—cold enough to shock him to consciousness.

Again, it had happened again.

He sagged to sit on the bed and let his head hang forward.

How many times had he ridden into the madness that day and managed, with strength that could not have been his own alone, to help another of his men to safety? Not enough times. He had not saved them all.

Many had died, too many, and it was his fault.

Would it never be over?

The crazed episodes came more frequently now.

A sharp, rapping sound almost stopped his thundering heart. Rapping at the door, God help him. The black thing he had become did not even recognize a knock at the door for what it was.

"Go away," he called.

Instantly the door opened and Bigun slipped inside. He closed the door firmly and turned the key in the lock.

"What is it?" Saber asked. His hair clung damply to his neck. Chilled by the icy cooling of sweat, his naked body shook. "Speak up, Bigun. What's the meaning of this intrusion? And why the locked door?" Had the faithful servant decided to turn on his troubled master—to become his jailer?

"You will drink, my lord," Bigun said. He carried a candle, and this he set beside the bed while he poured water from a pitcher into a glass. "Drink, my lord."

Saber pushed back his hair and took the glass. The water bathed his parched throat, and he gulped thirstily.

Bigun refilled the glass. "I regret I took so long to hear you. I was distracted by an event below." He moistened a cloth and pressed it to Saber's brow.

Saber closed his eyes. "No matter."

They had first met on the ship back to England. The dour Indian had tended the English lord in his almost constant delirium. At his own request, once ashore Saber had been transferred to Devlin North's care. It had been some months before Saber encountered Bigun again. On that occasion he'd saved Bigun from a crippling penance.

Coincidence had placed Saber on the same ship for his second trip to India. Bigun, too, was aboard, but this time another Englishman recognized the Indian as a fugitive from justice. Some matter of filching leftover food from the English officer's kitchens for beggars at the door. Evidently the paltry theft and the devastating punishment to which Bigun had been sentenced was all that concerned the pompous officer.

Bigun's wrist had been upon a block, a sword raised to ensure payment for crusts, when Saber intervened. Cousin to a duke, an earl in his own right, Saber's rank had "persuaded" the other Englishman to relent. Afterward the Indian insisted he must spend the rest of his life repaying the debt.

He looked critically at Saber now. "You will sicken, my lord," he said, wringing out the cloth. "Let me help you dress."

Saber shook his head. Still naked, he stretched out on the mattress and rested the back of a forearm over his eyes. He preferred to sleep without clothes—when he slept.

"There was the event," Bigun said.

"Hmm?" The answer might be to abandon sleep entirely. Only in his sleep did the specters rise.

Bigun cleared his throat. "The event. Below."

Saber slid his arm to the pillow above his head. "What are you talking about, man? Event below? Another of your damnable riddles."

The Indian drew himself up to his full, diminutive height. "A visitor."

"A visitor?" Saber peered through the dim light. "At . . . what? Two in the morning?"

"Well past four. Now."

Past four? Saber pushed to his elbows. "The devil you say. Who is it?"

Silently, Bigun produced a folded sheet of paper from a pocket in his tunic.

Glancing from his servant to the paper, Saber took it and turned on his side. A flood of sickness swept through him and he fell back.

"My lord!" Anxiety raised Bigun's voice.

"It's nothing. It passes—when the memory passes." There were few secrets between master and servant. Bigun had learned the nature of Saber's demons when he'd first tended him.

Saber rose to an elbow again, unfolded the paper, and held it beneath the candle:

"My dearest Saber," he read. *"I will not ask you to forgive my little masquerade last night. You would not agree to see me, so I found a way to see you without your permission."*

He arched his neck backward. "Bigun, do not tell me there is a female somewhere in this house—other than our incomparable housekeeper?"

Bigun shuffled his feet and said nothing.

Saber moistened his dry lips. "I see. There is another female in this house."

He read on:

"Once you said you were my friend. You told me you would never deny me if I was in trouble. I am in trouble, Saber. I need you."

He made a fist on his thigh. Yes, he had told her he would never deny her, but that had been when he was still a whole man, when he had dreamed of making her his, his beautiful bride—his wife, the mother of his children.

All gone.

"My lord?" Bigun said tentatively.

Saber grunted and continued reading:

"Tomorrow evening there is a soiree at the Eagletons'. No doubt you are also invited. Please relent from the solitary sentence you have assigned yourself—and me—and come. Please, *Saber. But first, will you see me now? Just for a moment? So that I may look upon you and know peace? With affection, Ella."*

"My God!" Sweat broke upon his brow again. "Get rid of her! Do as I tell you, at once."

"She is lovely. Lovely. Young. Serious, I believe."

"Serious, yes," he whispered through gritted teeth. "Serious, determined, willful, outrageous—trusting, gentle—and wasting her time on me."

"You could spare her a few minutes."

"No. How did she get here?"

"By carriage."

"And alone?"

Bigun sighed. "Alone."

"Send her home. Instruct her coachman to protect her at all costs. She should not be abroad at such an hour. What can Struan and Justine be about? First she appears at Sibley's to torment me . . . now this. She should be in the safety of her parents' home, not wandering in the night."

"Hmm. She insists she must talk to you."

Saber threw wide his arms. "Look at me. Look, Bigun. Soaked with my own sweat. Wild. A sick man."

"You, my lord," Bigun said very solemnly, "are a very strong, fit man."

"Not in my mind! I can never be free of the sickness in my mind. How could I ever subject a sweet female to such horror as living with me would represent?"

"You would like to live with her?"

"I—" Saber turned facedown on his bed. He let the note drift from his fingers. "I would like not to discuss this matter."

"Perhaps she would help. Mend you, my lord. Heal you."

"I am sick of soul," Saber said into the pillow. "A man with a sick soul can never have anything to offer—and he can never be healed."

"My lord—"

Tapping at the door silenced Bigun.

Saber turned his face in the direction of the tapping.

"Saber? Are you in there?"

"I cannot bear it," he muttered.

"Saber, it's me, Ella. Can you hear me?"

He shook his head, unable to trust his voice.

"I know you are there," she said, emotion trembling in every word. "Please could we talk? Please would you tell me what I've done wrong?"

He buried his face. To want. To want and to be able to have, yet to know the having would be utterly wrong . . . Torment.

"My lord?" Bigun said beside Saber's ear. "It grows almost morning."

"Go away," Saber muttered into the pillow. He raised his face and shouted, "Go away, Ella. Forget the past. Go."

"Saber, please—"

"Leave this house at once. Cease your persecution of me. I never wish to see you again."

He heard her cry out, a strangled, wounded sound that faded to rasping sobs. Then her retreating footsteps followed.

"You lied to me, Saber," she gasped through her tears. "You said you loved me. I was too young. I am not too young now, but you do not love me now."

Her feet hit the stairs in quick succession.

Saber looked up at Bigun. "See to it that she gains her coach safely."

Bigun's face took on the haughty expression he saved for moments of extreme disapproval. "I wash my hands of this."

"Do as I request," Saber roared.

"Saber!" Ella's voice reached him from the vestibule. "Today Papa is to see a man who wishes to ask for my hand. A stranger. I do not want this man."

He rose and approached the door, then remembered his nakedness. Blindly, he sought around for something to cover himself with. "Give me a robe," he said, yanking the door open. "I must speak to her. She must see that what she remembers was only a childish infatuation that could not last."

Bigun rummaged in a huge ebony wardrobe and brought forth a black silk robe.

"Hurry," Saber urged. A draft rose from the floor below. She had opened the door.

"I will die rather than be given to a stranger I do not love," Ella called to him in her broken voice.

He struggled into the robe and tied the sash. Without bothering with shoes, he threw the door wide and started for the stairs.

"I love you, Saber. I'll never love another."

The front door slammed shut.

He ran downstairs and outside into the stinging early-morning air.

Her coach drew away from the flagway.

"Ella!"

The shades at the carriage windows were drawn down. She neither saw nor heard him. Too late. It had been too late even before they met.

"Ella," he murmured. "My beloved Ella."

Chapter Three

No man was good enough for his daughter.

Struan, Viscount Hunsingore, turned the pages of a document his solicitor had left for signature that morning.

A calm manner would serve him well in the days to come. And an unruffled air would be mandatory in such matters as dealing with the callers he was expecting today. Yes, an air of nonchalant control.

He threw down his pen. He could not be dispassionate where Ella was concerned. "Absolutely not! No!"

"My lord?"

Startled, Struan looked up to see Crabley, the Hanover Square butler, standing before the mahogany desk. "I didn't hear you enter," he said, more sharply than he intended.

"I did knock, my lord."

"Are they here?"

"*They*, my lord?" Crabley's small, protruding black eyes magnified the question conveyed by his words.

Struan pushed to his feet and advanced around his desk.

This study usually brought him peace and pleasure. He felt neither today. "They, Crabley. The people I told you were calling on me this afternoon."

"It is not yet eleven, my lord." Doughy of complexion, his width and height similar, the butler had always performed his duties impeccably. Both Struan and his older brother, Arran, Marquess of Stonehaven, found the servant's manner irritating, but his loyalty and scrupulous attention to detail made him invaluable.

Struan eyed the man speculatively. "Are you a man of passion, Crabley?" There, let him come up with a suitably butlerlike response to that!

Crabley pushed out his lips and wriggled his snub nose as if some thought were necessary. "Considerable passion," he said without inflection. "Yes, my lord, I am a very passionate man. I would protect those I serve to the death . . . if such an extraordinary measure should prove necessary. Is that what you meant, my lord?"

Struan coughed, and waved a hand. "Um, yes, yes, I suppose it is." He smiled. "Very admirable, Crabley." And somewhat humbling—humbling enough to make a man a deal less angry at the world.

"This was delivered," Crabley said, extending a small bundle of silk the color of emeralds and bound shut with gold braid. "For Miss Ella."

"What is it?" Struan asked, deeply suspicious. "Who would send Ella gifts? She knows no one in London."

"I'm sure I couldn't say, my lord."

"Didn't the messenger say who it was from?"

"No, my lord."

"There isn't a card?"

"No, my lord."

"In God's name!" Struan roared. "Must you always be so—?"

Ella's entrance, with Justine at her heels, saved him from

losing his composure completely. "Someone sent something for me?" Ella asked.

Struan glared. "How do you know someone sent something for you?"

She had the grace to blush a little. "I was . . . I heard the doorbell and looked down to see who it was."

"Are you expecting someone?"

Ella, dressed in one of the overly simply-cut gowns she favored, swept to a little gilt chair and sat down. She twitched her lavender-colored skirts and crossed her hands in her lap. Too nonchalant, Struan thought. And too exotically beautiful for any father's peace of mind. Her eyes were particularly dark today, her skin translucent despite its burnished quality. Her blue-black hair had been tightly restrained in braids and knotted at her crown. Rather than producing the plain effect most would achieve, the stark style only accentuated her mysterious perfection. A man should not be burdened with such extraordinary loveliness to protect and guide.

He glanced at Justine. Their eyes met, and he saw her understanding of his feelings. They could not love this girl more. She and her brother, Max, were as dear to them as little Edward and Sarah.

"Ella?" he said sharply, flexing his shoulders. "Perhaps we should have a discussion. Certain matters are deeply concerning to me. Set that down, Crabley. Leave us, please."

He caught Justine's frantic gesturing and stopped himself from chastising Ella for her escapade at Sibley's. Justine kept no secrets from him, but she easily extracted a price for her honesty. She had made him promise he would not mention the episode unless it was repeated.

Once Crabley had closed the door behind him, Struan turned back to Ella. He studied her closely. "You don't appear rested," he said, ignoring Justine's grimace. "Are you well?"

"Very well, thank you, Papa," Ella said. Her attention was on the green silk-covered parcel.

"I understand your mama explained to you that I'm to receive visitors this afternoon."

Ella's carefully relaxed posture tensed.

"We don't have to speak of that now," Justine said in a rush. "After all, Struan, this is all very premature. Ella hasn't as much as showed her nose to the *ton* yet."

"The suggestion is that we should consider avoiding the Season altogether," Struan responded, uncomfortably aware of his own stress.

Justine came to him and rested her hands on his. "No Season? You cannot mean it."

"I didn't say I meant it, merely that the suitor's father did make the remark in his letter to me that a wedding would be a better use of a large amount of my blunt than what he termed pretty and pointless affairs."

"Oh!" Justine blinked rapidly and leaned closer. She lowered her voice. "She is upset, Struan. Please do not persist in this."

"Please don't whisper," Ella said. "I have no intention of marrying this person who needs his parent to speak for him. How very strange. A man too immature to deal with his own affairs, but who has the temerity to offer for me in marriage. Of course, you will not see him, Papa."

Struan smothered a smile. "Of course I will see them, young lady. I have made inquiries. Apparently the Wokinghams have very deep pockets and a fine estate in Lancashire. Lord Wokingham's letter refers to a previous meeting of ours. Although I confess that I have no memory of the event, courtesy demands that I at least entertain his suggestions." He wished he could recall the meeting to which Wokingham referred.

"Piffle," Justine said distinctly.

"Why," Struan said, anticipating an outburst of annoyance, "I do believe you sound more like your grandma every day."

Justine didn't disappoint him. "I shall ignore that comment." But she scowled darkly at the suggestion that she resembled her termagant dowager duchess grandparent in any manner. "Sin's ears, Struan, Ella's right. A creature who needs his father's voice is not ready to ask for any woman's hand in marriage, much less the hand of the most beautiful girl in England. Wait until she appears at the Eagletons' tomorrow. We shall be inundated with gentleman callers. Do not see these people today."

He found it almost impossible to deny Justine anything, but he had already agreed to see the Wokinghams. "We are in suspense, Ella," he said, patting Justine's hands and reaching for the surprisingly heavy gift. "No card came with this, but I understand it is for you. Open it."

"You're changing the subject," Justine whispered.

He kissed her elegant nose and whispered back, "Yes, I am, my love."

Ella took the bundle from him, set it back on the desk, and carefully untied the golden braid. She parted the silk and her hands went to her cheeks.

Within the silk rested a pouch of woven gold, heavy and soft—and shimmering richly. Here and there in the priceless fabric, cunningly placed diamonds winked with sly brilliance.

"Gad," Struan murmured. "A small fortune, I shouldn't wonder."

"You seem remarkably taken with displays of wealth today," Justine said sharply. "What is it supposed to be? Do look at it, Ella."

Ella bent over the exquisite thing. "The diamonds are woven into the gold—like beads into fine lace. So perfect."

"Very old, I should imagine," Struan said. "Look at the thing. There's got to be some sort of note."

His haste earned him another frown from both his wife and daughter.

Ella touched the gold and it fell open.

"Oh, how clever," Justine exclaimed. "It's an evening reticule. See the gold strings to close it—and the white satin lining. I've never seen the like."

"No," Ella said softly. She leaned over and picked up something that had lain hidden in the folds of white satin. "A red glass star on a chain. How strange."

Struan narrowed his eyes. "A ruby star. Incredible workmanship. I do believe the Wokinghams have decided to ease their way here."

Ella wasn't listening to him. She held the fabulous ruby star in her palm and gathered up the little golden web bag with its dusting of diamond sparkles.

"Perhaps you are more interested in Pomeroy Wokingham now?" Struan asked. "After all, he wouldn't send you such a priceless thing if he weren't very serious about his suit, would he?"

Ella held the bag to her face and sniffed deeply. "Pomeroy isn't a name I could ever come to care for in a man," she said indistinctly. "He did not send this." Without another word, she turned away and left the room.

If the beating of one's heart could make one deaf, then she would surely never hear again. Ella sped belowstairs and through the kitchens. Cook and three maids all paused and dipped curtsies. Curtsies, Ella thought vaguely. How her life had changed since the night when Papa had saved her from the horror in Whitechapel.

"Good morning," she said, smiling brightly. Every eye went to the treasure she carried. Ella held it aloft and said, "Isn't it a lovely thing? Useless, but lovely. Did Crabley come this way?"

"In his pantry, miss," Cook said, wiping her hands on a voluminous white apron. Red-faced from working over the fire, she blew at escaping strands of hair. The aroma of nutmeg and stewing apples promised delicious things to come.

Ella hurried on to Crabley's pantry and knocked. She waited for him to bid her entry. "Morning, Crabley," she said pleasantly once she was inside the comfortable little room. This was where he held court over the household's fine crystal and china, and dispatched orders to various underlings.

He got hastily to his feet and set down a book beside his brown leather chair. "Miss Ella?"

She held out the bag in one hand, the ruby bauble in the other. "This was delivered a short while ago."

"Yes, miss."

"There was no note?"

"No, miss."

"You don't know who sent this?"

"No, miss."

Yes, miss. No, miss. Ella swallowed the irritation Crabley always made her feel. She'd been unable to see who came to the door—or to make out more than her own name amid the low exchange. Her reason for looking down from the gallery at all was that she'd hoped to get a peek at the beastly Wokinghams. "Was the messenger liveried?"

"In a manner of speaking."

"Speak, then!" She rolled in her lips, then said, "I am too sharp sometimes, Crabley. Forgive me. This is a puzzle. I merely wondered if you could help me decide who sent such a gift." And prove that she wasn't imagining what she thought she smelled.

"Strange attire," Crabley said, setting his short legs apart and clasping his hands behind his back. He frowned in concentration. "Foreign, if you ask me."

"I am asking you," Ella said softly.

"Definitely foreign. Never did hold with foreigners myself. Not to be trusted—particularly that type. Turbans and tunics and baggy trousers. Most unsuitable in a servant."

Ella almost laughed aloud—with joy, not mirth. She pretended to be interested in the rows of Baccarat glasses in cabinets along one wall. "But there was no note, Crabley?"

"No, miss."

She closed her eyes and gritted her teeth. "Did this servant give his name?"

"No, miss."

Patience. "Very well, thank you, Crabley. You've been most helpful."

She hadn't been mistaken. Once more she held the bag to her nose. Roses. Rose-scented incense—the kind she'd smelled at Saber's house. And Bigun must have delivered the gift, which, in turn, must have been sent by Saber.

"I must return upstairs." And she must go at once to Saber and thank him for the gift. This was his way of asking her to forget their difficulties and go forward. She could scarcely breathe for happiness.

"Miss Ella," Crabley said as she went to open the door. "The foreign gentleman said I should tell you and no other."

She spun around. "Tell me what?"

"He said I should wait for an appropriate moment to tell you his master's comments. His master knows you will understand."

Ella held the bag to her breast.

"He said his master believes you need no written message, since you will look at the pendant and understand what it represents."

She stared from Crabley's little black eyes to the ruby. "I do not know."

Crabley cleared his throat. "You don't know what's happened to this man who gave you the gift—so the servant says. He has suffered, and it's changed him."

Ella felt her way to sit in Crabley's leather chair. "I do know that. I know it well. What does it mean?"

"The servant was instructed to let you know that the man you knew is gone. Someone you would hate is in his place now. More tender than the heart that sends it. That's what he said I was to say. The foreigner's master tells you that the red stone star is more tender than the heart that sent it."

She looked at the ruby in her palm. "How can he think such a thing?"

Crabley didn't respond.

"Was that all?"

"If you have kind thoughts of him still, this person doesn't want them. You're to look at the stone and remember how cold it is. Don't try again. That was the most important instruction, he said. You're not to try again, whatever that means. The gift is for the past and in thanks." Crabley coughed and looked blankly at the ceiling. "An exotic star for an exotic girl—one he will see whenever he looks at a night sky. A girl whose countenance will shine for him wherever he is, wherever he looks. There can be nothing more between you. That was the rest of the message."

Ella pressed a hand to her stomach. "Such a long message," she whispered.

"I have an excellent memory, Miss Ella."

Hiding tears, Ella got to her feet and walked past Crabley with her face bowed. "Thank you," she told him. "I'm sorry I disturbed you." The bag and ruby must be returned.

"The foreign gentleman had a message of his own," Crabley said.

Ella paused, but didn't trust herself to turn around.

"He said—rather presumptuously, if you ask me—but he said proud people could also be foolish people. He said you should consider that his master misjudges the condition of his own heart. That's what he said."

Powdered and pompous. Greville, Lord Wokingham, strutted into the study, his paunchy body upthrust by corsets into a pigeonlike form. No doubt his blue velvet jacket had cost a pretty penny, and the pink satin waistcoat embroidered with orange roses. His flamboyantly checked trousers didn't hide scrawny legs—or a widely braced stance and tottering gait.

Repulsive, Struan decided instantly, before meeting bloodshot eyes sunk into fleshy folds. One look into those eyes and he knew true revulsion—and he recalled the meeting to which Wokingham had referred.

As if reading Struan's thoughts, Wokingham sputtered, "Esterhazy's musicale. Seems like yesterday."

"More than four years ago," Struan said shortly.

Wokingham rubbed his drink-mottled nose. Slashes of bright rouge colored his flabby cheeks. "Your friend Franchot made quite a splash, eh. And it all began right there at Chandos House. Strange life, what?"

Struan nodded briefly. "Strange. But satisfactorily just in this case." His lifelong friend Calum Innes had seen his bride for the first time that night. And he'd begun the journey to resume his rightful place as Duke of Franchot—a title that had been stolen from him shortly after his birth.

"Hmm, well, I'd like you to meet your future, er, son-in-law?" Wokingham guffawed, leaned over his belly to slap in the general direction of his knees, and staggered to fall into a chair. "Don't mind if I sit down, d'you?"

"Not at all," Struan said, distractedly eyeing the man who had stood silently behind Wokingham. "Good afternoon to you, sir. I take it you are Pomeroy? I don't believe I heard what other name you use."

"Wokingham," the man said shortly. "It's also our family name. Pom to my friends."

His father's rumbling laugh burst forth again. "The Hon. Pom, they call him. My right hand, I can tell you. Couldn't run things without him. That gel of yours will be getting a prize."

The "prize" looked levelly back at Struan. Of average height and thin, there was about him a boneless quality—as if he would glide rather than walk. Thin hair that might be sand-colored shone in pomaded brown furrows against a white skull. Blond brows arched to sharp peaks that dipped to meet the corners of his eyes at one aspect, and arrowed toward an exceedingly long nose at the other. A rim of white ringed the man's small mouth. But it was the eyes that turned Struan's stomach. Utterly colorless, the Hon. Pom's eyes held no light. His stare was a flat as a snake's.

"I'd offer you refreshment," Struan said, hearing his words explode with his haste to be rid of these people. "Unfortunately, I've had something unexpected come up. I'm sure you understand."

Pomeroy approached, his chin pushed forward. He shot out a hand. "Good to meet you, Hunsingore. Pater's told me a great deal about you and your family."

Without thinking, Struan shook hands. Only with difficulty did he hold back an exclamation. The hand that enfolded his had the softness of a woman's. Soft, formless, weak and hot. Hot sweat coated Struan's palm.

Those hands touching Ella?

Never.

Struan swallowed. "We're flattered—that is, Ella's mother and I are flattered at your interest in Ella. Of course—"

"You're probably wondering what made us take this step," Wokingham interrupted. "Long story, and I won't bore you with all of it. Pom caught a glimpse or two of Ella. Love at first sight and all that."

"Glimpse? I can't imagine—"

"Shopping," Pomeroy said smoothly. "In Bond Street. Saw her and made inquiries. Simple as that."

"My boy knows what he wants when he sees it," Wokingham said, his fat lips pushed out. "No point beating about the bush, I say. If Pom's ready to find the same fetching little baggage waiting in his bed every night, then who are we to argue, eh?"

Struan gaped. Fetching little *baggage?* His Ella?

Pomeroy produced a small, purple velvet box from his pocket and opened it with a flourish. "Call her in, would you, old chap? Never met a female who didn't return a fella's ardor with this sort of encouragement."

A diamond-encircled sapphire as large as his own thumbnail winked at Struan. "Er, very nice. Meant to thank you for your gift."

"Could hardly thank us for it before we presented it, what?" Wokingham chuckled hugely.

Struan collected himself and, at the same time, checked any further reference to the ruby in the gold bag. Damn, but it was impossible dealing with marriageable daughters. Evidently this slimy, disgusting excuse for a man wasn't the only one to have caught a "glimpse" of Ella. She must be locked away at once. Sent back to Scotland. Made to wear a thick veil . . .

He was losing his mind!

"Let's get on with it, then," Wokingham said. "If there's any chance of the gel being disappointed about missing the Season, Pom can take her about a bit. She'll enjoy it all even more on his arm. After all, she'll be the envy of every unattached, grasping female in London. And they're all grasping, what?"

Struan cleared his throat. "We are flattered by your interest, but—"

"You're overwhelmed," Wokingham flapped a beringed hand. "We aren't doing this blindly, old chap. Let's be blunt. After all, we're all men together here. Saw the gel myself. Fine piece, I must say. My boy's got good taste."

"I hardly—"

"We'll take pleasure in decking her out, won't we, Pom? My boy will supervise that aspect of things himself." A huge wink eclipsed one reddened eye. "Of course, when he's got the unwrapped material in front of him, so to speak, he may forget to wrap it up again in time to go anywhere, what?" Laughter shook Wokingham's belly.

Deep loathing made Struan's legs weak. It made his temper roar. "I think this meeting is over," he said carefully. The less fuss he made, the less chance there was that Justine or Ella would hear and be exposed to this display. "I'll summon my butler to show you out."

"Out?" Wokingham struggled to his feet. "What the bloody hell do you mean by that, m'boy? Out? We're to be relatives. A man doesn't show his relatives out before they're ready to go."

"This man shows out whomever he pleases, whenever he pleases."

Pomeroy strolled closer to Struan. "Evidently you don't understand. I've seen what I want and I intend to get it. For the first time in my life I want to make a slut into an honest woman. I haven't been ready until now."

Struan could not believe he had heard correctly.

"Been too young until now," Wokingham said, apparently oblivious to his son's outright insult to a young female who was beyond reproach. "With his fortieth birthday behind him, he recognizes it's time to produce some offspring. Might as well choose a pair of thighs that promise endless entertainment in the process, what? To say nothing of the chit's other areas of possibility. Youth, succulent little tits—and an arse to match, I'll wager." The man finished with his tongue held between his teeth.

One more second and Struan would call them out—both of them. To do so would be more than they deserved. One could not deal in matters of honor with men who had no honor. "Out," he told them succinctly. "Never return. Put your bauble back in your pocket, sir, and go. How dare you suggest that an innocent creature such as Ella is a *slut*? *Out!*"

Pomeroy closed the ring box and tossed it casually upon the desk. "We're offering to take her off your hands and pay a fair price for the goods. With certain considerations in the way of a dowry, of course."

"Out!"

"After all," Pomeroy remarked, "it isn't as if she's got a solid pedigree. You know what we mean."

Cold chased the heat from Struan's skin. "I don't know what you mean," he said, watching their reactions with great care. "And neither, I'll wager, do you. This entire incident is an insult to the Rossmaras and it will not be forgotten."

Wokingham went to his son's side. Any trace of humor had disappeared from his face. "Insult? When did the truth become insulting? We're offering to take the female off your hands. Might not be so easily accomplished with any other eligible male—not under the circumstances. I'm sure you understand."

Struan forced his hands to remain relaxed. "Why don't you explain this to me?"

"Oh"—Pomeroy gestured loosely with a pale hand—"enough said, really, don't y'think? After all, we're all gentlemen here. Certainly wouldn't want to speak aloud of a ruinous past in one so physically titillatin' as Ella, would we?"

They knew something. Perhaps not everything, but something. Struan had convinced himself that a girl seen fleetingly in a certain setting when she was not even sixteen, was unlikely to be recalled in entirely different circumstances more than four years later. And she had lived a sheltered life ever since. She was not known in Society.

"Got your attention, have we?" Wokingham asked fatuously.

The man's satisfaction inflamed Struan. "Your innuendos make no sense, but they do make it necessary for me to issue a warning to both of you. I am tempted to call you out. Push me further and the temptation will become irresistible."

Pomeroy smiled—an exceedingly unpleasant sight. "Creditable attempt, Hunsingore. Most might cringe and run away—assume they were mistaken. Unfortunately for you, we know we are not mistaken. Oh, have no fear, our intelligence was gained in the most discreet manner. Does the term 'lady tailor' mean something to you?"

Wokingham giggled and hitched at the crotch of his trousers. "A certain innovative brothel, eh, Hunsingore. Expert work by ladies accomplished in satisfying gentlemen of any size—or *taste*?" He giggled again. "And entertainments not to be missed, eh?"

Restraint cost Struan everything now. Ella's only hope rested with absolute denial of her past. "I have no idea what you're talking about," he said, contriving to appear puzzled. "What could this establishment possibly have to do with my daughter?"

He saw the faintest uncertainty in Wokingham's eyes and pressed on. "I may manage to forget this incident. If you leave at once and never mention it again."

"You deny that Ella has a questionable past?" All expression had deserted Pomeroy's ferretlike features.

"Absolutely. You are wrong in your assumptions."

"Really? I wonder if you understand the word *wrong*." Pomeroy stroked carvings along the edge of the desk.

Damn, he must be circumspect. He must exercise more control than should be required of any reasonable man.

"She isn't your daughter, Lord Hunsingore, is she? Not *really* your daughter."

His heart thudded. If they mentioned that he had first seen Ella at a brothel auction where she'd been displayed—all but naked—as a virginal prize for the highest bidder, he'd have no defense but outraged denial. Then he'd have to throw them out himself. But what then? He couldn't risk drawing the issue into the cruel light of the *ton*'s avaricious *on dit* mill.

Lies were his only refuge, Ella's only refuge. "Ella and her brother were the children of a gentleman farmer and his wife. Their holding marched with an estate I once owned in Dorset. They both died of cholera. A terrible thing. Ella and Max were completely alone."

Wokingham and Pomeroy said nothing. They exchanged a sickeningly knowing glance and returned their scrutiny to his face.

"Every penny of the parents' estate went to pay debts. There were no relatives. I decided to care for the children myself. Then my dear wife and I adopted them. So you are misinformed, you see. I would have her ladyship confirm this, but to as much as know there had been any slur against Ella would quite undo Justine. Naturally, and appropriately, we consider Ella and Max as much our children as the two who are of our own blood. I'm sure you will agree that you have been misled—and that you will understand my horror at your suggestion."

One side of Pomeroy's mouth jerked upward. "So you say." He and his father nodded. "Very likely. And very admirable on the part of you and your lady, I must say."

"Very admirable," Wokingham echoed.

Pomeroy picked up the velvet box, opened it, and removed the ring. This he set on the mahogany sheen of the desk. "Nevertheless, such a girl would do well to marry into a fine family like the Wokinghams, don't you think? Marry and be tucked safely away from harm—from harmful tongues."

Wokingham shook his head and made a smacking sound with his lips. "Sad what some girls have to go through. Gossip can be such a destructive thing. Can finish 'em, can't it? But my Pom wants her regardless, don't you, Pom?"

Pomeroy raised his brows in assent.

Keeping his steps measured, Struan went to the fireplace and pulled the cord to summon Crabley. The only offense in this matter would be solid defense, and that defense would consist of the denial of any rumor these insects attempted to introduce.

"No need to bother the flunky," Wokingham said. "We'll see ourselves out. Take the ring, Pom. You can give it to her yourself and enjoy her gratitude." His giggle wrung out Struan's stomach.

"I'll look forward to that moment," Pomeroy said. "It's a pity you did not see fit to simplify this transaction, my lord."

"We will not speak of this again," Struan said.

Wokingham and his appalling son approached the door. "My Pom wants her," Wokingham said, his eyes red slits. "What Pom wants, he gets. I always make certain of that. You have nothing to fear. Our discretion is assured. But we will stay in touch."

"I don't think so," Struan said as Crabley appeared.

Pomeroy bowed slightly and said, "You may depend upon it."

Chapter Four

"I have no stomach for this." Saber stepped deeper into the shadows of the gallery above the Egletons' great hall.

Devlin North rested a hip on the carved stone balustrade. "You wish to be here. You do not wish to be here," he said in the damnable neutral tones he affected whenever he delivered particularly irritating announcements. "You wish to reenter society at last. You do not wish to reenter society at all—ever. You wish to see her. You do not—"

"I do not wish to listen to your goading twaddle, North. I asked you to accompany me here in case I decide to carry out a certain mission. Nothing more."

Devlin turned his handsome face away and crossed his arms. "And for this I got out of a charmingly warm bed—and certain other charmingly warm places."

"I have always detested London in the Season," Saber said darkly, refusing to discuss Devlin's latest dalliances. "I detest the games one is supposed to play."

"Seems to me you've managed to avoid London in almost

all seasons, old chap. We both know you wouldn't be here now if you could stay away from—"

"Margot said she'd been invited."

Devlin laughed shortly. "Determined not to confess the truth, are we? Very well. Yes, Margot was invited. A relative of hers was acquainted with the Earl of Eagleton's father."

"She probably won't come."

"Probably not," Devlin agreed. "I'm not particularly enjoyin' the evenin' myself, old chap. Lookin' down on the festivities has never been my idea of a scintillatin' experience. Prefer to be in the thick of it, so t'speak."

Saber didn't bother to disguise his disdain. "In the thick of a gaggle of warbling mamas and their twittering, downy chicks, you mean? To say nothing of rubbing shoulders with the chicks' bored papas, and an assortment of posturing, so-called eligible males."

"I think it is you who posture," Devlin said softly.

There was no answer to that, none that would please Saber. Devlin looked downward past a ring of rich banners swaying gently above the colorful scene in the hall below. "You came because you want to see her," he told Saber. "We don't have need to speak her name aloud, do we? And there must be some other reason that has compelled you here, but which you are not telling me. No matter. You may hold your little secrets."

His little secrets? His entire life was a secret now, a sick, fearsome secret. It must remain so. But Ella had spoken of his promise to come to her aid if ever she needed him. There would be no peace for him until he proved to her that he could not fulfill his promise because he was a changed man.

"Do you know what they say of you here in London?"

Saber frowned at Devlin. "No doubt you will tell me."

"They say that you and Margot are lovers, that you are her protector. Suggestions are made that the mysterious Earl of

Avenall has unusual sexual preferences and that you pay Countess Perruche well to fulfill them."

"Who are these chatterers to whom you refer?" He was aware that there was some talk, of course, but not that he'd become of any great interest to the *ton*.

"*They* are those who matter, Saber. You know how perverse our incestuous little circle of the Blessed is. The Upper-of-the-Upper feeds upon morsels such as a beautiful, widowed countess who spends large amounts of time with a reclusive earl—alone—in his house."

"Let them feed."

Devlin shrugged. "I'm simply warning you of what you will confront if you decide to proceed with this plan of yours to go about again."

"I never said I intended to go about again. One clandestine foray doesn't mean I shall make a habit of frequenting such absurd affairs. Not that my presence will be missed."

"*Au contraire.* You have become the most whispered about rake in Town."

"Rake?" Saber asked, amazed. "In God's name. They call me a rake?"

"Indeed. The enigmatic Saber, Earl of Avenall. The man your downy chicks cheep about behind their fans—and exchange deliciously titillating speculations about behind their mamas' backs. And their mamas are clucking about you, too, my friend. After all, you're quite a catch, old man."

"How can I be—"

"You are," Devlin said, interrupting. "I would not tell you lies. The moment you put in your appearance, you will be on every husband-hunting parent's list. At the top of their lists. So, be warned."

"And what of you?" Saber asked shortly. "Who doesn't at least guess at the depth of your pockets? North of the shipping

Norths, they must say. Man's related to Midas. Wonder you're still a free man."

Devlin raised his arms and stretched. "Let's say I sympathize with you, old chap. Fighting 'em off left and right is such a bore—but I manage."

Saber could not help but be amused. "As you say. I've no doubt you manage very well. However, I shall leave the pleasure to you. There is only one thing I need to accomplish here—with your help. I want to meet with Ella. Alone." He indicated the chamber behind him. "I will be in there."

Devlin dropped his arms. "I say. I'm hardly going to find it easy to get a gel to come upstairs with me on her own."

"You'll find a way," Saber told him. "Pull her aside and give her this."

"What is it?" Devlin asked, looking at the folded square of paper Saber had pushed into his hand.

"Ella rather likes notes. She sends a great many of them. One more should cause her no particular surprise."

"But—"

"Find a way to give her the note. Make a suitable opportunity for her to come to me. The matter will then be finished, I assure you. After tonight she will shudder at the very mention of my name."

Ella wished she could close her eyes and be somewhere far away when she opened them again. The handsome Earl of Eagleton and his lovely wife had greeted Mama and Papa as old friends. Lady Eagleton had treated Ella with particular kindness, but everything else about their elaborate soiree was horrid.

Why couldn't she go home to Scotland? Now that she knew she must give up on Saber, there was no point in remaining in London.

Mama nudged her and murmured, "Chin up, Ella, please.

And *do* smile. James and Celine will think you are not enjoying yourself."

"I'm not," Ella whispered back vehemently. "They are a charming couple. They also don't appear to notice anyone or anything but each other, so they won't know if I'm miserable, will they?"

"Ella." Mama's deep amber eyes clouded. "You should have warned me that you only agreed to come to London because you knew Saber was here. At least I could have been prepared. I could have attempted to coax him out of hiding."

Ella couldn't bring herself to tell Mama the awful story of what had transpired between Saber and herself on her second visit to his home. "I doubt he'd pay any attention. He is selfish, and foolish to boot. He deserves to have his ears boxed."

"His ears boxed?" Mama giggled. "What an odd notion. Something tells me you'd better not try any such thing, miss."

"How can I? He continues to cower in his dark house."

Mama turned to Ella. "How do you know about his house—dark or otherwise?"

Ella opened the white lace fan that matched her gown. "I was merely guessing," she said. "His behavior at Sibley's would make anyone think of dark places. I do not like this gown."

"I beg your pardon? You chose the gown."

Ella congratulated herself on a neat diversion. "I chose it to please convention. White makes me look sallow. I detest pale, lifeless colors. In fact, I detest dresses of any color. I shall not wear them again once I return home—which will be very soon. May we go back to Hanover Square now, please?"

Before Mama could respond, while her mouth was open to deliver what would undoubtedly have been a deservedly brusque retort, a narrow, brown-haired man thrust himself in front of Ella. He said, "Good evening, Miss Rossmara. I am Pomeroy Wokingham, a friend of your father's."

Ella gazed into flat, pale gray eyes. She could not seem to look away.

"Perhaps the viscount mentioned us? My father is Lord Wokingham?"

Ella heard Mama's sharp intake of breath before she said, "Good evening, Mr. Wokingham. How nice of you to introduce yourself. If you'll excuse us, Ella and I—"

"Lord Hunsingore suggested I come and speak to you, Ella," he said with an oily familiarity that turned her stomach. "He thought you'd enjoy being taken for a stroll in the gardens. I understand they're considered handsome."

A stout woman emerged from the richly garbed throng and touched Pomeroy Wokingham's elbow. She wore deep mauve satin with a turban that did not quite match, and clasped a buxom, very red-haired girl by the wrist.

Pomeroy spared the older woman a hooded stare. "Madam?" he said coldly. His chilling eyes moved on to the younger female. He glanced from her round, china blue eyes to her pouting lips, to her large, immodestly covered breasts. Ella noted that his attention lingered where tightly fitted, strawberry pink tulle strained over twin mounds of blue-veined white flesh.

"Mr. Wokingham, I am Mrs. Able. The Reverend Able's wife. Your father and my husband have met on a number of occasions, but of course, you know that. We don't see you in church, but your family has a long and happy history with St. Cecil's. I understand Octavius introduced our little Precious to you at the Rectory when you were last in Lancashire. I'm sorry I wasn't at home on that occasion."

Pomeroy hadn't had his fill of the red-haired girl's breasts. "Regrets are mutual on this occasion." Slowly, his attention slid to Mrs. Able. "Please give my regards to your husband." With that he contrived to stand between the Ables and Ella.

"As I was saying, Miss Rossmara, we should take a turn around the gardens."

"It isn't warm," Mama said. "I don't think Ella and I should enjoy being outside."

"Ella will have the benefit of my cloak," Pomeroy said, barely parting his thin lips. "Lord Hunsingore thought that an admirable idea."

Alarm flashed over Mama's face. "You cannot possibly be suggesting that the two of you . . . Well, can you?"

"Come, come now," Pomeroy said, very quietly. "We should not pretend about certain things, should we, my lady?"

Mrs. Able's red-haired daughter was not to be so easily dismissed. She thrust herself into the tight circle Pomeroy had accomplished with Ella and her mother.

Pomeroy ignored the girl.

"I'm Precious," she said to Ella. "My mama says we're both making our first Seasons. I scarcely know a soul but dear Pom, here. Do I, Pom?" She tucked a hand beneath his elbow and pressed against him.

"Don't you?" he said. A nerve twitched at the corner of his eye.

"You know I don't," Precious said. Her voice had a childish quality quite unsuited to her full-blown appearance. "You silly man. You remember perfectly well the way we talked about how lonely I'd be in London. Except for when I'm with you, of course."

A vein pulsed visibly in Pomeroy's temple. "Won't your mother be looking for you . . . *Precious*?"

"I'm right here, Mr. Wokingham," Mrs. Able warbled from behind him. "Don't give me another thought. I know my Precious is in good hands with you."

Ella felt closer to laughter than she had all evening. "I'm pleased to meet you, Precious," she said, smiling at the girl. She could hardly be blamed for poor dressmaking or an unfortunate voice. "Mr. Wokingham is anxious to walk in the gardens. Do say you'll accompany him."

"Oh, I will. I will, indeed I will," Precious said. "Come along, Pom. You can show me the shrubbery." She tittered giddily.

At that moment a striking, very familiar face came into view. "Devlin," Ella exclaimed. "Mama, it's Devlin North. You know, of Northcliff Manor." Devlin's Scottish home bordered Castle Kirkcaldy lands.

"I could hardly forget." There was a degree of reserve in Lady Justine's voice. "Even though it's been some years."

Devlin caught sight of Ella over the heads of the crowd and grinned. Nodding and murmuring to people who greeted him as he passed, he threaded a path to Ella and her mother.

"Devlin," Ella said, delighted. "I didn't know you were in London." She felt Pomeroy Wokingham's hovering presence but refused to as much as glance at him.

"I'm very often in London, my dear," Devlin said. He took Mama's unresisting hand and kissed it lightly. "It's always a pleasure to see you, my lady," he told her.

She breathed deeply and said, "I hope you're well, Mr. North."

"Please. It's Devlin."

Finally she allowed him a smile. "Devlin, then. It's been a long time since we last met."

A long time since Papa and Mama had mistakenly thought Devlin was seeking to court Ella—whom they'd considered much too young at the time. In fact, Devlin had been bringing news of Saber's condition following a battle injury in India.

"It was nice to meet you, Ella," Precious Able said. "Pom and I are going outside, aren't we, Pom?"

Ella looked at Precious with a kind smile. "Make sure he lends you his cloak. It's cool."

"Oh, he will, won't you, Pom?" Precious said, urging him away. "Come along, Mama."

Pomeroy all but trembled with barely restrained fury, but the odd trio progressed in the direction of French doors that opened onto a terrace. Ella watched only long enough to note that Mrs. Able did not accompany her daughter and Pomeroy outside.

"Nice affair," Devlin said, surveying the glittering company.

Mama shifted her weight. "Very," she agreed. When she stood for too long the childhood injury that had left her with a limp caused her discomfort.

"You look very lovely, Ella."

"Thank you."

"And the color of poppies always did become you, my lady," Devlin said to Mama.

"Thank you."

Have you spoken to Saber? "Have you been in London long this time, Devlin?" If only she could speak to him alone. He might know something—some way to reach Saber and make him explain his behavior.

"I've been in and out of London in recent years. My business brings me here."

"I see."

"Are Arran and Grace planning to be in Town to help with your launch?" he asked, speaking of Papa's brother and his wife.

"They'll come for the ball Papa and Mama intend to give for me at the end of the Season," Ella told him, trying to sound animated. "And Calum—I mean the Duke of Franchot, and Pippa are to give me a ball, too."

Devlin studied her intently. "The entire family gathering around, hmm?"

"My brother, Max, may not be able to come for either affair. He's at Eton. But Mama's grandmama is to arrive at any moment."

Devlin grinned. "The formidable Dowager Duchess of Franchot. We should all quake."

Ella raised her chin. "Great-Grandmama Franchot is my friend. We understand each other."

"Ouch!" Devlin pretended to ward off a blow. "Forgive me. I intended no insult to your venerable relative."

She did punch him playfully then. "You fun me, sir."

Mama tweaked the pleats at the waist of her full skirt. "Perhaps we should find your papa," she said. "The Marquess of Casterbridge wanted to discuss some matter with him, but I'm sure Struan will be missing us by now."

"He will be missing you," Ella said boldly. "Why don't you go and rescue him. I shall be perfectly safe with Devlin, won't I?" She turned innocently trusting eyes up to his. They were green, but not the deep, hypnotic green of Saber's.

Devlin's affable grin appeared again. Unfortunately, on Devlin's exceedingly handsome face, an affable grin took on a wolfish quality.

Mama's disapproving sigh could not be missed, but she addressed Devlin directly. "I entrust Ella to you for the moment, sir. She likes you. And she has not been happy. If your company pleases her and lifts her spirits, you will have done us all a service. But have a care. One false step and you will bring the wrath of the Rossmara men upon your head—and my brother, the duke, will be with them. However, I feel a certain warmth toward you. Why, I may never be certain. Prove my feelings warranted, if you please."

As Mama left them, Ella felt color mount in her cheeks. "I'm sorry," she told Devlin. "My parents are very protective of me."

"Yes," he said, his tone changed. He sounded sharp, almost angry. "I'm thirsty. Let me take you for refreshments."

Ella studied his face for some clue to his humor but found none, except for an odd lack of any emotion at all. "Thank you," she told him, frowning slightly. "That would be delightful."

He offered her his arm, and she placed a hand decorously upon it. She didn't fail to note the envious stares of both matrons and their unattached daughters as she passed with Devlin. "Shipping," she heard several times. And "She's dark. Like a gypsy" reached her ears.

Ella raised her chin even higher, but lengthened her stride.

"Do not hurry, little one," Devlin said softly. "They are jealous. You are the most beautiful creature in the room, and they hate you for it."

"I am nobody," Ella said before she could stop herself.

He glanced down at her and murmured, "There, you are wrong. You are most definitely somebody. I only wish—" He pressed his lips together for an instant. "It's imperative that we find a place where we won't be interrupted."

She drew in a short, sharp breath.

"I have something to give you. From a friend."

Rather than escort her into the banquet room where tables groaned beneath the weight of delicacies as pleasing to the eye as to the tongue, Devlin turned Ella toward a passageway that led to a door behind the foot of a great, curving marble staircase.

On the other side of the door, he held a finger to his lips and shut them inside a room lined with serving carts. "Read this," he told her, holding out a sheet of paper folded into a square. "Read it quickly. We don't have much time."

Ella opened it slowly.

"Hurry," Devlin ordered. "If you are missed, we shall both regret this."

With suddenly cold fingers Ella flattened the paper and held it where candlelight shone from a sconce. *"Ella,"* she read.

"Your persistence plagues me. If you can finally accept that what we might have shared can never be, forget that I sent this note. If you still doubt the inevitable, come to me now. Devlin will help you. Saber."

She grasped Devlin's sleeve.

"Ella?" He bent solicitously over her. "Are you ill?"

"No," she told him when she could speak. "Shocked, but not ill. Where is he? In Burlington Gardens."

"He is here."

Ella glanced around.

"No. Not here in this room. But he is in this house. Waiting for you in a chamber on an upper floor. Evidently you begged him to be here and he has responded to your request."

"Take me to him."

Devlin made as if to touch her hair, but let his hand drop. "You are certain you want to see him?"

"Yes," she said urgently. "Yes, yes. There is nothing else I want in life but to see Saber."

He bowed formally. When he straightened, his face was grim. "No more delay, then. I shall take you up stairs usually reserved for servants and pray we do not encounter any of them. They should all be busy with the Eagletons' guests."

Ella did not care who saw them. She followed Devlin past a heavy green curtain covering the entrance to a staircase so narrow that her full skirt brushed the walls as she climbed.

Turn after turn brought one short flight of steps after another until they arrived behind a second heavy curtain—this one screening a short passage and another door.

When Devlin opened the door, the muffled sounds of the soiree reached Ella's ears. They were on a balcony above the great hall.

Her heart turned. She paused a moment and Devlin stopped the instant he realized she was no longer behind him. He frowned and gestured for her to come.

Pressing a hand to the bodice of her gown as if to calm her heart, she joined him before yet another door, this one framed by a gothic stone arch.

The heavy, studded oak door stood slightly open. No light showed beyond.

Ella looked at Devlin.

He took her hand and pressed it between both of his. "Saber is waiting for you. Remember, he has suffered, Ella. He suffers still. If his manner is not exactly as you recall, be generous. Don't judge him harshly. He cares for you."

Saber cared for her, yet he repeatedly refused to see her. And now he would see her to prove she had been mistaken in wanting to do so.

"Thank you," Ella told Devlin. "I think it would be best if you returned to the company. I shall find my own way back."

He looked at her for a moment, then turned away and did as she suggested without another word.

Ella rested the fingertips of her right hand on the door and pushed it open.

Chapter Five

Nothing moved.

Beyond the leaded casement a cloud-covered moon cast the dimmest of light into a violet-tinged black sky.

Ella, her arms pressed to her sides, took a step into the room.

"Close the door."

She jumped and peered around.

"Close it, Ella." Saber's voice.

"Where are you?"

"Do as I ask."

"Yes." Yes, she had nothing to fear from her old friend. She pushed the door until the latch clicked like a gunshot in the room's heavy stillness.

"There is a key in the lock. Turn it."

Saber's voice, but not exactly as she remembered it. Ella turned the key.

"Come here."

Her hands went to her throat. "Where are you?"

"Near the window."

"Can't we light a lamp?"

"I find that when there is nothing to distract the attention—such as looking upon another—one may truly hope for the touching of minds."

He sounded . . . angry? "I have pressed you, Saber. You are annoyed with me, but I . . . I have so longed to be with you."

A slight movement caught her eye, a tall shadow, darker against the suggestion of draperies at the casement. "Come to me, Ella."

She could not force enough air into her body. The night and the room were one, one with the man she could not see—all pressing in, surrounding and drawing her. Deeper to a place she desired and feared at once.

"If you would rather leave—"

"No!" She advanced slowly, arms outstretched, feeling for obstacles.

"In God's name."

Ella stopped. He had spoken softly, but with such pain. "Saber, what has happened? What is it that has kept you from me? I love—"

"Do not say that."

She covered her mouth.

"Will you let me touch you, Ella?"

Touch her? "Of course you may touch me. You are my friend. You said you would always be my friend." Two more steps took her close enough for his shadow to become a presence. She felt his substance. A warmth emanated from the man, a warmth and an essence of him, of his body and spirit. "You sent me a message."

"You sent me many."

"And you ignored them all."

"Until now."

She took one more step. "You sent a gift. A beautiful gift."

"A cold gift. And another message."

"A false message. The gem is cold, but your heart is warm, my dear friend. Since the night in Cornwall when you returned from the fair to comfort a troubled girl, I have known your heart. What I felt for you at first has only grown, Saber. And I believe you spoke your true feelings then."

His tracing over her hair was so light, she reached to brush it away as she might a cobweb.

He trapped her fingers. "You said I could touch you."

"You surprised me."

"This will be the only time we can be together."

She reached for him, found his solid chest, and filled her fingers with his jacket. "Why do you say such things? There is no impediment to our being together now. I am no longer a child."

His hand moved from her hair to her face. With the delicacy of a butterfly's wings, he traced her brow, her eyelids, her cheeks—and settled a forefinger on her mouth. "I remember your mouth, little Ella. God help me, I remember everything about you." He breathed out, long and slow. "I remember the scent of you. Wildflowers. You still smell of wildflowers, and sun on warm grass—and sweetness."

She held very still, but inside she trembled. "And I remember you. Everything about you. Why did you go away after you had recovered from your injury? I wanted to be with you. You told me we would be together one day."

"I had to go. Please do not speak of that. I had to return to India."

"But you have come back again now, and—"

His finger on her lips sealed her words away. "This will be the only time, Ella. Should you prefer to leave me now?"

"I do not ever want to leave you!"

"What I want, I should turn from. What I want is wrong."

She pushed close and rested her cheek on his hard chest.

"Whatever you want should be yours. Tell me. I'll get it for you."

He laughed at that, a short, bitter laugh. "You have brought me what I want—and what will ensure that the remains of my miserable life will be a penance."

She did not understand.

"I struggled against coming here tonight. Struggled and lost. But perhaps that is as well. We are both in need of finding some peace for ourselves."

"You mean together?" She could not hide the hope she felt.

"No," Saber said. "Apart. You must give up this pursuit of me, Ella. I cannot bring you happiness."

"I will not give you up."

"Then I must make you do so."

He spoke in riddles. "There is nothing you can do to drive me away," Ella told him.

His sigh hurt her. "If only that were true." Saber settled his hand on the back of her head and held her to him. "You do not sound exactly as you did when you were that child in Cornwall."

She smiled. "Mama—Lady Justine, as you knew her then—she made certain Max and I learned not to embarrass the Rossmaras with our crude speech. Who would know that Max was once the property of a master pickpocket in Covent Garden? He's a gentleman now—at Eton, no less."

"I'm glad," Saber said, although he did not sound glad at all. He sounded ever more removed from Ella.

"And my owned wretched past—"

"You are who you were always meant to be," he said sharply, and his fingers tangled in her hair until her scalp hurt. "You are Ella. There will never be another like you."

Then why did he say they could not be together—other than now?

"May I touch you, Ella?"

"Yes. I told you so."

"And you have not changed your mind?"

"No, Saber. Do so. Please."

For moments he remained still, then he set her a little way from him. "Your skin is golden, Ella." He stroked her jaw and her neck, until his fingertips settled on her bare shoulders. "And so soft. I have seen it often. I saw it when I was in India—and on the ship—and I see it whenever I close my eyes and wish our lives had been different."

Ella did not dare speak. She tingled where their skin met. Was this what they spoke of, the girls who twittered about the way they felt in the company of men? Ella knew nothing of those feelings. She had never experienced them until now.

"Soft and golden," Saber murmured. "I promised myself I would wait until you were old enough. And I was so certain our time would come to be together."

"And now it has," she whispered, resting her palms on the smooth front of his shirt beneath his jacket and waistcoat. "I know Papa—"

"You said I might feel you. May I kiss you, Ella?"

Kiss. She had never been kissed. In her dreams, both waking and sleeping, she had imagined a kiss and it had always been Saber's.

"May I kiss you and forget that there has been any past—or that there will be a future?"

"Kiss me, Saber."

His head bowed over hers. His breath crossed her face, soft and warm. His lips met hers lightly.

Ella closed her eyes. She did not breathe. She thought her heart did not beat. She existed only where Saber's lips rested.

Back and forth his mouth brushed, the softest of brushing while a deep sound came from him. A groan. His lips hardened, sought she knew not what, pressed and parted, parted her lips also. Ella gasped, her breathing flowing into Saber, his breath returning to fill her.

Her eyes flew open. His tongue ran along the seared skin inside her bottom lip, and passed her teeth—and met her tongue. His tasting of her turned blood to water, bones to nothing. Her body and his—one. If he released her, she would fall.

"Mmm," she murmured.

"Mmm what, Ella?"

"I like this kiss."

"I like it too. I like kissing you."

"Then perhaps you should kiss me again."

He kissed her again, and again and again, and every kiss pressed deeper into her mouth. She clung to his shirt, his neckcloth, whatever she could hold. The heat of him beat through to her, reached her skin and beyond. Strange sensations. Pulsing in places she could not name but where she wanted to feel those sensations more and more—with Saber.

"It is not enough," he told her.

"No." What wasn't enough? He would make it plain.

"Is it all right if . . . I will not pressure you, Ella. You have already suffered enough in your life."

"And I have been very fortunate in my life, also."

"Brave little Ella. Just once—may I feel your loveliness just once?"

"I am not lovely. But whatever I am is yours, Saber."

He straightened, and she heard the rustle of his jacket as he took it off and tossed it aside. He moved more in the darkness, removed his waistcoat. His shirt shone white in the gloom—until that, too, was gone.

Cautiously, Ella slipped the backs of her fingers over his chest. Soft hair. Smooth, warm, firm skin over bone and muscle. So different in form from her own body.

Gently but firmly, he took her wrists and placed them at her sides. He turned her around and began unfastening her gown. She sucked in a breath, but made no effort to stop him.

Slowly, cool air swept over the skin he bared. Her gown was undone, and her chemise. He slid them slowly from her shoulders and down her arms, pulled the sleeves over her hands and let them fall.

Ella bowed her head and waited. If this was what Saber wanted, then she wanted it too.

She was naked to the waist. Never before had she been naked in front . . . Ella pressed away the memory that crowded in. It did not count that she had been forced to suffer the scrutiny of men while she'd worn only a transparent scarlet gown. Her mind had fled that moment, just as it had fled the sights that had surrounded her on that terrible night, in that terrible house of evil. And at least, thanks to Papa, she had been saved from the full extent of whatever dreadful fate had been planned for her in that house.

Saber kissed her again, this time on the vulnerable back of her neck. She shivered.

"Cold?"

She shook her head and hunched her shoulders, fighting an urge to cover herself. With Saber this was right, it was as it should be.

He urged her against him. Her back met his chest and she leaned. Then his caressing hands rose over her shoulders and across the tender place at the dip in her throat, and passed lower to stroke over her breasts.

Ella smothered a cry. This was Saber, the man she loved.

He covered her breasts, lifted and supported them, and rested the sides of his thumbs on her nipples.

She took little gulps of air. Her breasts ached. Her nipples grew hard beneath the flicking brushes of his thumbs. Hard and searingly aware. Arching against him, she rolled her head, seeking. Seeking? What could feel so? What could pass through a woman's body like white hot strands, strands of pleasure that demanded to be drawn through her without end?

His next kiss lingered on one shoulder, his breath slipping over her breast.

She did not need to see him to know his face, to know his form, to *feel* him.

When he took his hands from her breasts she was bereft, but waited patiently for his command. Very quickly he slipped her clothes from her hips until they fell about her feet.

Clad in only her stockings and slippers, she stood in a strange room, in a strange house, with the man she had loved since she scarcely knew what love meant.

Her ribs, her waist, her belly—he explored them all with reverent care. Her thighs received his patient attention.

They had no need of words.

There was no before. There would only be now and forever.

He touched her there!

"Hush," he said against her shoulder when she made a sound. "Whatever you have known is in the past. This is what I want you to know now—and to remember. My wish is to give you pleasure."

The place at her center burned at his probing.

Bewildered, Ella twisted to face him. She tried to hold him but could not. He bent and licked the tip of a nipple.

"Saber!" Her legs jerked, and she gripped his tensed arms.

Cupping her breasts, nuzzling between, he captured first one nipple, then the other. He drew her deeply into his mouth, and she was helpless. Nerve and flesh, all wanting—all taking.

He straightened, and claimed her mouth again.

Ella slipped her arms around his waist and pressed her breasts to his chest. His hair teased her nipples, inflamed the hot, white threads again, and this time she knew where they began and where they sought to bury themselves. The curls between her legs hid the source of tormenting desire that did not fulfill or release her.

Saber's hips met her belly. The part of him she knew was his manhood thrust against her. Huge in its strength, it sought her. Again the dim but awful images hovered in her memory. They had no place here. Those were other bodies, other mindless bodies that providence had kept from harming her.

With greedy fingers, she sought the weight of him, surrounded and held it, heard his broken moan, met the fresh lunge of his hips.

His mouth on hers swallowed her cry as he walked her backward. Her bottom met the edge of something solid.

Saber's mouth left Ella's, and she looked up at him. In the darkness his eyes glittered, and his teeth. She knew those eyes. They were the deep green of deep water. Then the light was gone again and once more his lips covered hers—and his fingers delved into the curls where pleasure hovered.

She felt the slick wetness of her own body and blushed. He would feel it too. He used that slickness to slip into her most private place, to slip in and slip out. He used her own womanly elixir to glide over a tiny hardened bud where all ecstasy was centered. The ecstasy hovered, begged for what she could not form in her mind.

Again he found the passage that closed without bidding around his fingers. Again he returned to the swollen bud. This time his mouth fastened to her breast, and while he took her nipple between his careful teeth, he worked the bud ceaselessly.

Tension brought her thighs together, clamped his hand.

White hot. It shattered, frayed, blossomed black and red and consumed her. Ella cried out—a scream she could not swallow. He had rent her, and she welcomed the wound, the beloved wound that needed no healing. Might she never heal from this moment.

"My beautiful Ella," Saber said against her breast. "I thought I could convince you—convince myself that our lives must never touch. Perhaps I thought I might do that through teaching you a lesson, poor fool that I am—teach you that I am a poison, to myself and to you. You must go on. But how shall I ever live now?"

She struggled to understand. While all her body throbbed, she fought to clear her mind. And she reached for Saber, for his strong arms and wide shoulders—for his broad back.

"I should like to touch all of you too," she said timidly. "Might I do that?"

He held still.

Beneath her right hand, a knot of flesh marred the skin of his shoulder. She pressed her lips together and felt his tension. "This is where you were wounded, my dearest. Let me soothe you. There is more to this thing between us, isn't there? What you have made me feel tonight. You need me to do for you what you have done for me."

"What have I done for you?" His tone was no longer gentle.

"Brought me so much joy."

"No," he said. "I have tasted joy to which I had no right. And I was weak enough to relish every stolen moment. It is more than I deserve."

"Never," she told him. "It will never be enough, not until our lives are over."

"Mine is over."

She grew still.

Abruptly, he withdrew from her. There was a flare, and the light within a lamp brightened.

Ella didn't care that she was naked. He was beautiful. His dark hair fell forward as he adjusted the lamp. The line of his long spine glistened and muscles rippled with the slightest movement. Her eyes went to the scar at his shoulder. White and twisted, it traversed in a curve to the center of his back.

So much pain. Her beloved had suffered so much. Where the knots bunched, the point of a blade must have sunk again, and again.

He might have died!

"Saber. Such terrible wounds. So deep. Let me hold you."

"Hold me?" He turned and caught her by the upper arms. "Hold me? Are you sure?"

"Saber!" Her heel caught the edge of the carpet and she overbalanced. All the room spun before her, the room and Saber's face, Saber's poor, viciously scarred face.

Chapter Six

He disgusted her.

Saber looked into her dark eyes, at the revulsion stamped there—and he knew that he had not suffered utter desolation until this moment.

He bowed his head, allowing his hair to cover what terrified her so. Swiftly, he retrieved her clothes and set them on the heavy, canopied bed at the left of the room.

"Saber?"

She still clung to the side of the chair where she'd all but collapsed at the sight of him.

"Can you dress in the dark, Ella? I would help you."

"In the dark? Yes. Why—?"

"Because I knew you would be repulsed by me and I couldn't bear the finality of that. So I stayed away. Go to the bed. I will deal with the lamp."

"Repulsed? I asked . . . I wanted to know why you would put out the lamp. Why should I dress in the dark?"

"I'd like to spare you the horror, Ella. I thought I could be strong. I had decided that I could meet you in this room, deny my feelings—sever with you forever and be done with it. But then I heard your voice. I felt your presence. I had to touch you, Ella. Once you were near, I had to know your scent, your tenderness. How wrong I was. How my selfish lack of restraint has wronged you. I should have done as I planned. You were never to see me as I am."

He approached the lamp.

"Ooh!" Her angry cry battered him. "Stop it! Stop it now, do you hear me?"

Saber paused but did not turn around.

"All men are cabbage-heads! All men *decide* what women do and do not want or think, without ever bothering to ask. You believe you have the right to pretend to see inside my mind. You have misused me, Saber!"

This angry female was not the Ella he remembered, but then, he had shocked her—and he had taken advantage of her ignorance about his condition. "I'm sorry," he said quietly. "It isn't enough, but I regret my behavior."

"I regret your behavior too." Her feet beat a path across the carpet. "I shall certainly require your assistance."

"Yes. A moment while I deal with the lamp."

"If you touch that lamp I shall . . . I shall . . . Well, I will. So don't. Now look at me."

She had always been brave. Only a brave young female would share what she considered to be her most shameful secret—her illegitimacy—with a man who was almost a stranger. Ella had done that, with him, when she'd been less than sixteen and so unsure of her future.

"Saber"—her voice softened—"look at me, please."

He did as she asked reluctantly. With his fists on his hips, he faced Ella across the elegant room and planted his feet apart.

"You've hidden from me because of your wounds, haven't you? Your scars?"

"I have apologized for my actions tonight. There is no more to be said."

"Nothing at all *has* been said. Nothing of honesty."

He drove a hand into his hair. "I tried to stay away from you. Now I shall do so—completely."

"You didn't simply try to stay away, Saber. You did so. You are only here tonight because I finally goaded you into revealing yourself."

He looked at her then. Not a tall woman, but straight, proud. Her black hair had slipped from its chignon to fall in partially unraveled braids about her shoulders.

Naked. Completely naked before him and watching him with those great, dark, exotic eyes.

Unashamed.

But then, this was not a virginal girl who had never known a man.

But she was shy in her way—he knew that. And he must never forget that whatever she had once been was not of her own making—and her extreme youth might well have made the acts she'd performed unreal to her then. Pain. She must have suffered pain at the hands of the monsters who used her. Pain and fear—and confusion. And now, after she had at least enjoyed a few years of comfort and protection, he had visited more distress upon the blameless creature he could not stop loving.

"Say something, Saber," she asked, wrapping her arms about her waist. "Am I displeasing to you?"

"Displeasing?" He averted his eyes. "You are the most lovely creature in the world. I have tried not to allow this to happen. As I have confessed, I should not have done so. I managed to keep what I have become hidden from you. To change that was madness. I would never have wished you to remember me as I am."

"They have hurt your soul," she told him. "If they had not

done so, you would not think a few silly scars could repulse me."

He gazed upon her fully. "Don't humor me, Ella. Condescension offends my manhood, and there is nothing amiss with that, I assure you."

She dropped her arms and raised her jaw. "There is no need to testify to the condition of your manhood to me, my lord."

He frowned, and could not stop himself from glancing the length of her slender but intoxicating body.

"I *felt* your manhood, my lord." Her breasts, round and pointed and pink-tipped, jutted with each angry breath. "It thrust at me. And it filled my hands. And its weight impressed me, as no doubt you were aware."

He felt himself redden. "I'm so glad you noted my proportions in such detail," he said, making sure his words bore sufficient sarcasm. A man of eight-and-twenty should not blush like a cub at the mention of his rod. "You speak as a connoisseur."

The words were no sooner spoken than regretted. Her smooth brow furrowed. She lifted her hair from her shoulders and remained with her elbows raised. "A connoisseur?" Upthrust breasts and a slender waist. Her hips flared gently and her long legs—in their provocative stockings—took his breath away. There was nothing about her that did not render him speechless.

"A connoisseur?" she repeated. "What can you mean, Saber? Why, that word suggests—"

"It suggests nothing," he told her rapidly. "This entire exchange should not have happened. You must return to the party. By now there will be searchers out looking for you."

"I'm never going back to the party," she said flatly. "Do you know Pomeroy Wokingham?"

"The Hon. Pom? A lecher. A debauched . . . Enough said.

He is not the type of man whose name should cross your lips. Get dressed."

"You dress me," she said calmly. "You undressed me."

Saber lowered his eyes. "Sweet Ella. You are determined to pretend I do not disgust you, aren't you? In the name of an old friendship, you will try to give me back some of what I've lost. Thank you, but I am at peace with my choices." *Liar.*

"My lord, you have recently completed a very thorough examination of my person. Do you deny that?"

Her manner with words was quite singular. "One does not voice such things."

"One might not. I do. Answer me, if you please."

"Your person suffered that treatment from me, yes."

"My person did not suffer at all—unless it was from the most marvelous ecstasy any woman's body has ever known. I adored every instant of it, and shall look forward to many more such explorations—from you."

Saber stared at her.

"Shocked you, have I, my lord? I suppose I should apologize for my forwardness, but since my newly found boldness has been brought about by your kisses, by your mouth upon my breasts, by your hands all over me—your fingers inside me—"

"Ella!"

"As I was saying. I might apologize for being brazen, but I'm naked because you took off my clothes. And I can scarcely help it if I've discovered I'm glad you did. Or that having your mouth on my breasts and your fingers in my body and stroking that place until—"

"Ella!"

"Oh, why must you keep shouting my name like that?" She marched toward him. "My mama believes a young woman should know all about the business of men and women. Men and women together—when they are entirely alone, that is.

Alone in their own . . . well, their own chambers, or whatever."

Saber found he could not summon a single word of response.

"She wrote a book on the subject, you know. And it was published."

It was published, all right. It was published and published and published, and all of the Polite World—and the not so polite world—had read the damned thing. They continued to read it. Poor Hunsingore, and Stonehaven—and Saber's own cousin Calum, Duke of Franchot—had suffered the notoriety of having their names emblazoned in the wretched book. Dear Justine's innocent study of a subject almost entirely lacking in that virtue had led to a most provocative book intended to be read by young women preparing for marriage. And Justine had *dedicated* the volume to her husband and his brother, and to her own brother—with her thanks for their help!

"In Mama's book," Ella continued when she must have decided he would not respond. "I have not been allowed to read it yet. She says I shall do so when I am betrothed. But I've been told by others who have read it that it says a woman should learn to enjoy the man she loves as much as—"

"I know what it says."

She came to stand before him. "So you've read it?" Her perfect skin glowed. Her eyes glistened with sincerity. "How very enlightened of you. I understand very few men will touch the volume."

Every man in London hadn't been able to wait to "touch" the volume. "I've read it."

Ella looked directly up into his face. "And did you consider it to have merit?" If she was repulsed by him, she hid the fact well.

"I considered it . . . enlightening."

"Enlightening how?"

He was growing hard again. No, he was already hard, had been so unceasingly since he'd first touched her. "There is insight into the female mind, I believe. Interesting from an academic point of view." Surely her apparent comfort while standing unclothed before him could not be natural? But then . . . Yes, but then.

Ella was frowning. "From an academic point of view? How very cool. A young lady who spoke of it said she experienced certain—*sensations*. I can hardly wait to discover its effect upon me. Anyway, I believe you found it more than academically interesting. Did it make your body feel some sort of longings?"

"Longings?"

Without warning, she stroked the length of his rod through his trousers and tucked her hands beneath to support him. "Like this, I suppose. I have considered the subject, and I think this swelling takes place because of longing. I've noted a similar reaction in a number of gentlemen—always when they are in the company of females who appear to engage them."

She amazed him. "Indeed," he said.

"Oh, yes. And the longings must come from some connection of the mind to the body. Those connections might well be caused by a certain stimulation that might arise from a discussion of a man and woman together in a condition of love, don't you think? As is presented in Mama's book, I understand?"

He thought he was about to disgrace himself, and to lose control—in either order. "Very likely. It's inappropriate for you to, er, handle me as you are, Ella."

She squeezed, a look of deep concentration filming her features with distraction. "Odd," she murmured.

Saber gritted his teeth. "Odd?"

Again she squeezed. "Definitely odd."

"How so?" He knew a moment's deep uncertainty. He also knew an even deeper need to remove his trousers and enter where his fingers had already ventured this evening.

Ella squeezed him yet again. "It responds to the touch. I mean, it actually, um, *pops up* whenever it's been compressed."

Saber snatched her hand away. "This is an unbelievable conversation. I'm going to assist you into your clothes and you will then go back to the soiree."

She turned from him, picked up the lamp, and walked to the bed.

Her straight back narrowed to the waist and her small bottom was round and smooth. . . . White stockings secured with pink satin, rose-encrusted garters worked an erotic spell on his senses.

"Obviously nothing can be the same as it was before this evening," she remarked. "And I, for one, am exceedingly glad."

How would he manage to assist her into her clothes without losing his head to passion again? He was a bounder, a man with nothing to offer, yet who had taken liberties with one who was innocent at least of heart.

"Your generosity humbles me, Ella."

She reached the bed, calmly used the steps to climb upon the mattress, and sat with her feet dangling over the edge.

"You have quelled your natural feelings in order to help me with mine," he told her. "That is generous."

She gathered her chemise and held it to her. "Come here, please, Saber. I need your assistance."

And he needed strength—very possibly much more strength than he could hope to possess. "Perhaps you could slip on that garment. Then I could tie—"

"Out of the question. You must help me."

Keeping his face averted, he approached.

"What are you doing? Saber, look at me!"

Perhaps his face wasn't so very terrifying—not to a young woman of apparently strong sensibilities. But she could not see where the true scars remained, remained forever open.

"I am cold." Her voice rose a little.

Repentant, Saber went to her and took the flimsy, lace-trimmed white gauze thing from her. "I cannot imagine that this would bring a great deal more warmth than your own skin."

Her hands, shooting around his neck, stopped his frowning perusal of the garment. Ella pulled his hair away from the scars on his face.

He lowered his eyelids.

"A cruel thing," she remarked softly. "A cruel, senseless attack on the most handsome face I ever knew."

He closed his eyes entirely. "Now you know why I prefer the darkness. Why I frequent a dim, old men's club where my disfigurement is of little note."

"Your disfigurement." Very gently, she smoothed her fingers along the raised white scar that made a crescent from his hairline, through his brow—blessedly missing anything but the corner of his eye—to plunge across his cheekbone and the side of his jaw. "An annoying little thing. But no doubt with a great deal of soothing—the kind of soothing it will receive from me—there will be some relaxing of the skin."

Saber tried to turn his face aside, but she quickly slipped a hand over his cheek. "Open your eyes, please."

He did so at once.

She did not flinch. There was no evidence of disgust in her expression now. "Does this hurt?" She rested a thumb on the webbing at the corner of his eye.

"No," he told her truthfully.

"And your eyes are not touched. I thank God for that."

"As do I," he confessed. "I should hate to burden some poor servant with the care of a blind man."

"I would gladly have become that servant," she told him. "I meant that looking into your eyes is the greatest joy I can imagine." She shivered.

"You are chilled, Ella. Come, let me help with your gown now."

"I should prefer that you hold me."

He would also prefer to hold her, but he was, after all, nothing more than a man—a man who had suppressed carnal needs for far too long.

Ella wriggled closer. She wriggled close enough to thread her arms around his body and settle her face beneath his chin. Her breasts pressed insistently against his chest.

"Ella, my sweet," he said, and immediately hoped she did not hear the desperation behind the endearment. "It isn't seemly for us to remain so."

"Nothing that has passed between us is seemly. I am not a green girl. I know perfectly well that my reputation is now ruined."

He held his breath. She spoke as if she had obliterated her past. Was it possible for such a thing to occur? Saber rested his chin on top of her head. "I intend to ensure that your reputation survives this evening. You will return to the company via the route you took to get here. And you will explain that you wandered off and couldn't find your way back."

"I don't want to."

Her nipples were hard against his skin.

His rod was hard, very hard.

"Pomeroy Wokingham is the man who is trying to get my father to agree to give him my hand in marriage."

Saber grew absolutely still. "Pomeroy?"

"Yes. I told you someone was to approach Papa. It was Pomeroy and his parent. And downstairs at the soiree he tried to take me out into the gardens—without Mama. He said Papa told him he was at liberty to walk with me. I do not believe him."

"Neither do I," Saber said thoughtfully. The Wokinghams were well-known among a certain set. Saber had heard talk of them from Devlin, who counted a number of questionable types among his acquaintances. "The Wokinghams shall never get their hands on you, my love." The father and son were said to have a predilection for sharing whatever female they procured.

"I like that."

He heard Ella only dimly. "What do you like?"

"That you called me your love. You see, we are both of a mind. We both know that this is absolutely what is meant to be. We will be together now. Nothing can separate us again."

There could be no question of the Wokinghams interfering with this girl.

Saber took in a shuddering breath. "It is imperative that you go back downstairs at once."

"Not unless you come with me."

He turned cold. "Out of the question."

"Then it is out of the question for me to go."

"Don't be childish."

"Don't you dare refer to me as childish! I have waited four years for this moment. I shall never allow you to leave me again." For emphasis, she placed a hard, openmouthed kiss on his lips. "There." She drew her face back triumphantly. The evidence of their kisses showed on her swollen lips and his beard had reddened her smooth skin. What could be done about her tumbled hair, he could not guess.

"You have to save me from the Hon. Pom and his revolting father."

Protective resolve, and an urge to seek the shelter of familiar shadows, warred within Saber. "Struan would not give you to such creatures."

"They are wealthy. Papa said as much. And well-connected."

"And out of the question," Saber retorted before he could temper his reaction.

Ella stroked his arms. She scooted up until she could plant kiss after kiss along the wretched evidence of his failure as a soldier, as a leader and protector of men.

Saber grasped her waist. "Ella—"

"Hush. This is very good for you. Mothers tell their children that kisses will make them better."

He laughed without mirth. "I am most definitely not a child. And you, my dear, spectacular woman, are not my mother."

"Of course not. How silly of you to be literal. I merely meant that if mothers have said such a thing for so long, then it must be so. Oh, Saber, I wish there was no need to leave this room—ever."

"We cannot have very many of our wishes," he told her.

"They've been telling lies about you, you know."

"Have they?"

"I know they absolutely cannot be true."

His mind responded sluggishly. The tips of his fingers played over the soft skin of her thigh above a stocking.

"Obviously there is no courtesan in your life. You would not ever consider having anything to do with such a creature."

Saber withdrew his hand.

"I heard those silly men talking about it to you at Sibley's. But you were just too kind to tell them they were being foolish."

"What are you talking about, Ella?" He had an unnerving notion that he knew.

"Countess Perruche. I asked Mama about her and she said

the woman is a French courtesan and considered practiced in . . . Well, I don't know exactly what she's practiced in, but it didn't sound at all suitable. But there is definitely talk about you and this Margot."

So the chatter was all over London, was it? So much the better. He and Margot had designed matters exactly that way.

"We shall soon put that tongue-wagging nonsense to rest," Ella said. "I'll help you with it at once."

"Ella, my dear friend, it is absolutely time for you to return to the others." With that he put her firmly from him, took up the chemise, and slipped it over her head. When she raised her arms, the sight of her all but brought him to his knees again. He would not be able to continue this incredible restraint much longer. For that reason, among others, this temptation must be removed.

Once she was dressed, Saber sat her on a stool before a small glass and sent up thanks for the silver-backed brush and comb that rested on a crystal tray atop the dressing table. He concentrated on brushing out her hair.

Her light laughter brought his attention to her face. "What amuses you so?"

"You. Playing the maid. Although I must say that no maid ever brought me such delight by simply brushing my hair. Now we shall see how you do with the braids."

He handed her the brush and comb. "We shall watch *you* braid your hair, little vixen. I'll stand ready with these terrifying pin things."

While she deftly plaited her hair, Saber retrieved his shirt and made a fair job of reknotting his abused neckcloth. "I will make sure you are safely on your way," he told her, slipping on his waistcoat.

"You will take me," she told him serenely. "I shall then go to work on these dreadful rumors about you and Countess Perruche—at once."

He could not talk to Ella about Margot. The relationship he shared with the French woman was something he was not ready to explain. "Ella," he said patiently. "You have helped me tonight."

She grinned. "I think you have helped me far more. But soon the time will come when I shall read Mama's book and know exactly how to accomplish my part of the bargain."

He paused in the act of putting on his black jacket. "Bargain? There is no bargain. Now you understand why I could not possibly go about again. And why it has been necessary for me to stay away from you. Despite my misgivings, I don't believe I shall always regret what has passed between us. Eventually I may find great pleasure in the recalling of it."

"You will not have to recall it." She bounced to her feet and twirled. "See? Good as new. But very different inside, of course."

"Ella—"

"You will not have to recall it because we shall repeat the event at least daily—possibly many times daily—from now on."

Saber gaped.

Her laughter rang in the room. "Oh, you goose of a man. Did you really think a silly old scar would make me stop loving you? You did, didn't you? In Scotland, when you sent me away from Devlin's house, you made sure I did not see the scars. And again at Sibley's. Your face was always in the shadows. I should be angry with you for thinking so little of me, but I cannot be angry with you."

"Thank you," he said through dry lips.

"How fortunate for both of us that early adversity made me a very determined person. In fact, my lord, I find your scars quite dashing. My goodness, I shall have to discourage all the females who will swarm about you. You will turn every head."

Saber did not smile. "I have had experience of the way in which I turn heads. I have seen the distaste. And you are recovered now, little one, but I have not forgotten that at first you all but collapsed at the sight of me."

"Collapsed?" She looked from him to the chair where he'd pleasured her, and back. "I was shocked, yes. A natural thing when one—thanks to a certain person's lack of trust—a natural thing when one sees the evidence of suffering on a beloved one's face, on his body—without warning. And I did not almost collapse, you twaddle-brain. I *tripped* on the wretched carpet and all but fell. You should have been concerned with catching me, not worrying about your silly little scars. So there!"

Her audacity—and her vehemence—rendered him speechless yet again.

"Now," she said, slipping her hand through his arm. "Are we ready to go down and deal with what must be dealt with?"

"I . . ." Visions of Pomeroy Wokingham rose abruptly and wholly clear. Struan wouldn't consider giving Ella to that libertine, would he? "Very well. I shall accompany you down."

"Of course you will. We will immediately set about stilling wicked tongues—and making certain the Hon. Pom turns his designs elsewhere."

"I shall take you to Struan and Justine. It has been far too long since I saw them." A brief flush of warm anticipation surprised him. He'd taught himself not to think of the relatives who had once been so close and so dear.

"They are going to be delighted," Ella bubbled, urging him toward the door. "Of course, Mama has always expected that this would come about. I have no idea what Papa may have thought, but I'm certain he will be happy for us."

Saber halted before the door and turned to Ella. "Happy for us?"

"When we announce that we are to be married!"

When he could speak, Saber said, "Ella, of course I have caused you to . . . No, Ella, no. For your sake I will return you to the company and ensure you are not bothered by further advances that do not please you. But, my dear one, that is all that may be between us."

Her lips parted and he saw her teeth come together.

He had to make her understand. "I . . . No, I confess that I *did* want to be with you as I was tonight. As I was, and more—much more. When I thought I set out to merely teach you to detest the sight of me, I deluded myself. For that I must bear the guilt. You are blameless. But no harm is done, and I hope you will forgive me."

"F-forgive you?"

He felt a flooding of resolve. "You have given me so much. I believe it may be possible for me to move about in Society again. If you can bear to look upon me, the rest are without importance."

"You promised you would always be my friend," she whispered.

"Yes. And I will. I am."

"I didn't know exactly what you meant at the time, but I did later. You meant friend of the kind who shared what we have shared. I thought . . . I thought you loved me."

"I do love you." His misery was something he did not dare reveal to her. Every word must be carefully chosen. "I love you as a sister."

Ella tore her hand from his arm with such force she staggered. "Posh!"

"I beg your pardon?"

"I said, Posh! Piffle! Twaddle! Poppyçock! I don't know exactly what is afoot here, but I will not stand for it! There. Now you know."

"Be assured—"

"I am assured. I am assured that you will not be allowed to

retreat to that dismal house in Burlington Gardens again. You will not be allowed to languish there with your two-headed monsters and nasty, lolling-tongued statues. When you languish, Lord Avenall, it will be with *me*!"

She did not understand at all, but how could she? The line must be drawn, and drawn very clearly, at once. He held her shoulders. "As I have told you—I am your friend and you may look to me for support in any trouble that befalls you. I will protect you."

"And I will protect you," she told him fiercely. "Husbands and wives are bound to protect each other."

It must be made clear now, before he took steps he would soon come to rue. "What husbands and wives do is of no relevance here."

Her eyes held his. "You would not have touched me as you did if you did not wish for us to be man and wife."

"Wishing has nothing to do with this. On this occasion, necessity must be the only consideration."

"Necessity demands that I be with you, Saber," she said with simple directness. "I want to be where you are at all times. When you are awake and when you are asleep. Always."

His gut clenched. He reached out and held her hand, closed his fingers around it so tightly he saw her wince. "Listen to me," he said, hearing the harshness in his tone. "Your little fantasy can never be. Accept what we have shared and be grateful I am not a man completely without scruples or control. Also, if you are moved to think ill of me, remind yourself that it was you who would not rest until you forced a meeting with me. You would not forget me even though I had begged you to do so."

"Saber—"

"No. No, let me finish. We will not be announcing a betrothal tonight. Not tonight. Not ever."

"Why?" she managed to choke out. "Please make me understand."

"Because it cannot be. I cannot now, and will never be able to marry you."

Chapter Seven

"*I cannot now, and will never be able to marry you.*" Ella emerged from the door to the servants' stairs on Saber's arm, his announcement still ringing in her ears.

When the rush of loud conversation, of laughter, and of music met them, Saber hesitated.

Ella didn't urge him onward but waited patiently. He must accomplish his reappearance in Society at his own pace. But there were other matters that would not be left to the uncertain fate of Lord Avenall's whims, such as his marriage—to Ella.

He placed his fingers over her hand on his arm and proceeded slowly. His fingers were long and firm and warm. Ella liked the sensation of his strength added to her resolve. She liked everything about the man—except his foolish belief that she would somehow forget what had passed between them, and be content to become his "friend."

"Why?" she asked conversationally.

His face, when he looked down at her, was rigid. He

dreaded confronting people who would stare. How could a man so devastatingly attractive doubt his power to overcome something so trivial as scars—even such cruel scars?

"Why, Saber?" she repeated.

"What are you asking?"

"Why can't you marry me?"

They had almost reached the stream of guests coming and going from the supper room. Saber drew to a halt and stared at Ella. "In God's name. Have you lost your mind?"

"Not that I'm aware. Why, have you lost yours?"

The look he aimed at her was decidedly strange. "My sanity is not for you to discuss. And kindly do not mention . . . do not embarrass yourself by persisting with a subject we have agreed never to mention again."

"I agreed to no such thing," she told him in the identical tone. "Good evening, Countess Ballard. How lovely to see you again."

The elderly, gray-haired lady paused on her way into the supper room and raised a gold lorgnette to her bright blue eyes. "Hmm," she said. "Young Hunsingore's gel. Pretty thing. Unusual. Make some man a fine wife." With that she leveled her blue gaze on Saber and blinked. She dropped the lorgnette and said, "At least you're not dead, young man," before continuing on, her voluminous black gown rustling, an excess of fabulous gems winking at her neck and on her hands and wrists.

"I suppose I ought to find that funny," Saber said through his teeth.

"One day we'll remember it and laugh." *Please.*

Saber's fingers gripped Ella's tightly.

"Come on," she told him. "Let's find Mama and Papa."

Ella took a step, and Saber walked with her until they reached the entrance to the great hall.

"This is a mistake," he murmured.

Those closest stopped talking and turned to stare. Ella saw female mouths fall open, and she didn't imagine for an instant that their owners felt only horror at the sight of Saber. She recognized fascination when she saw it.

He mesmerized them. . . .

"Hot," he said, his step faltering. "So hot."

Ella pressed close to his side and said, "It will be cooler once we reach the other side of the room." She slid her fingers farther down his hand until she could thread them with his. Surely he didn't tremble?

She glanced up at him. His gaze appeared fixed.

"Saber," she whispered urgently. "Are you ill?"

He started, and shook his head. "Ill? I am oppressed, not ill."

How typical of the male, to resort to any lengths to avoid what they did not wish to confront.

"Oppressed? Is that all? We are all oppressed, my lord. You have not answered my question yet." Smiling from side to side, she walked, so that Saber had no choice but to accompany her—or desert her and flee.

He accompanied her. "What question? This scrutiny is insupportable."

"How can you blame them for staring? You are the most mysteriously compelling man in the room. Some think they know you, but cannot be certain after so long. Soon one of them will be sure and the news will spread like fire through dry grass. And you will be fighting off the attentions of these young hopefuls and their mamas. Why would there be any reason for you not to marry me?"

"Ella," he mumbled. "*Not now.*"

"That's an improvement. At least you admit we shall have to discuss the subject further."

As they progressed, a swath opened before them with elegant men and women falling back on either side. Hushed comments slithered amid the sibilant whisper of satins and silks brushing together.

"They consider me a freak," Saber muttered. "And so I am."

"Lord and Lady Eagleton!" Ella said gaily. "Look who I found on my way back from the supper room."

Lord Eagleton surveyed Saber with interested gray eyes. His golden-haired wife smiled in surprised recognition. "Saber," the lady said, obviously delighted. "Why, it's been so long since anyone saw you. You were in India?"

"I was," he said evenly.

Lord Eagleton's clever face showed pleasure. "Avenall. Of course. Damned glad they didn't manage to finish you, man. And I'm glad to see you about again. Take care of Hunsingore's girl, there. She's the apple of her papa's eye."

"Understandably," Saber said.

Ella didn't dare risk looking up at him. "We're on our way to find Papa now," she told the Eagletons, whose attention was immediately captured by other guests.

Nearby, three young females clustered close together and peeked at Saber.

Ella glared at them, but they didn't notice.

He said, "Look at them. They can't take their eyes off me."

She giggled. "And of course it's because you're so repulsive. Sometimes I cannot believe the stupidity of men."

"You have never learned the value of respect, my girl. This is not an easy matter for me."

"Ella Rossmara!" One of the girls detached herself from her friends and tripped rapidly in front of Ella and Saber. "You are coming to my ball, aren't you?"

This was Ella's first formal outing of her first season. If she had been introduced to this female, she had no recollection of it.

"Verbena White-Symington," the girl said, looking not at

Ella but at Saber. Her perusal was avid. "My ball is to be in two weeks. Since my mama's sister was a lady-in-waiting to the King's sister, the Princess Mary, my ball is to be held at Clarence House!" Verbena White-Symington, brown-haired, somewhat plump and festooned with yards of green, pleated frills, all but capered with self-importance.

Saber said nothing. Ella felt the force of his desire to be anywhere but here. "How wonderful for you, Verbena," Ella said kindly.

"Isn't it, though? And you will come?"

If she had been invited to a ball at Clarence House, she would not have forgotten. That her parents were concerned by a lack of invitations had not gone unnoticed by Ella, who longed to tell them that all of the Polite World must know she was not their daughter by blood.

"I don't believe I've met your companion." Verbena looked even more boldly at Saber. "Are you the Earl of Avenall? The one everyone talks about?"

The girls behind her gave a combined little shriek of delighted shock at such forwardness.

"I am the Earl of Avenall," Saber said. "So I suppose I must be the one everyone talks about. If you'll excuse us?"

"You'll come to my ball at Clarence House, won't you, my lord? I think your disfigurement is ever so interesting."

Another little wail of pretended horror sounded.

Ella didn't wail, or smile. She turned from Verbena without another word and took Saber with her. "I told you every girl would be praying for your notice."

"Is that what they're doing?" He sounded so cynical.

"She wants you at her ball, Saber. Your presence would be a coup."

"Perhaps they hope I'll be part of some entertainment. A monster for display, possibly. Rather than a dancing bear."

"Don't—"

"I do not belong here. I should never have come."

"Stop it. I will not listen to this."

Young females smiled at Saber. He didn't notice. Neither did he appear to notice the calculating glances, the whispers behind fans, on the part of the girls' mothers.

"I think I see Mama's dress over there. Near the windows. It will be cool. Do you see Mama? There are gilded columns nearby. See? And such a crush of friends. Mama and Papa are so rarely in London. Everyone is always so happy to see them."

"What I see is that I appear to have caused the stir of the century," he told her quietly. "And I do not like it."

"The stir you cause on our wedding day will put this one to shame. You will look so handsome in your wedding clothes."

He squeezed her hand in warning. "That subject is closed."

"Oh. Are you already married?"

"What?"

"Do you have a wife?"

He stared straight ahead. "You know I do not."

"Do I?"

"You call me a liar, miss?" Saber asked her, narrowing his eyes to meet hers.

"Good."

"I beg your pardon?"

"Good. That is all. Simply, good. You do not have a wife, so there can be absolutely no reason for you not to marry me. Unless you hate me. Do you hate me?"

"No."

"Good evening, Sir Basil." She dropped a brief curtsy to a very elderly gentleman who had come to Hanover Square in search of Mama's grandmother. "Do you find me repulsive, Saber?" Evidently Sir Basil was still one of the dowager's admirers.

"Do you?" Ella persisted.

"May this monstrous event soon be over," Saber muttered. "Of course I do not find you repulsive."

"Did touching my body sicken you?"

"Oh, Ella. I was so wrong."

"Because you did not enjoy—"

"Be silent," Saber ordered.

She saw Mama clearly now. "I am merely trying to ascertain the true reason for your decision to use and then spurn me."

"Oh, my *God,* Ella. If you are heard, you will be ruined."

"I am already ruined."

"You are not. And I did not . . . I did not intend to *use* you."

"Hello, Sukey. Your dress is lovely." She smiled at a girl who had stopped to study Saber.

He averted his face. "Ella—"

"Promise me you will not hide away from me again." She checked her stride, pulling him to face her. "Promise me, Saber. I'm begging, but I don't care. I need you. I don't want to be without you again."

His eyes darkened and he gazed fully upon her mouth. A muscle in his jaw sprang hard.

Ella said, "And I think you need and want me, too."

"Here they are!"

Devlin North's booming baritone announced Ella's arrival with Saber. She turned reluctantly toward her parents and their friends.

Mama's lips parted. "Saber!" Her throat moved sharply, and when she surged toward him, her tear-filled eyes showed her intense emotion. "We have missed you, cousin. We have truly missed you."

Saber absorbed Mama's hug while Papa slapped him on the back and said, "Damn it, man, you've chosen to be a stranger from us all. Welcome back to the light."

"Thank you." Saber was slow to return Mama's embrace.

When he did so, Ella saw his eyes close and the shadow of pain pass over his features. "I have missed both of you."

Mama raised her head to look at him and held her bottom lip in her teeth. "Did you think that would matter? The scars? You are more handsome than ever."

"That's what I've told him," Ella said. "Isn't it, Saber?"

He lowered his eyes and didn't respond.

"Calum will be in Town shortly," Papa said. "He and Pippa intend to give Ella a ball in Pall Mall. He's mentioned wanting to see you."

"Yes," Mama said. "You've worried us all."

"For that, I'm sorry. These have been . . . unusual times."

"I expect they're glad to see you're in possession of your faculties, old man," Devlin said, laughing and showing his marvelous white teeth. "Probably afraid you aren't capable of handling your estate. Ripe for some unscrupulous type's shenanigans. Or an asylum. Now they can put those fears to rest, eh?"

Tension emanated from Saber. "I can't imagine why they should think such things. A man's got a right to prefer a quiet life."

" 'Course he does," Devlin agreed seriously. He raised his eyes—and his arched black brows. "There's Margot. I thought you said she wouldn't come tonight. I suppose she couldn't stay away once she knew we'd be here."

The woman who approached, her smile for no one but Saber, set Ella's pulse thrumming. Amber glowed in combs holding the copper-colored ringlets that cascaded from a plaited arcade at her crown. Even at a distance, Ella caught the glow of the woman's eyes as they watched Saber, the glow of joy at the sight of him. Eyes like fine brandy. A face as exquisite as a porcelain doll. And a body as voluptuous as Ella's was slender. Voluptuous in patent lace over satin the same color as cinnamon diamonds.

"Mon chéri," she said huskily when she arrived before Saber. "How happy this makes me." A wide, square neckline, edged with cream lace, revealed the tops of full, white breasts.

"Margot," Saber said, taking the woman's hand and bowing to kiss it. "It always makes me happy to see you."

Ella's arms fell to her side.

"This is Countess Perruche," Saber said to the assembled group. "We are old friends."

"Very old friends," Devlin said, his cheerful demeanor showing no sign that he'd noted the stiffness that had crept into the moment. "Saber and Margot inspire me."

Ella made herself look away from them and ask, "Inspire you, Devlin?"

He shrugged, and pushed his lips forward. "Devotion is always to be envied and sought after, don't you think?"

The countess smiled around the circle and moved to Ella's side. "You must be little Ella. I have heard a great deal about you."

Not so little, Ella longed to say. So it was true. Saber and this lovely creature were . . . Well, they were, that was all.

"Saber has told me that you were not even sixteen when he met you."

"Years ago," Ella said quickly.

Countess Perruche inclined her head. "As you say." She looked at Saber again. "Saber and I met in India. He has been most generous to me."

Ella noted how Mama studied the floor and Papa threaded his hands beneath the tails of his evening coat behind his back. Neither continued to smile.

A scuffle, accompanied by a high-pitched giggle, broke the tension. Precious Able trotted through the French windows and stopped when she saw the silent company that watched her arrive.

"It's lovely outside," she said in her high, coy voice. "Really lovely, isn't it, Pommy?"

Smoothing his thin brown hair, Pomeroy Wokingham followed her inside. He passed Precious as if she had ceased to exist and joined Ella's group—as if he'd been invited. "I'm damned," he said, staring at Saber. "Avenall? Thought you weren't quite . . . Well, to be blunt—and I do believe in being blunt—to be blunt, I thought you weren't quite yourself anymore, old boy."

"Pommy," Precious whined, pushing to the center of the gathering. "I'm cold. You promised me a little something to warm me." She did not wear the cloak Pomeroy had promised, and her pink dress was crumpled.

"It *is* cold," Ella said, suddenly feeling guilty that she might have caused this light-brained girl discomfort by abandoning her to the foul Hon. Pom. "You should go into one of the parlors where there is a fire, Precious."

Precious's eyes hardened on Ella. "Pommy's going to make sure I'm warm, aren't you, Pommy?"

He ignored her. His gaze lingered rudely on Saber's face, but he spoke to Papa. "It's good to see you again, Hunsingore. My father's a bit under the weather, or he'd be here. My father holds you and your lady in the highest regard. He said as much after we visited Hanover Square." Pomeroy turned his attention to Ella. "Not, of course, in quite as high a regard as I hold you, Ella."

Her throat closed. "Thank you," she muttered, loath to incite further unpleasantness. "Perhaps we should consider going home." She could not look at Saber again, or at the gorgeous Countess Perruche, whom he clearly admired—if that was the appropriate term for his feelings toward the woman.

"May I call upon Miss Ella tomorrow, Lord Hunsingore?" Pomeroy asked pretentiously.

"I have appointments with the modiste tomorrow," Ella said rapidly.

"Perhaps you would allow me to accompany you," Pomeroy said, his pointed teeth showing.

"The devil she will," Saber snapped. "What d'you think—"

"Ella's mother will accompany her," Papa said, his dislike for Pomeroy evident. He turned his attention to Viscount Hawkesly, a handsome Cornishman, and his lovely wife. "Calum has spoken of you often lately. I hadn't realized you were such close neighbors."

"I say," Devlin said, stooping. "Some lady's lost a gewgaw of some sort, what?" He flourished a piece of red chiffon aloft.

Ella could not move.

Devlin studied each of the females in the group. "Doesn't look as if it belongs here." He looked at the chiffon. "A lady's topknot's missing its crowning glory, I shouldn't wonder."

Ella met Papa's eyes. He smiled, and in his smile was reassurance, and a warning. She was not to react in any way to what might be a cruel joke, or merely a sickening coincidence.

"Oh, dear," Mama exclaimed suddenly. She reached for the wisp of scarlet material and took it from Devlin. "Now my surprise is out." She tucked the piece into her reticule.

Devlin folded his arms and grinned. "Surprise, my dear lady? Do you intend to appear at some masquerade ball as a harem girl? Dashed appealing you'd be, I'm sure."

Papa's frown was thunderous.

"Oh, no," Mama said, laughing self-consciously. "Ella has such striking coloring, I decided we would dispense with tradition and have her wear red for her ball rather than something pale. You do not enjoy pale colors, do you, Ella?"

"No." Her own croaking whisper appalled Ella. "I am tired,

Papa." Poor, dear Mama. She knew the story and she, too, had overreacted to the chiffon. Red chiffon.

She'd worn a blindfold as she was led into the room.

"Ella." The creature who had held her captive spoke imperiously and removed the blindfold. "It is time to take off your cloak."

Ella had clutched the neck of the velvet cloak tightly, but the voice barked out again, "Ella is an innocent. Such a prize. Take off the cloak, child."

The woman who had blindfolded Ella had issued a warning: "Do wot she says. Do it quick. It'll go easier wiv yer if yer don't fight. You'll be sorry if yer fight."

"Take off the cloak."

She'd pushed the velvet from her shoulders and let it fall.

And the men and women in the room—bejeweled and drunken, some half-naked, had gasped loudly. Men had begged her to come to them. Women had urged their partners on, demanding to "see more," while some had laughed and said that there couldn't be much more to see.

Clad only in a dress fashioned of transparent red chiffon, she had stood before a room crowded with lascivious strangers.

"Ella?"

She heard Papa say her name and managed to smile at him. Anger toughened his lean, handsome face. "Does the hour grow late?" she asked him, at a loss for a more inventive remark.

"Very late," he told her.

"Red chiffon for your ball, my dear," Pomeroy said, his heavy eyelids drooping. "What a delicious vision you'll make."

"We shall all look forward to that," Devlin said heartily. "What say you, Saber?"

Saber took a long while to answer, and when he did, it was

without as much as glancing at Ella. "Will you all excuse us, please? I must escort Margot to her lodgings."

Holding Countess Perruche's elbow, he walked away.

Ella watched him go.

"I shouldn't care to wear red for my ball," Precious said. "My parents would say it wasn't at all the thing."

Mrs. Able chose that moment to put in a belated appearance. With her came a tall, stoop-shouldered man dressed entirely in black.

"Mama and Papa," Precious trilled. "Do persuade dear Ella that she shouldn't wear red for her ball. Papa, you tell Ella and her mama and papa."

Devlin bowed his head. Taking advantage of the musicians' enthusiastic play, he spoke quietly to Ella. "I don't know what has happened here, but I want you to listen carefully to what I say. There is something not at all as it should be, and I mean to find out what it is."

Ella closed her eyes and shook her head slightly. He must not probe. No one must probe. And she would hope that the thing Devlin had found was, indeed, a gewgaw from some lady's hair.

"Leave it to me," Devlin persisted. "And do not think badly of Saber. He is very fond of you."

Very fond. So fond he had left with a woman who was obviously far more than the object of his *fondness*. And he had walked away with that woman without as much as wishing Ella goodbye—after what had happened between them in this very house.

Well, Lord Avenall had not heard the last of her yet. She had pursued him tirelessly before. Now she had even more reason to pursue him—at least until he had the courage to tell her he did not love her.

Saber had not said he didn't love her. He hadn't said he *did* love her—other than as a friend. But she would not give up yet. She might not know a great deal about such things, but she was aware that men often sought the companionship of a certain type of female for comforts of a kind Ella could certainly guess at now. The thought of Saber seeking solace with anyone but her turned Ella's heart, but she would be brave. She would prove to him that he didn't need a ladybird because he could have Ella.

"So deep in thought, Ella," Pomeroy Wokingham said as if he were her conspirator. "And so pale beneath that golden skin. Let me take you for some refreshment. There is nothing like a little confection to put roses back into lovely cheeks."

"That's another thing," Precious said. "Red wouldn't do a thing for someone with such a sallow complexion, would it, Mama?"

Devlin offered Ella his arm, and she leaned gratefully upon it. Her parents moved closer together and began moving through the crowd. Ella and Devlin followed.

"Well, it wouldn't," Precious said. "And you said you were taking me for refreshments, Pommy."

The last thing Ella heard "Pommy" say was "Shut up, Precious!"

Chapter Eight

Pomeroy Wokingham's father belched and spread his legs farther apart. "Fool," he spat at Pomeroy. "Never should have listened to you. Should have insisted on going with you."

Pomeroy leaned from the purple velvet divan to pour more Madeira. The drink slopped over the rim of the glass and splashed the knee of his trousers. "A pox on it," he shouted, screwing up his eyes to focus. "Not my fault, I tell you. How was I to know that damned North fella would be there to turn her head. Then Avenall, in the name of the devil! *Avenall,* with his destroyed face. And she looks at him as if he's a God!"

The faces of gaudy *putti* ran together on panels that covered the walls and ceiling of the salon in the Wokinghams' Grosvenor Street house.

Father hitched his embroidered, Chinese silk robe over his bare, skinny thighs. "Should have gone with you," he said into his glass, and sucked the contents greedily. "Never send a boy, and all that."

If only he didn't need the old bastard, Pomeroy thought. If

only he could find a way to get his hands on enough blunt to be free. He'd change things around here. And he'd have heard himself called a boy for the last time.

The room was warm. Satin-fringed green velvet draped the windows, closing in heavy Jacobean furnishings. Ornate crystal lamps shone on father's collection of statues. Nude females in sexual poses.

Pomeroy wanted a nude female in a sexual pose. He wanted a live one, and he wanted her now.

"You should have found a way to get her outside," his father said, and coughed, spewing droplets of liquor-laced phlegm. "You said Hunsingore was off talking to Casterbridge—and you couldn't have your way with a bit of a female?"

"I told you things went wrong. Then North was there monopolizin'."

Father waved his glass unsteadily. "North's a nobody. New money. *New* money, Pom! People like the Hunsingores don't waste even their so-called daughters on new money. I should have . . . What the bloody hell is that?"

Voices were raised in the hall, one female, the other no doubt belonging to Boggs, the useless butler father refused to dismiss.

"It's three in the morning," Father grumbled. "Damned impudence. Visitin' at this hour of the night."

"Morning," Pomeroy amended.

His father tried to point at him but succeeded only in stabbing the air in numerous places. "Respect, boy. That's what I expect from you. Respect."

"And I expect what you promised me," Pomeroy said, tired of pretending submission. "I want that girl. She's mine."

" 'Course she's yours. We'll get her—whatever it takes. Any way we can. Tell Boggs t'stop that racket. Tell him he's a whore's arse. Tell him that."

"My pleasure," Pomeroy assured him, but before he could rise, the object of his hatred entered.

Muddy of complexion, with a bulbous nose and eyes sunken between beetling brows and fat cheeks, Boggs puffed as he approached his employer.

"What's the bloody fuss?" Father demanded, flapping a hand toward the vestibule. "You're useless, Boggs. Nothing but a whore's arse."

"As you say, my lord," Boggs intoned, bowing. "There's a young female to see you. I've told her to go away, but she refuses. Very insistent, she is, my lord. Lord Wokingham will see her, so she says. Says you'd want to see her if you knew what she wanted to tell you. Whatever that means."

Boggs never used one word where four or five were a possibility.

Pomeroy sat straighter. "Young female, y'say? Name of?" Ella had come to her senses and decided to throw herself on his mercy. Her righteous papa had told her they'd better play along.

"Name of Precious," Precious Able said, giggling as she tripped into the room. At the sight of Lord Wokingham, she stopped and frowned. "Who's he? I thought you said this was your house, Pommy."

"Get out, Boggs!" Father yelled. "Explain yourself, Pom. Who's this baggage?"

"Baggage?" Precious shrieked as Boggs, still bowing, closed the door behind him. Her red hair was freshly arranged and she now wore a swansdown-trimmed blue cloak over a paler blue gown. "The old man called me a baggage, Pommy."

"The old man," Pomeroy said, smiling at her, "is Lord Wokingham. My father."

"Oh!" She dipped, and sent a pouting moue in Father's direction. "I should have looked more carefully. I'd have seen where you got your handsome face and fine physique, Pommy. Good evening, my lord. I must have forgotten you were in residence. In fact, I need to speak to both of you. Pommy and I have become friends. I hold him in the highest regard."

"Do you indeed?" Father's eyes rested on her breasts where they spilled from the low neckline of her gown. A row of little, blue-jeweled buttons strained against buttonholes the length of the bodice.

"Pommy and I understand each other, don't we, Pommy?"

"Do you, Pommy?" Father asked, his teeth bared in a lascivious leer Pomeroy recognized well. A thrill of anticipation raised his cock against his trousers.

"You were at our house in Lancashire, my lord. You visited my father. He's the Reverend Able of—"

"My father isn't interested in such matters," Pomeroy told her hastily. "I had intended to join you that day, Father, but I ran into Precious when I was stabling my horse and became, er, diverted?"

Lord Wokingham chuckled, his belly jiggling inside the fine, thin silk of his robe. "What's a clergyman's daughter doing in London for the Season, then? I take it that's why you're here?"

Precious undid the frog at the throat of her cloak and took it off. She draped the garment over a chair. "My mama and papa know I've got prospects. I'm their only child, and they decided to make sacrifices to give me a chance of making a—a happy match."

"Y'mean they've taken a flyer on some fool buying those big tits of yours for enough to keep the family in comfort."

Pomeroy raised his brows and enjoyed his father's reaction to Precious's satisfied nod. "Something like that, my lord. Can't blame them, can you?"

"Suppose not," Father said. "Hardly protectin' their investment by allowin' you to chase around London at this hour, are they?"

"They don't know. I've decided to take matters into my own hands. I've seen what I want." She dimpled at Pomeroy. "We'll do very nicely together. And from the looks of this place, there'll be plenty to spare for a little nest egg for my parents. Just to keep them quiet. If you make proper use of my possibilities."

Pomeroy steepled his fingers. The girl was no fool, yet she behaved as if she had something—other than a lush body—that might give her a hold over him. "Why should we be interested in an arrangement like that?" he asked her.

"We?" she said, walking toward the fireplace, her hips swinging with every step.

"Lord Wokingham and I. We share everything, y'know, Precious." He met his father's glittering eyes. Without his powder and rouge, the old man's face was a flaccid mask of crazed purple veins.

Precious turned to regard them, one by one. "Nothing would suit me better. I'm more than enough for two, I can tell you."

Pomeroy had already managed a brief sampling of what Precious was enough for—both in Lancashire and earlier in the evening in the gardens of the Eagletons' house. He wiggled a little on the divan. He hadn't sampled quite enough—and he was bored.

"What do you want?" he asked, suddenly tired of talking to Precious Able. There were other uses to which she could be put—then quickly discharged. No one would believe any stories she chose to tell later, especially since she'd been foolish enough to venture out alone.

"I've told you what I want."

"Preposterous," Pomeroy said. "But I see no reason not to enjoy this visit, do you, Father?"

"None at all," Father said, his tongue passing over his lips. One of his legs swung away from the other, opening the robe to show him ready for the enjoyment he anticipated.

"I'm sure you'd like it to be that easy," Precious said, strolling close enough to stare at Lord Wokingham's bared crotch. "Nothing wrong with your wares, my lord," she said, idly making circles with one forefinger over her left breast.

"Take your clothes off," Father ordered, his voice thick.

Pomeroy never failed to be impressed with his parent's appetite for sex—even when he was foxed.

"Now, now," Precious said. The outline of her large nipples showed through fine muslin, and she applied a massaging thumb to each one. "I didn't come here like the addle-pated girl you think I am. Oh, I want some of what you want, all right. Probably more than the two of you can give me. But there's other things I want, and I'm going to get them."

Pomeroy stood and took off his coat. "Come here, Precious."

"In my own good time. You've got yourself in a bad way, haven't you? Queer bungs, that's what they say about you. Hardly a penny between you. Pinched purses. Empty."

With his hand at the fastening of his trousers, Pomeroy froze. "The devil you say."

"I do," Precious agreed, tilting her head. "My papa knows the truth of it, because there's those who've come to him asking how to get payments from you."

Lord Wokingham cursed volubly. "And the clergyman violated things spoken of in confidence," he spat.

"But not in confession, my lord," Precious said. "Be that as it may. I know. You should be glad, because I'm going to help you."

Pom's cock wilted. "Get out."

Smiling, Precious sauntered to sit on the divan instead. She leaned back on her elbows. "I want one of you each side of me. Cozy, that'll be."

"She's dangerous," Father said.

Precious fingered the buttons on her bodice. "Little me? No such thing. You want Ella Rossmara, because she comes with so much money you'll never have to worry again. And I'm going to help you get her."

Pomeroy swallowed, and swallowed again.

"Lord Hunsingore's made it plain how much his darling bastard daughter's worth. We'll just have to make sure you and your papa are the recipients of all that lovely money. You, your papa—and me, of course."

Breathing heavily, Father got to his feet. Scarcely taking his eyes off Precious, he refilled his glass and then poured a second. This he took to Precious. "Drink it," he said.

To Pomeroy's amazement, she promptly drained the glass and handed it back to Father. "Another," she demanded.

"Why should you be any part of this?" Pomeroy asked her. "If there's a shred of truth to what you say, which there isn't."

"Which there is," she said. "I'm a part of it because I'm what you really need—not that gypsy of a girl who was probably born in a gutter. And I do know you're living on loans. You've a pile of notes, notes that are going to come due and cost you everything you own shortly."

Lord Wokingham supplied her with more Madeira and said, "Pull up your skirts, girl."

She ignored him while she drank. "My mama and papa do know where I am. If I don't return, they'll call a constable. They've got a letter from me explaining. And if you don't do what I say and take care of me, I'll tell all of London that you're ruined. And that you're trying to get your fingers into Lord Hunsingore's deep pockets."

Pomeroy trembled with fury. "You can't assist me with the Rossmara girl."

"Certainly I can," she told him. "Come to me. Both of you. We need to test how well we'll do together. Then I'll explain exactly what our plans will be. They'll work. Trust me."

Father dropped down beside her on the divan and hauled up her skirt.

Precious behaved as if her private parts had not been revealed to both men in the room. She patted the divan and beckoned to Pomeroy. "There's plenty to go round," she told him.

He longed to rip off her clothes and beat her white skin until she begged to be released, begged to be allowed to forget she'd ever had the temerity to threaten him. Instead, he did as she asked and sat beside her.

"There," she said. "That's better. This bodice is too tight."

Father guffawed and squeezed her breast. "Long time since I came across dugs like these. Particularly a pair offered so freely. I bet you've taught more than one chap a thing or two he didn't know."

She eyed him knowingly. "Only after a few chaps taught me some things I didn't know."

"A clever mouth," Father said, slipping a jeweled button from its hole. "I like that. Now you can teach us, right, Pom?" He winked at Pomeroy.

Renewed interest sprang between Pomeroy's legs. "And perhaps we can add to the young lady's repertoire," he said, helping with the buttons.

Precious rested her chin on her chest to watch while her huge breasts were revealed. Their pink centers were the size of little plates, each one offering a large, pouting berry.

Pomeroy took a nipple between finger and thumb and pinched.

Precious gasped and writhed.

Lord Wokingham played with the other breast.

Pomeroy's head bumped his father's when they bent to fasten their teeth and suck.

Never at a loss for means by which to spice the event, Pomeroy's father dragged Precious's skirts around her waist and pushed her flat on her back with her knees bent at the edge of the divan. He emptied the remaining contents of a glass of Madeira over the girl's belly and curly, red bush, and grinned up at Pomeroy. "Thirsty?" he asked.

Pomeroy fell to lapping the wine, never releasing his handful of Precious's breast. She bucked and laughed—and spread her legs.

Lord Wokingham chose to take his drink from a deeper place. He guzzled noisily between slick folds, discarding his robe as he did so.

The blue gown joined the robe. Pomeroy needed nothing more than to push his trousers past his knees.

She was tireless. And she did know a thing or two. His father preferred his pleasures in comfort—on his back—which suited Pomeroy. Wedged between the two of them on the floor, Precious grunted and squealed, tossed and begged—for more and more.

Pomeroy was happy to oblige.

When he finally fell back, wet with his own sweat, and with hers, he rolled to lie on the carpet and listen to his father thrust upward into her. The old man was game, but he took longer these days. Pomeroy smiled. Fair enough—the girl was welcome to the extra pleasure she so loudly enjoyed.

At last the groaning and shrieking ceased. They stretched out, side by side, breathing heavily.

Pomeroy turned, unable to waste a moment of fondling Precious's heavy breasts. "So," he said, and bent to enjoy a long, slow suckle that brought fresh cries to her lips. "So, what do you want, Precious? Really want?" As if he didn't know. She wanted what every unmarried female in London wanted—to marry him.

"First I want to help ensure our future," Precious said, holding up her breast to help Pomeroy's exploration. "I know things."

"So you've shown us."

"Other things. About all kinds of people. I've got a source now. Ella Rossmara—or whatever her name really is—will bring us what we need. She'll have to if she wants to save herself."

Lord Wokingham propped his mussed head on a hand and looked down at the girl. "How will you manage that?"

"You'll find out."

"Tell us now."

Her face hardened. "I'll tell you when I've done what needs to be done. Not before. And not before you give me what I want. To make sure you don't think of backing out of the bargain."

Pomeroy sighed. "Let me guess. You want a husband. You want marriage."

"Exactly." She made her blue eyes very round. "I want a respected place in Society. And I must say it appeals to me to have that wretched Ella at my beck and call. The men look at her as if she's something special. She won't feel so special when she has to do as she's told—by me."

Pomeroy could almost pity the creature her delusions. But there was no doubt that she had an idea, and it might be very useful. "Why don't you tell us exactly how you expect to accomplish all this. And what you'll expect from us in return. Then we'll just have to see, won't we?"

"I'd say you've already seen," Precious said, sitting up and pressing her breasts to her knees. "This is how it'll be. With my help. Pommy gets to marry Ella, who'll bring us all the money we'll ever need."

Pomeroy narrowed his eyes and thrust a hand between her legs.

She pushed him away. "And I get to be a lady." Turning to Pomeroy's father, she said, "You've been a widower far too long, my lord. It's time for you to take a new wife."

Chapter Nine

"Overreaction," Papa pronounced. "That's it. Pure and simple. You are both overreacting."

"Struan," Mama said gently. "I rather think it may be you who are overreacting. You've talked of little else since last night."

He threw up his arms and paced back and forth across Ella's little sitting room.

"Where could it have come from?" Ella asked, not for the first time by any means.

Mama smoothed the piece of red chiffon on her knee. "I wanted to believe Devlin's theory to be true. But no lady would wear a torn scrap like this in her hair. It is unbound." She fell back in her chair and stared into the fire. "A cruel jest."

"A *coincidence,*" Papa thundered. "You aren't thinking at all. Torn from the hem of a gown, I tell you. Trodden upon by some clumsy oaf and discarded without its owner even being aware, I'd wager."

Ella scrubbed at her face. "It appeared, Papa. It simply *appeared.*"

"You don't know that."

"I do. We would have seen it, just as Devlin did. It is so garish."

"No one knows about . . . about what happened," Mama said, closing the chiffon inside her fist. "Those who did are either gone from the country or in prison."

"Or members of this family," Papa said morosely. "Or in very high or very low places. And there was quite a crush around us when it happened. Anyone could have dropped it."

"Or someone who wished to press a point," Mama said. She frowned at Papa. "Given what passed between you and your visitors the—"

"No," Papa said sharply. "Too obvious, my dear."

"What?" Ella asked. "What are you talking about? Who?"

Mama shrugged and shook her head. "Nothing, Ella. I am simply overprotective of you. And perhaps overconcerned, too. We must put this behind us."

Ella caught Papa's sleeve. "You just said it was all a coincidence."

"And so it is," he told her. "I was only referring to those present at the time. Even if some were likely to be among our acquaintances now—in London—they could not possibly remember you as that child."

Couldn't they? She was dark, the whisperers said. Like a gypsy. The Countess Ballard had remarked upon how unusual she was. Papa might be right, but he might equally well be wrong. Someone might remember. And someone might have a reason for wanting her to know they did. To warn her? Because they wanted her to . . . to go away?

"Ella?" Mama said. "You must not fret so, my dear. This is all supposed to be fun. A wonderful time. And it will be. We must see about the gown for your ball at Pall Mall."

"It will *not* be red chiffon," Ella said. She plucked at her full, leaf-green skirts. "Even the thought of such a thing makes me weak."

"Of course it shall not be red chiffon," Papa agreed.

"Oh, but of course it most certainly shall." The fire continued to hold Mama's attention, but her fine features tightened with resolve. "Absolutely. Red will become you."

Ella flung aside the embroidery hoop she'd been carrying. "I detest red. I will always detest red. Have you lost your mind, Mama?"

"That will do, young lady. Apologize to your mother."

"No," Mama said, shaking her head. "She does not have to apologize. I should have explained myself at once. By wearing the very thing that someone may—please note that I say *may*—wish to use as a threat against you, that threat will become as toothless as an ancient dog—and as dangerous."

Only the tick of the small ormolu clock on the mantel broke the silence that followed.

"Don't you agree?" Mama turned her bright amber eyes upon them. "Ella will look lovely and she will toss any ill will back into the face of its perpetrator?"

The chance to reply was lost in Crabley's noisy entrance. He coughed and puffed, showing his annoyance at having to climb the stairs. "Her grace, the Dowager Duchess of Franchot, my lord," he announced to Papa. "I suggested Her Grace might await you below, but—"

"But I am not so decrepit that I can no longer hobble up a flight of stairs." Tiny, white-haired, rod-backed, and formidable, the dowager duchess progressed into the room. Garbed in unrelieved black, she raised her ivory-headed cane and pointed it at Crabley. "That is more than I can say of you, my man. Never saw a servant take so long to make his way up a few stairs. Disgrace, that's what I call it. You're feeding your flunkies too well, Justine. But what else would I expect. You never had the sense you were born with."

"Good afternoon, Grandmama."

The dowager peered at Mama and repeated, "Good afternoon, Grandmama," in a parody of her granddaughter's voice. "Is that the best you can do, girl? I'm probably a hair away from me coffin and you can't as much as kiss me? Hmph." She waved Crabley from the room. "Fetch tea. And tell my companion to remain downstairs. Take her refreshment there. We won't be remaining long. I have a great deal to do at Pall Mall."

Mama got to her feet and placed an arm around her grandmother's rigidly held shoulders. She bent to kiss a papery cheek. "You will put each of us in a coffin, Grandmama," she said, not quite suppressing a smile. "You are indefatigable. Sit in my chair."

"Nonsense," the dowager said, glaring. "You sit in your chair, madam. You are the cripple."

Ella did not dare look at Papa, who didn't allow an instant to pass before saying, sharply, "Kindly do not refer to Justine as a cripple, Your Grace. You know it is not true, and it offends us all."

"Piffle." The dowager turned her sharp scrutiny upon Ella. "Well. Met someone yet, have you?"

"Someone?"

"Don't shilly-shally with me, my girl. You're here to find a husband. The sooner that's accomplished, the better. The longer you wait, the narrower the field, and the better the chance of falling into a bounder's bed."

"Grandmama!"

"Silence, Justine," the dowager ordered. "We are all grown up, here. You, of all people, should be comfortable with anything I may decide to say. You and your wretched *book*. I never thought to see the day when a granddaughter of mine would *publish a book*. The shame. It's a wonder I'm still breathing. And a book on *that* subject! Oh, the shame." She shook her head, and flames in the fireplace shone on jet beads beneath her bonnet brim.

"Ella has attended a single event," Papa told the old lady, "We have in fact received one offer for her hand."

Ella's lips parted in horror.

"We have?" The dowager proceeded to a straight-backed chair and perched on the edge of its Aubusson tapestry seat. "This is most encouraging."

"It is not encouraging at all!" Ella burst out. "Pomeroy Wokingham is hardly—"

"Pomeroy Wokingham?" The stick rose in Papa's direction. "Make certain I do not hear that name again. A prancing popinjay. Like his father. Despicable man."

"I didn't say we were considering the proposal," Papa said sheepishly. "I merely wanted to keep you apprised of events, as it were."

"I wish to return to Scotland," Ella said.

An awful hush fell.

Ella pointed her nose in the direction of the molded, pale pink ceiling. "In fact, I think we should all go home—to our various homes—forthwith. Before any more time is wasted on this pointless undertaking."

"What is she saying?" the dowager whispered, as if Ella were demented and likely to turn into a wild thing at any moment. "Has something happened that you're not telling me about? Has some male person offended her—*forced* himself upon her?"

"Oh, fie! Not nearly enough." The words were out before Ella could contain them.

Another cavernous silence followed. Then Mama's grandparent pounded the carpet with her cane. "I might have known it," she said. "Like mother, like daughter. And like father, like daughter. She's as impulsive as both of you." She looked from Papa to Mama. "Who is the man who has compromised her? Compromised and abandoned her?"

"No man!" Ella's parents said in unison.

The dowager eyed Ella. "Is that what you say, gel?"

For the briefest of instants Ella considered telling the truth, that she loved a man and could never love another. "There is no man who has compromised me." To admit the truth would accomplish nothing, other than trouble for Saber.

Crabley reentered the room, a heavy silver tray in his hands and Rose, Ella's maid, at his elbow. Rose, as small and quick of movement as the dowager, busied herself with the tea things.

She began to pour milk into Sevres cups.

"Ella can do that," the dowager said, gesturing for the fair-haired girl to leave.

Rose glanced at Ella, saw her encouraging smile, and quickly lowered her eyes. Crabley had already departed. Rose withdrew, almost colliding with Saber in the process.

He carried his hat and still wore a long, caped overcoat. If he saw his grandmother, he gave no sign. Saber looked piercingly at Ella. "Forgive me for intruding," he said. His long dark hair brushed the collar of the black coat. "I promised I'd come, but I don't believe we discussed the time?"

He had promised no such thing. He'd walked away from her on the previous evening as if he'd forgotten she existed at all.

"You aren't intruding," she told him, scarcely able to breathe. "How could you?"

It was the first time in four years that she had seen him in daylight. His stark countenance dominated the room. White linen gleamed against the black overcoat and the dark clothing he wore beneath. There was about his features a saturnine slant, a hollowness cast beneath his full bottom lip, his high cheekbones. The scars, partially hidden by his hair, were an insult upon so compelling a face.

"Well," the dowager said. "My grandson, Saber. Returned from the grave, or so it seems."

He turned to her, obviously noting her presence for the first time, and bowed slightly. "Grandmama. You look well."

"I am. And you look as handsome as the devil—more so. Pity about the wounds. Why wasn't I told?"

"Because none of us knew," Papa said shortly. "Take your coat off, man. I'll ring for another cup."

Ella looked into Saber's green eyes.

He stared back—and made no attempt to remove his coat.

Papa cleared his throat.

Mama got up and began pouring tea. "You still take it as you did, Grandmama? With—"

"Oh, don't chatter, Justine. A woman as old as I doesn't suddenly decide to take her tea differently. The very idea. Saber, you must know all the eligible men in London."

With evident reluctance, he turned from Ella. "I used to know them, Grandmama," he said.

"Just like your father," she told him. "He was deliberately evasive, too."

Saber's father had married Justine and Calum's aunt. Both had died at an early age and had apparently not been among the dowager's favorites. Not that the dowager admitted to having favorites at all.

"You do know these men," she persisted. "Of course you do. Or you know *of* them. Their identities, at least. Their pedigrees. Their holdings. The type of thing we have to know in order to decide if they're worth bothering with."

Saber's high brow furrowed. "Exactly why do we want to know?"

"I am surrounded by idiots! Because we have to select a husband for Ella, of course. Why else would we wish to know?"

Ella studied Saber closely. The only sign of emotion was a clenching of his fingers on the brim of his hat.

"Of course you understand what I mean, Saber. That's settled, then." The dowager duchess accepted tea from Justine. "You will start tomorrow."

Saber set the hat down carefully on an inlaid marquetry table. "I'm sure you intend to explain the nature of my duties, Grandmama."

"Ella is a prize," the old lady announced in ringing tones. "She is very much like myself at her age. Strong. Determined. A backbone to be contended with. And she's beautiful, to boot."

Stunned, Ella could only gape.

"Close your mouth," the dowager ordered.

Ella did so with a snap.

"Any man who gains her as his wife will be more fortunate than he deserves. Our job is to ensure that the least undeserving candidate wins the prize."

Ella raised her eyes to Saber's face. He looked steadily back.

"Which is exactly where you come in, young Avenall."

"Yes, Grandmama," he said, still holding Ella's eyes with his own.

"I do not want Ella to go into marriage as I did—without the benefit of choice."

Mama made a noise.

"Speak up, Justine," the dowager demanded. "Don't snuffle, girl. Speak your mind."

"Oh, no," Mama said. "It wasn't . . . Yes, it *was*. What I wished to say was important. I don't seem to recall your being concerned about my choices before I was married. Except that you did not think I should marry at all."

"That is all in the past," the dowager duchess said shortly. "These are more modern days."

"Three years later," Mama muttered.

The dowager ignored her. "Ella needs to have her options openly presented. A gel of such spirit cannot simply be parceled out like a box of confections. That's where you come in, Saber."

His expression was bemused.

"You will make a list of possible candidates. Then you will go over that list with Ella. By the way, Ella, have you developed any unsavory interests?"

"Unbelievable," Papa said clearly. "Incredible."

"Interests such as Justine took up," the dowager continued. "Writing books for women on subjects they've got no right to explore. Anything of that nature?"

Concentration had become difficult. "I wish I could think of something to write about," Ella said. "But Mama has done the greatest possible service to women. So I'm told. I haven't been allowed to read it yet, of course."

"You soon will be," the dowager said, pretending not to hear Papa's explosive laugh.

"I hope to work with homeless children," Ella said. "I have great hopes that I shall be able to make a difference to—"

"Forget that nonsense," the dowager said. "I'm glad I asked. Better to nip tendencies of that kind in the bud immediately. You will be a wife and a mother. A difficult task, I assure you. Difficult, consuming, and thankless."

"Yes, great-grandmama," Ella said dutifully.

"Good. That's understood. Now to your part in this, Saber."

He inclined his head. "Always willing to serve, Grandmama."

"Hmm." She pursed her lips. "We shall soon see. You will make your list, go over it with Ella, then present me with what we need."

"And what," Saber asked, "do *we* need, exactly?"

"A husband, of course! You, Saber, are to see to the business of selecting Ella's husband!"

Chapter Ten

"There you are," the dowager duchess said, peering around at mementos of Saber's travels.

"Good evening, Grandmama," Saber said, closing his sitting-room door. He was still recovering from her request of the previous afternoon. "I hadn't expected—"

"What can possibly be wrong with you, my boy?" the old lady interrupted him. "This is . . . It defies description."

He looked at Bigun, who had neglected to warn his master that his grandmother had arrived, accompanied by Viscount Hunsingore—and Ella. Bigun had neglected to warn Saber, or to ask if he wished to be foiled in his attempt to withdraw from Society once more.

"Amazing room, Saber," Struan remarked, walking between the collection of ivory, jade, and gold statues Saber had gathered in the Far East. "You don't find it a little oppressive, though? Your man, here, said this is where you prefer to spend your evenings."

Saber felt pugnacious. "He's right—if careless about his duties—I do prefer to spend my evenings here. Alone. And, no, I do not consider my salon in the least oppressive." Ella wore a brown, fur-trimmed cloak over russet-colored silk. She hovered at the edge of his awareness. If he did not look at her directly, he might avoid finding her image even more clear in the hours after she left.

He had already made more than one impulsive and ill-advised decision. The deliberate encounter at the Eagletons' would never leave his mind. He'd given in to urges he had no right to own. Going to Hanover Square to assuage his guilt with some sort of apology had led to further difficulty—to this present difficulty.

Ella must leave. They must all leave, quickly. He was tired from not having slept in almost three days. Saber feared the night to come when fighting sleep, yet dreading exhaustion, might throw him into the protracted nether state he had experienced on several occasions, and would never cease to dread.

"Well, I do not find this room at all pleasing," Grandmama announced, marching firmly around a golden goddess from Burma and taking up a post beside entwined jade snakes. She averted her face from their forked tongues. "A dismal, disquieting place. I repeat. What is the matter with you, my boy? I sent word that you were to join us at Pall Mall this evening. To consult with Ella."

Ella's muffled exclamation captured Saber's full attention. She held her bottom lip in her teeth, and her eyes shimmered too brightly.

"Your Grace," Struan said, approaching the old lady with measured steps. "You did not mention that you had invited Saber to Pall Mall. You said—"

"I know what I said." She settled herself in an ebony chair with gold feet shaped like eagle's claws and with spread golden wings painted upon the back. "I have responsibilities here. Something others seem capable of forgetting all too easily."

Struan frowned down at her. "Under the circumstances, that hardly excuses—"

"It excuses whatever I say it excuses."

"Great-Grandmama did not mention that you had been invited to Pall Mall," Ella said to Saber in a small voice. "I'm sure she forgot. Papa and I thought *you* had invited us here. We shall leave you alone at once."

Saber stood by the fireplace. He watched Ella's discomfort with mounting agitation. She should not suffer, not again after suffering so much already. He should stop it. "Ella—"

"Silence," Grandmama ordered. "You would not come to us. So we had no choice but to come to you."

Struan was oddly silent, an observer. But there was no doubt that he thought a great deal. Saber's sense of dread mounted at the prospect of a sudden outpouring of Struan's anger. Saber feared that anger because he doubted his ability to control his own.

"We did not agree that I would do what you asked me to do," he said to Grandmama. He could not, would not, help find another man to be with Ella in a manner he could not contemplate.

"Pish, posh," Grandmama said. She sent Bigun a ferocious glare. "Does your man always insinuate himself into family discussions?"

Bigun bowed and moved to the center of the room. "Is this the moment, my lord?"

Saber frowned at his old friend and servant.

"You said you would instruct me on the matter of responding. In good time, you said, my lord."

"Responding?"

From beneath his multihued silk tunic, Bigun produced a painted leather pouch. From this he took a handful of envelopes and cards. "Very strange, the English," he said, riffling the papers. "They call. They call a great deal. And all at the same time of day. So very odd."

"Is there a point, Bigun?" Saber and his servant had an unspoken vow of mutual respect. They owed too much, one to the other, for the expected relationship between master and servant.

Bigun made much of producing wire-rimmed spectacles. These he perched upon his thin-bridged nose before reading: "The pleasure of your company. Yes, yes, yes. At Carlton House on, yes, yes, yes." He replaced the card in the pouch. "Then there is this one. A musicale for Lady Johanna Bunkum. There are so many, my lord. We really must respond. I have it on good authority that the English set great store by these little social annoyances."

Saber could feel his guests' bemusement. "Thank you, Bigun. But we don't really have to deal with this right now."

"Well, my lord. At least in the matter of the proposals of matrimony I thought we might make some reply. Where I come from, people would shudder at the thought of making such a suggestion by messenger, but—"

"Matrimony?" Grandmama said loudly. "Proposals of matrimony? Who have you proposed to, boy?"

"No, no, Your Grace," Bigun said serenely. "These are proposals made *to* the earl, not *by* the earl." He spoke slowly, as if Grandmama might be either hard of hearing or somewhat light of brain.

Resolving to get to the bottom of Bigun's preposterous behavior—later—he sent a warning glance, at which the servant inclined his head and closed the pouch.

"As I have already asked you, Saber, does your man always assume he is welcome at family gatherings?"

"I have not yet dismissed him." Neither would Saber do so until he could send his visitors with him.

"Dismiss him, then. How dare he prattle about nonsensical invitations at such a time."

"Great-Grandmama," Ella said. *"Please."*

"Please. One wonders what exactly you are begging me for. Since I doubt you will explain, I shall have to guess that you wish me to hurry. I shall do so—as quickly as pleases me. Why does this man of yours dress in such an outlandish fashion, Saber?"

Bigun bowed to the duchess, his expression showing nothing. "I am from a province in India, Your Grace."

"I hardly think that excuses—"

"Great-Grandmama!" Ella rushed to the dowager's side. "This is appalling. Outrageous. We cannot possibly intrude upon Saber's privacy in this manner. And we cannot presume to criticize—"

"I can criticize whatever I please," Grandmama said, but she raised the hood of her cloak over her bonnet. "However, since the two of you must work together, it's as well you seem to agree on all this privacy nonsense. And upon your disapproval of me. Well, I wish you joy in it. Come along, Struan. We shall leave them to the task."

Avoiding Saber's eyes, Struan bowed and offered the dowager his arm. "A good notion. We'll return later."

"Later?" Ella said. "It is already past eight."

The dowager raised her lorgnette to peruse first Ella, then Saber. "I hardly think either of you is too frail to spend an evening hour or two on a project of extreme urgency."

They were going to leave—without taking Ella with them!

"When should you like to discuss your social calendar, my lord?" Bigun asked. "Clearly you have become a man in great demand."

Saber shook his head. "Leave the cards, if you please, Bigun."

"Amazing behavior," Grandmama said. "Come, Struan."

Saber stepped away from the fireplace. “May I point out, Grandmama, that Ella does not have a chaperon?”

The old lady paused in her regal progress toward the door and tapped Bigun sharply on the back of his hand. “You will chaperon Miss Rossmara. Is that understood?”

For once Bigun did not produce an instant response.

Struan looked grave. “After all, Saber, you’re a member of the family. You should feel some responsibility to help out in this matter. Your man here will be answerable to me for Ella’s safety and reputation. D’you understand, Bigun?”

“The young lady’s safety and reputation?” Bigun repeated.

“Exactly,” Struan said. “Purely a formality. Just in case there should be any question. We’ll send a coach for Ella at ten. Is that agreeable with you, Saber?”

He felt the intensity of her gaze. “Yes,” he said shortly. How could he deny her in front of others?

Bigun left to show Struan and Grandmama out.

“I do not believe this!” Ella said. “She lied. Papa accepted the lie, and left me here as if it were the most normal thing in the world. They’ll send a coach for me in two hours? Your male servant is to be my chaperon? How bizarre.”

Saber regarded her. He could not look away now even if he tried. She captivated him. Mesmerized him. *Terrified him.*

“Say something,” she demanded. “What do you make of their behavior?”

“It is your behavior that interests me more. Only a short while ago you were using any possible means to force your way into this house—or to pester me at my club—yet now that you are all but thrust upon me by the family, you complain. What is it, Ella? Does the fruit become less desirable once it ceases to be forbidden?” He was cruel, but honest. “Or did the sight of me by day finally convince you that I am no longer the stuff of your childhood dreams?”

Ella said, “You are petty. And mean-spirited.”

"I am direct. I do not say pretty words to hide the ugliness beneath."

She lowered her eyelids. "And your directness brings you many invitations. And proposals of marriage? I have never heard of such a thing."

Neither had Saber. Bigun should answer for that piece of fiction. "Are you jealous that I should be invited about?"

"Why should I be jealous? I, too, have many invitations."

"No doubt. Perhaps that is why you are suddenly so uninterested in your little charade with me."

"You have made it plain that you want no part of me, Saber."

"And now you are ready to accept this?" He should feel grateful.

"I am not ready to accept it. We should prepare to spend the next two hours together."

Two hours together. Alone. Saber fiddled with a fob on his watch chain. He must be vigilant. Any slight drifting in concentration might be disastrous. He did not know exactly what he was capable of when the darkness overtook him.

Surely he would never do Ella harm. . . . No, he was not certain of that. Yet there was no evidence that he had ever actually . . .

"Saber. Oh, I am *so* out of patience. What I want is of no matter to anyone."

"It certainly matters to you," he remarked. His voice did not sound at all like his own.

She placed her hands on her hips beneath the cloak and approached him. "I suppose that's the best I can expect from a man who regards me as a joke."

"I do not regard you as a joke."

"No, no," she murmured. "You are right. Not as a joke, but as one to be taken, but not taken seriously."

"This is pointless." As far as he knew, he had never, even

in the throes of one of his worst attacks, inflicted harm on another.

As far as he knew. There were those—the only ones who knew of his affliction—who would not tell Saber about the lost minutes, or hours, for fear of sending him further into the abyss.

Ella swung away from him. "So, we are to sit here—you, Mr. Bigun, and I, and pretend for two hours?"

"Bigun," Saber said. "He does not care to be called 'Mr.' "

"Ooh." She stomped toward him once more. "Silliness. Little things. And at a time when my life holds no sign of light."

"And mine does?" Slowly, he undid her cloak and swung it from her shoulders. The strings of her bonnet fell undone at a touch and he removed the wide-brimmed velvet confection. She neither helped nor resisted. "Do you find this room unpleasant?" he asked.

"I find it unusual," she said promptly, studying it with narrowed eyes. "I confess that I might rearrange your treasures. And they are indeed treasures. But, no, I do not find it unpleasant. In fact, I find it fascinating."

"You can be comfortable here while we await your coach?"

Her answer was to settle herself on a low, green-leather-covered hassock, tuck her reticule into her lap, and hold her hands toward the fire.

The small, exquisite gold and diamond reticule he had sent to her. He had not noticed she carried it until now.

Ella took the bag between her hands. "A beautiful thing. You were generous to give me such a gift."

He had wanted to give her something. Even as he'd told Bigun to deliver the message that was supposed to dampen her interest in him, Saber had reveled in the thought of her owning something he'd intended to give her anyway. The bag and the ruby were only two of many treasures Saber had looked forward to showering upon Ella . . . before their worlds had spun away from each other.

"Well, then"—he took the chair his grandmother had vacated—"it's good that you're comfortable. How shall we proceed, I wonder?"

"We shall not proceed. Mr. Bigun is taking a long time."

"Bigun."

Her breath blew out noisily.

"He will not return."

Ella looked at him sharply. "Of course he will return. Papa instructed him to chaperon me."

"Bigun will return when I signal for him to do so. He has other duties to perform. He will be in attendance when the coach comes. Struan said Bigun was to assume responsibility for your reputation and safety. He does not have to be in this room to do so. Perhaps I should write down the names of possible suitors."

"Tell me about India."

He deliberately relaxed his hands on the arms of the chair. "Nothing to tell."

"How did it happen? Your injury?"

"We shall make a list." He got up and went to a black-lacquer secretaire that had once belonged to a Chinese prince. "Stay by the fire. It is cool over here. I'll write. If you have any suggestions—"

"Don't waste your time."

"Tell me if you have any suggestions."

"I suggest you speak to me about India. About the reason you went back a second time when you'd already been wounded."

He pulled paper in front of him and dipped a pen into the standish. "Sir Knowlton Carstairs is a fairly innocuous fellow."

"A glowing recommendation!"

Saber wrote the name. "Someone who will please you—"

"There is no one!" He heard her move behind him. "You know there can be no one but you."

"Ella, please."

"Why would Grandmama think you should help me find a husband?"

"She does not always make her thoughts plain. But Struan led a quiet life until he left the priesthood and married Justine."

"He was not a priest. He never took his final vows."

"Nevertheless," Saber said patiently. "He *was* a priest, in all but his final vows. And he did not spend a great deal of time going about in Society. Now he and Justine are happy with their quiet life in Scotland, and with their family. Am I not correct?"

"Yes," she told him, standing at his back now. "And I have told them that is where we should return."

Saber drew a deep breath. "I believe Grandmama asked me to assist in this matter because she thinks I am better acquainted with those men who might make you a suitable husband."

She rested a hand on his shoulder. "This is a sham, dear one," she said softly. "By all means, write names upon your paper. They will satisfy the dowager. She wants only the best for me, I know. She has always championed me—even though she knows I am nobody."

"You *are* somebody." He gripped her hand on his shoulder. "You have not been dealt the finest of cards, Ella. But you are the finest of women, a prize any man would be proud to possess."

"Any man but you," she said, taking her hand away. Moving beside him, she idly picked up a brass box from the desk. "Make your list, Saber."

He looked at the box and had to restrain himself from taking it away. "That will make your fingers dirty."

Ella opened the lid of the box and gave a short laugh. "Why, a button collection. I had a button collection when I was . . . My mother collected buttons and gave them to me. I loved them then, before I was old enough to know that they had been lost from the clothing of people who visited that house."

"Don't . . . Ella, don't speak of that."

"It doesn't hurt anymore. It's over."

Was it? How could such a thing ever be entirely over?

"Where did these come from? They appear . . . military?"

Saber could not look at the buttons. He began to write. "They are military. More mementos."

"Quite the collector," she said. "I had not known that side of you. They all appear . . . Most of them are the same in design."

"Are they?" All cut from the coats of dead men, all men under Saber's command. "I can't even remember where I got them now. I should have Bigun get rid of them." Never. He would keep them as long as he lived.

Ella snapped the box shut and set it down. "I hate London."

"I am not fond of it myself."

"Then why are you here?"

Because here he usually found anonymity. "It is what I'm accustomed to."

"What of Shillingdown? Who cares for it?"

"My estate commissioner."

"You do not like your estate?"

His estate reminded him of his need for a family, for a wife, for children to carry on when he was dead. The only wife he would ever want was Ella, and he could not have her, even if he could forget the past—his own, and hers.

"Saber?"

"I like Shillingdown well enough. I'll return there in good time—I visit occasionally."

"Kirkcaldy is the closest I've come to having a home."

"A beautiful estate. You like living in the lodge?"

She actually laughed. He'd forgotten how her laugh had the power to make him smile. "I adore the lodge," she told him. "You did not visit, but it is quite the most wonderfully eccentric building in the world. Papa and Mama love it too, and we are so close to the castle and to Arran and Grace and their children. Oh, yes, I do love living there."

"And Edinburgh? Do you like to visit that fair city?"

"Yes. Charlotte Square is always filled with visitors and music."

"But you have not met some young buck who could capture your heart? And keep you happily living in your beloved Scotland?"

"No."

He should not feel relieved by the promptness of her response.

"I spoke to you once of Papa and the way he rescued me—and Max."

Saber bit back the impulse to tell her he didn't wish to discuss that issue again. "I remember."

"You know, I was offered at an auction in that house. The house where my mother and my uncle had a room."

"You don't need to speak of it."

"When my mother was younger, and there was not enough money, she had been . . . I believe she did some work at the house."

She was offering him honesty without any notion that he already knew a great deal about her early years—and guessed the rest.

"I was paraded before a lot of people—"

"No, Ella. Do not say more, little one. You were cruelly used."

"We have both suffered, Saber. Could that not be reason for us to draw close together? To comfort and heal each other?"

So sweet. So ignorant of the nature of the man at her side.

In a rustle of silk, she knelt by his chair. "I should like to comfort you, Saber."

"Thank you for your concern." He could not relent, even for an instant.

One of her cool hands settled on his cheek, caressed his neck. She said, "There is something you're not explaining to me, isn't there? Something you think I should not care for?"

Tenderness rushed through him. He covered her hand and turned his mouth into her palm.

"I could not help myself." Her voice shook. "There was nothing I could do but stand there and allow them to stare at me with only—"

"No! No, Ella, I cannot bear it. I cannot bear it for you." Or for himself. One more cause for shame—he could not obliterate what she had been from his mind and pretend she was untouched. Poor child, that she had been. Poor, helpless child. They could not bring each other happiness. He could bring no woman happiness.

"Is it that? Is it my past that makes you shun me?"

"No!" He lied, and yet he did not lie. "You think you know me, Ella. You don't. If you did, you would not want me."

"I want you no matter what you are." She rested her face on his shoulder. "I know what you are, Saber. You are a man. Good and bad. Strong and weak. Brave and afraid—like any man. But you are more than the rest to me."

She spoke, and with her words, touched his heart—or whatever there was where his heart was supposed to exist. "How I would like to accept what you seem determined to give."

"Then *do* it," she whispered, turning her face up to place a lingering kiss on his jaw. "*Do* it, Saber. Take me for your own."

Take her? He clasped her head, held her cheek to his neck. He breathed in her scent of wildflowers, and new-mown grass beneath the sun—and wind on her Scottish moors. And he knew the sweetest cut of all. To love and be loved, yet to be denied.

Saber held Ella's face between his hands and looked down into her eyes, eyes the same color as the deep russet silk pooled about her legs.

Her soft lips parted.

He watched her lips, the glimpse of white teeth.

Ella lifted her chin.

Saber felt her breath on his face.

Her eyes drifted shut.

He flinched at the rapid thunder of his heart and rested his jaw atop her head.

She trembled.

"Ella. One day I will find the strength to make you understand."

Her hands folded around his wrists. "Why can't we just be us."

"Oh, but we are just us." He released her and stood up. "That's it, y'see. We are us, the sum of what we have been and have become."

She remained at his feet, holding his wrists. "And what we've become is good, Saber. It always is, because we learn from it."

Gently, he raised his arms until she was forced to let go. "True for you, sweet one. But there are those for whom the result is not good."

Her hands came together as if in prayer. "You are good. We

will be good together. You told me we would always be together."

"I told you that a long time ago. Before I became what I am. And you do not want to know what that is, Ella."

She pressed her steepled fingers to her lips. "I do know. You are . . . You are the best man in the world."

Shaking his head, he backed away. "No. No, Ella. I am the worst. What I have become, you cannot even imagine. What I have become—"

"Saber!"

"Don't you know what I'm telling you?" he shouted, and hated himself for the shock on her face. "I am not . . . What I have become is unspeakable. I cannot even be called a man. I no longer know the nature of my life—or my living death!"

He left her.

Chapter Eleven

Ella remained where Saber had left her, crumpled beside the chair at the secretaire.

She could not imagine what he'd become? He'd become something unspeakable? Not even a man?

"Why did you leave me?" she asked the air where he had been. "Why won't you listen to me? Why won't you let me listen to you, really listen to you?"

Where she rubbed her silken skirts, her moist palms left marks.

He no longer knew the nature of his life? Or his living death? Because he was scarred?

Ella flattened her lips to her teeth. He made her angry. She would like to follow him to his precious hiding place and demand that he open his heart to her.

Not again. She must not allow herself to run after Saber again. If he did not want her, she must accept his wishes.

And if she accepted those wishes, she would accept no other man! She got to her feet. No other man could ever be what Saber had become for her. And she did not care what everyone else wanted for her. What they thought she wanted for herself.

Fie! Great-Grandmama Franchot wanted Saber to help find Ella a husband? What bitter irony.

Ella went closer to the fire. Her body was cold, yet she still felt Saber's warm chest on her cheek and the texture of his coat, smelled his clean masculine scent.

He had pressed his mouth into her palm. She looked at the place. When he'd brushed his lips over her skin, there had been an expression of longing on his face, longing, and struggle within.

It was because her childhood made him angry that he would not let her speak of it. What he didn't know was that much as she detested her past, she feared her present more. She feared her present if the scrap of chiffon meant someone had indeed recognized her and intended to make her secrets public.

Why would anyone do such a thing, other than to victimize her, to control her?

If she told Saber her fears, what would he do? Tell her family to take her away from London? Tell them that he would be what they wanted for her, a loving husband? That he would protect her from vicious tongues?

She turned her head sharply.

Fool. If he wanted her, he could have her. He did not want her.

Ella picked up the reticule he'd given her and sat on the ebony chair to wait for the coach to come for her.

Saber would return before it was time for her to go back to Hanover Square.

Coals in the grate snapped. Flames wound up the crooked chimney, red and purple and blue.

From somewhere came a creak. She stared at the door. The house pressed in around her, heavy, still, and silent.

Mr. Bigun might have forgotten all about Papa's request and gone to bed. The servant might even have left the house altogether.

Saber was in the house. Ella could feel him.

He had gone away because he was troubled. But he could return at any moment. Surely he would not simply leave her alone here.

A long case clock ticked in a corner.

The flames shrank a little lower.

Saber *would* come back.

Ella's next breath quivered into her chest. He would come to her and she would be glad.

But . . . He was right, he was not the same.

She drew her bottom lip between her teeth and slipped to sit far back in the chair. Saber would never do anything to hurt her.

"Oh, come back," she said. "Where are you?"

Saber was not the same.

Brave Ella was frightened.

"Get out, Bigun!"

"The young lady has already left, my lord?"

"I told you to leave. Now."

Bigun produced the small bottle he seemed always to carry somewhere about his person, and poured a measure of brown liquid into a glass. "Drink this, my lord, and lie down."

"And sleep?" Saber laughed. "Thank you, Bigun, but no. In that direction lies only disaster. Go to your own bed."

"Your family does not appreciate you, my lord."

"What?" Saber swung from looking through his bedchamber window at the dark roofs of the stables behind the house. "What in God's name are you jabbering about?"

"They treat you badly."

"I have no idea what you mean. My family has not been

part of my life in recent years because of certain misunderstandings."

"And now they think of you as someone who has no life of his own, master."

Saber shook his head shortly, and winced at the pain in his temples. Ella was alone and confused in this house—in his house, where she should never have to feel anything but comfort.

"Perhaps I have done some good in that area," Bigun said.

The sound Saber dreaded started, very low, very far away, but growing louder and closer.

Hoofbeats.

"Now they will know that you are in demand, too. And perhaps the young lady's ardor will return."

He squinted at Bigun. "Speak plainly."

Bigun looked pained. "I am plain. Invitations, I told them. Proposals of marriage. It is known that nothing makes a commodity more precious than scarcity."

Saber went to the chest beside his bed and slid open a drawer. The emeralds in the handle of the dagger shone dully. "You talk nonsense, and I have no patience for it now, my friend." The dagger had severed the threads that held the buttons.

"Not nonsense at all. Now they will think of how many females desire you, my lord."

He glanced up. "Was that what all that invitation and proposal rubbish was about?"

"Not rubbish. A calculated move on my part, master. And I saw the young lady's face. She was jealous at once. The old one will think about it and come to the appropriate decision too."

The dagger had been in his hand, retrieved from a fallen enemy. He'd seen a bare arm upraised, a similar dagger clasped in a strong fist.

"Oh, yes, the old one will stop, and cast about, and say, Saber is receiving proposals of marriage. He does not have time to waste on lists of suitors for Ella. And then she will—"

"Please go away."

"Drink the potion, master."

"Leave me."

Bigun, the glass in one hand, turned down Saber's bed. "Miss Rossmara's head has been turned by the attention she has received at her first event, master. But now, because of Bigun's ploy, she will want you even more than she did before."

The Indian's voice droned and blurred.

That strong arm had descended, and another Englishman's last scream split the air. Saber scrambled after the assailant, grabbed his arm, tore at him. He held the wrist where the Englishman's blood trickled from the killing knife, and stared into a foreign face.

Young. Younger than Saber by far. Like the lad he had taken to safety.

Bigun's voice ceased to form words.

"Go to your bed," Saber told him, forcing himself to walk to the door and open it. "Thank you for your efforts. Most . . . Most inventive. Good night."

"The young lady?"

"She is safe. Her father will return for her." Perhaps by then he could hope to have collected himself.

Bigun held up the glass. "Drink—"

"Leave it. I'll drink it in good time."

Bigun hovered a moment longer, then did as he was commanded.

Saber waited for the sound of his servant's slippers to recede before lifting the dagger from the drawer. The three emeralds in the hilt shone mysteriously.

Hoofbeats.

He was awake and hearing the horses—just like the last time when exhaustion had claimed him after too long a fight against sleep.

How could he subject Ella to this?

Even if he could push the acts she had been forced to perform from his mind and take what she offered him, how could he ever take her to his bed knowing she might see what he had become?

His mind was changed forever.

Ribbons of color wound about his brain. Pain and horror sickened him. He closed his eyes and saw a gush of bright light—and the light pierced his head.

He sweated and tore, gasping, at his neckcloth—and slipped to his knees beside the bed.

Aieee!

The face of a youth. Saber had hesitated.

Hoofbeats.

A second, surely only a second of hesitation. But a rearing animal caught Saber's shoulder and the dagger had flown to the shredded earth.

And in the heartbeats that followed, that youth with cold eyes and white teeth between snarling lips, had driven his weapon into the breasts of two more Englishmen. Two more had died.

The boy's laugh jarred Saber. He shuddered, and lunged for the dagger. Words he did not understand streamed from the mouth in the blood-spattered face. The moment Saber's fingers would have closed upon the dagger, the stranger reached it first and snatched it up, and slashed at Saber's face.

"Stop it, stop it!" Saber stumbled to his feet and staggered to lean against the wall of his bedchamber. He could not bear the memories.

The dagger tore his face, his neck. And then he fell, tried to turn and grab the boy's legs. But the blade descended, plowed through his back, and rose. Again it plunged, again and again.

All pain, all blood. Face-to-face with a dead Englishman in the mud. A man as young as the stranger Saber had thought to spare.

He had betrayed his own. Mothers and fathers had lost sons. Wives had lost husbands, children their fathers, brothers and sisters, their brothers—because Saber had failed them all.

He had been attacked with the knife that would have saved the lives of comrades. Attacked and left for dead.

The coals were all but spent. Sparks crackled where flames had curled.

Ella shivered. An hour had passed since Saber left her. Fifteen minutes had been spent before that and after the dowager and Papa's departure. So much time remained before she could hope to be taken home.

On an upper floor something thudded.

Ella held the reticule tightly against her stomach. She was safe here. Nothing would ever happen to her in Saber's house. He would not allow it.

Footsteps, heavy and slow, sounded on the stairs leading down to the vestibule.

She wetted her dry lips. Of course. Saber felt guilty at having deserted her and was coming to ensure her comfort. He would be angry at Mr. Bigun for allowing the fire to burn so low.

The footsteps met the flags in the vestibule. Heels clipped on stone.

Ella rose and moved to stand behind the chair. Her eyes strained against candlelight burning low in the vessels offered up by Saber's statues.

Her heart rivaled the crack of shoes on tile. Her heart beat much faster.

Then the door opened and Saber stood there.

"Oh." Her relief at the sight of him all but buckled her legs. "Oh, Saber. Thank goodness you are returned."

He didn't reply.

The door slammed shut behind him and he approached her across carpet that swallowed his footsteps.

"Saber, there are things I want to tell you. Please will you listen to me now?"

He raised his right hand.

Gripped in his white-knuckled fingers, a gilded dagger gleamed.

Chapter Twelve

Gripped in his white-knuckled fingers, a gilded dagger gleamed.

Ella held the back of the chair. "Saber?"

His eyes stared past her, vacant, yet not vacant—seeing, yet not seeing anything of this world.

"Saber, what is it? What's happened to you?"

Slowly, his blank gaze settled on her face. She saw the sheen of perspiration on his brow.

Unable to resist, she took a step backward, and another. Saber wouldn't hurt her. . . . She retreated until she bumped into a bronze figure of a man in flowing robes. Ella grabbed the statue and it wobbled.

Saber advanced. Never looking away from her, he wiped his brow with a sleeve—and closed the distance between them.

Was he awake? What had she heard about people who walked while asleep? *Do not awaken them.*

Ella held very still.

The dagger caught the light. He held it so tightly, his fist shook.

He would not hurt her. Transfixed, she stared at the glinting blade. Closer and closer. Saber walked as if his feet were weighted, or pulled back by water.

And then he was before her, above her, watching her with eyes as deep green as glimpses of emeralds in the handle of the dagger.

Ella screamed. Her legs would not hold her any longer. She stumbled against Saber, grasped his coat and began to slide downward.

One strong hand clasped her arm. "Ella? My dear girl—are you ill?" His voice sounded as if it hadn't been used in a long time. "Ella?"

He had stopped her fall. Keeping her hold on his coat, Ella steadied herself and raised her face. "You . . . Saber, the knife. You frightened me."

Pulling down his brows, he studied the weapon in his hand. "Cuts skin and flesh," he said, "and spirit—and soul."

Her teeth chattered together.

His arm went around her waist. Their bodies pressed together, his solid chest to her soft breasts, his unyielding hips and thighs against her stomach, her legs.

Ella slipped her hands beneath his arms, rested her face on his shoulder and clung. "Is that the knife that . . . Is it the one that wounded you?"

His grip on her tightened. "What? No, no, of course not." Saber's trembling matched her own. He was like a man returning from another place. "The knife? The dagger? I brought it down to show you. Another memento of my travels."

Ella simply held him and struggled to control her quaking limbs.

"Isn't it pretty?"

She shook her head. "I hate it. I don't like the way it feels. Evil."

His laugh was forced. "Such an imagination. You and Max must both have fed on dreamers' milk when you were infants."

That brought a fleeting smile to her lips. Max had a shocking reputation for falsehoods that were not exactly falsehoods. His imagination had often all but brought him to disaster—it had also saved him. Ella knew how her younger brother had used his flights of fancy to escape the degradation of his early life.

"You would find Max changed," she told Saber, hugging him the tighter. "When he comes to London to visit, you will not believe how he has grown up."

"Should you like to have the dagger?"

Amazed, she opened her eyes to look at the elegantly wicked thing that now rested across his palm. "Thank you, but no." What would he say if she told him she had thought—for a time—that he might use it to harm her? "I wish I need never look at it again. It's hateful."

Reaching, he put it on the mantel and wrapped both of his arms around her. "I'm sorry I left you alone here. I am confused, Ella."

Confused? About his feelings for her? How easily hope blossomed. "I'm confused too. These years when I have tried not to think of you have been terrible."

"But you did manage not to think of me, surely. Not too much of the time?"

"All of the time," she said shortly. "I cannot make you feel as I do, but I'm helpless to feel otherwise. On an evening that seems long ago, yet perhaps only yesterday, I saw a young man at Franchot Castle."

"Don't, Ella."

"I was newly come to this world of ours. A lucky girl rescued by a kind man. A girl who spoke like a street urchin—like the urchin I was. And the young man was in his cups."

She smiled into his jacket and felt him sigh. "He was in his cups and angry because his wicked cousin—or the man he thought was his cousin—would not give him what was rightfully his."

"All past," Saber reminded her. "Etienne was a usurper. Not my cousin at all. Calum is that cousin and, thank God, Calum has been returned to his rightful place as Duke of Franchot, so all is well. He gave me what was mine."

"And now you do not care a whit for it."

"Ella—"

"No," she told him gently. "This is my story. Then you can tell yours. That young man—foxed as he was—looked at me as if I was like no girl he had ever seen."

He stroked her shoulders, rubbed the back of her neck. "You were like no other girl I had ever seen. You still are."

Ella could scarcely swallow. "That night you wanted to accompany me back to my rooms." She laughed. "Mama—although she was not yet my mama—but Mama was most firm. She put you in your place."

"She did indeed," Saber said. "Were you glad?"

Ella buried her face in his coat and chuckled.

"Were you?"

"Were you, Saber?"

"In some ways females are all the same," he said with mock gravity. "They like to push a man to indiscretion. No, I was not glad. In fact, if I remember my drunken thoughts of the time, I was decidedly put out. An exotic creature came into my company, only to be snatched away so quickly."

Ella withdrew her hands, then replaced them—beneath his coat this time. "I thought you the most handsome man I had ever seen. I wished we were alone—even then when I didn't know you at all. I wanted to go somewhere with you and just look at you."

"You would not wish to look at me now," he said with bitterness in his voice.

She squeezed him as hard as she could. "Pish, posh, as Great-Grandmama Franchot would say. If I say too many pretty things to you, I shall turn your head. But looking at you is still the greatest pleasure of my life."

His breath moved her hair. "So much promise. All gone."

"No! Not all gone. Now it can be ours, Saber."

He rocked her, rested his chin atop her head, played the tips of his fingers over the sensitive skin at her nape.

"You came to me at night—in the garden at Franchot. I was little more than a child then. I didn't understand how gallant and honorable you were. You were already a man with a man's desires, yet you treated me with such gentleness, with such reserve."

"Don't, Ella."

"Why? It is true. And it brings me gladness to speak of it. I cannot tell anyone else. You spoke to me and listened to me. And you made me a promise."

"Ella—"

"You promised me you would always be my friend. You said you would be there if I needed you. And you meant much more, didn't you?"

His long, powerful hands splayed wide over her back. Spreading his fingers, he let his thumbs come to rest against the sides of her breasts.

And Ella trembled anew.

"India was a cruel place to me," he murmured.

She held her breath.

"I had never seen . . . I saw things I had never seen before. I cannot forget them, Ella, and they have changed me."

"They changed you when you were wounded, didn't they?" Raising her face, she gazed up at him.

Saber looked over her head. "It wasn't the wounds."

"What, then?"

Like a man rising from sleep, he shook his head. "It's past now."

"Is it? Is it past for you? Over?"

Saber glanced down into her eyes, tilted his head, and bent to kiss her neck. Always he turned the scars away from her.

She melted against him. Her body was not the same with Saber—it was not her own. Where his touch met her breasts, she ached, and the ache filled her with burning, with longing. She remembered the caress of his bare skin on hers and pressed her eyes shut.

With maddening care, he made circles on her breasts, through silk and muslin. His mouth was both firm and gentle on her neck, her shoulder.

The still room was only a place to contain their bodies, their spirits—the sensations Saber evoked in Ella. She stood on tiptoe and wound her wrists behind his neck. He kept his face turned away and she could only kiss the jaw he showed her, the cheek, the corner of the mouth she saw, waking or sleeping.

"The other night," she said. "When you and I were together."

"I was wrong," he breathed.

"You were right. It was right for us. I want to be with you like that again. Saber, is it unnatural for me to want to be naked and for you to be naked?"

"No," he said indistinctly.

"Then I want it now."

His chest heaved. "Please don't . . . Ella, your carriage will return soon. Even if . . . It isn't proper and it must not happen again."

"Why must you fight me?" She tried to pull away, but he held her fast. "You are impossible!"

"I must be sensible. For both of us."

"Kiss me." She was forward, but he was her love.

"Close your eyes," he told her after a moment's hesitation. "Ah, ah, don't argue. Close them."

Ella did as he ordered and lifted her face. She lifted her face and waited.

"Do not open them. Promise?"

She screwed up her eyes. "I promise."

"You are the loveliest creature I have ever seen."

Ella started to open her eyelids.

"No! You promised. I am going to tell you things I have no right to tell you. If your eyes are closed, you can pretend you are simply listening to a creation of your female imagination. A character from one of the novels you no doubt enjoy."

"One of the novels men should also enjoy so that they can know what women would enjoy."

He laughed shortly. "As you say, my dear. No doubt you are right. I must let you select some volumes for me. Meanwhile, I shall have to improvise."

She pressed even closer. "I thought you were going to kiss me."

"Patience. When your eyes are open—which, of course, they will not be until I say so—they are the darkest of browns and they shine. Like cinnamon diamonds. Cinnamon diamonds would suit you. You should wear them often. Your brows remind me of birds' wings, and your nose is straight and a little tip-tilty."

She wrinkled the part in question. "Tip-tilty?"

"In the nicest possible way. Your neck is soft, as soft as the skin on your shoulders and arms—and on your breasts."

His fingers, applied to her eyelids, stopped them from popping open.

"Hush, beloved," he murmured. "There may never be another time for us. Your breasts are soft yet firm, and when I filled my mouth with them my manhood was not the only part of my body to leap. I should be damned for speaking so to you, but it leaps now."

"I know," she said before she could stop the words. Her hips tilted into his.

"Do you indeed?" He brushed his mouth over her brow. "Do you indeed, my girl? Do you know that as my body quickens, it longs to feel again the soft curls between your legs?"

She let out a small cry.

"There you become wet. You are wet now, perhaps?"

Heat blazed in her cheeks.

"Mmm. I see that you are. That is as it should be, Ella. To be fully with a man—as it is meant to be—your heart and soul, and body, should be open and welcoming. The entering for the man is the receiving for the woman. It is the joining of their bodies as something more than flesh. If that is not the way of it, then the joining is only for passing pleasure and when the pleasure is over there is nothing remaining."

"The pleasure is wrong?"

His laughter was deep. "Oh, no, beloved. Not wrong at all. The pleasure is unbearably sweet. The thought of it turns my loins to fire." He covered her breasts, tucked his fingers beneath the neck of her bodice, and flirted with her straining nipples. "Fire that will consume me when you are gone."

"Then keep me," she told him, breathless with her need. "We could go away from here now. I need nothing but you. I want nothing but you."

"And your mouth"—his lips covered hers in a deep, deep kiss—"your mouth is the stuff of my dreams as well. I look at your soft lips and feel them on mine. When they part, mine part also." He kissed her again, slipping his tongue into her mouth, moaning softly, deep in his throat.

"Saber," she said when he nuzzled his way to her ear. "Don't send me away again."

With both hands, he cradled her head and pressed her face to his chest. "I can't keep you. Not ever."

She made fists against him. "Why?"

"You could not understand. I don't want you to."

"I will not allow you to send me away again."

"The choice is not yours."

"You speak such beautiful words. Then you puzzle me. You break my heart, Saber."

"There are things I cannot share with you," he told her. "But I can ask you to forgive me for not being what you need—not anymore."

"You are—"

"No. Not ever. We must let each other go."

With unbearable pain? She could not do it. Somehow she would find the way to destroy whatever stood between them. The gold reticule hung from her wrist. "I have brought the ruby star back to you."

At first he didn't respond. Then he said, "Why? It was my gift to you. I got it for you."

"I brought it back because you said it is not as cold as your heart. A lie, Saber. And I do not accept gifts that are lies."

"I wish it to be yours."

She heard a new edge in his voice—desperation? Hardening herself, she said, "You should save it for someone you can love."

He grew quite still. "I have no reason to save it any longer."

Because you love me?

"I have given it to you, Ella. Wear it and think of me."

"I always think of you. Saber, let me heal you. Please."

His response was to embrace her more ardently, to enfold her as if he would absorb her into him.

Ella took his face in her hands and pulled it down to hers. He tried to avert the evidence of his wounds. "No! No, Saber. You have not heard me." She eased his scarred skin against her cheek. "I asked you to let me heal you. There is nothing of you that I do not love."

"There are scars you cannot see."

She smoothed his shoulders, his back. "I have seen them. I want them for my own."

"Ella," he murmured. "Please accept that we cannot be together. Regardless of what we may both long for, it cannot be."

Her head bowed to his shoulder. "What if you discovered that someone wanted to do me harm?"

Beneath her hands, his muscles stiffened. "Do you harm? Is there . . . Has someone tried to harm you?"

She should not do this, but desperation had stolen her choices. "Possibly. Look." Catching at the reticule, she contrived to remove the latest secret delivery to Hanover Square. "This was sent to me today. Left in a packet on the doorstep. Rose—my maidservant—gave it to me when I returned from Pall Mall. There was no note."

Saber looked at the scrap of red chiffon she fluttered near his face and frowned. "Someone sent it to you?"

"It is a warning, Saber. Someone wishes to frighten me—to let me know my past is not a secret and that it can be used to ruin me."

He shook his head. "Used how? A piece of material?"

"To shame me. To spread rumors."

Saber took the gauzy thing from her fingers. "You will have to be more plain, Ella."

How could he know the details? He had not been there. "This is what I have always feared," she told him. "I never wanted to return to London—in part because I had met you and wasn't interested in meeting other"—she silenced him with a forefinger on his lips—"I did not want to meet other men. I still do not want to meet other men. But I also knew there would be a risk such as this, that someone would recognize me."

Understanding darkened his gaze, hardened his features.

"Yes," she whispered. "Papa and Mama were convinced that it would not happen because I was so young. But I am . . . different. Like a gypsy, they say. And I have been noticed, and remembered by an ill-wisher."

Saber spoke through his teeth. "Who could wish you ill? Who would *dare* to try to hurt you?"

His vehemence shocked her. "I only want it to stop." And she wanted Saber at her side—by whatever means now. "Shame is the weapon here. I wore red chiffon for—"

"No!"

"For the auction," she finished, and felt tears fill her eyes. Her voice broke when she added, "Transparent red chiffon that did not hide my body."

Saber closed the material inside his fist. "No one will shame you because of this. Do you understand?"

His intensity shouldn't thrill her so. "It could happen." *Take me away.*

"I would not allow it."

"How would you stop it?"

He settled his thumbs at the point of her chin. "You are guilty of nothing. Remember those words. Hold them in your heart. You have been a victim." Bending, he kissed her escaping tears. "There will be a man—a man who is truly a man—who will not be swayed by idle chatter."

"It is not idle chatter," she reminded him. "And I have already met a man who is truly a man."

"Not the right one, my dear. Not yet."

Her heart grew tight. "So I am to face the *ton* and wait for the whispers to begin. But I should take comfort in the knowledge that you, and my family, consider me blameless. I shall be a very lonely, very vulnerable creature, Saber."

"You will not be lonely." He turned to see the longcase clock. "It is almost time. Let me help you with your cloak."

Ella caught his hand. "How is it I won't be lonely? When they shake their heads and point at me?"

"You will not be lonely," Saber said grimly. "Never. Because I shall never be far away."

She raised her brows quizzically.

"Grandmama will be delighted to hear that I am completely committed to assisting with your launch into Society. Where you go, I shall go—your devoted childhood friend who wishes to make certain you are well-matched."

"But—" Words failed her.

He smiled thinly. "No questions. Anyone who speaks ill of you, or tries to hurt you in any way, shall answer to me. This much I can do for you, little Ella."

Not exactly what she had dreamed of—or planned to accomplish—but better than might have been. "You will accompany me during the Season."

"I shall be close at hand—always. Justine will be more than willing to supply me with a list of your engagements. Those engagements will become my own social calendar—God help me."

She eyed him innocently. "Poor Saber. You really don't like going about, do you?"

"I shall not be *going about,* as you put it. I shall be caring for you until you have a husband to take my place. In the meantime, any woman who seeks to smear you will do well to find a hiding place from me. And I will *kill* any man who offends your honor."

Chapter Thirteen

"I shall go in when I'm certain the establishment is empty," Saber told Devlin. "Please speak to the proprietor. Tell him you wish to engage his services for a very lucrative commission."

Devlin glared through the coach window at the bustle that was Bond Street in the middle of a sunny but cool afternoon. "You have avoided explaining this piece of foolishness to me. Why should I be your lackey?"

Saber studied his friend's impeccably fine profile. "Because you know this is difficult for me, this appearing in public."

"If I am to believe you, the weeks to come will be a veritable round of high living for you, Saber. Why should you need me in this matter?"

"I don't. Except to help me make certain I am not seen."

"Then why not give me your dratted mission and let me accomplish it? Why come at all?"

The shop windows held Saber's attention. "Because I wish to make my own selections. Then I shall return to the coach and leave you to do the necessary. If anyone should inquire, the owner will think you are the buyer, and he may even say as much to anyone interested. There must be no suggestion that I have any part in this."

"Bloody hell! In *what*?"

"Now," Saber said forcefully, and threw open the carriage door. "That man was the last customer to enter, and now he has left."

"Well, we've certainly sat here long enough to know an entire afternoon's custom hereabouts," Devlin remarked without humor. He followed Saber to the pavement and into the shop, with its two mullioned windows flanking a highly polished oak door.

Saber shut the door behind them. A man stood behind the counter with his back to his new clients. Surreptitiously, Saber turned over the sign that would now pronounce Cox's Flowers "closed," and gently shot home a bolt.

The man turned around. Saber swept off his hat and held it before his nose and mouth while he studied billowing heaps of fragrant blossoms in vases on every surface of the room.

Devlin cleared his throat and returned the man's greeting. "Mind if we look around?"

"Take your time, gentlemen."

Saber hovered beside a crystal vase filled with brilliant spring blooms. "Unusual," he murmured behind his hat brim. "Elegantly simple, yet so full of life. Like Ella."

Devlin's hand came down heavily on his shoulder. "Is that what this is all about? A bloody *posy* for Ella?"

"No," Saber told him. He gestured for Devlin to bring his ear close. "Not a bloody posy, friend. Dozens of bloody posies. I am going back to the carriage. You are going to order—and pay for—six vases of spring flowers to be delivered to Miss Ella Rossmara every day."

"You want me to send—"

"No, you rattle-brain. Not *you*. Not from you. Anonymously." He glanced about. "And single red roses, each differently presented. And a bowl of cream roses. Yes, cream roses would suit, too."

"In God's name—"

"In no one's name, Devlin. And please don't curse so. It doesn't become you. The stock here is pleasing, just as I thought it would be."

"Then send it yourself."

"And risk some busybody finding out they're from me? And then having the laugh on Ella. No. This way the worst that can happen is that you appear the ardent suitor. That alone should be enough to make any number of young bucks vie for the attention of Miss Rossmara. Do it, please. If all goes as planned, the assumption will be that she is besieged by admirers. We have only to arrange for a remark to be dropped here and there. We know what happens when a female is perceived as the most sought-after creature in all London."

"Yes," Devlin said under his breath. "They will make fools of themselves trying to capture her. Very clever, Saber. Also damnably expensive."

"I can afford it," Saber reminded him. He did not say that he had nothing else to spend his money on, other than the simplest of lifestyles.

He let himself out of the shop and immediately entered the carriage again.

Nothing would give him more pleasure than to shower Ella with flowers—in his own name. What lay ahead of him, giving her to another man, was the cruelest cut of all. He had no choice.

For two nights past, the darkest hours had claimed him for hell. His affliction only grew worse. Surely the time when he would pass over into madness forever must be at hand. Before that happened, he must make sure Ella was safe.

He stared at the windows of the flower shop. How he would revel in giving her every flower, every jewel, every beautiful thing in the world that might make her heart glad.

She would take you and leave the rest.

Fate's knife was sharper than any living assailant's dagger. He no longer gave a damn about whatever had happened in her past. With every moment spent in her company his love for her deepened. So deep had that love become that he knew he must move quickly to remove the temptation of Ella Rossmara from his life—whatever was left of it.

Two young females and a black-clad maid paused before the florist's windows. Saber stiffened and drew back into the shadows of the coach.

One of the girl's blond ringlets bobbed as she turned toward her companion.

He didn't recall her name but she'd been at the Eagletons'. Saber sent up thanks that he hadn't encountered her upon leaving the shop. She laughed and hurried on with her unknown friend, the parcel-laden maid scurrying to keep up.

Devlin was some time in completing his business. As soon as he reentered the coach, Saber rapped for the coachman to carry on. He opened the trap and shouted, "Number Nine Regent Street. Howell and James."

"Howell and James?" Devlin moaned. "Now what am I to send her? Fans? A clock or two?"

"No."

"Sweetmeats? Pounds and pounds of sweetmeats a hundred times a day?"

"No," Saber said, pulling on his gloves. "Jewels. Jewels every day. Then on to Fifty-two Pall Mall."

"Dodsley's?" Devlin tossed his hat on the seat beside him. "You're going to send her *books,* man?"

"Not at all." Saber examined the stitching on his cuffs. "I'm going to select a few volumes for myself."

* * *

Pearl and diamond earbobs nestled in a bed of ice-blue velvet. Ella touched the stones briefly before closing the satin box and setting it with three other boxes containing jewelry that she'd received as gifts in recent days.

"Girls can be so difficult." Blanche Bastible, Grandmama Franchot's companion, sighed hugely. She picked up the box Ella had just discarded on an inlaid chest in the cream and gold drawing room at Hanover Square. Blanche opened the box again. "Really, Your Grace, I am amazed at your patience in these matters."

Seated on a gold brocade chaise, Great-Grandmama behaved as if she hadn't heard Blanche. The arrangement between the two had followed the upheaval when Great-Grandmama had arrived in Scotland to try to stop Papa from marrying Mama. In fact, Blanche Wren Bastible was the Marquess of Stonehaven's mother-in-law. Arran, Marquess of Stonehaven, Papa's brother, had married Grace Wren, a charming sprite of a woman cursed with an overbearing mother—Blanche Wren Bastible. An alliance between Blanche and the dowager duchess of Franchot should have been a fantastic impossibility. In fact, the two suited each other very well—for reasons no one at all understood.

"Young lady," Blanche said ominously. Voluminous and inappropriate daffodil yellow gros-de-Naples encased her substantial body and a row of matching yellow bows adorned the intricate loops of her chestnut hair. "Young lady! You are behaving badly. Do you think that this dying-wraith act makes you interesting?"

"I rather thought wraiths were already dead," Ella said, wishing Blanche would go away—preferably all the way back to Cornwall and Franchot Castle.

"Disrespectful," Blanche muttered. "Did you hear that, Your Grace?"

"Ella has wit. I like that. Someone has taken your fancy. That's it, isn't it, Ella? Come along. No coyness, if you please. Doesn't become you. Tell me the man's name at once."

And wouldn't that ensure the silence Ella so longed for? Unfortunately, the silence wouldn't last. The uproar to follow could be all but endless.

A footman knocked and entered with a bowl of cream roses.

Blanche clapped her hands and jumped up and down, for all the world as if she were sixteen rather than nearing her fiftieth birthday. "I declare," she warbled. "More roses. One gentleman sends cream roses. Another red. Then there are those gaudy springy things that keep coming. But they are interesting in that I'd simply *swoon* to know the message he seeks to convey. And the jewelry! Although that need not come from the same man. And the fans. The most beautiful fans imaginable. Have I told you about the way my first husband courted me and—"

"Yes," the dowager interrupted. Blanche had a magpie's attachment to shiny baubles. "You most certainly have told us, Blanche. Who is the man for whom you pine, Ella?"

Ella bent to smell the latest bouquet.

"Answer me," the dowager demanded with some asperity.

"I cannot," Ella said, turning to look at the old lady. "If it were possible, I would." Mutual understanding passed between them. The dowager would not press further—at least for the moment.

Blanche sniffed loudly. She removed an earbob from its box and slipped it onto her own ear. "Cannot tell?" she said. "Will not tell, more likely. Oh, the trial of ungrateful daughters. As the mother of just such a one, I know the difficulties. And after all this family has done for—"

"That will do, Blanche, dear," Great-Grandmama said

firmly. "If Ella says there is no one she favors, then there is no one she favors. Put the earbob away, my dear."

Huffing, Blanche did as she was instructed and set the box down with the others once more.

The door opened and Devlin North was shown in. He wore a gray cloak and still carried his hat and riding crop. The wind had ruffled his thick black hair. " 'Morning, lovely ladies," he boomed. With him came fresh air and the atmosphere of power-in-motion that Ella felt whenever she saw him.

"Good morning, Mr. North." Great-Grandmama extended her hand and accepted the touch of Devlin's mouth—which he repeated with Blanche.

He turned the full vital intensity of his gaze upon Ella, and his smile disappeared. "Good morning to you, Ella," he said gravely, approaching, holding his hat and his crop before him. "Lovely as ever. Even lovelier, in fact. How are you, my dear?"

Ella frowned a little. "I'm well, thank you." His piercing regard disconcerted her.

"It is very important to some of us that you be not only well, but happy. I'm sure you understand what I mean."

She didn't. Behind Devlin, Great-Grandmama had grown still. Ella felt the old lady straining not to miss a word. Blanche, on the other hand, didn't hesitate to hover close by.

Devlin glanced around the room as if he hadn't noticed its contents before. "Wonderful flowers," he said. "No doubt there is a man who thinks a great deal of you. How could there not be?"

Ella also looked at the flowers. "They're beautiful, aren't they?"

"And jewels, I see. Oh, indeed, quite marvelous."

"They're beautiful," she repeated. "And more than a little overwhelming."

Devlin picked up a white box and opened it to reveal an

emerald bracelet. "Whoever sent this knows how well such strong color becomes you," he said, smiling at her. "May I put this on for you?"

Suspicion wheedled its way into Ella's mind. She extended her left hand and snuffed out the thought. Ridiculous. Devlin North wasn't a man likely to be attracted to Ella as anything more than a family friend. On the other hand . . . Excitement fluttered in her breast. Perhaps Saber . . .

Devlin concentrated on fastening the bracelet and held her wrist toward sunlight streaming through the window. "See how it shines?" His attention shifted from the bracelet to her eyes. "But beside you, it is pale. I'm certain the man who sent this would say as much. If he were here, that is. And I know he wants nothing more than to be here with you."

Ella couldn't find words.

His fingers lingered on her wrist, hovered over the deep green stones of the bracelet, slipped around to hold her hand. "Of course, he knows he is with you whenever you spare a thought for his gifts—and his regard for you." The tips of Devlin's fingers caressed Ella's palm.

Blanche's enormous yellow skirts swayed, and she sighed loudly.

"No messages?" Devlin said, releasing Ella as if he loathed to do so. "No evidence of the admirer's identity?"

A single admirer? Why would Devlin assume all the gifts were from one man? "No messages at all." Unless Devlin knew that only one man was responsible for the deluge of expensive tokens.

Fleetingly, he touched the point of her chin. "When I first saw you—at the lodge at Castle Kirkcaldy—you were a beauty. I told Struan and Justine as much. You have only become more so. And you are a delight, to boot, Ella Rossmara. Any man would count himself blessed to have you for his own."

Thoroughly embarrassed, Ella fussed with one of the vases of spring blossoms. Papa had been disquieted by Devlin's attentions to her at that time. But surely Devlin wasn't, by these obscure means . . . No, he couldn't be.

"Nothing to say, little Ella?" He pulled a red tulip from the vase. "Someone knows your affinity for simple things. Simple, elegant things."

Ella studied his face. "You think so?"

"Oh, yes." Slowly, his eyes moved from the tulip to her face. "Someone wants to see you surrounded by simple elegance. An emerald bracelet of impeccable design, cream roses in crystal vases, an ivory fan with diamonds where only you will be the one to see them—earbobs of pearls and diamonds that will be warmed by your skin. The man has studied you well, Ella."

"More than one man, I should say," Blanche said excitedly.

Great-Grandmama said, "Hush," in a voice that brooked no argument.

Devlin ignored them both. He rested the head of the tulip against Ella's cheek. "Have you noted how the petals of a tulip resemble velvet?"

She nodded, unable to move.

"This one is red velvet. The texture of your lips, but not as subtle in color." Openly, he studied her mouth. "Not as subtle at all," he murmured, his own lips remaining parted.

Momentarily mesmerized, Ella heard her sharp intake of breath. "The gifts are quite lovely," she said faintly. The box containing the earbobs had been closed by the time he entered the room and the ivory fan was upstairs in her bedchamber. . . .

She was imagining nothing. A woman would have to be made of wood not to feel the passion in Devlin's words—in his actions. He was wooing her!

* * *

“I do hope you have made the right decision in this,” Margot told Saber. “Perhaps you should reconsider, *mon chéri.*”

Saber tucked her arm through his elbow and climbed the steps to the front door of the Stonehaven Mansion in Hanover Square. “You trusted me to get you out of India, Margot. You have trusted my every decision since those dreadful days. Do you suddenly doubt me now?” Regardless of his dear friend’s opinion, there could be no turning back.

“I trust you in all things,” Margot said quietly. “You are the best of men, Saber. The most honorable and kind. Without you I should have been branded a bigamist and cast out entirely.”

“Don’t think of it now,” he told her, patting her hand. “That is all behind you. And it is—as I so often tell you—it is hardly your fault that you were a young girl taken in by a man who promised you a wonderful life.”

“A man who married me when he was already married and—”

She broke off as the door opened to reveal the Stonehavens’ squat butler.

Crabley’s mashed little nose wrinkled and his shiny black eyes took in first Margot, then Saber before he said, “Come one, come all,” in his peculiarly toneless voice, and stood back for them to enter.

He led the way to a closed door, knocked, and went in. “Lord Avenall,” he announced, “and . . .” His wave toward Margot was delivered with a flourish before he departed without waiting to hear her identity.

Margot gave an astonished laugh.

Saber was more astonished to see Devlin seated with Ella on a gold brocade chaise. A woman in yellow whom he had never met sat in a chair near the chaise.

Devlin leaped to his feet and strode across the room. "Saber! This is a surprise!"

"Evidently," Saber muttered.

Devlin drew down his arched brows. "I came to pay my respects to Ella and her family." He inclined his head significantly, and Saber followed the motion to an array of stunning bouquets set upon a gilt console between two windows. "Struan and Justine are out visiting. The dowager duchess is here, but she's gone to rest."

"Overwhelmed by so much coming and going," the woman in yellow said fatuously. "I'm the dowager's companion, Blanche Bastible. I'm also the Marquess of Stonehaven's mother-in-law."

At that Saber spared the woman an interested look. "Grace's mother?"

A large bosom rose beneath the yellow gown. "Such a trial," she said. "Daughters. One cannot rely upon them to provide for one's comfort in times of difficulty. Such a cruel stroke that I should have been granted only a daughter, when a son would have known how to ensure that his mother never worried for a moment of her days."

Saber remembered the story of Blanche Wren Bastible and how she had all but forced her daughter into marrying Arran to secure her own good fortune. Good fortune had truly come in the form of the eventual outcome of Grace's stormy courtship—if that was the correct term for what had been described—with Arran.

"I am Countess Perruche," Margot said suddenly. She nodded at Blanche but went directly to sit beside Ella. "We met briefly at the charming soiree at the Eagletons'? There was no opportunity to get to know each other."

If Ella was delighted to meet Margot, she disguised her happiness well. "A memorable evening," she said, looking not at Margot but at Saber. "Unforgettable."

He absorbed the jolt that struck him in places best forgotten at this moment. "Indeed," he agreed stiffly. "I wanted you to meet Margot. She is a very dear friend of mine."

"Is she?" The chill was unmistakable.

"We met in India," Margot told Ella. "Saber was so very kind to me."

Ella's face became marble cold. "Saber can be very kind, it seems." She threaded her fingers through pleats in her deep-green dress. "I'm lucky today. First Devlin. Then you, Saber. So much attention."

There was something in her voice, something completely unlike her. Annoyance, perhaps? Suspicion? He favored Devlin with a long, contemplative stare. His friend had made no mention of any intention to visit Ella.

"A girl making her first entry into Society should receive much attention," Margot said, twinkling as only Margot could twinkle. Today she was utterly charming in a blue-gray promenade dress and wide-brimmed, matching bonnet. "Of course, in France things were not so—er—not so simple is perhaps the word I search for. I married my husband, Count Perruche, and went to India. But that is my story, and it is not interesting, I assure you."

Blanche Bastible's avid attention irritated Saber. "We are detaining you, Mrs. Bastible. I'm sure my grandmother must depend very heavily upon you. Please don't let us keep you from her."

"Oh, you aren't," she said, her round blue eyes very wide.

"Please check on her," Ella said flatly. "The countess will be an excellent chaperon, won't you, Countess?"

"You must call me Margot. Of course you must go to the dowager, Mrs. Bastible. It has been a pleasure to meet you."

Blanche opened her mouth, obviously about to protest, but shut it again and left the room without another word.

When the door had closed, Saber said, "I'm here for the

reason we discussed, Ella," and detested the formality in his voice. "I have decided—and Margot has kindly agreed—that with her in attendance there will be no question regarding my attentions to you at upcoming functions."

He saw the immediate glitter in Ella's eyes. She quickly looked at her hands in her lap.

"Isn't Saber clever?" Margot said at once, covering Ella's hands but flashing a warning glance at Saber. "He does always think of all things. He has persuaded me that if he is apparently escorting me, his attendance upon you will be seen as nothing more than appropriate family concern."

"I see," Ella said. She extended a slender wrist upon which a bracelet—the bracelet he had selected—of emeralds winked. "I love this, don't you? Devlin was kind enough to put it on for me."

Saber cleared his throat. "A lovely thing, indeed." He scowled at Devlin. Had he come here and overplayed his hand? Did Ella suspect her tributes had come from Saber? "Looks as if you've already gathered a gaggle of admirers, young Ella."

"Does it?" She looked at him from beneath lowered lashes. "A gaggle, do you think? Or perhaps just one very determined man?"

Devlin became exceedingly interested in carvings along the mantel.

"What would make you think one man had sent so many gifts?" Saber asked, staring at Devlin's back.

Ella said, "Oh, the notion has been suggested."

Damn Devlin's eyes. He'd overstepped himself this time.

"May I see what you have been given?" Margot asked, getting up and offering her hand to Ella with the natural friendliness Saber so admired in the woman. "Come, I will not deny that I do adore pretty things."

Ella allowed herself to be led to a collection of jewelry

boxes on the table with the flowers. Margot was soon exclaiming over the contents.

Saber went to stand at Devlin's side and said, "Why did you come here?"

Devlin straightened, but did not look at Saber. "To pay a friendly visit on Ella."

"What would make her think so many different gifts might come from one man?" Saber asked softly.

"Can't imagine."

"You can't imagine? It couldn't be that you decided to turn my little plans around, could it?"

"No idea what you mean."

Saber itched to force Devlin to turn around. "Are you sure you haven't . . . ? Well, have you?"

"Have I what?"

"Don't be obscure with me, man. Did you say to Ella that . . . Did you?"

At last Devlin gave his full, apparently puzzled attention to Saber. "You're not making much sense, old man. Did I? You'll have to do better than that."

Saber felt Ella glance at him and lowered his voice even further. "Did you *say* anything? To her."

"Oh." Comprehension spread over Devlin's face. "You mean . . . Oh, you can't mean that."

"Did you say I sent all these things? Did you decide you know better than I what is good for her—and for me?"

"Damn it all, Saber," Devlin exclaimed under his breath. "I don't like your tone. Or your suggestion. A man spends his valuable time trying to help a fellow out. Only to be accused of mischief? I say, that's rum."

Saber's spine stung. "Well . . . Oh, forget I made any such suggestion. I'm on edge."

"So you may be. But there's no call to start doubting your friends. As it happens, I don't agree with your decision on this matter. But I wouldn't go against your wishes, old chap. Good God, I'm not your father, am I?"

"Hardly."

Margot was chattering louder and louder while Ella openly, and curiously, watched Saber and Devlin.

The arrival of Justine, a newspaper clutched in one hand, was a welcome diversion. Radiant in pale mauve, Saber's cousin puffed with obvious excitement. "Struan has gone on to attend to some business with his solicitor. I came back to be here for your appointment with the modiste, Ella." She smiled around, nodding recognition at Margot. "We're about to have Ella's gown made for her first ball."

Ella muttered something indistinct.

"But I must share this with you," Justine said, unfolding the paper. "I am simply amazed. Lord Wokingham's puffed off his intentions to marry . . . Guess who? Come along—guess, all of you."

Her question was met with slowly shaken heads.

"Oh, come along," Justine said, her smile broadening. "Make a teeny guess. But make it a wild one."

"Mama!" Ella chuckled. "This isn't like you. Tell us at once."

"Oh, all right. *Precious Able.* That very garrulous girl. The clergyman's daughter. Can you imagine such a thing?"

"No," Ella said. "Surely you mean Pomeroy Wokingham."

Saber shared Ella's wish to hear that they could forget Pomeroy's suit. "Read it again, Justine. It can't be old Wokingham."

"Well, it is," Justine said, sounding aggrieved. "Says as much right here. Greville, Lord Wokingham, to Miss Precious Able, daughter of, et cetera. There, you can't have it plainer than that, can you?"

Crabley, entering once more with measured steps, interrupted the conversation. "Come one, come all," he droned, bearing a box before him. The box was fashioned of beaten silver and shaped like a large heart. "Another delivery. Don't have to say who it's for, do I?"

Silently, Ella received the box.

"Open it!" Margot bobbed. "Quickly. This is so exciting."

The hinged lid lifted to reveal iced confections, each decorated with a sugar flower.

"Oh," Margot said, awed. "How extravagantly wonderful."

Justine folded her newspaper. "You are already a toast, Ella."

Saber watched Ella closely and all but exclaimed when she took a small card from inside the rich box. "You didn't actually put a message in?" he whispered to Devlin. "What name did you use?"

"You didn't select sweets," Devlin whispered back.

"No, but I thought . . ." He looked sideways at Devlin. "Didn't you select them?"

"No. You didn't say anything about sweets."

"But—"

"Who are they from?" Justine asked. "We should all like to share this treasure, Ella."

"Who the *devil* are they from?" Saber muttered.

Ella opened the card, read it, and replaced it in its envelope. She slipped the envelope inside her sleeve.

"Well?" Justine said.

Margot smiled and covered her mouth.

Saber went to Ella. "Who sent the sweets?"

She looked up at him. "Does it matter?"

"Yes, it damn well does matter. Who?"

Saber heard Devlin say, "Saber, old chap," but ignored him.

Ella sighed and produced the envelope again. She handed it to Saber. "Read for yourself."

The heavy cream envelope contained a matching card on

which, in a spidery hand, was written: "Your humble servant, Knowlton Carstairs."

"Carstairs," Saber exploded. "The bloody nerve of the man!"

"Saber—"

"I'll deal with this, Devlin. I didn't think you'd even met Carstairs," he said to Ella.

"The man who was your first suggestion as a husband for me?" she said. "I met him briefly at the Eagletons'."

"And he has the gall to approach you like this?"

Ella looked around the room. "Evidently he is not the only one who has the gall."

Saber narrowed his eyes and finished reading the card aloud: "I hope I may call upon you." He tossed envelope and card aside. "He *hopes he may call upon you.*"

"Well," Ella said, selecting a sugary morsel. "We must expect a visitor, then."

"Over my dead body," Saber said through gritted teeth.

He looked at Ella. She smiled, and popped the confection into her mouth.

Chapter Fourteen

"Turn around," Pom told Precious, twirling one forefinger. "All the way around, my pet."

She did as he instructed, wobbling a little. Her hair hung loose tonight. In the glow from wall sconces in Father's study, the long tangle of ringlets shone a harsh red.

"Slower," Father mumbled around a mouthful of dates. He all but reclined on a brass-studded leather chaise near the fire. "Do it again. Much slower." His voice was slurred, his eyes rheumy.

Pom made a slow circle with his finger. He sucked hock from his goblet, watching Precious as he did so. The smell of her was strong. Some French concoction she'd bought on one of the Wokingham accounts in the Burlington Arcade. She'd already bragged to him about "Woky" telling her to have whatever she pleased.

The girl made another somewhat ungainly revolution.

"Not so bad," Father said, scooping up more dates and eating them from his palm. "Nice pair, hmm?" He made a vague gesture toward Precious.

A pair meant to be used, Pom thought. And he intended to use them well. After all, the debts arising from this speculative venture would be his if it failed. But the venture would not, *could* not fail. His turn to win had come, to win and to wreak vengeance.

Father waved his free hand again. "Always was partial to red there, y'know. Your mother's was red." His vision cleared for an instant.

Pom didn't like it when his father talked about the mother Pom didn't remember. "I was surprised you decided to puff it off in the *Times*, Papa," he said, changing the subject. "Makes it more difficult later, didn't you know?"

"How so?"

Shrugging, Pom pushed to his feet and filled his glass. "Official. Means there'll have to be a lot of explanations later."

"Round you go again, m'girl," Father said, then, "I meant it to be official, Pom. Didn't I, Precious?"

She giggled.

Pom detested her giggle.

"We haven't told you what we're about this fine night," Father said to him. "Shall we tell him, Precious?"

"Ooh, yes," she said breathily. "Better hold on to yourself, Pom. Wouldn't want you to lose precious jewels in your trousers."

She was coarse. Ladies might be carnal, but they were never coarse. Precious was no lady—and he did not like what he thought his father was telling him. "This so-called betrothal," he said carefully. "We must be certain it in no way affects Precious's chances for a good match afterwards."

Precious giggled again.

"Stop there," Father told her when she faced away from him. "Plenty to hold on to at the back door, too. Man of my maturity appreciates a well-developed female arse."

A soft arse, Pom decided, at the same moment when he

threatened to do exactly what Precious had warned he might. His trousers bound him. He adjusted himself.

"Look at him!" Precious dropped back her head and laughed raucously. She peeped at him over her shoulder and laughed again. "Do you have an itch, Pommy, darling? Should you like me to scratch it for you?"

"Mine's the only cock you'll scratch until I tell you otherwise," Father said, sounding petulant. "There'll be no calling off the betrothal, m'boy. Before the night's out you'll be rutting with your future mother-in-law. The next Lady Wokingham. Don't tell me the thought doesn't appeal."

"You can't be serious."

"Never more so. Shall we tell him now, Precious? After all, this is going to be our present to Pom, isn't it?"

Pom's stomach clenched. Conspiracy. His father had entered into some sort of conspiracy with this willing whore. Pom's last swallow of hock rushed back up his throat, acid, foul.

"Oh, don't give me that look, Pom, m'boy. You know the way the land lies. That'll never change." Father winked, and his other eye drifted shut to match. "You're my heir. You'll get everything."

"There isn't anything," Pom snapped, approaching Precious. And older men than his father had produced offspring by females who'd found ways to press their sniveling brats' claims. "Not a bloody penny, Father dear. So far we've pulled off an amazing feat—almost no one guesses, certainly no one of account."

"That's what this is all about," Precious told him, her chin resting on a plump shoulder. "It's all part of the plan. A sort of rehearsal, isn't that correct, Woky?"

Woky.

"Absolutely correct, my luscious little sweetmeat."

Pom took one of Precious's ringlets and wound it around

his finger. "You two seem to have been busy with your planning. In private." He wound and wound, until Precious winced.

"Planning for you, Pomeroy," Father said with some asperity, asperity ruined only by a hiccup. "I've got to give our Precious a great deal of the credit, too. Mostly her idea."

Pom released the ringlet slowly. "I'm in suspense."

"It's a practice," Father said, grinning, spittle spraying with each word. "Isn't that right, Precious?"

"A practice," she said. "We're going to make sure you get it right on the day."

What interested him now was a real performance. "I tire of this," he said, fumbling at the fastenings on his trousers. "Enough talk."

"Step away, Pom," his father said, good-naturedly enough. "Sit down and do as you're told."

"I said—"

"Sit *down*, Pom. Be gracious. It's unbecomin' for a man not to be gracious when he's given a gift."

"I want to—"

"*Sit down,*" his father roared. "We're going to rehearse your weddin' day, you ungrateful whippersnapper."

Pom narrowed his eyes, but he subsided into a wing chair that matched his father's chaise. For some moments there was silence but for the crackle of the fire. The room was overwarm. Heavy green damask draperies covered the windows. A worn, green and brown silk rug almost obscured the dark floorboards.

Precious stood on a wooden footstool from which the cushion had been removed.

She was naked.

Lord Wokingham mumbled and sniffed, and struggled to a more upright position on the chaise. He said, "That's what we're going to do, isn't it, my luscious? We're going to ensure he makes the very best of his opportunities."

"Yes!" She squealed and drew up her shoulders. "It's going to be delicious, Pommy. I can hardly wait. We're going to go through every teensy thing tonight. Will you help your Precious?" She pouted.

"Help her," Father ordered. "Bring out the clothes."

Pom raised his eyebrows and asked, "What clothes?"

Father waved toward a leather screen arranged across one corner of the room. "Behind that thing."

Spread on a bench behind the screen lay a creamy satin gown and various other female garments. Pomeroy gathered them up and carried them out. "What am I supposed to do with these?"

Father guffawed and snorted. "Dress the girl! Dress her for her weddin'—to me."

Pom folded his arms. "The hell I will."

Precious pointed a toe. "Wouldn't you enjoy putting on a stocking for me, Pommy?" Her high voice wheedled and she teetered precariously on her plinth. A plump, pink ballerina on a too-small music box—turning, turning. He could almost hear the tinny sound of a clockwork waltz. "Pommy?" she repeated.

He looked from her foot to the red bush that so pleased his father.

"Help her," Father said. "It'll be worth it. Get you in the mood, so to speak."

Scowling, Pom selected a lacy white stocking from the pile of fabulously expensive clothing and bent over Precious's wriggling toes.

"Easier if you kneel down," she told him. "Better view, too, if you know what I mean."

"I'm damned if I'll—"

"Just tell yourself she's Ella," Father said slyly. "That's

what we're doin' here, Pom, making sure you do this perfectly with Ella."

"With Ella?" He grew even warmer.

"Yes," Father said. "With Ella. Take your time, m'boy, but do it. With Precious's help we'll soon manage to deal with that little problem. To our great advantage. And to your satisfaction. But, in the meanwhile, we might as well enjoy the anticipation, what?"

Pom's heart speeded. He went slowly to his knees and pulled the stocking on, unrolling it over Precious's limb, smoothing it past her knee, stroking the soft, bare skin of her thigh.

Sweat broke out on his face, his back.

"Naughty, naughty!" Precious smacked his hand when it reached her red curls. "If you go too fast, you'll spoil it. And Ella isn't as passionate as me, remember. She'll need a bit more persuading."

Pom took the other stocking and repeated the process before tying a silver garter above each of Precious's dimpled knees.

Ella's legs would be long and slender beneath his hands.

He wiped the back of a wrist over his brow.

The very air in the room had grown warm.

"The stays," Precious said, and held her arms straight out.

Pom picked up the gusseted, boned garment. "I doubt Ella Rossmara wears stays," he said.

That brought a wrinkle to Precious's smooth brow. "She will wear stays on her wedding day. We want to see her in them, don't we, Woky?"

"Mmm?" Father had dozed. He roused himself. "Mmm. Yes, 'course. Whatever you say."

"What does she mean, *we* want to see Ella in stays?" Pomeroy and his father had certain rules where these things were concerned.

"Tell him, Woky."

"Precious will be with us when you take your Ella."

"No!"

"Yes," Father said. "Be guided, Pom. The Rossmara girl will be the more vulnerable in the presence of another female. We've no doubt she'll appeal for help, for understanding. Titillatin'."

"She'll want me," Pom said, pursing his lips. "She doesn't know herself yet, her passion. I'll make her know it, and want it. She's mine."

"Put"—Father indicated the stays—"put 'em on."

Pom hesitated, then spread the heavy cotton garment open and wrapped it around Precious's very soft, very pink and white body. She lifted her breasts and leaned toward him. "Ooh," she said, "won't you like putting stays on Ella and making her do this for you?" She brought a chubby pink nipple to his mouth, but withdrew quickly when he went to suck it.

"Lace her in," Father said shortly.

Pom ran his tongue around Precious's nipple. He sprang even harder inside his trousers.

Father scooted to the edge of the chaise. "You're not doing it the way it's supposed to be done. You don't get to this part until *after* the ceremony."

Ella's breasts were smaller, firmer, more pointed. Pom's legs trembled with lust. He closed his eyes and filled his mouth with Precious's turgid female flesh. Ella would taste sweet. She'd moan and push against him.

"Do as I tell you," his father said. "Do it now."

"He's thinking about Ella, aren't you, Pommy?" Precious said, gasping, clutching his head to her.

Reluctantly, he pulled away. He regarded her wet nipple, before turning her around and beginning, awkwardly, to lace the stays.

"Nice," his father said, grunting as he got to his feet. "Very nice. I believe I'll have you in those, m'dear. Later."

Precious's giggle was predictable. "Come and help me get comfy, Woky."

Pom held his teeth together and yanked the laces till Precious gasped. Her future husband amused himself with her breasts, and the red "there" that so pleased him.

By the time Pom fastened the bodice of the satin gown his sweat ran freely all over his body. Precious had contrived to taunt him to bursting arousal while Father mewled and bleated, and pawed at her.

Finally dressed, she stepped down off the stool and swept away from them. "Now." She swung around. "The practice has gone well so far, wouldn't you say?"

Pom couldn't speak. He looked at Precious and closed his eyes, and saw Ella before him, her arms outstretched.

"On the day when Ella stands in this room, we'll be very close to getting everything we need. Her dear papa's money will keep us as we deserve to be kept. And he'll keep on paying us, won't he?"

He opened his eyes.

"If he doesn't, the truth about Ella will come out, and the viscount wouldn't like that." Precious smiled. "Woky and I have everything worked out. She'll get ready for the ceremony in this very room."

Fury overtook Pomeroy. "Have your fun. But I shall have Ella. Not as my wife the first time, I realize—I'm no fool. But I'll have her anyway, and afterward no other man will take her. Then Hunsingore will be happy enough to make sure she marries me."

"He's *so* clever," Precious said, her eyes growing ever more round. "He's guessed what we had in mind, Woky."

"Not exactly what you had in mind, evidently," he told them both. "Why not let me in on your clever plans?"

"We're going to!" Precious turned her back on him again. "Come on, Woky, let's show him."

Father's face grew red. He took short, raspy breaths. "Well, I didn't think . . . I'll do the honors first, m'dear."

"No!" She beckoned her fiancé impatiently. "We can wait. Pommy needs something to keep his mind busy for a while."

"Hmph." Father filled his cheeks with air and puffed it out before trotting in front of her. She promptly bent over and thrust her head between his legs.

"Put your knees together," Precious said indistinctly. "She'll try to get free. This will keep her where we want her."

Pom's father obliged, clamping Precious's head between his skinny knees.

"Now the skirts," Precious said, flailing her arms ineffectually.

"What if she kicks?" Father asked. "Could hurt a fella."

"You'll hold her legs," Precious informed him. "I'll do the honors with her head and deal with her dress. Do come *on,* Woky."

Father leaned over Precious and pulled up layers of satin and cotton and lace-edged lawn until the gown gathered in heaps to frame a plump bottom.

"The drawers," Precious shrieked, rocking her hips back and forth. "Rip them."

Obligingly, Father ripped the divided drawers asunder, presenting Pom with Precious's ready private parts.

"Get it out, then!" she cried. "I know how ready it is for me. Do it, Pom."

"Do it, man," his father said, panting loudly now. "Do it and don't take long about it."

Pom struggled and freed himself, letting his trousers fall around his ankles.

Precious's next shriek had a different tone. "This is how it'll be," she told him breathlessly. "With Ella. She'll think she's coming here to help me. I've got it worked out. Then we'll get the money."

The money. *With Ella.*

"Come on," Pom's father said impatiently. "Get a move on."

Pom did as he was told.

Chapter Fifteen

"I am beside myself," Justine said, sitting down on Great-Grandmama's favorite gold chaise in the old lady's Pall Mall boudoir. "Edward has always been such a happy child. And Sarah. I cannot believe they are *pining* and that they cry for me constantly. What can I do? They need me. But Ella needs me here. Especially since Struan has been recalled to Scotland."

"This is why I asked you to attend me this morning." The dowager leaned on her cane and favored her granddaughter with a sharp-eyed stare. "Struan must respond to his brother's request and return to Kirkcaldy. They have need of him there, and matters of estate always come first. You, my dear Justine, belong with those children you insisted upon giving birth to at such an advanced age. When you should have been considering my welfare, I might add."

Ella expected Papa to explode as he invariably did when Great-Grandmama commenced to berate Mama. Instead he nodded gravely. "How right you are, Duchess. There is no doubt that Justine must return to Scotland with me—

to Scotland and the children. This pining we've been informed of, this refusal to eat, demands the presence of their mother."

Ella smiled a little behind her hand. Papa would do anything to have Mama at his side—even tolerate Great-Grandmama's waspish insults.

"No, I cannot leave Ella," Mama insisted. "At this time as at none other before, my daughter needs her mother at her side."

Ella knew an instant's deep, old pain. Quickly eased. Her own mother had been dead four years since, but Lady Justine and the viscount had taken an orphaned boy and girl and made them their own. Fortune had breathed on Ella and Max, who had never before possessed a family name, or known those of their respective fathers.

"As always." Blanche Bastible sighed hugely. Her eyes, as round, blue, and baleful as those of a painted china doll, filled with easy tears. "As always, it is the mother who must deny her own needs in favor of her children's. It was the same for me with Grace. Such an ungrateful, uncaring, willful—"

"Charming, long-suffering, and dear woman," Papa finished, his mouth drawn into a grim line. "You will remember that Grace is my brother's wife, and a more faithful, giving, talented woman does not favor the earth—with the exception of my dearest Justine, and Calum's Pippa."

Ella knew Grace, Marchioness of Stonehaven, Uncle Arran's wife. Aunt Grace was a lovely lady whom the entire family regarded as a saint to tolerate her hoydenish mother.

"Enough of this prattle," Great-Grandmama said, pounding the floor between her feet with her ebony cane. "Both Justine and Struan are needed in Scotland. Arran would not have sent word to that effect had it not been so. I am more than capable of attending to the business of seeing Ella properly launched. After all, I've had considerably more experience with Society than you, Justine. You barely made your Season, if that's what you can call that pathetic attempt—"

"I do not care for these things," Mama said, her voice unusually sharp. "But it is entirely possible that I should have been less of a failure had you not insisted upon repeatedly reminding me of my . . ." She glanced at Papa. "Of my slight limp."

Papa grinned his approval. He had worked diligently to improve Mama's view of herself. Not so long ago she would have referred to her "slight limp" as a "deformity," and managed to add the word "cripple" to boot.

"Struan," Mama said. Her fingers hovered over a dark red curl escaped at her temple. "Please tell me what I should do? I—"

"We shall all return to Scotland." Ella heard her own words before she'd finished forming the thought. "I want to go too. I hate it here." Why stay if she couldn't have Saber?

"Pah!" Streaks of pink appeared on Great-Grandmama's thin, papery cheeks. "I'll not hear of such a thing. I've already arranged everything."

"Everything?" Papa said, his black brows raised.

The ebony cane rose to jab the air in his vicinity. "Everything," Great-Grandmama told him. "As soon as I learned of Arran's letter—yesterday—word went out that all communications regarding Ella shall be delivered here. That will include the extravagant gifts she is receiving."

"No gift could be more than she—"

"I *approve.*" Great-Grandmama interrupted Mama. "Evidently Ella has already captured a good deal of attention. Mountains of flowers, gems, fans, golden clocks." She sighed. "Reminds me of my own Season. Naturally, I only required one, and that one was merely a formality for my own amusement and satisfaction. Justine's grandfather had already secured my hand."

Mama, who showed signs of extreme agitation, gave her full attention to Papa. "Struan, please help me in this."

He sat beside her and took her hand in his. "I am as torn as you, my sweet," he told her simply. "But I believe we should be grateful for your grandmother's kind assistance and return to Scotland."

"We shall all go together, I tell you," Ella said, moving to stand beside her parents. "I don't care a fig for London or the Season. Empty people doing empty things."

"Oh, darling," Mama said. "It's time for you to marry, and this is where you will meet your husband."

"I've already met . . ." Ella crossed her arms and massaged the spot between her brows. "I do not intend to marry, thank you."

Blanche Bastible made a twittering sound. "Did you hear her?" she asked, breathless. "I did. She's trying to rush on, but I heard her say she's already met someone. Oh, girls are such a bother. She's been sneaking around behind our backs. You must tell us everything at once, young lady. Who is this man?"

"No man," Ella said, beyond patience with Blanche's foolishness. She had met Saber and no other man mattered, but Blanche should not know that her heart was broken. "Papa, I can be very useful at Kirkcaldy. I can be a great help to Mama with the little ones—and to Aunt Grace. I have small needs and I promise never to be a burden."

"Enough!" For a very small, very frail-looking lady, Great-Grandmama had a very big, very penetrating voice. "The girl will do as she is told. She needs launching and I shall launch her. This discussion is over. Get ready to travel, Justine. Struan, take your wife and leave the rest to me."

"Well," Papa said, smiling into Mama's troubled eyes. "It appears that all is in hand. We must certainly be here in time for the ball Calum and Pippa wish to give for Ella. If necessary, the younger children will travel with us. Meanwhile, the dowager is capable of taking care of our girl."

"No," Ella said. "I hate it here."

Great-Grandmama approached Ella and stood looking up into her eyes. "You do not hate it here," she said.

Ella moistened her dry lips.

"There is something you want and which you do not think you can have."

Shaking her head slightly, Ella frowned.

"You and I shall do very well," Great-Grandmama said, the faintest of smiles twisting up the corners of her colorless mouth. "Justine and Struan will return to Scotland, and you and I will become a formidable alliance. Do you understand me?"

Ella shook her head again.

Great-Grandmama made certain her back was to Mama and Papa. She raised a finger to her lips in silent warning. "Of course you do. We have a common goal."

A common goal? Ella smiled politely. Possibly Great-Grandmama was not as spry of mind as they'd all supposed.

The old lady's eyes narrowed. "Our goal is your happiness," she said, spearing Ella with her gaze. "Yours and that of the man who will be your beloved. I may be old-fashioned, but I still believe these matters may be preördained. I believe there is only one man for one woman in this world. Finding that man and woman can be a problem. One simply has to persevere."

"Yes," Ella almost whispered. "Oh, yes."

"Finding them, then convincing both parties they have been found?" Great-Grandmama cocked her perfectly coiffed head.

"Yes," Ella agreed.

"Quite. Trust me in this, my child. All we have to do is help events along a little."

The dowager's affinity for a girl with no pedigree puzzled those who knew of Ella's lowly beginnings. Ella only knew that in the dowager she had an indomitable, if irascible, ally.

A discreet tap at the boudoir door diverted everyone's attention. The butler, Finch, entered with an envelope and a card on a silver tray. These he delivered to Ella before announcing, "There's a Miss Able here to see you, Miss Ella."

Ella glanced at the card, then began to open the envelope. Invitations had started to arrive at Hanover Square almost hourly. Evidently Great-Grandmama had indeed managed to divert deliveries to Pall Mall.

Finch cleared his throat. "Should I show Miss Able up?"

Ella started and studied the card again. "Able? Oh, Precious Able." She looked to Mama. "Why would she come to see me? She obviously doesn't like me."

"Why?" Blanche asked baldly.

"Blanche, dear," Great-Grandmama said. "Why don't you run along and check that cap the maid was supposed to be mending for me?"

"But—"

"I want to wear it this afternoon," Great-Grandmama said firmly.

Blanche opened her mouth but clearly thought better of persisting. She left the room in a great rustle of orange taffeta skirts.

"Why doesn't this Precious person like you?" Great-Grandmama asked as soon as Blanche was gone.

"I don't know," Ella said, knowing all too well but reluctant to as much as think about Pomeroy Wokingham.

Great-Grandmama wrinkled her sharp nose. "Probably jealous. Who wouldn't be?"

"Couldn't agree with you more," Papa said. He stood, urging Mama up with him. "We must prepare to leave at first light tomorrow. Will you at least give London a little more time, Ella? I know it would bring your great-grandmother pleasure to assist you here."

Ella considered. She might merely be wishing, but she had a strong feeling that when Great-Grandmama spoke of persuading a man that he was the "right" man, there would seem to be a definite possibility that she referred to Saber.

The envelope in her hand bore only her name—in a spidery hand. She extracted the paper inside.

"Ella?" Papa persisted.

She glanced up. "Do you think I should stay?"

"Yes," he told her. "And so does your mama."

"I do," Mama agreed. "And we should not keep Miss Able waiting indefinitely."

"Show her up," Great-Grandmama told the butler. "If you don't need me, Ella, I think I shall retire until dinner. And you should busy yourself preparing to leave, Justine."

"Roses have been delivered," Finch said. "Red and cream and yellow. And lilies. And a box wrapped in silver cloth. In the dining room. All for Miss Ella. I'll show Miss Able up." With silent, measured steps, he departed.

"Tell me you will make this a happy time," Mama asked Ella.

Ella felt Great-Grandmama's gaze and met her eyes. "I shall do very well with Great-Grandmama," she said, noting how the old lady's shoulders relaxed a little. "I should be upset if I thought I had kept you from my little brother and sister when they need you so."

"That's that, then!" Papa smiled hugely. "Let's leave Ella to her visitor. Isn't this the girl who's engaged to old Wokingham?"

"Yes," Ella and Mama said in unison.

Mama laughed. "I believe I shall come with you at once, Struan."

Great-Grandmama went through the adjoining door to her

bedchamber and Mama and Papa left the room, passing Precious Able as she came in.

Awash in a froth of flounced, lavender gros de Naples with a profusion of silk violets beneath her bonnet brim, Precious bobbed and lowered her eyes demurely. The instant she was alone with Ella, she closed the door and rushed forward, arms outstretched, as if to meet an old and treasured friend. "I told that creepy old butler he needn't come up with me," she said breathlessly. "I said we knew each other really well and didn't need him. Did I act precipitately?"

Ella evaded Precious's embrace by turning and indicating a chair. "This is a surprise," she said, also evading the girl's question. "Sit down. I'll ring for some refreshment." What could they possibly talk about? Why would Precious Able come at all?

Precious plopped down, fluffing her skirts around her and settling a little velvet reticule on her lap. "No refreshments for me, please. I simply couldn't eat a thing. I am beside myself, Ella. Beside myself. I searched my mind for someone to turn to—for a friend—and found none. But then I thought of you and I remembered how kind you were to me at the Eagletons'."

Kind? Ella remembered little kindness in their exchange. "Are you sure you wouldn't care for some coffee? Or chocolate?"

"Absolutely not." Precious splayed a hand on her ample bosom and fluttered her red lashes toward the gold and cream plastered ceiling. "I could not force a single thing down my throat. I am in such a fuss, Ella. I've come to you because I sensed you have a good heart and that—although we do not know each other well—you may consider being a friend to someone who is alone and very troubled."

"Surely—" Ella broke off, torn between compassion and suspicion. "Surely your mama and papa—"

"No!" Precious spread her arms and lay back in the chair. A tear coursed each cheek from wide-open eyes. "You do not understand. No one does. Not even my dearest Woky."

"I see." Ella didn't see at all. "Is this Woky—?"

"Lord Wokingham. My intended. He is the very best of men. His extreme concern for my well-being—and my reputation, of course—may even be partly to blame for the agony of loneliness to which I am doomed."

"Agony of loneliness?"

"Absolutely," Precious said. "Ella, you are so beautiful. And green does become you so. What a perfectly lovely dress."

"Thank you." Ella blinked at the change of topic. "Please don't cry." She produced a lace-edged handkerchief and took it to Precious.

"Would you be my friend?" The girl leaned forward. "Would you?"

Refusing friendship was outside Ella's experience. "Why don't you explain what has happened?"

"Mama and Papa had to return to Lancashire." The velvet reticule claimed the attention of Precious's plump fingers. "You see, we are not particularly well off. I wouldn't mention such a vulgar thing, but I feel a generosity in you. You are not a person who judges others on the basis of their wealth—or lack of it."

"No." Ella understood a kind of desperate poverty Precious could not be expected to as much as imagine.

"I am entrusted to my fiancé's care." Precious clutched the reticule. "I am lodged in his house until our wedding."

Uncertain as to what her reaction should be, Ella said nothing.

"My companion is a boring woman provided by Woky. Agatha. A drab elderly maid who never speaks a word, except to chastise me."

"Surely you could speak to your fiancé—"

"I could *not,*" Precious said, the picture of misery. "He is so good. And so kind. I cannot bring myself to complain about a single thing he does for me. He is providing for my every comfort. He spares no expense."

"But you are not happy."

"No." Precious's high voice soared even higher. "Woky is so concerned with propriety that he does not even allow himself to see me—except for brief moments with wretched Agatha in attendance."

Ella murmured sympathetically.

"He *never* speaks to me other than in polite platitudes."

Warming a little to the other's sadness, Ella pulled a chair close to Precious's and sat down. "Evidently Lord Wokingham is determined to treat you with the utmost respect." Even thinking about the Wokinghams turned Ella's stomach, but she kept all hint of revulsion from her face. "Once you are married it will be different." What a perfectly dreadful thought.

"But I should like to know him a little first," Precious wailed. More tears erupted from her eyes. "And I am so lo-lo-lonely."

"Pomeroy doesn't talk to you?" Ella managed not to grit her teeth.

"He's angry." The red lashes flickered downward. "He wanted me himself, but Woky would not have it."

"And you're glad?" Ella asked softly. "Glad because you want to marry Lord Wokingham."

"Oooh!" Doubling over, Precious sobbed loudly. Her back heaved and her hands pawed at her voluminous skirts. "Oooh, what shall I do?"

Horrified, and moved, Ella caught Precious's hands and smoothed their backs. "Hush," she said firmly. "Hush, Precious. Tell me what I can do to help you. I will if I can, you know." The poor creature was undoubtedly the victim of her parents' willingness to abandon her to strangers. Ella was too familiar with the tearing hurt of being tossed aside as if one had no worth.

Gradually, the sobbing subsided. Precious sniffed and raised her head. Large, wet smudges marred her lavender skirts. She clutched Ella's hands as if to hang on to life itself.

"That's better," Ella told her, smiling reassurance. "You aren't alone anymore."

"Th-thank you," Precious said, and her face crumpled again. "You are so k-kind."

"Let's be sensible." This showed signs of being an even more trying day than had already proved to be the case. "You are to marry Lord Wokingham and this makes you happy. We must concentrate on that and find ways to help you deal with any loneliness."

"You don't understand." Precious made strangled sounds. "Can I tr-trust you, Ella? Am I right to assume you are good and true and would never divulge a confidence?"

"I am not a gossip," Ella said shortly. "I find no pleasure in the unhappiness of others."

"Oooh," Precious whimpered, squeezing her eyes shut and crying afresh. "I think you will make what I must do bearable. I am so grateful to you. I don't want to marry Woky. He's good to me, but he's old—and h-he drools a little."

Ella's stomach made an entire revolution. She swallowed. "Then why are you marrying him?"

"I must. I must do what my parents tell me to do. I must marry for money and position, and my prospects have seemed poor because we have so little wealth of our own. Mama and Papa say Woky is an answer to our prayers—a dream come true."

The stuff of nightmares rather than any dream Ella could

imagine. "You should not do this thing if it is so distasteful to you."

"There is no choice. I am committed and I will do it." Shifting forward on her chair, Precious blinked against moisture on her lashes. "And it will be all right, I know it will. It will be now that I have your friendship. I so needed someone honorable to trust, and I found you! This must seem strange, my coming to you like this. But I believe in divine providence, don't you? I believe I was guided to come to you and that it was exactly the thing to do. You are the sweetest, most generous person I've ever known. With you as my helper and friend, I can bear the weeks to come."

Perhaps, if she was more concerned for another's happiness than for her own, she would be more able to bear the pain of Saber's rejection. "You may come here whenever you please," Ella said, smiling, and patting Precious's hands. "But I do believe you should contact your parents and explain your true feelings for Lord Wokingham."

"I cannot." Precious shook her head until her red curls bounced. "This much I can do for them. They have been so good and generous to me. They sacrificed everything to give me this Season. I am fortunate that a man of Woky's standing noticed me at all. I am resolute, Ella. He has honored me with this offer of marriage, and I shall honor him. I shall be a faithful, obedient wife. He will be proud of me."

How awful.

"And I shall manage well enough if you will attend me."

"Attend you?" Ella frowned inquiringly.

Precious clung to her. "My parents cannot be in London for the wedding. I shall have no one—no one but you. Will you attend me? Will you help me prepare and be with me during the ceremony? It is to be private—performed at Lord Wokingham's mansion here in London."

"Ah." What could she say? How could she refuse—despite

her loathing at the prospect of being in the Wokinghams' home?

"You will come, then? You will help me prepare and stand with me for the ceremony?"

Ella regarded the other's anxious face and said, "Yes, of course I will."

Chapter Sixteen

"*Do you remember Lushbottam's?"*

Sickened, Ella stared at the words on the single sheet of heavy notepaper and sank slowly into the chair Precious had vacated minutes earlier.

From below came the hollow boom of the front door closing behind the departing visitor.

Ella settled shaking fingertips on her mouth and tried to breathe deeply enough to calm herself.

"An exotic girl in red chiffon. Transparent red chiffon. A virgin for auction, Mrs. Lushbottam said. We both know that was fabrication, don't we, my dear one?"

"Who are you?" Ella said aloud, barely able to breathe at all now. First strategically dropped scraps of red chiffon, now this dreadful note. "Why are you doing this to me?"

"No virgin you, exotic girl. Just one more of Mrs. Lushbottam's 'lady tailors' who were skilled in accommodating any size or shape of gentleman. Such a clever notion. Did you have fun in that house of debauchery? Did you revel in the acts you performed there?"

She had performed no acts. A victim. A helpless victim paraded before the eyes of cruel men and women who stared at her body and made lewd comments. Even the nature of what those acts might be was not clear to her. She had been blindfolded most of the time. The women, the *tailors* had spoken of certain things, but Ella had not understood.

"Do you think everyone has forgotten what you were? What you are? Impossible. Your breasts are pointed, the tips sharp and uptilted. The hair between your legs is as black as the hair on your head. An invitation. But you know that, of course. A neat conspiracy. "Virgin!" And now you hope to trick some upright man into marrying you. You think to evade your past."

Ella surged to her feet. She must get away from here. This evil person could shame not only her, but her dear family. *Max.* Max must never be touched by this. If he were to as much as get a hint of this subversive attack upon his sister, he would be almost impossible to restrain. He'd try to search out the culprit and deal with him.

Saber, Saber.

If only she could just feel his warm arms about her, look into his serious eyes and know he would be there to help her be strong.

She would not cry. There was no time for tears, and tears would not heal this oozing wound of horror.

"Well, lady tailor, you must wait for my next communication. Fear not, I am not ready to send you back to threading needles. Not yet. Perhaps never, if you do as you are told."

This mad person intended to control and manipulate her. For what purpose?

"I have not yet decided the exact nature of how you will pay for the wrong you have done me."

Wrong? She had done nothing wrong. Her brow became

hot and damp. Mama and Papa had not yet left. Perhaps she should go to them at once and show them the note.

No. They had already done too much for her.

"I know you will be anxious to serve me. Be patient, my virgin, be patient. I cannot tell you when I will come to you, but I will come. Best stay away from public places—and from any man you would not wish to be embarrassed before. After all, if I encounter you publicly, I may not be able to stop myself from warning any gentleman of your true colors. Red chiffon. Accommodation to any gentleman's needs. Large gentlemen particularly welcomed. That is how the sign over the door of Mrs. Lushbottam's read. But, of course, you remember such details well. Do you prefer large gentlemen to thread your needle?"

What did it mean? Oh, what did it mean?

Running footsteps sounded on the stairs.

"I am, my dear virgin, your ever-attentive master. Await my pleasure."

She thrust the note and its envelope into the pocket of her gown and pressed her palms to her cheeks.

"Ella! Ella!" The door flew open and banged against the wall. "It's me, Max. Footsore and exhausted, but at your service, sister. Why are you in residence here instead of Hanover Square? Crabley would scarcely speak to me."

Ella fell back a step. "Max? What on earth are you doing in London? You're supposed to be in school."

"Sick," he said, staggering comically. "Surely you see I'm sick and have been returned to you in hopes you can save my life."

Settling her features into an older-sisterly frown, Ella studied her fifteen-year-old brother from the top of his unruly red hair, to the toes of his highly polished and very fashionable bespoke boots. "I am here because Papa and Mama are returning to Scotland in the morning. Edward and Sarah need them, and Papa must deal with some questions about both Kirkcaldy itself and the lodge. He needs Mama with him. Great-Grandmama is to be my mentor for my Season. But enough of that. What is all this with you, Max? Surely you haven't been expelled from Eton."

"Expelled? I'll thank you to take back such a suggestion. I am a model pupil in every manner. My masters gasp at my brilliance. They have never seen the like. That's what they say daily."

At fifteen Max was over six feet tall and, rather than gangly as most youths so quickly grown might have been, he showed a fine, strong figure. Max lived with vigor, confronted every experience with curiosity and energy. His once carrot-colored hair had darkened to a rich, deep red and, although thick and tousled, no longer stood up as if in a condition of perpetual shock. Green eyes now showed a developed humor that could sometimes be tempered with acute seriousness. Max Rossmara had become a handsome young blade, and Ella looked upon him with pride.

Today Ella also looked upon her brother with suspicion. He could not possibly be ill and he could not possibly have any right to be here unless he'd been sent away from Eton.

"You wrote," he said, standing before her, resting a big hand on each of her shoulders and looking down into her face. "You are not happy."

Having to tilt up her chin to regard her young brother's face disconcerted Ella. "I did not tell you I was unhappy."

"Precisely. You did not tell me anything at all. Only that you were in London. Nothing more. That was because something is amiss. You are unhappy. Otherwise your words would have bubbled with interesting news. There. That's the way of it. You need me, so I am here."

Ella looked away. She could almost feel the horrid note—even through her layers of petticoats.

Max examined his fingernails. "I suppose this has something to do with Saber."

"Saber is wonderful!" She closed her mouth tightly.

"Wonderful, but?"

Ella shook her head.

"He has done something to make you sad, hasn't he?"

"Do not persist in this," Ella said. "You must return to school before you are missed."

"I am already missed. They sent me home because I am sick."

"But you are not sick, Max. What can you be thinking of, running away and coming here after all Mama and Papa have done for you?"

He withdrew his hands and let his shoulders sag. His eyelids lowered until he appeared almost asleep. "Matron gave me leave to return home," he said weakly. "Apparently she feared some sort of epidemic. The fever, you know. When it became so high, I saw demons. By coincidence that was after I dampened my shirt with hot water, and placed a heated stone beneath my pillow. But I saw small purple demons dancing on Matron's shoulders and disappearing inside her bodice. They shrieked. Apparently they were overwhelmed by what they found there, I suppose. I told her so."

"Max! You are not changed at all." Ella barely contained her mirth. "You continue to tell the most frightful stories. That poor woman. You shall return to her and apologize at once."

"Not until I have made sure all is well with you," he said, absolutely serious now. "I have been given leave to rest here with you until I am recovered. I will be recovered once I am no longer concerned for you."

"What will Papa say? And—"

"Leave them to me. Finch said they have gone out to visit friends and will not return until late this evening. By then I shall have thought of an appropriate excuse for being here."

"No doubt," Ella said wryly. "Just leave out the purple demons and the bodice of your matron's dress."

Max ignored that. "Tell me what Saber's done to you."

"Nothing."

He rested his chin on his chest. The lines of his face were sharp and clever. Despite his youth, in his black, tailed coat and high, starched white collar, he was a figure bound to command notice. "And therein lies the answer, I think," he said in measured tones. "Yet again Saber has failed to act. You love him, don't you, Ella?"

She blushed and averted her face.

"Quite," Max said. "I know exactly how that feels now."

"What?" Her head snapped in his direction again. "What does that mean?"

He gestured vaguely. "Nothing. Only that a man of my experience understands these things. Not that I have known love, but I have felt the small twinges that might be mistaken for that emotion. However, we are not discussing me. Tell me about Saber."

"You speak so well now, Max. One would never imagine you had once been . . . well, one wouldn't, would one?"

He grinned. "No, one wouldn't, would one? No more than one would imagine you had once been . . . well . . ."

"Very well," Ella snapped. She must not be further reminded of the other. "We have made that point."

"And you tried to change the subject. I take it you have seen Saber?"

Oh, indeed she had seen Saber. Seen him and much, much more. "Yes."

"How is he?"

"Marvelous." She bit her bottom lip.

"Good. If he's so marvelous, why do you look so sad?"

"He does not want me, Max." Tears stung her eyes. "He has

vowed to help find me a husband. Can you countenance such a thing? Saber is going to help find another man for me."

Max paused in the act of perusing a small portrait he'd picked up from a tiny marquetry table. "Surely you jest? *Another* man? Saber is trying to find someone else to be your husband?"

"Yes," Ella said in a small voice. She did not feel particularly like the older, more mature sibling at the moment.

The gilt frame of the portrait met the table with a sharp clack. Max said, "Then he is a fool or mad—or both."

"Don't," Ella implored. "I cannot bear to hear you speak of him so. Oh, Max, he was wounded in India."

"Yes." Max's straight nose rose. "Years since. We already knew of this. What has it to do with the situation at hand?"

"I think . . . I think it has everything to do with it. His face is quite severely scarred."

"Really?" Rather than revulsion, Max's expression showed impressed interest. "How very dashing."

"I couldn't agree with you more. I would not wish him to have suffered such pain as must have been his, but he is still the most handsome man in the world, not that I should care what he looked like as long as he was my Saber."

"There is another female, perhaps?"

Ella swayed a little.

"There is?" Max declared. "Who is she?"

"Well, he does have a friend, a Countess Perruche. Margot. But I don't think . . . No, I don't think so."

Max took Ella's hand and led her to the chaise. Once she was seated he leaned over her. "Then what, sister dear? What is keeping the rattle-brain from sweeping you to the altar?"

She shook her head. "It's mysterious. *He's* mysterious. He says he cannot be with me. We cannot be together. It is not *possible* for us to be together. And he appears desperate when he says so. Desperate and unhappy. Then there is Devlin North."

"What about Devlin? He's in London too?"

"In London and possibly courting me."

"Possibly?" Max snorted. "Either a man is courting a woman or he is not."

"I just don't know," Ella said. "The most beautiful gifts have been arriving. Lots and lots of them. I was suspicious that Devlin might be sending them." She considered before she said, "But I am not at all certain Saber isn't the one."

Straightening, Max puffed up his cheeks and made his green eyes round. "Too complicated for a simple mind like mine, my dear sister." He bent closer again. "What is it? What aren't you telling me?"

Ella's heart leaped. "Nothing!"

"Oh, yes, there is," he told her, pinching his nostrils and assuming an air of wise concentration. "I feel it. I see it. Something else is afoot here. You are not just unhappy. You are troubled. Frightened even."

He could not possibly know. He was guessing or fabricating. Max had been a master fabricator all his life. She composed herself, arranging her skirts and settling a calm expression on her face.

"Oh, no, you don't," Max said, tapping the tip of her nose. "You may try to appear calm and removed, but I know better. We have been everything to each other, Ella. Without you, I should not have survived. Without you—and Papa, whom you persuaded to rescue me—I might still be picking pockets in Covent Garden. Although by now I'd be rotting in prison, if I were still alive. I'd be little better than an animal. Tell me what makes you pale beneath that lovely golden skin of yours. Other than unrequited love."

She pressed a hand over the pocket where the letter rested. "Nothing, I tell you."

"Nothing, hmm."

"Exactly. Nothing at all. I'm a little fatigued by all the revelry is all."

Before she guessed his intention, one of Max's large, strong, nimble hands descended upon hers—on top of the letter in her pocket.

"Max! What are you thinking of? Let me go."

He transferred her hand from his right to his left and deftly removed the letter from her pocket. "I think this is the something that bothers you? It is, isn't it? You were never good at hiding things from me."

"That is private." She made an unsuccessful grab for the envelope. "Give it to me."

"I saw the way you touched it when I pressed you for information. Whatever is so private here is also a great trial to you."

"It is not. It is nothing but a personal note from a friend. Kindly—" She made another grab, but he turned his back and she heard him pulling out the notepaper. "Max, I beg you, do not read it. Oh, please, do not read it!"

He kept her at bay with infuriating ease—and read the letter.

A dull red gradually rose up his neck and over his face. "Please sit down," he said to Ella in a voice not at all like his own. "Sit down and collect yourself."

"You had no right to take what was mine and read it!"

Max pounded the back of a chair. "How dare this foul creature write such filth to you."

She trembled so, her teeth clattered together. "What does he . . . ?" How could she ask her fifteen-year-old brother to explain what must be the truly horrifying suggestions of the letter writer?

Max flattened his lips to his teeth and stared at her. "You do not understand this, do you?" He waved the paper. "Of course not. How could you?"

"How could *you*?" she snapped back.

He pushed his fingers through his hair. "I am a man. I became a man when I should have been a child. The world made it so for me. Now. Be calm."

"You are not calm." Her voice was a squeak. "You are not calm at all. You are angry."

"Angry does not describe my feelings at all fittingly. Sit down, Ella." When she had reluctantly done so, he continued. "What did you intend to do about this?"

She was helpless to stop tears from falling. "I don't know. I had only just finished reading it when you arrived. Who can have sent it to me?"

"A fool," he said shortly.

Ella wiped at the tears.

"I shall kill him," Max added.

"No!" This is exactly what she'd been afraid of. "There will be no violence. It is against the law. And you, rather than he, might be hurt. I will discover the identity of this creature and reason with him. I will make him understand the error of his ways and apologize to me."

"Hah!" Max's eyes were narrow slits of green fire. "You will *reason* with a sick, mad man? Will you do that while he ravishes you?"

"Max! How could you speak to me so?"

"Someone must speak to you so. You have lost your senses. These are not the words of a sane man who might be reasoned with. A creature with evil designs sent you this. He guessed, correctly, that you would attempt to hide it and deal with him yourself. And, when you did, he would have accomplished what he wanted—he would have you, Ella."

"But—"

"Saber will help us."

"Saber?" Saber must never know exactly how dreadful the story of her life at Lushbottam's had been. "Saber doesn't want any part of me except as a helpful family friend."

"Come, we shall visit him now. Where does he live?"

"No. It would only be as before. He would refuse to see me—if I could persuade his man Bigun to announce us—which I doubt after the last fiasco."

"Fiasco?"

"I cannot recount it. The event is too painful even to consider."

"I suppose you have some soiree this evening?"

"I declined all invitations. I couldn't face another round so soon after the last. One has no time to as much as catch one's breath." She turned her face away. "And I don't want to go out at all unless I can be certain I shall see Saber."

"Do you mean he may not be attending an event this evening, either?"

"He goes nowhere. He came to a party at the Eagletons', but I think it was merely to make a point with me." She trembled at the memory of what had passed between them. "He wanted to make certain I understood we could have no future together."

Max paced, coming to a halt in front of her. "Rest."

"I beg your pardon."

"*Rest.* Go to your bed. Mama and Papa will retire early to prepare for the long journey on the morrow. Great-Grandmama always retires early, and so does Blanche. Who attends you?"

"A maid called Rose. She is to come to me from Hanover Square."

"Can she be trusted?"

"I . . . Trusted in what?"

"Tonight, when the house is at rest, we shall go to Saber. It will be late, so late that we can hope he will at least be at home—if not in bed. I would prefer to come upon him unawares."

"Oh, no," Ella moaned.

"I thought you loved him."

"I do, but—"

"Then help me to help you. And we *need* his help with this." Max waved the letter. "He will know how seriously we should take it, and what should be done."

Ella covered her face. "I am so ashamed."

"You have no cause for shame. You are blameless."

She bowed her head. "You speak as if you, not I, were the eldest. I do not understand what will be gained by pressing Saber when he has made it so clear he does not wish to have anything further to do with me."

"Has he made that clear?" Max asked softly. "Are you sure?"

A coolness slipped over Ella's heated skin. She dropped her hands, clasped them between her knees, and regarded her brother.

"Well," he said, smiling a little. "*Are* you?"

"No. No, I'm not at all sure. I think he may just be so foolish as to think I am disgusted by his disfigurement. Inside me, I feel—I feel he may love me, Max. Oh, it is all such a puzzlement."

"No matter."

She looked up sharply. "No matter?"

"No matter. Your puzzlement is about to be removed."

"*You* are a puzzle, Max."

"While you rest, I shall explain my presence here to Mama and Papa—and to Great-Grandmama, of course. At midnight you are to be dressed—in simple clothing that will not draw too much attention. We will make our way on horseback. Do you know the interior of the house?"

"Yes." Her stomach squeezed. She felt too cold now. "But

what would be the point of riding to Burlington Gardens? Even if Saber will see me, he will only repeat that he has decided we can have no future together."

A great smile of confidence transformed Max's serious expression. Confidence and guile. "He may repeat what he pleases. While I keep watch, you will persuade him otherwise."

"I've tried," she told him passionately. "He either does not hear or does not care."

"He will hear and he will care."

"How? Why?"

"My mind is made up." Max pushed back his coat and planted his fists on his hips. "Yes, quite made up. We'll make certain he's in bed."

"Oh!" Ella bobbed on her toes with agitation. "What on earth can we accomplish if he's in bed?"

"Simply"—Max said, raising one arched, dark red brow—"you will seduce him. He will compromise you."

Saber looked into the secret herbal draft Bigun had prepared for him and smiled—a cynical smile. What kind of man had he become?

"Drink, my lord," Bigun said, although the little man was supposedly busy with Saber's clothes and should not have been able to see his master. "Drink deeply and sleep deeply."

"Drug myself, you mean."

"We do what we must."

"And we must be drugged in order to become unconscious."

Bigun faced him. His gold turban shimmered in the subdued light of Saber's bedchamber. "You must rest."

"I never rest."

"At least your body gains strength. I arranged for the ruby earbobs to be delivered tomorrow."

"Good." Saber would like to place the rubies on Ella's ears himself. He tossed back the draft and set down the goblet. "I must busy myself with the matter of securing the young lady a suitable husband."

"A very simple matter, my lord."

Saber glared at Bigun. "Simple? Finding a man worthy of one so . . ."

"Of one so charming, so beautiful, so perfect of mind and soul—and body?"

"Hmm. Yes, yes exactly."

"As I said," Bigun remarked, brushing imaginary annoyances from the coat he held. "A very simple matter. Such a man is readily to hand."

"Who?" Naked—as he preferred to be in bed—Saber threw back the covers. He should not feel angry whenever he contemplated securing a man to take his place with Ella. "Who is readily to hand, Bigun? Speak up, man."

"You."

Saber stopped in the act of getting into bed. He rested his knuckles on the mattress and closed his eyes. "I thought we had covered that topic. It cannot be me. And we both know why."

Bigun made much of hanging the coat in the large, carved ebony wardrobe.

"We both know why, don't we, Bigun?" Saber said loudly.

"We both know why you *pretend* it cannot be so." Bigun's tone was silken. "I do not agree with you. I think the young lady is exactly what you need. Someone who loves and wants you and—"

"Silence!"

"Do you love her?" Bigun continued as if there had been no explosive interruption.

Saber turned and fell, spread-eagle, onto the bed. "Leave me. Leave me in peace."

"You love her."

"I told you to leave. Get out. Now."

"You, my lord, love Miss Ella Rossmara. You desire her mind and her body. You wish she were beside you—"

"Out," Saber roared, rearing onto his elbows. "And never mention her name to me again."

"As you wish." Bigun bowed and backed toward the door. "But you do love her."

"Out!"

"But of course, my lord. Love does strange things to men, but it can be most healing."

"Get out!"

"A woman's soft hands upon a man's fevered body—"

"Get—" The door slammed before Saber finished shouting his order.

His head ached.

His head invariably ached when he'd fought sleep for more than a few days, as he had since his last confrontation with his demons.

Bigun was right. The need for rest was desperate now. Sleep must come at any price.

Warmth spread through Saber's limbs. He doused the light and rolled toward the windows where, as he insisted, no draperies had been drawn over the casement. Outside was utter darkness. A wind slapped tree limbs against the panes and light rain tapped the glass.

The wind hummed.

The humming rose and fell.

The tapping rain was as the music of tiny silver finger cymbals. The finger cymbals of dancing Indian women. Dancing and turning, dancing and turning. Undulating bodies. Silver and gold—silk—soft.

Saber drifted.

Ribbons of silk wafted about him—slipped away.

Drifting.

The wind hummed, and hummed.

The rain fell harder.

When the wind would have cooled his body, a covering was drawn over him. The cover settled softly over his shoulders, molded to his legs.

Warm softness curved around his back.

Soft.

A hand slipped beneath his arm and around his chest, and held him.

How long had he lain there?

The thunder of hoofs came again. Blood filled his eyes and he could not see who rode toward him—friend or foe.

Saber rested his head on the churned earth once more. From all around him came the stench of sweat. Sweat, fear, and death.

Moaning and wailing, screams of pain rose on every side. Screams from the living who felt life draining away. Then the sounds ebbed, save those of approaching horses.

He held very still. Those who came might think him already dead.

He was dead.

His heart hurt. It pounded, twisted, pounded. It would stop and he would be dead.

He was already dead.

"Aiee!" The cry rose to a shriek. Hoofs fell so close to his face, he felt the earth give beneath the animal's weight.

The horse pawed the ground. Tack creaked and jangled.

Saber held his breath.

At last the hoofbeats started again, leaving, galloping away.

Perhaps he was safe.

But he was dead. Pressure on his chest pushed the last air from his lungs. His own sweat broke to run and mingle with the blood that burned his eyes.

Screaming. Oh, God, screaming again. They had all held their breath, just as he had, hoping their lives would be spared. Why? Why pray for a life that was all pain, a life that would end soon, anyway?

He wasn't dead.

He could try to get away, to get help—for himself and his wounded men.

They screamed.

More horses. Thundering again—coming this way. Men's voices raised. Shouting. They had returned to finish what they started.

"No. Leave them. No!"

An arm clamped tightly about him, clawed at him, pawed at him. Warm breath puffed against his spine. He felt his enemy's face.

"Get off. Get off, I tell you!"

He rolled toward his assailant and struck out with his good right arm. "Damn you! You've done your worst."

"Stop it!"

"Not again," he yelled. His sweat made his hands slick. He needed a knife. "Never again, do you hear me?"

"Please!"

"Beg, you bastard!" Saber scrambled over the other's body, searching for his knife, for any knife. There had been one close by. *"Beg."*

"Please! Oh, *please.*"

His fingers found the place where the knife would be. He remembered now. He'd placed it where he could always find it. Sobbing his relief, he grabbed the cold handle and sat astride the body of his tormentor.

Fists pummeled his belly.

He lashed back, striking an unseen face, and raised the knife.

"Saber!"

Saber. His name. He pinned the other's neck.

"Saber! Please. What is it? Saber!"

He grew still. He was cool again.

Looking around, he saw moonlight, moonlight through undraped windows. Moonlight on tumbled white sheets.

The rain had stopped. "It isn't raining," he murmured. "It was raining."

"I'm sorry."

Saber looked down at his "enemy."

Crushed beneath his weight, her great dark eyes glittering in the moonlight, lay Ella.

She looked not at him, but at the knife poised to strike at her heart.

Chapter Seventeen

Ella.

He opened his mouth, heard her name within his mind, but could make no sound.

Beloved.

She would be his only beloved for as long as he lived.

Slowly, as if in a trance, she raised her arms and wrapped the fingers of both hands over his on the handle of the dagger. For an instant he didn't guess her intention, didn't guess that she meant to help him take her life. . . .

"No!" He wrenched the gleaming weapon away and threw it across the chamber.

"You want to kill me," Ella whispered. "So kill me."

"No, no, no. Don't say it."

"You hate me. I am disgusting in your eyes."

He fell down beside her and gathered her in his arms. "You are beautiful in my eyes. You *are* beautiful. You are my only beloved one."

She sobbed silently, her slim body heaving. Her dress and petticoats had been removed, but she wore a modest chemise of some fine stuff.

"All my life I have been a mistake," she said into his chest. "I caused my mother pain. For me she was forced to do things she hated to do—to keep me, and Max. I am worthless."

My God! This was his fault. He had known how fragile his Ella was. He'd known from the first moment they spent alone. Then she'd trusted him with those secrets that tore at her heart, and he'd felt disgust. Yes, then he'd felt disgust—or disappointment so deep it could not be ignored. But now he felt only his need for this girl. He needed her so desperately that he could not conceive of drawing another breath once he left her presence for the last time. And he would leave her eventually, and forever—once he had dispatched his duty and made certain she was under the protection of a man who would love and care for her.

"Why do you hate me, Saber?" Her voice was indistinct.

He stroked her tumbled hair. How could he not? "I don't hate you. I told you, I love you."

Her tears wetted his chest. He rolled to his back, pulling her on top of him, and covered them both with the sheets.

Gradually her sobbing eased. As she relaxed she grew heavier, and warmer—and Saber became very aware of his nakedness, and the flimsy nature of her chemise.

"If you love me," she said. "If you love me, keep me. I ask nothing of you but that you let me stay with you."

Saber pressed her face into his neck and squeezed his eyes shut. "No."

"But you said—"

"I cannot."

"Stop it!" Her fists descended on his shoulders and she forced her head up until she could look down at him in the moonlight. "Over and over you have said we cannot be together. Tell me *why* we cannot be together. I love you. You say you love me. Please. Do not send me away again. I can have no life except with you."

"I might have killed you." He spoke the words aloud, heard them in the night—and died inside. "Why must I say more to make you understand? Another instant and you would have been dead." Sickened, he turned his face from her.

"But you didn't kill me," Ella said. "And you did not intend to kill *me.*"

"How can you be sure?"

"You were asleep when I came to you. I was wrong to do such a thing. You thought I was an enemy and that I had attacked you. You fought back."

How close she came to the truth. "You do not understand. Think what you saw. What manner of man did you see when I held you down and raised a knife against you?"

Her thick hair fell forward. Firelight and shadow played over the fine bones of her face, over her shoulders and the deeper plane between her breasts. The white chemise gleamed, as did her skin where it blossomed above her bodice.

Ella held motionless, her elbows locked, her fists still clenched on his shoulders.

"This is not seemly," he told her quietly. Try as he might, he could not contain his body's response to her. She would feel him. "How did you come here?"

Her fists unfurled and she slipped her hands around his neck. "Max helped me. He diverted Bigun while I slipped in. We were wrong, but I don't care. I want to stay with you, Saber."

He grimaced. Her belly, her sharp hipbones, her thighs pressed his body. She was a slight enough creature, yet her weight was a burning presence.

"I don't care what anyone thinks anymore," she said. "I am nothing anyway. Only let me be where you are."

"Nothing?" He tried to concentrate. "You are everything. I

asked you a question. What did you see when I attacked you?"

"A man surprised," she told him, settling her breasts against his chest once more and nuzzling her face to his neck. She kissed him there. "Had you been accustomed to my presence, you would not have behaved so. You thought you were alone, but then there was a stranger in your bed."

She could not know the truth. He would not, could not tell her all of it, but she must learn enough to make her leave and never want to come back.

"I wrote to Max. We have shared so much and he guessed I was unhappy. Today he came from Eton and pretended sickness to be allowed to remain with me. When he suggested we come to you tonight I was afraid, I thought it a poor idea. Now I'm glad. Hold me, Saber. Does it make you feel as it makes me feel?"

"Ah . . ." His wretched brain refused to do battle with the demands of his body.

She wiggled on top of him.

"N-n-no," he moaned. "Don't move, Ella."

"Oh, it makes the feelings for you too? The burning. The aching." She took a hand from his neck and pushed it between them. "Here in my breasts there is the most extraordinary sensation. And down here." Her fingers worked downward until they met his rod—and grew absolutely still. "We spoke once before of how this part of you leaps. It leaps again—because of me. I want to feel it, to hold it to me. You touched my breasts before. You kissed them and sent a fire into me. I want you to kiss them again."

By God, he was only a man!

He slipped his fingers through her hair and drew her face down to his. "Hush. Long ago you were a victim," he said against her lips, and teased them open with his tongue. "You—had—no choice." She pressed her mouth to his and he moved his head gently, brushing skin on skin, mingling breath with breath. Kisses that bound. Kisses that did nothing to quiet the clamoring urgency in his belly.

Her breasts, innocently offered, teased him—the stiffness of her nipples warning him that the arousal was not his alone. In this he must have strength—for both of them.

"Ella—"

She kissed him to silence. Kissed him, copying the motions of his tongue, meeting each firm thrust of his with one of her own.

He should stop.

He should make both of them stop.

Ella moaned. She still touched him most intimately, and he did not possess the will to stop her.

The acts she'd performed with . . . A child forced. Acted upon but never instigating. It was a miracle she could respond to him, want to respond to him.

"Show me what I should do," she murmured. "Exactly what would please you?"

He embraced her fiercely. Enough time would never pass to obliterate the memories entirely, yet she trusted him enough to want to please him. The others . . . Those creatures who had used her had done nothing other than take her. Now she wished to give—to him. She sought his teaching.

"Kiss me, Ella," he told her. "Kiss me again, my darling."

She sealed his lips with hers so sweetly, his belly grew tight and his throat constricted with tenderness. He raised his jaw, urging her mouth to open wider. With her head anchored in his hands, he deepened the kiss.

Moments more and he would lose himself in her.

"Ella"—he drew away, still holding her face close to his, but putting distance between their lips—"Ella, sweet, I asked you a question. You must answer."

He could not see her expression. Her hand moved upon

him, exploring. Saber closed his eyes and said, "I should like you to put your arms around my neck."

Instantly she stopped. "You do not like me to touch you—there?"

He swallowed and tried to will away all feeling. Impossible. "Your arms around my neck, please."

"Yes, Saber." She did as he asked, and as she did so her breasts moved against his chest, and her hips pressed the harder into his—and he fought for control.

"I will repeat my question. When I held you beneath me, what did you feel?"

"Your legs and . . . that."

He frowned. "My—"

"You have very strong legs. I should like to feel them about me like that again. And that, well, it is—"

"Ella!" He was in danger of disgracing himself. No man could be expected to endure such provocation and yet to exert willpower enough to resist that provocation. "Ella, when you looked into my face, what did you see?"

Her legs moved. Just as he had clamped her hips between his thighs, she now clamped his hips between hers.

Nothing separated him from the entrance to her womanhood.

Saber shifted. He released her face and slipped his hands down to lift her from him.

Rather than her waist, his hands spanned her ribs—spanned the place where the soft undersides of her breasts swelled.

A soft "ooh" sighed over his lips.

So soft. So lovely. He sprang harder—a disaster. The tip of his penis met the maddening texture of hair, the inflaming smoothness of aroused flesh—and the sleekness of her readiness.

Saber filled his hands with her breasts, played his fingertips over her budded nipples.

And if he took her, and fell asleep with her in his arms, he could be claimed once more by the unspeakable—and the next time he might not awaken in time to stop his violence. The next time, he might wring the life from her before consciousness found him.

"My God! No!" Twisting violently, Saber turned until Ella fell onto the mattress. "No, do you hear me? *No.*"

"Saber, please—"

"No." He loomed over her, trapped her wrists against the bed. "I am not a man."

"You are a man. You are the best of men. You are—"

"Stop it." He shook her. "When you looked up at me after I awoke, you saw a man unworthy of trust."

"I saw you." Her breasts rose and fell rapidly. "You are the dearest of men."

"We shall not discuss this further except for you to hear what I will say—once. There is a reason why I cannot love you."

"You already said you loved me," she told him in a small voice.

"As a sister," he lied.

She struggled against his grip—to no avail. "No brother loves a sister in such a way."

"The flesh has its own way," he told her. "I cannot help my body's betrayal. But it is not the betrayal of my mind. I shall never marry, Ella. Not you, not anyone. This is as I wish it. I have more important matters upon which to spend my life." Such as mourning the loss of the treasure that might have been his.

"I need you."

What if he had not fully awakened? What if a few more seconds had passed in that hot, bloody place to which he was doomed to return again and again? Saber looked down at Ella, grateful in the knowledge that the moonlight could not reveal the depth of his self-disgust.

"Saber?"

"I almost killed you."

Ella stopped struggling. He saw the glint of her eyes, of her teeth—the pale sheen over her cheekbones. Quiet enveloped them.

"At this moment I am naked and holding you to my bed. You are little more than a girl, and you are not my wife. If anyone were to discover us, your reputation would be gone forever."

"That's what Max . . ." Her voice faded to nothing.

Saber peered at her more closely. "Max? Max *wanted* this to happen?"

"He thought that if I was compromised, you would marry me and then I should be safe."

"He is fifteen," Saber said, incredulous. "What would possibly make a lad of fifteen have such thoughts?"

"You forget," she said, her voice breaking. "You forget that we have not lived as people of your class live at such ages. And fifteen is not an infant, is it?"

"No," he said, remembering his own earlier years and the clamorous longings he suffered. "But for Max to plot against me—and with his own sister."

"You do not understand. We are afraid. And he believes you care for me—that you will keep me safe."

"Safe from what?"

"I am afraid!" She began to cry, low, keening sobs as if wrenched from her. "He w-wants to hurt me, to destroy me. I don't know why. Do you understand me, Saber? He wishes me ill and I don't even know why!"

Her body bucked upward. Immediately he released her wrists and caught her against him. Cold moisture coated her skin.

"What are you telling me, Ella?" he said into her hair. "That Max wishes you ill? I don't understand."

"Not Max. The other one."

"Explain yourself. Who wishes you ill?"

"I don't know, I tell you! But if there were no hope of his capturing me—if I belonged to you and he knew that if he hurt me he would answer to you—then he might leave me alone."

She panted, and clutched him. He grew hotter—and more desperate. "Please, Ella, hush. Oh, hush." He heard his own harsh breathing. "If you do not know who this—who it is who wishes you harm, how can you be sure such a person exists? Surely you aren't still worrying about the scraps of chiffon?"

"Not that."

Saber shifted with her to the edge of the bed. He covered himself and cradled her in his lap, her head upon his shoulder. "More chiffon. Is that the trouble?"

"My dress," she said. "In the pocket there is a letter. It was delivered earlier today. Finch said he found it on his tray. No member of the staff remembers taking delivery of it."

"All right," Saber said, deliberately calm. "I'm going to find some clothes and light a lamp. You're shivering." He set her carefully aside and left the bed, conscious of his nakedness as he had not been in his memory.

"You are very beautiful," Ella remarked in a clear voice.

He grabbed for trousers. "Close your eyes."

"I shall not."

"Do as you are told, miss. Quite enough has happened that should not have happened tonight."

She made a sound of disagreement and announced, "Not nearly enough has happened to please me, sir."

In other circumstances he would have laughed. Instead, he stepped into the trousers and fastened them rapidly.

"I wish you would not dress, Saber."

"I wish you would hold your tongue, Ella. Either you are a designing minx, or a very foolish one. Be assured that to lose one's reputation among the *ton* is anything but pretty. How should we hope to secure you a suitable husband under those circumstances?"

"No one will have me."

He paused in the act of donning a shirt. "I beg your pardon?"

"I said, no one will have me. He has all but promised as much."

Saber picked up a silk robe and carried it to Ella. He spread it around her shoulders and pulled it together in front of her. Then he lighted the lamp beside the bed.

The burst of yellow light revealed what the moonlight had disguised. Ella's face was pale, her hair a shiny, black mass that fell past her shoulders. Her eyes, as dark as her hair and filled with haunted intensity, followed his every move. When he went to move away, she shot out a hand to twine in one of his.

"What *is* it?" he asked. "I cannot help you if you will not explain."

Still clutching him, she slid to stand on the floor and pulled him with her to the clothing she'd piled on a chair. She turned her dress until she could feel in a pocket and remove an envelope. This she offered him.

Saber sensed how badly she needed to cling to him. He contrived to remove a piece of paper from the envelope.

"He intends to embarrass me," she told him. "See? If he sees me with another man he will speak up. He will tell about my early life. He will make sure no man would want to be seen with me. Everyone will—"

"Please," he said evenly, while rage mounted in his gut. "Let me read, Ella."

"Yes." She swayed, pushed her hair back from her face, watched him closely. "He will, won't he? If I accept any invitations and go about in public, he will humiliate me. And any man—or woman—who might be with me."

"Let me think." Let him be calm. Fury swelled through him. The words on the page ran together before his eyes.

"You hate me too."

"Be *silent*!"

She jumped, and covered her face.

"I must think, Ella."

"Think how to distance yourself from me." She dragged her hand from his. "No need. I shall make certain there is no need."

"Ella—"

"I could not bear it if Max's life were tainted by mine. He can overcome it all. Everything that happened to him."

"And so can you." Fear attacked him. She no longer sounded like the Ella he knew. "Whoever this man is, I shall find him and silence him."

"Mama and Papa have already done too much for me. I am not worthy of all they've sacrificed for me."

"They love you. Of course you are worthy. They would not change any of it."

"They would change who I am. *What* I am." With hands that shook, she caught up her petticoats and began to struggle into them. "I must go. I must return Max to Pall Mall."

"Struan will wish to deal with this person."

She turned eyes the shade of dark fire upon him. "Even if you hate me, you will not bring me even lower."

He shook his head. "Ella, please—"

"You will not speak to Papa of the letter." She snatched it from him and turned her back to put on a brown velvet gown of restrained cut. "I will leave you at once. Please return to your bed. Forgive me for intruding. No, you cannot forgive me, of course. What I did was unforgivable."

"You are not yourself. Allow me to—"

"There is nothing you need do for me except pretend to forget you ever met me."

Her frantic fumbling struck terror into Saber. "I will not abandon you. Please, Ella, be calm—"

"Do not tell me to be calm." Dressed, she swung toward him, her face rigid with anger and some other—removed—emotion. "Good night to you." She thrust the letter back into her pocket and made to go around him.

Saber stepped into her path. "You are right," he said, reaching for her. "Of course you are right."

Ella evaded him.

"You intend to return to Pall Mall?" From somewhere deep in his senses came a warning. "Do you intend to return to Pall Mall?"

"What I intend to do is no concern of yours. You have been kind to me. Remember me as generously as you can."

Saber lunged, and this time he caught her. She struggled so fiercely she almost twisted free, but he held her, backed her to the wall, and pinned her there. "You aren't listening to me. And you aren't answering me."

"Don't forget to replace your dagger in the drawer. You may need it if some other villain attacks you."

He smarted at her words. "I deserve your cruel tongue."

"You deserve only the very best in this world. You do not deserve to be affronted by an aberration. Aberrations should not exist at all."

It was as he'd feared. He was no stranger to the meaning behind her words. She had come to him because she loved him. Ella loved and believed in him, and believed he would protect her. And he had denied her. Now she felt there was nowhere else to turn—nowhere to turn and no reason to continue alone.

Saber looked down into her face. With a finger and thumb he tilted up her chin. "There will be no need for Struan and Justine to see the letter."

She stared back at him.

"We must make certain Max never mentions it."

"He will not," she said. "I need to go to him."

"In good time. First you and I have business to conduct."

Without warning, Ella slumped. Her eyes lost focus and she became limp.

Saber swept her into his arms and carried her to the bed. The room was too cold. He chose to be cool, but shock and disappointment—the disappointment he had heaped upon her—had affected Ella. She needed warmth. He pulled sheets and blankets over her and sat beside her, chafing her hands, leaning to kiss her brow.

"Ella," he murmured. "My Ella, you do not swoon. You are not the kind of girl who swoons."

She opened her eyes.

He smiled. "Hello again, Ella. Now we shall complete our plans."

Confusion clouded her face.

Loud pounding at the door made him wince. Ella's expression scarcely changed.

"I know you've got her in there." The voice from the corridor was unmistakably Max's. "Open up, Saber, or I'll come in anyway."

Ella blushed and turned her head away.

"It's all right, my sweet," Saber said. What must be done, must be done. "I understand now."

"I'm coming in!"

The heavy door creaked open, revealing Max. The tall lad

stood with feet braced wide apart, a thunderous frown on his young face.

"Hello, Max," Saber said. "Good to see you. I thought you were away at school."

"Don't try to divert me. Our parents cannot be here, but I am here and I shall insist that you do the right thing by my sister, you cad."

Saber's attention was caught by a bobble of gold behind the boy. "Is that you, Bigun? Nice of you to show our guest up."

"I forced him," Max said pompously. "He tried to throw me out. Didn't get far, I can tell you."

"So I see."

"Don't blame him," Max said. "I lured him into the street while Ella . . . That is, your servant isn't responsible for my discovering your foul deeds. I was too clever for him."

"Very true," Bigun said, his face popping around Max. "Too clever, my lord. Couldn't have guessed the young gentleman's intention."

Nor would he have decided to help the entire process?

"Max," Ella said. "Please go downstairs and wait for me. I'll join you very quickly."

"Go downstairs? Leave you with this defiler of innocents? Allow me to deal with this, Ella. You are only a woman."

"I could do nothing, my lord," Bigun insisted, hopping to see Saber. "Nothing. But perhaps—"

"Perhaps you should go to your bed, Bigun," Saber said. "We will discuss this tomorrow."

Ella sat up. She attempted—unsuccessfully—to tame her hair. "There is no point in persisting, Max."

The boy advanced into the room. Saber could scarcely believe this was the same lad whom he had last seen in Cornwall as a ten-year-old with skinny arms and legs and a stream of unlikely stories.

"You will hear me out, Lord Avenall. Hear me and do what must be done."

"Of course."

"There's no point in arguing further."

"No point at all."

"Max—"

"Leave this to me, Ella," Max said. "Some things must be settled between men."

Saber turned to Ella. He lifted her hair and settled his hands loosely about her neck.

"How *dare* you, sir," Max said loudly. "Kindly . . ."

Saber kissed Ella, slowly, deeply, lingeringly. Her fists beat his chest, but he kept on kissing her—until she stopped pummeling him.

"Dash it all!" Max's boots smacked the bare, cold boards of Saber's bedchamber. "Unhand her at once."

Saber raised his head and smiled into Ella's dazed eyes. "Why?" he asked Max.

"My sister is not some trollop for you to use and cast aside! You may think there is no reason for you to restore her honor, but I think—"

"I think so too," Saber said. "Your sister is to be my wife."

And he would devise a way to protect her from any foe—and from her husband.

Chapter Eighteen

"Kindly wait for me in the vestibule," Ella told Max.

He took several steps into the room. "You showed him the letter. Praise be! I told you he'd help us."

Ella felt Saber's eyes upon her but would not look at him. "Please do as I ask, Max. And you may go with him, Mr. Bigun."

"Bigun."

"You may go with him, Bigun." She felt faint again, but she would not swoon. She would not. She was not a woman who swooned. Saber had at least been right in that. "Go, now!"

Bigun's slippers scuffed rapidly away.

Max stood fast. "We should stop Mama and Papa from leaving London before you speak to them," he said to Saber. "I'll make sure they don't. Will you come directly? Or in the morning?"

"I'll be there at the appropriate moment," Saber said.

He rested the back of a hand on Ella's cheek. She felt something close to pain at his touch and closed her eyes. She wanted, more than anything, to turn her lips into his palm and kiss him. She averted her face.

"Ella," he murmured. "It's all right now, my dear. I will make sure everything's all right."

"We knew you would." Max sounded excited. "Damn me, but I'm glad I came to London when I did. If I hadn't—"

"I wouldn't have forced myself on Saber tonight," Ella finished for him. "Kindly do as I've asked and leave this room."

"Ella—"

"*Leave* this room, Max. Please."

Saber found her hand and gripped it firmly. "Do as your sister asks, Max. We'll join you shortly."

Mutiny tightened Max's features, but he did as he was told and shut the door with a bang.

Ella flinched and said, "I should not have spoken to him so. His concern is for me, and I could have refused to come here."

Rather than agree or disagree, Saber studied her, his head on one side. "So," he said. "It seems we are destined to make a pact, Ella."

"You are an honorable man. Honorable and kind."

He pressed both of her hands together between his. "You are honorable and kind. And you have been misused. But no more. From now on I shall be the one to deal with your comfort, my dear."

So calm, so passionless. He was a man confronted by what he viewed as duty. Saber, Earl of Avenall, did not shirk duty. And she had what she'd wished for. What a very happy girl she should be.

The dying fire crackled. The sulfur scent of the coals prickled Ella's nostrils. A chill settled over her and she glanced about the spartan room with its heavy furnishings and bare floor. A cold room for a man grown cold.

"Thank you," she told Saber simply. "I hope you will forgive me for the wrong I did you tonight."

"You did no wrong."

"I forced your hand. Not an easy thing to live with."

"But I shall not allow such self-recrimination. I assure you that I intend my wife"—he paused, and she saw his throat move as he swallowed—"my wife shall spend her time in gentle pursuits and she will certainly have no cause to regret anything."

Passionless and trapped.

"I'm certain I will appreciate such a quiet life, Saber. I should like to stand now. If you'll excuse me?"

He frowned at little at that, at her formality.

"Saber?" She tried to ease her hands from his.

"I find I enjoy looking at you exactly where you are," he said, increasing his pressure on her fingers a little. "A small enough pleasure, wouldn't you say?"

"There is no need to be generous," she told him. Despite her resolve, her mouth trembled. "You have been tricked—we have tricked you into something you wanted no part of."

For once he forgot any attempt at hiding his scars. He raised his chin and light played over the ferocious evidence of a knife's cruel efforts. The curved welt at the corner of his eye and over his cheekbone shone pale. This time Ella noted a healed gash beneath his ear and disappearing into his hair. Where his white shirt hung open at the neck she sighted yet another scar that followed the line of his left collarbone.

"It is a marvel you lived," she murmured.

Abruptly, he turned back to her. "After an attack that left me such a hideous monster?"

"I cannot believe you think that of yourself."

He laughed harshly. "I *know* that of myself. It doesn't matter, except when I consider the revulsion I must cause you."

"Oh, yes." A surge of anger inflamed Ella. "I feel so much

revulsion that I came begging you to keep me with you under whatever conditions you choose."

"Only because you need me."

Ella blinked against an instant rush of tears. "If that's what you wish to believe, so be it. The attack hurt you more inside than out, didn't it?"

He narrowed his eyes. "What do you mean?"

"You know my meaning. Your skin and flesh have healed, but your mind is still bleeding."

The corners of his beautiful mouth turned down sharply, grimly. "The condition of my mind is not for you to wonder at, Ella."

"As you say." A cowering flower she would never be. "Kindly allow me to get up. I must return Max to Pall Mall."

"You fainted."

"I am quite recovered. Let me by, please."

"The fire is burned low." He released her. "At least let me add coals and make you warm before we leave."

Ella threw back the covers, contrived to gather her skirts modestly about her legs, and slid to the floor.

"Very well, we'll leave at once." Saber stood also. "I'll finish dressing and help you. Please sit close to the fire, such as it is."

He had become larger, even more maturely made in the years since they'd met in Cornwall. Ella felt tiny beside him, tiny and vulnerable—and filled with longing. Tonight Saber had finally declared that he would be her husband. This should have been the most treasured night of her life, rather than the most bitterly sweet.

She pulled on her half-boots and pushed her stockings into her reticule. A moment more and her cape was settled firmly about her shoulders.

"Good night, Saber. Thank you for agreeing to become my champion."

"Wait." He stopped her from approaching the door. "I will see you and Max home. Should you prefer me to speak with Struan now, or in the morning?"

"There is no need to make a fuss about this. Come at your convenience." What had she done? He could not help but detest her for forcing his hand.

"Damn it, Ella. Let's not have coy behavior now."

"Coy?" She snorted and pulled up her hood. "Coy is something I've never been. Never will be. Life has not allowed me an opportunity to develop the ability to be coy."

"What, then?" He leaned against the door and crossed one foot over the other. "Are you going to insist that I go through the expected courting ritual? Shall we dance a few dances at a few balls and simper through a few walks in a few gardens?"

His sarcasm cut Ella. Her legs felt fluid and shaky. "You have every right to chastise me."

"Dash it all!" Even in the gloomy glow of a single lamp she saw a flush of anger in his cheeks. "You have what you wanted. What the devil is this contrary behavior?"

She would never be without pride. "You, my lord, can be a crass, pompous, condescending ass. Good night."

If he'd railed at her, she'd have managed to leave with her dignity intact.

Saber didn't rail. He laughed. He opened his eyes wide, drove his fine white teeth into his bottom lip, braced his hands on his knees, and burst into bellows of laughter.

"Laugh, sir. Go on, laugh. Asses bray, don't they? So bray, sir, bray."

He squeezed his eyes shut, and she saw the glitter of tears at their corners. Finally he wrapped his arms around his lean middle and rested his head back against the door. "It's—hardly—ladylike, ladylike to call a man an—ass." Once more he dissolved into a chuckling, rocking, *infuriatingly* amused rattle-brain.

"Let me pass, I tell you," Ella demanded. "You are hysterical, my lord." Her throat grew tighter by the moment. Any tears she allowed to fall would not be tears of mirth.

"I thought you were different, not a woman likely to be offended by a man who thought you didn't expect the niceties. I took you for granted, didn't I? That's what you thought? I didn't get down on my knee and ask for your hand. And I was supposed to do that even though you came here and asked for mine." His laughter faded to spasms of chuckles. "Really, Ella, you disappoint me."

"How unfortunate." The tears came and she could not stop them. "You understand absolutely nothing. Do you understand that, you cabbage-head? I need no pretty courtship. I need nothing but you, your love, your wanting to be with me. You once led me to believe you wanted that too. All I longed for was to know I could stay where you are. But you decided to *bestow* your hand in marriage upon me. And I do thank you for that, Saber. As I've already said, you are an honorable man. Thank you."

"Ella, Ella—"

"I do not ask you to forget that I love you—there is no need because you will want to forget that. But I do love you. I will always love you. And I think that in your way you love me."

"Ella—!"

"Good night."

"No."

"Don't be ridiculous. You can't respond to 'good night' with 'no.' Good night."

"No."

She spun away, and spun back to face him. "I need time to think—alone. Get out of my way."

"No."

"I'll scream."

"Scream."

Ella wetted her lips, pressed them together, then opened her mouth . . .

She couldn't scream, had never been able to scream even when she'd needed to. "Very well." The hood was hot, and she pushed it back. "Let me out of here."

"Make me."

"Oooh." Ella paced before him."You'd like that, wouldn't you."

"Would I?"

"Yes. You are excited by violence—" She knew her mistake at once.

Saber dropped his arms and stood aside. He opened the door.

"I only meant that you seemed to become quite overwrought when you thought—"

"That will do, Ella. Don't speak about something you don't understand. I shall take you and Max home now."

"No, thank you." Mortification at her own indiscretion made her spine tingle. "We came on horseback and shall return that way."

"Then I shall ride with you. It's dangerous for you to be abroad alone at this hour."

She walked past him. "I wouldn't dream of disturbing your routine further."

"You have no more idea about my routine than about any other part of my life."

"No," she agreed tonelessly. "You are right. I know nothing about you, but I shall endeavor to learn."

They reached the top of the stairs and Ella started down, preserving what dignity she could by not running.

Saber was right behind her. "I'll return to Pall Mall in the morning. I hardly think my visit would be welcome now. Or will you encounter some difficulty upon your return, do you think? If so, I'll come in with you, of course."

Ella gained the hall where Max stood, a wide grin on his boyishly handsome face. "I think Saber should come now, don't you, Ellie?"

"No," she said, sweeping past him. "Not now. There is no need to make a fuss over this. More fuss than I have already made." Shame overwhelmed her.

"But—"

"Bigun," Saber said to the hovering servant. "I need my horse."

"At once, my lord," Bigun said, scuttling toward the back of the house.

"I've decided to see your parents now." Saber had grabbed a cravat and coat and was hastily, and not very efficiently, tying the former. "There need be no mention of what you witnessed upstairs, young Max. You and Ella merely came for a visit at my invitation. You were present when I made my intentions clear to her."

Max saluted and pretended not to see Ella's glare.

"You have your life, Saber," she told him. "Please know that I'm aware of my selfishness. I will not allow our liaison to interfere with the comfortable regimen you have evidently established."

"I assure you that there is no regimen that would interfere with my being a husband to you."

"Hush, Ella," Max said. "You've got what you want, why be a widgeon about it now?"

"I do not have what I want." She covered her eyes, shamed by the tears that refused to be suppressed for long. "I have what I deserve." The promise of a loveless marriage.

"*Women.*" Saber pulled on his coat and snapped his shirt cuffs straight. "I shall never understand a single one of you."

"Neither shall I," Max said.

Ella scowled at her brother but addressed Saber. "No doubt you have had plenty of opportunities to be puzzled then, my lord. But I expect there are other females who make up for their lack of intellect in other ways."

"Not in my life, Ella. Not a single one."

She glanced at him and away again.

"Ella?" His voice became softly, sweetly wheedling. "Look at me, Ella."

When she did, he smiled and came closer.

"This may not have been the most romantic proposal in the world, but it will do, won't it? After all, you did surprise me somewhat."

Ella wound the strings of her reticule around her fingers and nodded.

"Of course you did," Max said. "Admit it, Ella. A chap's got to fess up to his part in things, y'know."

"I'm not a chap," Ella told him indistinctly. In other circumstances she might be moved to giggle. "But you're right. I did surprise Saber and I ought to take responsibility for it."

Saber stood over her. "Good. That's fixed, then. Home now, then a morning call on your parents?"

"Yes," Max said. "Good idea, Saber. But I'll make sure they're warned to wait until you get there."

"Is that to your liking, Ella?" With a knuckle, Saber raised her chin. "We'll deal with your demon together, you and I. And I am glad, my dear. What I told you about my feelings is true. There is no one but you. We shall do very well together."

Her heart lightened. After all, she had pushed him—not that a little pushing wouldn't have been necessary at some time if she were to make him know how much he wanted her. . . .

"Very well." Folding her fingers over his, she managed a wobbly smile. "We'll do as you say."

She heard the sound of hoofs on cobbles outside, and Max

opened the door. He had tethered his own horse and Ella's nearby.

Rather than a horse for Saber, a beautiful silver cabriolet pulled by two elegant grays drew up before the house. A particularly small Tiger in striped livery jumped from his platform at the rear and ran to assist the occupant of the carriage to the flagway.

Dressed in a dark, swirling cloak trimmed with soft black fur, the female passenger tripped rapidly up the front steps, but stopped abruptly when she encountered Max framed in the open doorway.

"Ah," she exclaimed. "A new servant at last, Saber, darling? You took my advice. Really, Bigun could not be expected to continue to do *everything.*"

Ella slowly replaced her hood. Saber slipped an arm around her shoulders.

Countess Perruche's coppery hair was unbound and flowed from beneath her hood. She sighed and then smiled at Saber. "I could not sleep, my love, and I knew that meant I should be with you."

"Margot, I don't think—"

"Ella," the countess said, suddenly frowning. "I didn't notice you. How nice to see you. Saber is comforting you, I see. He is a great comfort to all of his friends."

"I'm sure he is," Ella said stiffly. She stepped from beneath Saber's arm. "I'll leave you two to enjoy each other."

"Ella, please," Saber said. "This is not at all what it appears to be."

"Don't let me drive you away," Countess Perruche said. "Oh, my dear, you care very much for Saber, don't you? I should have known as much at once. Please, you mustn't think . . . Saber, explain to her that we are . . . She thinks we are other than, er . . . Ella, you must try to understand certain things."

Ella gripped Max's arm and thrust him through the door and down the steps. "Don't give it another thought, Countess," she said. "I'm sure you and Lord Avenall have important business together. Our business can certainly wait. Sleep well."

When Max refused to help her mount her horse, she managed to haul herself into the saddle and ride away. Max caught up before she reached the corner.

Max preceded Ella into the Pall Mall house. They entered through the old potting shed and used the back stairs, which had been all but forgotten for years.

"Why did you do it?" Max said, breaking the silence he'd maintained all the way home. "Why did you rush away like that when Saber was ready to come tonight?"

"Because he didn't want to come," she hissed.

"Bosh! Of course he did. Sterling chap, Saber. Gad, those scars are impressive."

"And I suppose his *ladybird* is also impressive?"

Max's steps faltered. He turned to look down at Ella. "Ladybird? I thought she was some sort of friend."

Ella rolled her eyes. "Of course she was. Forget I mentioned it. Let's get to our rooms, and get there quietly and quickly before the whole house comes down on us."

"Do you mean you think Countess Perruche is Saber's—?"

"Go on! Quickly!"

"I say. She certainly is a luscious piece, isn't she?"

Frustration and hurt tore at Ella. "Isn't she, though."

"Sort of the way it is, I suppose, isn't it?" Max's brows shot up. He turned quite pink. "I mean, isn't it expected that a man of his class should—"

"I don't give a fig what's expected." She sniffed—too loudly. "I want to go to bed."

"Saber will probably get rid of her after—"

"Stop it! If you think it's all right to share one's attentions with more than one woman, that's your affair. I shall never be happy with such an arrangement."

"I *don't* think that," Max said hotly. "When I marry, it'll be for love and there'll be no one but her. And we'll have children and they'll never know want or worry, and . . ."

Ella regarded him openmouthed. "And?"

"Nothing."

"You are a dear brother and I adore you," she told him gently. "Your wife will be very lucky and so will you, because you'll choose someone wonderful. Now, hurry up before someone hears us."

A step behind Max, Ella emerged from the low doorway into an upper hallway. Cobwebs draped her hair and face. Brushing at the sticky threads, she crept rapidly in Max's wake toward the stairs leading up to their rooms.

"There you are."

She jumped and spun to see Great-Grandmama—in a voluminous, ruffled black robe and a nightcap—standing on the threshold of her boudoir.

"Gad," Max muttered. "That's torn it."

"Come here," Great-Grandmama said, entirely too pleasantly.

Ella straightened her back, did her best to restore order to her hair, and walked resolutely to meet her fate. "Max need not be present," she told Great-Grandmama. "He has no part in this."

"Dash it all, Ella," her ungrateful sibling said. "I'm hardly a child, y'know. I did come home to look after you. And this is all my doing anyway."

"Brilliant," Ella muttered under her breath.

The dowager said, "Follow me, both of you. And be quick about it."

Max and Ella walked with the old lady into her sumptuous

gilded boudoir. She shut the door and arranged herself on her chaise.

"Come here," she said. "Pull up those two little chairs and sit where I can see you plainly."

Max got the chairs. He and Ella sat on the Aubusson tapestry seats and folded their hands in their laps.

When the old lady's silent scrutiny had bored past Ella's restraint, she said, "I'm sorry if we've caused you concern."

"Where have you been?" Great-Grandmama said as if Ella hadn't spoken.

"There's no point in pursuing this," Ella told her.

"There's every point. What do you say, Max?"

"I don't understand women."

"Oh," the dowager said. "Such wisdom from one with exceedingly wide knowledge of the subject must mean that women are indeed inscrutable. Where have you and Ella been?"

"I can't tell you."

Ella slumped against the back of the chair. "Why prolong this? We've been to Saber's."

She smiled! Great-Grandmama smiled as if she was vastly pleased about something.

"I've told you the truth. My going there may have been a mistake. It was certainly folly and unforgivably presumptuous. I suppose you'll want to tell Mama and Papa before they leave."

"Do you realize what time it is?"

Ella frowned at Max, who shrugged. Sometimes Grandmama's conversations were anything but linear.

"Look at the window. It's almost dawn."

A suggestion of gray light peeped through the draperies. "I didn't realize it was quite that late," Ella said, contrite. "You remained up because of us, didn't you? I'm so sorry."

"I *arose* to see your Mama and Papa off on their journey. They decided to leave early, before you and Max were up."

Ella felt disoriented.

"That silly Justine . . . Your mama was afraid she would be upset by the good-byes. Actually, I'm being too kind. Struan is a sensible man. He knew she might make another ridiculous fuss about leaving you, so he did the wisest thing by bearing her away too early in the day for her to rouse you."

"Oh." Ella rubbed at the space between her brows. Mama and Papa gone already, before they could learn that their daughter was to be married—to a man who'd chosen to sacrifice himself even though he did not want her.

"So," the dowager said. "What progress has been made?"

Utter misery weighted Ella. Exhaustion made her ache.

"Answer me," Great-Grandmama demanded. "What have you accomplished?"

"I don't know what you mean," Ella responded, more sharply than she'd intended. "Forgive me. I'm tired. I don't understand what question you are asking."

"Your progress? With Saber?"

Ella stared at the dowager. Max made an odd sound, but Ella wouldn't look at him.

"I assume you went to see him to try to push the corkbrain into taking action."

"Action?" Ella said cautiously.

"Action. *Action.* On the issue you went to see him about in the middle of the night."

"She knows," Max said, heavy awe in his young voice. "How d'you suppose—?"

"Hush, Max!"

"Kindly allow me to decide who shall or shall not speak in my presence," Great-Grandmama said. She pulled a red and gold silk blanket over her knees and tucked it about her waist. "It grows cold."

"You should be in bed." Ella's response was automatic. "I cannot imagine Papa and Mama leaving so early."

"I assure you that I do not tell lies."

"Quite," Max said, sounding too old.

"Quite," Ella agreed. "And now we should—"

"Now you should answer me. What—"

"He asked her to marry him," Max said in a rush. "He said he wanted to take care of her every need from now on and he asked her to marry him."

"Wonderful!" Great-Grandmama did the unthinkable. She clapped her hands together and she laughed. "Ah, I knew I could rely upon that silly boy to eventually realize what's best for him. Oh, I am delighted. You will make an excellent couple. Good, fresh blood for the family. Saber's mother was my only daughter, you know. But you'll be the one to bring the new vitality into the line, Ella. Handsome children you'll—"

"I should have refused him."

"Don't interrupt me. I said—"

"I should have told Saber I would not marry him."

Great-Grandmama leaned slowly forward. She'd set her cane aside, but now the tip met the carpet between her feet once more. "What?"

"He did not ask me willingly."

"Oh, yes he did," Max blurted out. "He asked and asked, and she behaved like a perfect ninny. Women. I can't imagine how we men put up with them. After—"

"Shut up!" Ella ordered.

"Stop interrupting everyone," Great-Grandmama said, banging the cane against the carpet. "Let's be calm."

"Everyone tells me to be calm," Ella said through her teeth. "I am calm. He is impossible. Cold, bitter, vain, *deluded.* And he is also . . ." She thought better of mentioning Countess Perruche.

"He is still being difficult, then?" The dowager's lips formed a grim, thin line.

"What do you mean, difficult?"

"Refusing to admit he loves you."

Ella's mouth fell open and she sucked in sharp breaths.

Once more the dowager showed a rare smile. "He does love you, y'know. I could tell as much when I saw you together that day."

This was beyond all. "But you asked him to find me a husband."

"Only as a means of making certain the two of you spent a great deal of time together. But he loves you. And you love him. And I approve."

"Well, I'm not sure I do," Ella said.

"I wanted to be certain there was an opportunity for Saber to realize that he wants to marry you."

"But he doesn't."

"I'll send for him in the morning."

"I should probably tell him I don't want to marry him after all."

"Probably," Great-Grandmama said.

"Please do not make fun of me."

"You're right, Great-Grandmama," Max said, and Ella saw him try to hide a grin. "They love each other."

"Which is exactly what I set out to accomplish."

"And you did," Max said, sounding incredibly happy. "You're an out-and-outer, Great-Grandmama, a brick."

Chapter Nineteen

"You look dreadful, Saber."

"Thank you, Grandmama."

"Do not"—his grandparent said, anchoring his hand to her breakfast table with a bony forefinger—"do not use your unpleasant wit upon me, young man."

He knew better than to provoke her further. "You sent for me and I came—despite the horrendous hour of the morning."

She peered at him and motioned an under-butler forward. "Kindly bring Lord Avenall some kidneys. He's in need of having his blood strengthened. A glass of claret might also . . . No, after breakfast."

Saber said nothing as his plate was filled.

"You were not asleep when my man arrived at your house," Great-Grandmama said. "I questioned him, and he said he heard you in your study when that—that *person* you employ took my message to you."

Saber pushed a piece of kidney around his plate. "I fail to see the importance of whether or not I was asleep when your man came for me."

"If you weren't asleep, it hardly matters that he came early, does it?"

"I merely referred to civil behavior, Grandmama. Nothing more."

"Posh! I shall be the judge of what you were referring to."

He hadn't slept at all. Margot's comforting visit had been short, but his thoughts had remained with Ella. He'd watched the morning arrive and thought of her—couldn't cease thinking of her.

Ella needed him—his name, his protection. Once that was accomplished, he'd find a way to provide for her future. He could not trust another man to do what must be done.

Unless he could move quickly to establish security for Ella, it might be too late. Too late because her persecutor might have found a way to intimidate her into hiding, or too late because he, Saber, had succumbed to the madness completely and been . . .

"Are you listening to me, Saber?"

Incarcerated.

"Saber?"

"I'm listening." In the years since the attack, the years of his descent, deeper and deeper, into his dark other world, he had never as much as allowed himself to form the word that spelled his worst fear. *Incarcerated.* He had not even thought the word before.

"What is wrong with you?"

"Nothing!" His eyes followed hers to his right hand. Curled into a fist, it shook steadily. He opened his fingers. "There is nothing wrong. Why should you think there is?"

She withdrew her forefinger from his left hand, then hesitated and patted him instead. "I understand these things, my dear. Forgive an old lady for seeming heartless. My advanced years make me impatient sometimes."

Saber stared at her. Never, ever, had she retreated into the wiles of the aged. He did not believe she was doing so now. She sensed something . . . Yes, she sensed there was something wrong with him and it frightened her, just as it would frighten anyone exposed to the horror of his . . . madness.

Last night Ella had become the victim of his condition. And she had made excuses for him.

"Eat," the dowager said sharply. "At once."

"I find I am not hungry," Saber said, eyeing the congealing lumps of meat with distaste. "Why did you wish to see me?"

The door opened and a rumpled Max came in. At the sight of Saber he brightened. "Morning," he said, and yawned hugely. "Finch said you wanted me, Great-Grandmama."

"Sit there." She indicated the chair beside Saber, who sat at her right. "Be quiet and eat."

"But—"

"You heard me," Grandmama thundered, if in a somewhat thin voice.

"Hardly been in my bed," Max grumbled, slipping into his appointed chair and casting Saber a conspiratorial sidelong glance.

The dowager harrumphed and raised her thin shoulders. "Seems to me that none of us has been abed, my boy. We will not go into the disgraceful events of last night. Not yet."

She knew of Ella and Max's visit to Burlington Gardens. His aged grandparent was up to something. "I'd intended to call this morning anyway," he told her. "I need to speak with Struan."

"You will speak with me."

"I shall certainly be most happy to have you present," he told her, deliberately soothing. "But I should appreciate having Struan awakened."

"Not here," Max said. "They left for Scotland. Decided to go without waking us—not that we were asleep."

Saber frowned. "You told me you'd make sure they did not leave before I spoke with them."

"Did he indeed," Grandmama said. "They'd already left London when this young rogue and his willful sister returned. Regardless, this will be a lesson to you, Saber. There are certain conventions to be adhered to in these matters. Entrusting a task of such importance to a child could never fall within those conventions."

"I say—"

"That will do, Max. I sent for you because you are Ella's brother and the two of you are very close. I admire that and wish to honor your friendship."

"Yes, but—"

"You will thank me for my consideration, eat what is put before you, and keep your mouth closed."

Max rolled in his lips.

Saber hid a smile and waited for the inevitable.

"How can I keep my mouth closed and eat?"

Saber laughed.

Grandmama reached past Saber with a spoon and rapped Max's knuckles.

The door, opening again, drowned the boy's pained exclamation.

At the sight of Ella, Saber stood.

She met his eyes and appeared confused.

"Stop gaping, child," Grandmama ordered. "Sit beside me at once and have your breakfast. You're looking as dreadful as Saber."

"Grandmama," he said under his breath.

"Don't reprimand me, young man! I say you and Ella look dreadful and you do look dreadful. Exhausted eyes, pallid skin, no life in either of you, I—"

"Ella looks beautiful," he said without the caution he knew

he should employ. "Sit down, my dear. Eat. You haven't had enough sleep."

"I have it on good authority that you haven't had *any* sleep," Grandmama told him. "You sit down and eat."

Ella's black hair had been loosely braided and wound about her crown. Her dark eyes glittered almost feverishly in a face that was, indeed, unnaturally pale. Ella was beautiful. Ethereal, vulnerable, touching places within Saber that he'd thought dead.

She began to turn away.

"Ella," Grandmama barked out. "Come here at once."

A violet morning dress with a demure white chemisette fitted Ella perfectly. Her breasts were a tender fullness, her waist small beneath a satin ribbon tie. The pleated skirt reached, but did not hide, narrow ankles.

So lovely, such an enigma—so impossible to banish from his mind ever again.

Slowly, she turned back to the table and walked to take a place beside her adoptive great-grandmother—across the table from Saber.

"That's better," Grandmama said, waving the flunky forward again. "More kidneys. See if cook has a little liver."

Max made a barely disguised choking sound, which Grandmama chose not to notice.

"Fading away," the old lady said. "And at a time when a young woman should be building herself up. Childbearing requires all the strength a female can have, my girl."

Saber looked into Ella's eyes.

She stared back, a grim tightness about her lips.

"Gad," Max exclaimed. "You never told me you were . . . Well, you know, Ellie."

"Got to build up your blood, or you won't have enough to give the offspring."

"I've always wanted to ask some questions about certain

aspects, you know," Max said, blissfully unaware of the tension in the breakfast parlor. "Naturally, I'm a man of the world and there's little I don't know. But the business of infants? I asked Mama if I could read her book, but she said I'd be bored until I was 'of an age,' whatever that means."

"It means," Saber said quietly, "that your mother, quite correctly, considers such information unnecessary at this point."

"That's just it," Max continued, brimming with cheerful interest. "I ought to know the nature of this information, don't you think? At least to a degree that would make a fella well-rounded in matters of the world. I'm not quite clear about how one thing leads to another. Or what exactly happens then. In fact, I'm not clear about a number of things. In fact—"

"Do shut up, Max," Ella said in a voice barely above a whisper. "When will you learn to be appropriate?"

"He's only interested," Saber told her. "Interested and probably uncomfortable, just as you are."

She looked at him then, and his stomach fell away. "I am not uncomfortable," she said. "Why should I be? I've made my apologies."

Exhaustion snapped Saber's reserves of patience. "I'm almost surprised to find you here, Ella. I feared you might have fled back to Scotland with your parents."

"Grandmama, would you please explain to Saber that Mama and Papa left unexpectedly early so I couldn't accompany them."

"Don't be a sapskull. Saber is perfectly aware that they have left."

Ella drew herself up. "Perhaps I should leave for Scotland."

"You will do no such thing," Grandmama said.

"Probably shouldn't travel if you're . . . Well, not a good idea if you're in an interesting condition, is it, Ellie?"

The girl pushed aside the plate that was put in front of her, and crossed her arms.

"Ella is not in an interesting condition," Grandmama said, with surprising patience. "I was referring to the need for her to become strong for when she *is* in such a condition."

"Oh," was all Max said.

"Rather than the foolishness your mama entered into, I should hope that you and Saber will waste no time in producing offspring."

The arousal Saber felt might have shamed him, had it not brought him the pleasure of recalling Ella's sweet body in his arms, her sweet lips upon his own.

Their offspring.

Their children—the fruit of his seed within her.

"I had a particular reason for asking Saber to be here this morning," Grandmama said. "Eat your kidneys. Both of you. And you, Max."

Keeping his eyes on the proceedings, Max ate with evident relish.

"We have arrangements to make," Grandmama continued. "There will be no more shilly-shallying. I shall deal with no more moonish nonsense. We are going to proceed with all haste."

"Proceed with what?" Max asked around a mouthful of kidneys.

"Saber." Grandmama raised her coffee cup and took a sip. "It's time you—"

"Don't say it," he told her, making certain his voice conveyed enough command to stop her. "Do not go too far, please, Grandmama. It would be a mistake."

For a moment the old lady considered. She set down her cup and pushed out her pale lips into a thoughtful little bunch of wrinkles.

"If you'll excuse me," Ella said.

"I won't," Grandmama said. "It's time some changes were made. Saber and I are agreed on that."

He forebore to argue.

"I've heard from Calum and Philipa," Grandmama said, as if the diversion wouldn't be noticed. "They have decided to visit earlier than planned. They'll be arriving in a few days to give your ball, Ella."

Ella showed no sign of having heard a word.

"Did you hear me? Calum and Pippa are on their way to London to give you a marvelous ball. As we speak, the ballroom is already being readied. Hasn't been used since Justine's pathetic attempt—"

"Don't say nasty things about Mama," Ella said. "There is no one as special as our mama."

"I should say not," Max agreed, forking in more kidneys and following them with a bite of toast recently cooled in the silver rack. "Mama is the best. So is Papa. Saber's a brick too."

Saber gave the boy a grateful half-smile. "Too bad your entire family doesn't agree with you, young Max."

"They do," Grandmama assured him. "No matter on that score at the moment. To our earlier discussion."

"About offspring, you mean?" Max asked, his attention on his plate. "Jolly good show that Ella and Saber are going to have some. When, exactly? I ought to at least read—"

"You will *not* read that outrageous book," Grandmama said. "Now be quiet, all of you, so that I may finish. It's inappropriate for women to be alone in London."

"Alone?" Ella gave the dowager her full attention.

The old lady raised her chin. "Yes, alone. With your father gone and no other male relatives in residence, we are alone."

Max sputtered. "I'm here!"

"You are not a man."

"I am—"

"Quiet! A mature male presence is essential—for the look of things as well as for protection and guidance."

Saber regarded her with interest. While helping Calum assume his responsibilities as Duke of Franchot, the dowager had shown herself as more than capable of administering the huge castle and its surrounding estates. Surely she wasn't becoming too feeble to deal with a London house.

"The staff is very reliable," Ella said. She patted Grandmama's arm and smiled. "And I have no fear in any situation. We are perfectly safe here."

"We *will* be perfectly safe here," the dowager duchess replied. "We need a man in the house and we shall have one. Saber is moving in at once. I shall act as chaperon until the marriage."

Chapter Twenty

Ella watched her visitor and longed for her to leave. Uncharitable, she knew, but this was a day when any intrusion would be unwelcome.

"This is the loveliest room." Precious Able positively bubbled as she bounced around Ella's sitting room. "The loveliest house. Lord Wokingham's is *so* stuffy. And so . . . Oh, dear, how very wicked of me. I should never speak any wrong of my dear Woky. He is so good to me."

"I'm glad," Ella said vaguely. "That is a particularly becoming gown on you, Precious."

"Do you think so?" Precious clasped her fingers together beneath her bosom and surveyed the yards of flounced, rosebud-pink muslin that foamed around her. "Woky said it was too provoking. I can't imagine what that meant, can you?"

"No," Ella said with complete honesty.

"Anyway. I didn't come to presume upon your hospitality for long. I only want to know what's happening to you. You haven't been about for *ages.* And I've missed you." Precious pouted prettily. "You promised to be my friend. You can't be if I never see you, you know."

Surely he would not do it.

"I was invited to Verbena White-Symington's ball at Clarence House! Can you believe it?"

Saber couldn't possibly agree to move in here at Pall Mall.

"Well, actually, Woky was invited to the ball and, of course, since I am his fiancée I went too. I was so certain you would be there."

With Saber under the same roof she would see him at every turn. Ella looked into the fire—seeing him now. Great-Grand-mama intended to do all in her power to promote a marriage that should not take place.

Ella glanced at the small, pearl-encrusted watch pinned to her bodice. Two in the afternoon. The house had been utterly still since Saber left—in a thunderous silence—and everyone else had removed themselves to their quarters. Even Max had absented himself.

"Of course," Precious said, walking toward Ella with springing steps that set her skirts swaying. "Perhaps you weren't invited."

"No," Ella said. "No, I don't believe I was. Although I'm not sure."

Precious giggled and spun in a circle. "You are such a silly puff-head sometimes, Ella Rossmara. Of course you would remember."

"Of course I would."

Whatever happened, she must work very hard to be a good wife to Saber, to make him glad he'd married her. He was marrying her out of nothing but duty. And she would let him do it because she was too weak to do otherwise.

Oh, her mind twirled around and around.

"You aren't even listening to me, are you?"

"Hmm?" Ella raised her eyes to Precious's and encountered

a frown. "Oh, I'm sorry, Precious. How thoughtless of me. I'm a little preoccupied."

Precious grew still and her frown deepened. "All right, I'm going to be honest. I'm just going to be absolutely truthful and explain exactly why I came today. I did try to persuade myself that I didn't need to, but I do and so I'm here."

Bewildered, Ella tried to become more comfortable in one of the stiff pink wing chairs.

"You aren't saying *anything.*" In a billowing, rosy cloud, Precious sank to the floor beside Ella. "I am your friend. You're troubled and you need help. I want to give you that help."

Ella's concentration centered on her visitor. "Troubled? Of course I'm not troubled. I was simply listening to you and there didn't seem too much to be said."

Precious pressed one of Ella's hands. "I know why you've been absent at absolutely every event for almost two weeks."

"Do you?"

"I don't believe a word that they're saying."

Ella gave the girl her complete attention. "I'm sure I don't understand what you mean."

"Oh . . . Well . . . Oh, forget I even mentioned anything. I'm sure I've got it all wrong anyway. My wedding is to be in four weeks—at Woky's house. But I already told you that."

"Yes. Precious—"

"Will you help me with all the shopping, Ella? Will you assist me in choosing my trousseau? You have such exquisite taste."

"I'll help you. Precious—"

"And you absolutely *promise* you'll be there on the day? My mama and papa cannot return from Lancashire, so I'll be all alone if you don't come, and I'm convinced I shall quite faint away if that happens."

"I'll be with you." Ella leaned forward. "Precious, what did you mean? About people saying things?"

Precious's blue eyes filled with tears. "Why, oh why did I mention it?"

"You did mention it. Now, would you please explain?"

"Oh, it's not really anything. They're all jealous of you because you're so beautiful—and so different-looking." Precious paused. She got to her feet and stroked Ella's hair. "Exotic. Not quite English, really."

Ella resisted the temptation to mention the word *gypsy*.

"They say you are not really the Rossmaras' daughter."

Ella breathed deeply. "I am the adopted daughter of Viscount and Lady Justine, Viscountess Hunsingore." Trying to avoid the truth would only result in more speculation. "My brother, Max, is also adopted."

"How kind of the viscount and his wife."

"Yes," Ella agreed. "How kind of them."

"So that much is true."

"That much?"

A tap at the door was an unwelcome interruption. Ella's maid, Rose, entered with a bowl of cream roses. "There's more new ones downstairs, Miss Ella. Will I bring 'em up?"

"No, thank you, Rose," Ella said. "In fact, why don't you take a nice vase of flowers to your room. And there is another box of sweetmeats on one of the demilunes. Please share that with the rest of the staff."

Rose bobbed and smiled her pleasure before departing again.

"Lots of gifts?" Precious said, moving to sniff the roses. "They weren't wrong about that either."

Irritation shortened Ella's temper. "Why don't you just tell me everything you've heard, Precious. It isn't kind to taunt someone you supposedly count a friend."

Precious swung around, her mouth turned sharply down at

the corners. "Ella! Oh, my dear one. I'm sorry. It's only that I spoke too hastily, I thought, and then I couldn't take back my words. Are you to have a ball?"

Ella wasn't distracted, but she said, "Yes. Two, I believe."

Precious puffed up her cheeks and looked doleful.

"You shall come," Ella told her in haste. "If you'd like to, that is. You and Lord Wokingham." But not the revolting Hon. Pom.

"Yes, yes, we should enjoy that so. When—"

"Precious, we were discussing what you've heard about me."

Max entered without knocking. "I say, Ella, this household has gone quite mad!" He stopped at the sight of Precious.

Precious regarded Max with avid interest and said, "Mad?"

"This is Precious Able," Ella said. "Precious, my brother, Max. Precious is telling me that there are unpleasant rumors abroad about me."

"Oh, Ella, I was *not.*"

Max's green eyes studied Precious intently. He strolled closer and stood, looking down at her. "What rumors would those be?"

"Really, there aren't—"

"Come along," Ella said, pretending jocularity. "Out with it, Precious. You're among friends."

"Your brother obviously has more important matters to discuss than gossip," Precious said, plopping herself on a rose-colored damask couch and smoothing her skirts. "I shall just sit and wait until you've finished your business."

Ella didn't miss the assessment in Max's gaze. "Not at all, Miss Able. After you, of course."

"No, no, you have some urgent news for Ella. Little me can wait."

"Not at all," Max insisted. "We are gasping to know what you know, aren't we, Ella?"

"We are," she agreed.

Precious turned very pink. "It was silly. I only wanted to let you know that I have absolutely denied all rumors on your behalf."

Ella met Max's eyes. Neither of them spoke.

"Can you imagine anything as outrageous as suggesting you had ever been in . . . Well, you couldn't imagine, could you?"

"How would we know?" Max said. "Since we don't know what we're not supposed to be able to imagine."

"Well, I don't really understand exactly what was meant, but I know it wasn't nice."

"Try to explain," Ella said.

"Try," Max echoed. "Try to understand, or at least repeat what you heard and *I* will try. Men often understand things that are beyond females."

Ella allowed that arrogance to pass.

Precious fiddled with beads that decorated her bodice. She glanced anxiously at Max, who continued to stand over her. "They talked about you not being any better than you ought to be, Ella. And I told them they were wicked. Wicked and wrong. They said you had once had a very different life and that you . . . They said you'd lived in an evil house and that you were no longer an innocent." She finished in a rush and pressed her hands to her cheeks.

"Really?" Max's voice was silky.

Words eluded Ella.

"Who exactly said these things about my sister?"

Precious puffed up her cheeks. "Ooh, *girls.* At several routs and things. You know how they do love to gossip. But I stopped them. So you don't have to worry anymore."

"No." Ella swallowed with difficulty. "Thank you for defending me."

Precious beamed. "I should just have come right out with it. Silly me. I could have put your mind at rest sooner."

"Thank you," Ella said again. She wanted to creep away and cry. Shame washed her in hot waves. "I shall be very happy to assist you with your shopping. Why did you say your parents cannot be present?"

"I didn't." Precious rested her chin on her chest—a simple enough feat. "They simply cannot afford to return to London."

"Surely Lord Wokingham would assist them."

"They have their pride. Papa has told Woky that parish duties make it impossible for them to return to London. I think Woky was glad to accept that excuse. He's quite possessive, you know."

"I'm sure," Ella said. "And I've kept you from him for too long. Allow me to ring for your carriage."

"I'll go down soon enough," Precious said, making much of opening her fan. "You two just talk and then you and I can make plans for our next meeting, Ella."

"But—"

"No, I insist." Precious's round eyes moved rapidly between Ella and Max. "Tell your sister what you came to say, Max. I assure you I'm more than discreet."

Ella wanted only to be rid of Precious.

"Precious," Max said, in a voice Ella had never heard him use before. He picked up one of the girl's red curls and wound it around his finger. "How the name suits you. You are indeed precious. Precious as a gem is precious. Precious as a clear blue sky is precious. Precious as a perfect flower is precious."

Ella remembered to close her mouth.

"Why, thank you, Max," Precious said, dimpling. "You didn't tell me your brother had such a way with words, Ella."

"This gift comes upon me rarely," Max told her, lifting a

none-too-clean boot to rest on the seat beside Precious. "Most difficult when it does. Extremely so. A factor of my age, so the doctors say. In fact, Matron—at Eton—Matron said she had never seen quite so extreme a case."

Precious drew against the back of the couch. "Case of what?"

"Oh." Max made an airy gesture, then leaned down until his nose almost met Precious's. "They don't really know." His voice dropped deep before he actually brought his nose to hers.

Precious jumped backward.

"Purple demons," Max said. "Small ones. Many of them. That was the manifestation on that occasion. They crept down inside her bodice. Matron's, that is."

"Demons?" Precious shrieked and clamped her hands to her bosom.

"It isn't demons this time," Max said, falling to his knees before Precious. "No, this time it is something quite different. You are glorious. Oh, I am in ecstasy. Such exquisite perfection. It is more than I can bear. I am overcome. Ella, Ella, help me before I disgrace myself completely."

Ella rose to her feet but couldn't seem to move.

"Look at her ankles," Max said, hauling one of Precious's substantial feet into the air and revealing several inches of a limb. "I would *die* just to be allowed to gaze upon such an ankle for the rest of my life. No, no, I must restrain myself. I begin to fear for . . . I begin to fear."

"Max," Ella said weakly, quaking with silent laughter. "Do sit down, my dear. I'll call Finch. He'll help."

"The house has gone mad," Max said. "Finch is gone. Dispatched for a rest at Hanover Square while Crabley takes his place here. Papa's idea evidently. Crabley has yet to arrive, but do not worry. I'll be all right soon enough."

"What is this sickness?" Precious's voice was a breathy croak.

Max leaped to his feet, staggered backward, and fell into a chair. "I am hot, sister, hot. I burn. I burn for her. Perhaps you should leave and allow me to declare myself." He panted.

"What is the matter with him?" Precious all but screamed.

"She is the embodiment of my dreams—of certain dreams I have started having of late," Max wailed. He convulsed in the chair, flung his feet over one arm, his head and arms over the other, and jerked. "I am yours, Precious. Yours and no other's. It does not matter that carbuncles grow on your breasts."

Precious screamed loudly. She looked down at her breasts.

"I don't care that you walk naked for all to see. What man could truly call himself a man if he were not willing to share his good fortune with the world."

"Ella, what is wrong with him?" Precious scrambled to her feet and grabbed her reticule.

"As long as I do not care how tightly you are corseted to squeeze you into your dress, what can it matter, my love?" Max's hips jolted up until he was a bridge between the arms of the chair. "Do not concern yourself that the others laugh at you. To me you are perfect. Your foolishness enchants me."

"Well!" The toe of one of Precious's slippers caught in a silk rug and she tripped.

Ella scarcely managed to stop the other girl from falling.

"Oh," Precious exclaimed. "How horrid he is. First he compliments me. Then he insults me. He is mad, absolutely mad."

"I am on the *verge*!" Max announced. He raised a face nicely reddened from having hung upside down. "On the *verge,* my precious, Precious. Come here and help me fly."

Precious wrenched open the door and rushed from the room. Her footsteps hammered the stairs, and within moments the front door slammed.

"Max!" Ella went to him and grasped his collar. She hauled him to his feet. "What on earth is the matter with you?"

"Nothing." He straightened his hair, pulled down his coat, and cleared his throat. "Not a thing."

"You dratted boy. You scared poor Precious to death."

"Not quite to death, unfortunately. Don't you think I should go on the stage?"

"Undoubtedly. Why did you do such a dreadful thing?"

He gently disengaged her fingers from his collar. "Because she did a dreadful thing to you. She made you unhappy and I do not like her."

"She thought I ought to know about these rumors."

"And she enjoyed telling you about them. She is a jealous, spiteful creature."

"She's just lonely, Max. You ought to apologize to her."

He shrugged. "Can't."

"Can't, or won't?"

"Can't. She's gone."

"Max—"

"Great-Grandmama has taken to her bed. Finch has been dispatched to Hanover Square. He's in a horrid huff because he thinks—correctly—that Papa prefers Crabley. I know perfectly well Papa thinks Crabley will take better care of things while he's gone. Anyway, Crabley's coming here, and Bigun's down in the vestibule sitting in some sort of red basket thing. And all the staff's threatening to leave if he doesn't."

"Bigun?" Ella said. "I don't understand."

"Neither does anyone else—except me. I understand perfectly. Useful, having a dramatic turn of mind. One understands the dramatics of others, even if they don't seem particularly dramatic."

"Oh, good," Ella said. "Then perhaps you'll explain them to your poor, not-at-all dramatic sister."

"You can be dramatic when you want to, Ella. I have it on good authority that you make a perfectly splendid ghost."

"Do not toy with me further. You've done quite enough damage for one day."

A tap on the doorjamb made Ella jump. She spun to face Devlin North.

He grinned engagingly. "Max has been up to no good? Is that what I just heard?"

"Been on the verge," Max said, all innocence. "You may remember how it is for a fella of my age."

Devlin's arched brows rose. He strolled in. "Not sure I do. On the *verge*? On the verge of what?"

"Did you come to talk to me?" Max asked.

Devlin, more handsome every time Ella saw him, crossed his arms over his massive chest and contrived to look ominous. "Actually, I came to see Ella. In the absence of her father, I thought she might welcome a little manly support—and guidance, perhaps."

"Unchaperoned?" Max asked as if horrified.

"You're here, aren't you?" Devlin reminded him.

"So I am. I shall sit over in that corner and doze. But have a care, Devlin. Even when dozing, I am ever vigilant. I should defend my sister's honor to the death—should such an eventuality become necessary."

"I think you have become demented," Ella said wearily. "Do sit down and behave yourself, Max. Be quiet. Let me at least *think*. Good afternoon, Devlin. May I ring for some coffee, perhaps?"

"Ring," Max answered as he settled himself in a shadowy corner of Ella's sitting room. "By all means ring. You might possibly get Bigun out of his basket thingie, but I doubt if he knows how to serve coffee. The rest of the staff is hiding until Crabley arrives. And dear Blanche is mopping Great-Grandmama's brow."

"Thank you, Max," Ella said. "Will you have sherry, Devlin?"

Rather than respond, he regarded her seriously. "You are very special, Ella," he said quietly. "No wonder Saber is so fond of you."

There seemed no suitable reply. Ella fingered her watch and smiled.

Max cleared his throat, but if Devlin noticed he gave no sign.

"Forgive me if I embarrass you," Devlin said. "But a man feels helpless sometimes and then he may say things he might not otherwise say—things that ought to be said anyway. If you take my meaning."

Ella didn't.

"I would do anything to help you, Ella. You know that, don't you?"

"Th-thank you." The events of this day only grew more confusing.

"Saber has"—Devlin drew closer and held out his hands—"he has confided all his deepest concerns to me."

Ella hesitated, then placed her hands in Devlin's.

He enclosed her fingers in a firm, warm grip. "I know about recent events," he said, raising his brows significantly. "You have been through a great deal."

Saber had told Devlin, told him things Ella never wanted another soul to know.

"Don't look so stricken," Devlin said, bending to look into her face, and waiting until she returned his gaze. "Like Saber, I regard certain matters of the past as just that—past. You are not responsible for . . . Children cannot defend themselves."

She bowed her head.

"Ella, Ella." Devlin rubbed the backs of her hands with his thumbs. "How could you be ashamed with me? I am your friend. I will always be your friend. I—I am very fond of you.

Because of that fondness, and my friendship with Saber, it is my duty to tell you not to pursue certain areas of his life. You already know what can happen if you do."

Saber had reported *everything*. "Did Saber tell you to come and speak to me about these things?"

"He has had need of a close ally, one in whom he could place absolute trust. I have been—and am that for him. I would do anything for Saber."

"So would I," Ella said without thinking. After a moment she repeated, "So would I," and felt no regret for her declaration.

"Even if it means letting him go?"

Her spine tingled. "What do you mean?"

"Nothing," Devlin said, shaking his head. "Nothing . . . and everything. Listen, my dear, you are more mature than your years, so I may speak plainly. I understand your needs at the present. Do you know what I'm saying to you?"

A glance at Max caught him sitting at the edge of his chair, staring back at her in anticipation. "Why don't you explain more clearly?" she said to Devlin.

"You have need of a protector," Devlin told her. "I would never wish this to sound so . . . so calculated. I assure you that although there is an element of calculation, there is far more willing . . . What I am trying to say brings me pleasure, Ella. I do not regard it as an onerous duty."

Ella grew warm—and angry. "Saber should not have confided my secrets to you. To you or to anyone else. I'm mortified that he's done so, and shall tell him as much."

"I think you fail to hear what I'm really telling you—*asking* you," Devlin said. He brought one of Ella's hands to his lips. "Never be mortified that I know your needs, my dear. And please do not be cross with Saber. He has certain problems that are beyond his control."

"You confuse me," Ella said. "Thank you for coming,

Devlin, but I believe I shall have to excuse myself. I find I'm very tired."

"Of course," he said, smiling broadly. "But not before I make sure you do understand me. I said I would do anything for Saber, and for you. And I will. With pleasure. You need a champion—someone to make certain you live the life you deserve. Saber wants that for you, Ella. He cannot help it if . . ."

With heat throbbing in her face, Ella waited for Devlin to finish.

"I must help my friends and will do so gladly."

"Gad," Max muttered.

Devlin frowned at him. "We shall do well enough together, Ella. It's time I settled down. Our match would answer your dilemma, bring me satisfaction, and give Saber peace of mind. What could be more fitting?"

Ella stared at him.

"So? What do you say? I understand Struan's on his way to Scotland. With your agreement, I'll send a messenger to present my offer for your hand."

"Gad!" Max slapped his knees. "If that don't beat all." He got up and went to open the door. "If that don't beat all. Bloody household's gone mad. Didn't I tell you that, Ellie? Now the whole world's gone mad with it."

"That's enough from you, young Max," Devlin said, but he smiled affably enough. "Overwhelmed the pair of you, have I?"

Devlin didn't see the next arrival on the threshold of Ella's sitting room.

"This has been so nice of you, Devlin," Ella said, speaking rapidly. "Thank you for coming."

Saber braced himself against the door frame. "No need to try to help the sly devil out," he said, his green eyes narrowing. "*Overwhelmed the pair of you, have I?* You haven't overwhelmed me, friend."

Devlin swung around.

"I ought to kill you for this," Saber said, surging forward. "Get out of the way, Ella. I'm going to make Devlin regret this piece of business."

Max fell back.

Ella tried to step between Devlin and Saber, but Devlin pushed her behind him and said, "You're posturing, Avenall. We both know you—"

"We both know I'll defend what's mine, North. Ella is mine. Mine! Do you hear me?"

Her legs threatened to buckle. Horror vied with joy.

"You know you can't have her," Devlin shouted. "For God's sake man, I'm only trying to put your mind at rest. At least you won't have to worry that she's in good hands."

"Damn you!" Saber launched himself at Devlin. "Ella is to be *my* wife. The only hands she'll be in are *mine.*"

Chapter Twenty-one

"The devil take you, Avenall," Devlin said through his teeth. With both fists raised, he came at Saber. "Got your trusted dagger somewhere about you, have you? Ready for the sight of more blood at last, are you?"

Saber had never thought to hear his best friend speak aloud of secrets they'd shared in private. "I do not need any dagger to squeeze out your life, *traitor*."

"Stop it! Both of you!" Ella rushed at Saber. She collided with him. "Stop it at once. I cannot bear it."

Saber was helpless to check his forward momentum—or his impact with Ella. Arms flailing, she fell backward—into Devlin's arms.

"I say!" Max didn't attempt to mask his glee at the proceedings. "Jolly good scuffle. Out of the way, our Ellie."

Hitting Devlin while he held Ella was out of the question. Saber opened and closed his hands in frustration. "Unhand her," he said, furious with his loss of control. "Come here, Ella."

She was lovely in green, lovely, flushed, and bright-eyed. And, despite her wrathful words, she looked at him with the love he so wanted yet so feared. With only a backward glance at Devlin, she came to Saber, stood before him, and rested a trembling hand on his arm.

He covered that hand on his arm and glared at Devlin over her head. "Explain yourself."

"Nothing to explain," Devlin said, his face tight and pale. "Trying to do a good turn for people I care about. Too bad a fella can't do a good turn without being held to ridicule."

"He asked Ellie to marry him," Max said. "Wanted to save you the trouble, evidently."

"Hush, Max," Ella said. "Don't inflame matters. I'm sure there is a perfectly good explanation for this muddle."

Saber wished he knew what that explanation was. "Don't interfere, there's a good chap, Max," he said, never taking his eyes from Devlin's. "We'll take this up later, hmm?"

Devlin nodded. "As you say. But I want it known that my intentions were honorable. And I also want Ella to know that I hold her in the highest esteem—and that what I know will never go farther."

"Bit late," Max said.

Saber eyed the boy.

Max thrust his hands into his pockets, rolled upon his toes and jiggled. "Just stating the truth. Wretched female visited earlier. Name of Able. Jabbering about rumors. Rumors about Ellie. She said they were all over Town. Talk of the *ton*."

"The devil you say," Devlin said. "She's got to be stopped."

"Ella's concerns are my affair," Saber told him quietly. "I don't know what you were thinking here, friend—really thinking—but—"

"He thought to help me," Ella said. "To save me because he believed you had decided you could not—could not. That you could not."

"He thought to marry you because I *could* not?" Saber held Devlin's gaze. "But I can. And I will. Just as soon as the arrangements can be made. And I do so with your family's blessings." At least with the dowager's blessings, but the rest would follow, of that Saber was certain.

Devlin set his lips together. He strode around them all and made his way rapidly from the house.

"Dash, that was splendid," Max said. "The two most eligible men in England fighting over you, Ellie!"

"There is only one man whose regard matters to me," she said. "And he chooses to make me happier than I had ever thought possible."

Rage had briefly banished dread. Now it returned. Happy? He would make her a bride, then a widow whose husband lived yet did not live. But he could not let her go again.

He would give her his name and his fortune. And he would watch over her—until the sickness claimed him forever. By then he must have made her his heir. As a rich woman in her own right she would be safe. And perhaps, God help him, she would ease his way to the end. Ella loved him, he must never stop believing she did.

"Saber? I will be a good wife to you. I will care for you always."

"Because I am an invalid? Because I am crazed?" The words were spoken and could not be recalled. He wrenched his arm from her. "You've got what you wanted, now leave me be."

"Saber!"

"I have matters to attend to." He left her and didn't look back.

"Saber, please!"

Damn his selfishness. His life was forfeit. Now, with his promise of "happiness," he condemned Ella to walk with him into hell.

* * *

"Follow me, Bigun," the dowager heard Blanche Bastible announce as she opened the door to the bedchamber. "Such a great deal of fuss. Lord Avenall's staff is upsetting this household entirely. Why there should be such commotion over a little thing like moving one man's possessions, I cannot imagine. It must cease before the dowager is reduced to complete collapse. But Her Grace will insist upon seeing you now. She is in bed, trying to rest. Do nothing to excite her."

The dowager made a hasty check of her beribboned nightcap and closed her eyes.

"Did you hear me, fellow?"

"Yes," Saber's odd servant said. "Oh, yes, dear lady, I hear you."

Blanche asked, "What is your country?"

The dowager contained an irritated puff.

"India, if it pleases you, my lady."

"India, hmm? Well, I particularly like your hat. I shall have my modiste make one like it for me. And regardless of the staff's opinion, I consider your red chair quite marvelous."

"Thank you, my lady."

From her vast and heavily carved mahogany bed draped with dark tapestries, the dowager decided it was time to make her presence known. "Out, Blanche," she said loudly. "Quickly. And do not strain your back listening at the door. Go directly to that foolish creature, Rose. Ella's maid. Tell her I should like to see her also." She opened an eye in time to see the Indian peer in her direction while Blanche flounced from the room.

"Come closer," the dowager told Bigun. "Be quick about it."

Bigun advanced cautiously, then appeared very much relieved. "The cross lady!" he said, beaming. "Cross and unpleasant. Your humors have made you sick, I see. It is often the way."

"Your Grace," she told him. "Kindly refer to me as Your Grace."

"Ah, yes. The old duchess—"

"Oh, what this family of mine brings me to. Disrespect. Reliance upon strangers. Come closer, I tell you."

Obligingly enough, the gaudily dressed servant went to the side of the bed. He peered at her. "How may I help you, lady?"

She scowled more fiercely. "I will not lose my temper!"

"Most wise."

"I wish to whisper to you. That fool Blanche is probably listening, even though I told her not to."

Bigun blinked and bent over her. "My attention is yours, lady. Your Grace."

With one small, bony hand, she caught him by the ear. She put her mouth next to that ear and murmured, "Good. This is what you will do."

Almost twenty-four hours had passed since Saber announced his intention to marry her. In the unlikely company of Margot, Countess Perruche, Ella rode in the Park. The countess had sent a message requesting that Ella join her, and Ella had been too curious to refuse.

Beneath skies the color of blue crystal, they trotted, side by side, along Rotten Row. Ella spared a sideways look for the countess, whose elegant black veil enhanced rather than hid her perfection.

Behind them on the crowded path trotted a groom who had come with the countess.

"I couldn't think of a safer place for us to talk," the countess said when they had been riding for some minutes. She inclined her head to a gentleman who rode toward them. He brought his crop to the brim of his hat in a smart salute. "I fear there may be some misunderstanding about my relationship to Saber. Under the circumstances, I'm sure you agree that we should make sure that is no longer the case."

Yet again she was in the company of someone whom Saber chose to take into his confidence on exceedingly personal matters. Ella had not seen him since he declared to Devlin his intention to marry her. He'd absented himself immediately and hadn't returned, yet he'd found time to seek out this woman's companionship.

"First, I must tell you how glad I am that you and Saber are to marry. He is a fine man and will make you a fine husband."

A fine man. The countess might try to sound dispassionate, but she cared for Saber. And Saber cared for her. Max had spoken of how natural it was for men of a certain class to maintain relationships with women other than their wives . . .

It did not have to be. Ella could not bear such a thought.

She studied the other woman's gray habit, the way it showed off a lush figure. How could she compete with a woman of such grace and experience?

"No engagement has been announced," Ella said. Sun through tall oaks painted a chiaroscuro across red earth churned by many hoofs.

The countess looked at Ella. "But it will be, surely?"

Ella spurred her gray to a less sedate pace. "Are these matters ever truly in the hands of women?"

"You are younger than I by far," the countess said, keeping up. "But I believe you are no less determined. Unless I much misjudge you, you are not a woman who will accept any fate thrust upon her."

The countess understood her quite well, Ella decided. "I think you remarkably brave to initiate this outing," she said. "In light of our last meeting."

"It is because of the last meeting that I asked you to join me today. There must be no misconception about my visit to Saber the other evening."

Ella looked straight ahead.

"I see I was indeed wise to seek you out. I am not, nor have I ever been, Saber's . . . When I refer to him as my friend, I mean that we are friends and nothing more. We have both known great trouble. I was also in India. That is where we met. There is a certain empathy between us—of a completely pure nature. I seem to sense when he is troubled. I sensed it the other evening and went to him. Evidently I was mistaken."

"You were not mistaken," Ella said, keeping her voice level. "He had suffered some sort of nightmare. And then there was the emotional event between us."

"Nightmare." The countess was not asking a question. "Ah, yes, the wretched nightmares."

"Did you know Saber is moving into the Pall Mall house?" Ella asked, raising her voice over the thud of their mounts' hoofs. "Bigun is already in residence—at least in the vestibule."

"How interesting. You seem determined not to address the subject of your betrothal."

"There is no betrothal." She did not intend to give any personal information to the woman who felt obliged to deny that she was Saber's mistress.

Mistress. Even the word stung Ella.

"Very well," Countess Perruche said. "You still do not trust me, do you?"

At least her flushed cheeks could be blamed on the wind. Ella pulled to the side of the trail to allow a yellow phaeton to overtake them. The occupant grinned at her as he passed. She noted how the man's grin became assessing, avid, and she looked away. The attentions of other men were unwelcome—men other than Saber.

"You are wrong, you know." Countess Perruche swerved to draw alongside Ella. "I am not his ladybird."

Ella ducked her head to hide a blush too brilliant to blame on any wind.

"I am not," the countess repeated. "What I have told you is true. We are friends. And because we are, I want to be your friend. I want to help you and Saber. But first, I must find a way to make you like me."

"One cannot *make* a person like one," Ella said, slowing down. She looked directly at the countess. "It is common knowledge that you and Saber are more than *friends*."

"It is common *gossip* that we are more than friends. And that gossip is a lie. If you will allow me, I will explain exactly how my acquaintance with Saber began. Then I think you will understand."

Ella took deep breaths and willed her heart to cease its hammering.

"We met in India. After he returned for a second visit."

"I already knew you met there."

"I was in terrible trouble. I had been duped into giving myself to a man who . . . He misused me terribly."

"I'm sorry," Ella murmured, casting a sympathetic glance at her companion.

The countess pulled up her mount.

Ella also stopped. She turned her gray around and trotted back to the other woman, who guided the chestnut she rode from the trail and into a patch of shade beyond the sweeping skirt of a willow tree.

The countess's groom stationed himself dutifully, just out of hearing distance.

"Are you feeling unwell?" Ella asked.

"I'm . . . I was never married," the other woman said, drawing in her lips. "I went through a wedding ceremony with Count Perruche, but we were not married."

Bewildered, Ella could think of no reply.

"You don't understand, do you?" the countess said bitterly. "We were not married because he was already married. He was a bigamist. He wanted me and knew I would not be his unless he married me."

"How dreadful," Ella whispered, alarmed at the countess's pallor. "Please do not feel you must continue."

"I want to!" The other woman glared at Ella. "You have judged me a bad woman for something I have not done. The *ton* judges me for the same invalid reason. The world would judge me a bad woman for something I did without knowing it."

"Do not overset yourself."

"Saber helped me. The count married me in Austria and took me back to India—where he had *another* wife to whom he was really married. I was to live in the same house with that poor woman and tolerate such behavior because if I revealed the truth, I would be cast out of polite society."

Ella was overcome with distress. "The count broke the law," she said indistinctly. "He could have been prosecuted."

"That would not alter the fact that I was a ruined woman in the eyes of all Europe. I had no choice but to be treated like a servant by that desperate, spurned woman and like a . . . And used by a man I had come to hate."

"Countess—"

"I had no money and nowhere to turn. Saber was invited to dine with the Perruches and, quite by chance, I encountered him on his own. He was still not at all well—just as he is not yet entirely well—and had gone to find solitude in the grounds of the house.

"I felt his goodness and I cast myself upon his mercy. He went to the count and told him he intended to pay for me to come to England. When the count protested, Saber warned him that unless he let me go, he would be unmasked as the villain he is."

Ella saw tears in the other's eyes and reached impulsively to touch her arm. "How very like Saber. He was very kind to me when I was a girl."

"As you say. How like Saber." Bitterness didn't become the countess. "Will you try to accept that I've told you the truth? It has cost me dearly. I am a woman without station, except a false one as the widow of a man to whom I was never married."

"You are a brave woman," Ella said staunchly. "Brave and dignified. Countess—"

"No. Margot, please." She found a small handkerchief and reached beneath her veil to blot at tears. "My name is Margot. Saber said I should continue to use that man's title to provide myself with some protection. Perruche will never dare to show his face here or on the Continent again, but I should like you to call me Margot."

Ella said, "Margot."

"And in case you think that my tragedy means I am more than Saber's indebted friend, I assure you that he is above taking advantage of such a debt. Also, much as I love Saber—as a friend—I would not ever wish to taint that friendly love with any other sort of liaison."

"No," Ella said. She believed her. "How do you live?"

"Not by Saber's generosity," Margot said, raising her chin. "Once I returned to Europe I contacted my father, who is glad to pay to keep me away from France. The money is mine anyway, from an inheritance made me by my mother. Papa lives in fear that I will return and shame him."

"I have known great unhappiness," Ella said simply. "I can feel yours. I can only pray that you will eventually find the joy you deserve."

Margot smiled. Sunlight caught the glitter of tears in her

thick, coppery eyelashes. "I am happy enough as I am. I have Saber and Devlin as friends. And now, I think, I have you. Am I correct?"

"Most certainly," Ella said, almost overcome with empathy and relief. "And I know my family will also be glad to welcome you."

"Do not be too sure." Margot's smile was wry. "We must pursue these changes slowly. Isn't that the man Saber has spoken of? Over there?"

Ella turned about and searched among the riders coming and going on the Row.

"Where?"

"On the bay. On the opposite side. He's looking at us. At you, I should say. He was at the Eagletons' that night."

Even as Margot spoke, Ella spied the Hon. Pom. Even at a distance she could not fail to feel his singular concentration upon her.

Pomeroy Wokingham spurred his horse to a trot and crossed the Row, incurring more than one oath from riders whose paths he entered.

"Good morning, lovely ladies," he called as he drew near.

Margot nodded.

Ella looked away.

"All alone? What's the world comin' to?"

"We're not alone," Margot said. "My groom accompanies us, Mr. er—"

"Pomeroy, Pomeroy," the Hon. Pom said, all too heartily, sweeping off his hat to reveal the sparse sand-colored hair he wore combed slickly over his shiny scalp. "Pomeroy to my friends, and certainly Ella regards me as a friend, don't y' know. How are we today, Ella?"

"I'm well, Mr. Wokingham," she said, wishing herself far away. "The countess is also well, I believe. As to you, well, I'm sure you know your own condition."

His left eye twitched. The stiffness of his smile suggested he retained it with difficulty. "I am also well, thank you," he said. "Nice of you to be concerned."

"We'd best get on," Margot said, making to return to the trail.

"Actually, I came down to look for Miss Rossmara," Pomeroy said, his tone becoming formal. "I called at Pall Mall and was told I might find her here."

Ella's stomach turned over, then repeated the process.

"A fine day for a ride, I thought. I'd intended to invite you to join me, Miss Rossmara."

"I already have company for the ride," Ella pointed out.

Pomeroy spared Margot a sweeping stare that took her in from head to toe and lingered at points in between. "Yes, well, no doubt the countess will understand if I take you away from her. Surprisin' that your family would permit you to be in the company of . . . Well, surprisin', that's all. You wouldn't understand, Miss Rossmara, but I'm sure the countess fully comprehends my meanin'."

"What are you suggesting?" Margot asked. She circled Pomeroy, causing him to turn in order to keep her in his sights.

He smiled, his thin lips drawing away from stained teeth. "No need to go into that here, madam. Ella and I have business to conduct. I'm sure you'll excuse us."

"And allow you to ride with a lady unchaperoned?" Margot said. "I hardly think that appropriate."

Ella could not seem to think at all. Her mind spun. He had gone to Pall Mall and been told he'd find her here? Who would tell him? Who would give him permission to follow her here?

"Come along my dear," he persisted, ignoring Margot. "No fault will be found with our keeping company in so public a setting. And there are things we must discuss. In private." He looked significantly at Margot.

Ella finally found her voice. "Countess Perruche and I are enjoying each other's company. Let us get on, Margot." She led the way back onto the Row.

Pomeroy contrived to bring his horse in front of hers. He narrowed his colorless eyes. "You would do well to do as you are told," he said, taking her breath away with his audacity. "I have already said that I come with blessings from Pall Mall."

"Pay him no heed," Margot said, but Ella noted that the other woman's voice trembled.

"There are incidents I'd like to help you recall," Pomeroy said to Ella. "Not that I imagine you can have forgotten them. Much as you might like to think you have."

Ella wound her reins tightly about her hands.

"But we shall speak of that soon enough. Good day to you, countess."

Incidents? Incidents she might like to think she'd forgotten? Ella envisioned scraps of red chiffon—and a letter filled with foul implications.

Pomeroy Wokingham?

"Come, Ella," he said, looking down his very long nose. "We have a great deal to talk about."

"We have nothing to talk about," she told him, breathless. "Good day to you, Mr. Wokingham."

The corners of his mouth jerked down. The Adam's apple in his thin neck bobbled. "Do as you are told." His voice had the quality of a gust through gravel. "You are in no position to be high and mighty, miss. It's time you accepted that. Any woman would be grateful for my attention. *You* should be overwhelmed at your good fortune."

Margot made a strangled sound.

"Must I speak of your shortcomings in front of others?"

"Go away," Ella said.

Rather than obey her wishes, Pomeroy put his horse between Ella and Margot's and said, "We'll be on our way. *Now*. I'm bloody tired of being told what to do and when to do it. Time a fella took matters into his own hands." He reached for Ella's reins.

"Hold up there, Ella!" a man's voice shouted. "Ella!"

A second voice called, "Ella and Margot!"

Ella looked over her shoulder and saw two men approaching at a gallop. One, mounted on a black, was unmistakably Saber, and her heart pushed toward her throat. She sucked in great gulps of air.

"If you know what's good for you, Mr. Wokingham," Margot said quietly, "you'll take yourself off. With all haste."

"The devil I will," Pomeroy said. His nostrils pinched and his lips turned white. "I've more right to be here than any other I see."

The second man raised a hand and Ella recognized Calum, Duke of Franchot, her mama's brother. Hatless, he had hair the same dark red as Lady Justine's, and eyes of a similar shade of amber smiled his pleasure at seeing Ella.

"If they discover you are pestering us," Margot said to Pomeroy, "this will not be pretty."

"Tell them you are otherwise engaged," Pomeroy said.

Ella gazed at him and knew a moment of the purest disgust she had ever felt. The man was a reckless oaf. "A reckless *oaf*," she told him. "Do you hear me? You are a reckless oaf who doesn't know he is about to be run off by two of the most powerful men in the kingdom."

"A sight I'd rather not witness," Margot muttered. "Blood sports have no place in Hyde Park."

The possibility of an unpleasant scene dawned on Ella the moment before Saber and Uncle Calum would have arrived. She glanced nervously from Pomeroy to the other two men.

Then Pomeroy's wild shout captured the attention of all in sight.

"Damn you!" he yelled, all but losing his seat. The bay had reared. One of Pomeroy's feet shot from its stirrup and the bay surged forward.

"Oh, my goodness," Ella said, quieting her own restless animal. "I called him a reckless oaf, but I had no idea . . ."

Calum pulled up at her left. Saber walked his black to the right of the gray.

Pomeroy's bay bucked once more and took off at a furious gallop. The instant before the pair rode around the bend and out of sight, the rider wrapped his arms around the animal's neck. Anguished curses floated on the pristine spring air.

"Did you indeed, young Ella?" Uncle Calum said.

She looked questioningly into his lean, exceedingly handsome face.

"Did you tell that bounder he's a reckless oaf?"

"Well, yes." She shrugged.

"Good," Uncle Calum said. "Our beloved Blanche confessed he'd been sniffing around Pall Mall, asking where you were. Said she'd told him you'd come here. Saber's been filling me in on the Hon. Pom. I remember his father."

"I'd rather forget both of them," Ella said.

"Let's hope he doesn't break his unpleasant neck," Calum said. "Can't imagine why his horse took off like that."

"No," Margot said. She studied the point of the pearl stickpin that had formerly secured her satin stock. "I think it was the rider's fault. He jumped and shouted so. Upset his mount evidently. I do believe a bee may have stung Pom's . . . Well, stung him in a rather vulnerable spot."

Chapter Twenty-two

Saber could scarcely bear the bright hope in Ella's eyes. She stood beside Grandmama's chair in the green salon at Pall Mall, and never stopped gazing at him.

"Such a fuss," Grandmama said, not for the first time that evening. "And that man of yours is a savage, Saber. Turbans and tunics and red chairs. The idea."

"Bigun rather likes you, although I can't imagine why." Sometimes baiting Grandmama was irresistible. Saber leaned back in his chair and stretched out his legs—and caught Ella's dark eyes once more. "Bigun is my right hand. I'd probably be dead without him. But that's not a subject we need to discuss here."

Ella smiled.

Saber could not take his eyes from hers, but he could not smile. "I wish you hadn't banished Blanche before I had time to remind her of her place, Grandmama," he said. "She had no right to send that vermin, Wokingham, after Ella in the Park."

Grandmama waved a hand. "Leave Blanche be. Doesn't always think. She means no harm."

"No more harm than a passing bee," Calum said.

Saber did grin then. Ella giggled.

"I fail to see why that comment is amusing," Grandmama said. "A bee often inflicts painful harm."

Calum leaned on the mantel, crossed one powerful leg over the other, and said, "Exactly as I suggested," with a completely straight face. "Ella, I'm to tell you that Pippa intends to take complete charge of this ball we're to give you."

Calum had already explained that he was on his way to Scotland to assist Arran and Struan, but that Pippa would be in London within a week.

When Saber first saw Calum, he'd thought to be relieved of the necessity to move into Pall Mall, but, as Calum seemed pleased to point out, Saber's presence would continue to be required for the ladies.

"Pippa and I want this to be an occasion to remember," Calum said, winking at Ella. "We met at a ball, y'know."

"We all know," Saber said.

"I do like Margot," Ella said. Her lips curved softly in Saber's direction. "I'm very glad she thought to seek me out. I believe we shall become fast friends."

The idea pleased Saber too. Margot could use more friends, particularly any who could ease her way in Society. "She's a charming lady," he remarked. "And brave."

"Margot who?" the dowager asked.

"Countess Perruche, Great-Grandmama," Ella told her, resting a hand on the old lady's shoulder. "She's delightful and very sensible. I know you will like her. She shall come to my ball, of course."

"Of course," Calum said expansively. "You shall invite anyone you please."

"And a great many more she neither pleases to have nor knows at all," Grandmama said, sniffing. "Everyone shall come. Everyone who *is* anyone."

"Aha," Calum said, propping his chin. "The famous people who are someone. How well I recall the days when I was not considered to be anyone, as you put it, Grandmama."

"Calum," the dowager duchess said sharply. "There are things best left forgotten. How could I be expected to know you were someone when I thought you were someone entirely different? . . . That is, when I thought that rogue Etienne was you and you were . . . ? Oh, you dratted boy, you revel in toying with a poor old woman."

Saber and Calum exploded into laughter and Ella pressed a hand over her grin.

The dowager gave a small smile. "You will not allow me the small considerations of the aged, will you?"

"No!" Calum and Saber said in unison.

Calum added, "You have the wit of a statesman. Would that you were a man. I should promptly put you forward to straighten out the mess in this country. A fine prime minister you'd make, Grandmama."

She lowered her eyelids and waved a hand at him. "Don't try to win me with flattery, my boy."

"Flattery?" Saber said. "You are a marvel and you know it."

"A marvel," Ella agreed. She wrapped her arms around her middle and strolled—apparently idly—across the room, tapping out the hem of her skirt with each step.

Soft gathers crisscrossed the bodice of her celestial blue tulle gown, drawing the eye to her breasts. Fleetingly, Saber's gaze settled there, on narrow lace that rested against the suggestion of full flesh above the neckline. A belt of woven gold studded with sapphires surrounded her waist. This gift he had sent yesterday, openly, and she had thanked him with sweet reticence. When he'd held the belt, he'd imagined it touching her—imagined his hands about her waist instead.

He would marry her.

He would marry and bed her.

When next he lay with her, there need be no drawing back. He tensed the muscles in his thighs. The memory of the weight of her breasts in his hands stiffened his rod to bursting.

Saber sat up abruptly.

His rod would slip into her soft moistness while he held her breasts and looked into her black eyes.

He remembered to breathe.

Each time Ella moved, her skirts rustled. He heard the sibilant whisper of fine fabric against her legs. Her slim ankles showed in brief flashes with every step.

The slightest instruction on his part as she lay beneath him and she would wrap her legs around him, cross her ankles behind his waist, raise her hips to open herself to him.

He stood up and strode to the windows.

"Moon fascinating you, is it?" Calum asked.

Saber didn't miss the amusement in the other man's voice. "Fascinating, indeed. Always did enjoy a good moon."

"There isn't one," Grandmama said. "What's the matter with you, Saber? You haven't been yourself since you finally decided to put in an appearance again."

He raised his eyes to the dark sky, a sky devoid of moon or stars, and felt the beginning of the darkness in his own soul.

"It's been a long day," he said. Facing people in daylight in the Park—tolerating their stares—had cost him dearly. "I think I'll excuse myself if you don't mind. No doubt you're tired, too, Calum. Journey and all that, hmm?"

"Don't let me keep you up" was Calum's response. "Grandmama and I have some catching up to do. I rely on her to keep my head level on estate matters."

The dowager actually made a gratified sound. "Are your quarters to your liking, Saber?"

He grunted, and continued to stare at the night sky until he felt Ella join him. She stood close enough for her shoulder to touch his arm.

"I understand you chose to take rooms at the very top of the house. Those rooms haven't been used in years," the dowager said. "Off on your own. Can't imagine why. Harder on the servants."

"Bigun will be the only one to attend me," Saber said. He couldn't risk alarming anyone with some irrepressible outburst.

"I'm glad you are to be here," Ella said softly. "I didn't think I should be, but I am."

"Why wouldn't you want me here? I thought—"

"I thought you didn't want to be here. I was mortified at the prospect of your being forced to come because of me."

He *was* forced to come because of Ella. "We shall have decisions to make shortly."

"Yes."

"I think we should marry without delay."

She didn't respond.

Behind them, Calum and Grandmama carried on a spirited conversation about who was or was not *anyone*.

Saber looked down at Ella. "Does that prospect displease you? Marrying soon?" He found he wished to hurry, for his sake as well as hers. Since yesterday he'd become obsessed with binding her to him. Only a fool would believe he'd be able to hide his deteriorating condition from her forever, but his heart told him that when she did know, Ella would defend rather than abandon him. She might very well help him keep his secret from a world that would surely want to lock him away if the truth became public. As long as his attacks remained confined to the night, making certain he remained in his bedchamber . . . Oh, God help him. Let him do what was right, for everyone, but especially for Ella.

"Whatever you want pleases me," she said at last. "I would marry you tonight, if that would make you happy."

He turned back to the pressing blackness outside.

"But it doesn't make you happy, does it?" she continued. "You are marrying me because you believe you ought to, not because you . . ." She stopped speaking and swallowed.

Blindly, he sought her hand and pulled it beneath his arm. "I have already told you that I love you. There are things you do not know about me and I'd hoped you never would."

"But if we are to be married we must have no secrets," she murmured. "What are these things?"

He'd already said too much, much more than he'd intended—yet. "Are you sure you love me, Ella?"

Her fingers tightened on his arm. "Yes, oh, yes, Saber. I have loved you from the moment I first saw you."

Saber closed his eyes. "And I have loved you. When you were a child I told myself I must wait, and that I could wait because I could do anything if I should eventually claim you for my own."

"And that wretched war almost took you from me." Her voice broke. "I thank God you were returned."

He laughed shortly. "Returned. How appropriate. Rather like a parcel. I was returned, but damaged en route."

"Not to me," she assured him. "To me you are as ever you were."

"And you"—he inclined his head to study her—"you have only become more beautiful. In your heart as well as in your beautiful body. There is no part of you that does not make me long to bear you away."

She blushed. Saber adored Ella's blushes. "Does Calum know what's been happening?" she asked. "About the chiffon? And—and the letter?"

"Struan had already written to him about the chiffon. I

think it better that we not share the contents of the letter if we don't have to."

Ella felt giddy with relief. "I should rather no one else need ever know about it." Her fingers traveled down to entwine with his. "What did he say about the chiffon?"

"That we shall discover this creature and deal with him."

"I have wondered about Pomeroy Wokingham," Ella said. "He has made certain unpleasant suggestions."

"The man is besotted with you. Justly so."

She didn't appear reassured, even by his little compliment. "He referred to my past. He said he *knew* things about me and that I'd best accompany him wherever it was he wanted to take me. There was a threat there, I know there was."

"The younger Wokingham is no more than a puffed-up popinjay. He may have got wind of something mysterious concerning you, but I don't think he's our man. If he'd written that letter, he wouldn't show his hand by approaching you direct. I believe that if he knows anything at all of substance it's no more than the fact that you were adopted by Struan and Justine. He may have tried to find out about your parentage and discovered nothing. There is nothing to be discovered. But that wouldn't stop him from deciding to make evil trade upon unsubstantiated innuendo—just to force you to grant him your company."

"I hate him."

"Forget him. He is no threat."

The shadows in her dark eyes suggested she wasn't comforted. "What does Uncle Calum say about our being married?"

"That he approves. In fact, he is delighted. He will present my offer to Struan in Scotland."

"I see." If Ella was delighted, she disguised her enthusiasm well.

He brought their hands to his mouth and kissed her fingertips—and felt a tremor pass through her. "You are passionate, my Ella."

"Hush." She colored again. "We shall be overheard."

"Passionate, but not overwhelmed with joy at the prospect of our wedding."

Her grip tightened until he frowned and glanced at her face. "What is it?"

"I should like to show you how overwhelmed I am."

Saber raised an eyebrow in question.

"Tonight, if that will please you."

She could not mean what he thought she meant. "Would you care to explain that to me?"

"May I come to you?"

She meant exactly what he'd surmised.

"May I?"

"I hardly think—"

"I do. You say there are things I don't know about you. I wish to learn. At once. Rose sleeps too far away to know if I leave my rooms. As you see, Max is involved in who-knows-what, but elsewhere. Why should I not be with you tonight?"

She took his breath away. Saber found he could not restrain himself from looking at her lips, at her neck and breasts. "A lady does not share a man's bed until they are married."

"I have all but shared your bed already. For short periods of time, it's true. I wish to rest with you, to hold you in my arms and have you hold me. I want to stay with you all night."

"My God," Saber breathed. "You are a temptress, Ella."

"Then I may come to you?"

"*Keep* your voice down."

"I feel a darkness in you, Saber. A struggle."

He stiffened.

"There," she said. "It's there again. *They* are there again."

"They?" Sweat broke out on his back. "What do you speak of?"

"Please don't pull away from me. Trust me, Saber. You harbor some devils. The night when I was so foolish as to surprise you, you attacked."

"Because—"

"Because you thought I was come to attack you. You did not know who I was and you expected me to be an enemy."

"Ella—"

"And you once came to me in a trance. Did you think I didn't know your condition, my love? When Papa and Great-Grandmama left me alone at your house, you came to me with that dagger upraised and you were not yourself. When you first entered that room, you did not know who I was. On that occasion, as on the other, it was my cry that stopped you."

He rubbed at his brow. "We'd best say good night, Ella."

"You are ill, aren't you?"

Saber withdrew his hand from hers. "Don't presume to speak about matters that are beyond your comprehension."

"I would rather comprehend," she told him. "So I shall come to you tonight and learn the cause of this darkness of yours—this affliction."

"I have no affliction!" The others would hear, but he no longer cared. He turned from Ella and walked swiftly across the room. "I shall bid you all a good night. Kindly warn the staff that the doors to my rooms will be kept locked. A habit from living abroad among strangers."

"We are hardly strangers," Grandmama said.

"Nevertheless, it's my preference. I prefer that no one disturb me. Privacy is of the utmost importance to me. Good night to you all." He made certain Ella—who appeared stricken—understood his implication.

"Hah!" Grandmama rose to her feet. "No doubt you will be glad enough to allow your bride into whatever *private* sanctum you decide to share with her."

Saber opened the door.

"I think your ball for Ella would be a perfect time to announce the betrothal," the old lady told Calum. "The sooner we get on with this, the better."

"No!" Saber spun to face them. "No. Under no circumstances will you announce a betrothal at the ball."

He heard Ella's small cry of distress but did not as much as glance in her direction.

"Would you care to explain your reluctance, old chap?" Calum said. He watched Saber narrowly. "Other than some perfectly appropriate desire to have Struan and Justine present."

"That is exactly the reason," he lied. He could not tell them that when Ella spoke of his "darkness" he doubted his decision to marry her at all.

Ella could not sleep. She'd opened the casement and sat upon the window seat where she could allow the night breeze to cool her skin.

For all Saber's declarations of ardor, he was still uncertain he wanted her to be his wife.

She knelt and crossed her arms on the sill. Somewhere an owl screeched. The scents were of stocks and sweet williams, and the other flowers massed for cutting in the kitchen gardens.

Somewhere above her Saber slept.

Ella sighed. Each time she thought of him, the most extraordinary sensations tingled in her breasts and ached deep in her belly, and almost pinched in the unmentionable—the unnameable—place between her thighs. Saber had touched all of those places and elicited the very feelings she longed to feel again.

And he wanted his own feelings. She just knew he did.

Mama's book.

That was it. She would obtain a copy of Mama's book and read all the things she'd been told she must not read until she was to be married.

She *was* to be married. Most certainly she must read the book. Then she would understand what made Saber act so strangely. And she would know exactly what to do when . . . when they . . . She'd know what to do when they did *It*. There was definitely an *It* that was beyond all they had experienced together already.

Oh, the breeze was so sweet. The thought that there was more than they had already experienced seemed incredible, yet there was that . . . that . . . There had been an insistent something deep inside her. And why would Saber's manhood grow so large and hard, just for the sake of growing large and hard?

No. No, she would not continue without discovering the truth of it all, and Mama *knew*. Everyone said her book was innovative and enlightening, and it was time for Ella to become enlightened. She had seen naked bodies cavorting at . . .

Enough of such thoughts.

A light tap came at the door.

She grew absolutely still.

Saber had come to her. Ella's heart leaped. Her throat dried.

With a whine, the door opened a little. "Ellie? Ellie, are you asleep?"

She slumped and rested her head on her arms. "Max, what are you doing creeping around in the night? Go away."

Rather than go away, he entered and closed himself inside. "This is really important, Ellie. I've just been having a chat with Bigun, and I came to you direct."

"Bigun?" She turned to sit on the seat. "Come here. What are you talking about, having a chat with Bigun? It's the middle of the night."

"He caught me."

Ella peered through the gloom at her brother. "Explain yourself."

He sat beside her. "Nothing to get overset about, our Ellie. I'd popped out to try my hand at a few cards. Bigun was in his damnable chair when I tried to make my way upstairs."

"*Cards?* Oh, Max. You're only fifteen. Where have you been?"

He shrugged and hung his head.

"Tell me at once."

"White's is incredible, Ellie. A man feels like a man at White's. Too bad old Beau Brummell no longer sits in his window. Should have liked to see that, I can tell you."

"White's?" Ella whispered. "*White's?* You've been gambling at White's?"

"Any club good enough for the cream of Society is good enough for me. I have a certain eye—a certain *second sense* when it comes to games of chance. Faro is a particular favorite of mine. I have that *dramatic* flair required to play with the required command."

Ella cringed and drew her knees up beneath her night gown. "Gambling." She shook her head. "At White's. What did you use for money?"

He shrugged.

"Answer me, Max. At once."

"Oh, all right. I didn't," he finished under his breath.

"You didn't gamble?"

"I didn't get into White's. But only because I didn't like the way the porter spoke to me. Told him off, I can tell you. Told him I had better places to be than his club anyway."

"You are a trial," Ella said, weak with relief. "You tried to get into the best club in London and failed. You had no right to sneak out of this house in the middle of the night and make a cake of yourself. You should be returned to Eton at once."

"I'm not strong enough yet."

"Fie! There is nothing wrong with you but your mischief. But no matter. What is all this about Bigun? I expect he told you off."

"He told me he was on his way to deliver a message to you. I offered to do it for him."

Ella peered at him. "A message? At this time of night?"

"I merely said I would bring it. I cannot be expected to understand why it was sent so late. But I'll gladly take it away, if you prefer."

"You vexing boy!" Ella presented a hand. "Give it to me at once. And light a lamp, if you please."

Max did as he was asked and brought the lamp close enough for Ella to read her note:

"Ella," it began. *"We are in need of time together. I wish to court you as you should be courted at such a time. Please accompany me to the theater this evening—"*

Ella looked up. "Obviously Bigun was supposed to deliver it in the morning. The lazy man decided to save himself a task."

"What does it say?" Max asked.

Excitement made Ella's hands shake. "Saber wishes me to accompany him to the theater this evening."

"Which theater?" Max asked with audible envy.

"Drury Lane," Ella told him, too happy to think. "He thinks I will enjoy seeing how beautiful the building is now. Oh, Max, he is becoming his true self again. I knew he would."

She slept somewhere below him.

If he hadn't been such a fool, she'd be beside him now.

Bigun rapped the door lightly and entered. "My lord?"

"Who else should I be?" Saber asked irritably.

"As you say." Bigun was his usual imperturbable self. "I will prepare a relaxing draft for you."

Saber made no protest.

Brown liquid gurgled from Bigun's ubiquitous bottle into a goblet. "Pleasant night, is it not, my lord?"

"Pleasant?"

"Not too cold. Not too warm. A certain *snap* in the air, as the English like to say."

"Really? I hadn't noticed." All he'd been aware of was that he could actually feel Ella's presence under the same roof.

"Well, then," Bigun said, setting the goblet on the chest beside Saber. "There is a note here, also, my lord. You won't want to bother with it until morning, but I'll leave it anyway."

Saber watched Bigun place something white upon the chest. "Note? What note, Bigun? From whom?"

"My lord, you are not to concern yourself with it now. Respectfully, of course, I suggest that you take your potion and sleep."

"I asked you a bloody question!"

"You are overwrought." As he shook his head, Bigun's gold turban caught flickers of firelight. "Rose was going to bring the note in the morning. I said I would save her the journey up so many stairs. I should not have brought it in until you awoke."

"Rose?" Saber pushed himself up against the pillows. "Is that Miss Rossmara's maid?"

"It is indeed, my lord. A most excellent maid, too, if I may remark on it. Modest and, unless I am much mistaken, very shy. She does not like to converse. But—"

"Miss Rossmara's maid gave you a note to give to me. From Miss Rossmara, I presume?"

"That would seem—"

"The lamp." Saber snatched up the envelope Bigun had placed beside the goblet.

Bigun lighted the lamp and stood by, sighing as if greatly burdened.

Saber pulled out a sheet of paper and read the few lines of writing it contained. "I'm damned," he muttered.

"Bad news?"

"I'm *damned*."

"Oh, my lord! It *is* bad news. I should have waited—"

"Thank you for bringing this, Bigun," Saber said. "Nothing to be concerned about, I assure you. Quite the reverse. I won't be requiring anything further. Good night to you."

Bigun bowed and said, "Good night to you, my lord," as he retreated and left Saber alone.

Saber read the note again. The lady had spirit and ingenuity—but then, hadn't those been two of the qualities that had drawn him to her?

"Saber," her note read. *"You always knew what was best, and how best to accomplish it. Of course we need more time together. Going to Drury Lane this evening will be wonderful. I should very much enjoy seeing a performance by Edmund Kean's son. Thank you."*

"Drury Lane and Charles Kean it shall be." He chuckled. *Ella, Ella, Ella!*

Chapter Twenty-three

"It's ever so romantic," Rose said. She put the finishing touches to strands of pearls threaded through Ella's arcade of braids. "They say 'is lordship is so . . . 'E's so *sad*, somehow. No, not sad, but broodin'. A bit like that Lord Byron was when he was first about 'ere in London, they say. Only Lord Avenall's much more 'andsome."

"Yes, Rose," Ella said, too excited to consider an appropriate answer.

"It's a shame as how they did . . . When Lord Avenall was in India. Well, I 'aven't seen it for meself, mind you, but they say 'is face—"

"His lordship has a scar on his face." A scar that had already become part of him to Ella. There was nothing about Saber that she did not love. "It is insignificant. Certainly it is nothing to be gossiped about belowstairs, Rose."

Rose lowered her eyes and bobbed. "No, miss. I'm sorry, miss."

Ella hunched her shoulders and shivered with anticipation.

"You need not be sorry at all, Rose. I think this is all very romantic, too."

"You love 'im, don't you?"

She ought to refuse any answer.

"Oh, there I go again," Rose said, puffing. "I always did say whatever I thought. Gets me into more trouble, I can tell you."

"I do love him," Ella said. "And I have always admired impulsiveness when it was without malice. You are much appreciated, Rose. Now, tell me, how does all this frippery look?"

"Just a minute." Rose untangled the two pearl tassels that lay against Ella's sleek, black hair. "Up you get and we'll 'ave a good look."

Ella stood up and held out her arms. Rose draped a shawl of black silk painted with clusters of violets the same shade as Ella's crepe dress. Pearls edged a wide lace ruffle from shoulder to shoulder at the neck of her bodice, and around the full skirt's hem.

Rose stood back and sighed. "You look a treat, miss." She straightened Ella's black ribbon belt. "Ever so lovely."

"I feel . . . as if I'm going to pop! Isn't that silly?"

"No, miss. I feel as if I'm going to pop too!"

They laughed, and Rose ran to answer a knock at the sitting-room door.

Crabley, red-faced from his climb, glowered at Rose. "The carriage is here for Miss Ella," he said. "I can't even trust a member of this household staff with a simple message. Might as well do everything myself."

"Crabley?" Ella hurried into the sitting room. "The carriage is early. Is his lordship waiting for me? Oh, dear, I do hate to keep anyone waiting." Thank goodness she was ready.

"His Lordship's been detained on business elsewhere. He's sent a carriage."

"But—"

"He'll be at the theater to meet you."

"Oh." Being disappointed over a little change in plans was foolish. "Very well, then."

Rose ran behind, plucking at Ella's skirts and tugging the shawl a little this way or a little that way, until they reached the carriage. Then she stood beside Crabley on the flagway and waved.

What a day this had been. Lonely, and bubbling with frantic excitement at the same time.

Max, the wretch, had actually feigned feverishness and managed to elicit sympathy from Blanche Bastible, who liked Max as much as she disliked Ella—or any female for that matter, save Great-Grandmama.

And Great-Grandmama had taken to her bed again, evidently angry with Saber for his abrupt departure to his rooms the previous evening. She would, she'd let it be known, reappear when suitably mollified.

Uncle Calum had left for Scotland before first light and Ella hadn't caught as much as a glimpse of Saber all day.

As the coach rolled noisily over cobbles, Ella watched the buildings they passed. Nightfall was almost upon the scene and a purple blush across the rooftops made the sun's final bow.

Ella did not even know how long it might take to get to Drury Lane.

But Saber would be there.

The coach made great speed. Ella clung to the edge of the seat. Outside the windows, daylight failed entirely, replaced by a dusky, smoke-laced haze. A wide swing around a corner brought narrower streets into view.

Those people Ella saw with the aid of streetlamps appeared more meanly dressed. Impressive buildings gave way to less splendid structures, then to narrow, crowded dwellings above businesses with shuttered windows.

The coachman had taken a wrong direction! Ella stared

from the windows, but could scarcely make out anything between the streetlamps now. Definitely the wrong direction.

She attempted to rise and knock for the coachman's attention, but was promptly thrown back into her seat by another reckless turn.

Her heart thumped so hard, she heard its beat in her ears.

"It will be all right," she said loudly. Sometimes, as a child, she'd found that speaking in a large voice drowned out the fears inside her head. "I don't know the way to Drury Lane. But Saber will be there. Saber will be there!"

The wheels clattered and the coach bounced. Each abrupt tip of the carriage flung Ella to the right or to the left. Her reticule shot from her lap and slid beneath the seat opposite.

"Saber!" she cried.

No, this was not right. This was wrong. Something was wrong.

The coach slowed as unexpectedly as it had speeded up. Ella's back pressed into the squabs. Squealing, the brakes took hold and the wheels ground more slowly. A great clatter of hoofs sounded, and the whinny and snort of the horses.

"Whoa!" The coachman's voice rose above the rattle of tack.

Ella pressed her hands over her ears, closed her eyes, and waited until all movement ceased. She would have a thing or two to say to the driver.

"Out you come, then." The door swung open. " 'Urry up. Can't 'ang around."

"How *dare* you?" Ella was forced to sink to her knees and scrabble beneath a dusty seat for her reticule. "You drove wildly. Lord Avenall shall hear of this."

"Whatever you say, miss. Right now I want you out of my coach so's I can be on me way."

Trembling, brushing at her skirts, Ella emerged from the

carriage to confront a taciturn man who handed her down none too carefully.

He slapped the steps away and slammed the door. "Right then. 'Ere you are, safe and sound."

"Safe—" Ella avoided scanning her surroundings. She knew what she felt here. Danger. "This isn't right. I'm supposed to be met by Lord Avenall. You should have taken me to Drury Lane."

"I follows orders," the man said, rubbing the back of a sleeve over his brow. "You're Ella, ain't you?"

She ignored his impertinence. "Yes."

"Then this is where you was supposed to come."

Ella breathed slowly and made herself look about.

Two lighted bay windows set apart by a gilded front door. A bronze cat on each side of that door.

"Take me away from here," Ella said weakly.

Even as she spoke, she heard the coach move on.

A sign in one of the windows read: *THE PERFECT SIZE AND SHAPE FOR EVERY GENTLEMAN. OUR LADY TAILORS FIT TO YOUR DEMANDS. WE WELCOME THE MOST SINGULAR DESIGNS. NO REQUEST DENIED.*

"No!" Ella whirled around—and confronted a gathering ring of ragged, begging urchins with outstretched hands. "Saber!"

Surrounded by the chanting children, she swung back toward the building. Women sat in the rosily lighted windows. Each female appeared engrossed in her sewing.

"No! No! No!"

The gilded door opened. A stooped, white-haired man came to Ella and took her wrist in a clawlike grip. "Welcome, Ella," he said. "I've been looking forward to this. You've been missed, my dear. Welcome back to Mrs. Lushbottam's."

The satisfied set of Grandmama's face amused Saber. "A small glass of sherry, perhaps?" he suggested. "Since it seems we are destined to wait a little longer for our vision to appear."

"Just a small one," Grandmama said. A message delivered to her bedchamber, informing her that Saber and Ella would be at the theater this evening, had brought her downstairs to the green salon in remarkably short order. "I must say that I'm gratified by your decision to be sensible, Saber. Not that it's anything less than I expect of a grandson of mine."

"Sensible?" he asked innocently, bringing her the sherry.

"Deciding to do the expected thing. Taking the girl about a bit. Courting her a bit." She sipped. "Always knew this was the right thing, y'know. You and Ella."

"Really?" What would the old lady say if he told her it had been Ella, rather than himself, who had been "sensible" enough to set the wheels of conventional courtship in motion?

Saber glanced at his watch. "Don't suppose you could explain to me why females take so damnably long to dress?"

"Kindly refrain from cursing in my presence."

He grinned.

"You are a disrespectful whelp," Grandmama said, not quite hiding her own smile. "A female requires time to make certain everything is just so. Unless I am very much mistaken, dear Ella will make our wait very much worthwhile."

A missed heartbeat suggested Grandmama was anything but mistaken. But they were in danger of missing the opening curtain.

Max strolled in and pulled up at the sight of Saber. "Thought you'd gone to the theater."

"I will be going to the theater," Saber told him. "Just as soon as your sister puts in an appearance."

"She's gone."

Saber frowned.

"Well"—Max turned away, then back—"I was just at her rooms. Rose said Ella had left."

"Stand still, boy!" Grandmama demanded. "And speak sensibly. Ella cannot possibly have gone anywhere. She will be leaving with Saber and, as you see, Saber is still here."

"Crabley!" Max's sudden shout rang through the house. "Crabley!"

The butler appeared almost immediately. "You *called*?" he said to Max.

"Ellie. My sister." Max's face had paled. "Where is she? Did she leave?"

Crabley's round black eyes darted past Max to Saber. His face worked before he said, "Lord Avenall? Oh my. Oh dear."

"In God's name, man," Saber said, striding toward him. "What's going on here?"

"You sent a carriage for Miss Ella, my lord. Because you . . . The coachman said you'd sent him because you were detained on business and that you'd be at the theater to meet Miss Ella. She went with him. More than an hour since."

She'd never expected to see Uncle Milo again. When her mother died he made no attempt to contact her, although he'd known where she was at that time and finding her would have been simple enough.

"I expect this feels like coming home," he said, when they'd passed through a vestibule carpeted with the big pink roses and lattices Ella had hoped never to see again. "Not quite as elegant as you'll remember it, but times were . . . Well, they were *difficult* for a while after I took the place over from Mrs. Lushbottam."

At last Ella managed to speak. "That . . . I thought this place would be gone."

"No, no, no. Lushbottam owed your mother and me. All came out afterwards. This was the only asset, so it came to me. But I've had hard times. Oh, yes, very hard times. Come in here and sit down, my dear. I can't tell you how relieved I am to see you."

The past curved forward. All that had been, all that Ella had tried to forget, blossomed around her. She walked without feeling her limbs move, entered the sitting room that had been Lushbottam's without feeling herself pass from the vestibule.

"Right here," Uncle Milo said, his thin fingers digging into her arm. "You sit here and I'll tell you what we're going to do."

She all but stumbled backward into a chair covered with roses of a different variety from those on the floor.

The door slammed shut.

"Now." Uncle Milo faced her. The years since she'd last seen him had brought little change. He might be even more stooped and his ragged eyebrows might jut more ferociously over his still bright-blue eyes, but he was the man who had always been at her mother's side.

"Why are you in this place?" Ella asked, disliking the faint sound of her voice.

He rubbed his hollow face. "Instead of roaming the fairs in a wagon? Mystical Healer? Detector of Ills? Bearer of Forgotten Powers? Needed your mother for that, girl. Never was much for mixing up whatever went into those bottles we sold. Anyway, time comes to settle down. You know that. By all accounts you found yourself a comfortable arrangement."

"What do you want?" Ella said. Her throat was so dry, it burned. "Why have you done this?"

"*Done?* What d'you mean, *done*? I haven't done anything but bring someone I've missed to visit me."

Ella's mind began to clear. "How did you know—about this evening? How did you know I would expect to go out in a carriage? You did know, of course. And you took advantage of the opportunity to snatch me away."

"Oh, come, come, now. I didn't 'snatch you away.' It was

only that I happened to hear something about your plans for the evening. I didn't think you'd mind a little change in the name of family feelings."

Family feelings? "I'd like to leave now, please."

He shook his head. "You wound me, Ella, really you do. I come to you in distress and you don't even want to talk to me."

"You didn't come to me . . ." What did it all mean? "Let me go."

"In good time. I'm in a very bad position, Ella, very bad. I need you. And I know you'll want to help out in any way you can. For old times' sake."

She made to get up, but he pushed her back. The smile was gone now. "Did you hear me, miss? I need money and I know you'll want to help me. In your dear departed mother's name."

Ella struggled to order her thoughts. Someone had found out she was to go to the theater with Saber, someone . . . someone who knew about her ties to this horrible place. That person had arranged to intervene and have her brought here. But who? *Who?*

"You'll do as I ask," Uncle Milo said. "Then we'll all get on with things as they were and forget this little piece of business."

"What can I possibly do to help you?" Ella said, evading his hand and getting to her feet. When he reached for her, she stepped back. "Kindly do not touch me. I can listen as well standing as sitting."

"Oh, we have become a lady, haven't we? At least on the outside. We do know what you are on the inside, don't we?"

Ella held herself erect.

"Daughter of a whore." His eyes flickered. "A woman who sold her body to any man willing to pay the price of using it."

"How could you?" Disgust made Ella cold, but blessedly

unafraid. "My mother was your sister. She is dead. You will not speak ill of her to me."

"Such a lady." Uncle Milo shook his head. "We'll just have to get through our business and let you go back to primping and pretending, won't we?"

"I'm late for an appointment," Ella said. *Nothing*. This was the nothing she had come from, and from which she could never be entirely free.

"I know all about your appointment," Milo said. "But never mind that. I'll put this to you simply. I've got a customer who's willing to pay a great deal for some of your time."

Ella squinted at him. "I don't understand."

"Don't you? Oh, I think you probably do if you think about it. After all, if it was good enough for your mother—when she needed to help out—then it's good enough for you. What you've got to offer isn't any different from what she had. Younger, that's all. And probably prettier. Who knows why this customer wants you rather than anything else I've got to offer, but he does."

"Who is this—this person?"

"You'll find out soon enough."

"Let me go!" Ella moved toward the door. Milo hobbled to bar her way. "I don't have any idea what you can be asking of me. I do know you're insulting my mother's memory. I hate you for that. I'm going home now. You may expect to be called to reckoning for this."

"Called to reckoning." Milo mimicked her. "I don't think so, my lovely girl. You just listen to what I've got to say. Then we'll understand each other and everything will go much better."

"I won't listen."

He approached until his face was only inches from hers. "If you want to continue with this lovely life you're pretending you've got a right to—you'll listen. Understand?"

She crossed her shawl tightly over her breasts.

"That's better. The customer wanted me to tell you that you'd better remember how easy it was to take you away from your *family* tonight. And it's going to happen again."

"No!"

"It's going to happen again," Milo repeated. "But if you play the game quietly—and generously—you'll only be borrowed now and again."

"Borrowed?" Ella clutched at her throat. She would be sick.

"Borrowed for a few games. That's what was said. And in return I'll be free of any worry about money. Seems fair enough, doesn't it?"

"You are nothing to me," Ella said. How would she get away from here? "Do you hear me? Nothing."

"I'm wounded," Milo said. "But I'll get over it. My customer will borrow you—just occasionally. And he'll always send you back—unless you disobey him."

"This is beyond all!"

"You must never give yourself to any man—unless you're told you can. Do you understand that? It means you mustn't spread your legs for anyone who isn't paying me for the privilege. Think of it as family loyalty—loyalty to your *real* family."

Ella looked into the cold eyes of the man she'd once thought of as her only male relative, and knew desolation.

"I see you understand me very well," he said. "That's a good girl. If you did allow a man to claim you, we'd have to take steps to make sure he didn't want you afterwards. Anyway, I'll send you back to your fancy house now. All you've got to do is remember what you've been told—and be ready to oblige my customer." He opened the door to the curious faces of several women wearing few clothes.

Throbbing with embarrassment and fear, Ella turned her head away.

"Blushing flower we've got here, ladies," Milo said. A round of raucous laughter followed. "Yvette, give the coachman the word, there's a good girl. Outside the back door."

"And what if I refuse?" Ella said without looking at him.

"My customer's already thought of that. If you resist, then we'll have to think of some different way to deal with you. I was told to tell you to think about that."

The horses were being brought around.

"I should never have interfered," Grandmama said. "I shall never forgive myself if something has happened to Ella."

Saber's eyes met Devlin's. What else could they think, other than that something had happened to Ella?

"Where shall you look?" Margot asked. She had been at Devlin's when Bigun went to ask his help in searching. "Surely the staff here knows *something*. Ask them who they spoke to."

"My fault," Grandmama muttered. "I only thought to give the two of you time together. Doing ordinary things expected of a courting couple. But I should not have written those notes."

Saber pressed his lips together.

"It was my fault too," the little maid, Rose, said in a quivering voice. "But I thought it was ever so romantic to help two people who love each other."

"You merely did as you were told, you foolish girl." Grandmama's snap returned.

Bigun and Max were helping with the horses. Later there would be time to discuss what exactly Bigun had thought he was helping by delivering forged notes.

The man in question rushed into the room. "Ready, my

lord—Mr. North. Max is with the horses. Crabley also insists upon accompanying you, and of course I shall—"

"You shall, indeed," Saber said, pulling on his gloves. "Margot, I should much appreciate your keeping company with my grandmother."

"I can ride, Saber," she said, moving toward him. "Let me search too. I should feel so much more useful."

"No—"

"I'll take care of Her Grace," Blanche Bastible said. She'd been utterly silent since she entered the room amid the uproar following the discovery that Ella was missing. "The countess is right. You'll need everyone. I don't ride very well, so—"

"Thank you, Blanche. Please remain here also, Margot," Saber said. "Enough time has been wasted. Let's go."

He led the way into the cold vestibule to be confronted by the extraordinary vision of Crabley wearing a cape and with boots over his stockings. The man stood before the open front door.

"We must choose directions," Devlin said.

Saber said, "Agreed. And when the constables decide to arrive, someone should tell them the entire story—such as it is—and explain what we've set out to do."

"Leave that to me," Grandmama said, joining them. "Oh, my goodness!"

Saber frowned at her, then turned to see what had made her stare so.

Devlin grabbed his arm and said, "Steady, man, steady."

Ella, exquisite in deep violet and black, walked slowly into the vestibule. Her eyes sought and found his briefly.

"Ella!" He surged to take her in his arms. "Where have you been? We've been beside ourselves."

She felt limp and insubstantial. Dread alerted every muscle and nerve within Saber. "My sweet," he said quietly. "Say something, please."

"I'm tired."

He looked from Devlin to Margot. Margot's lips were parted, her eyes wide.

"Ella—"

She pushed firmly against his chest until he dropped his arms. "What a fuss," she said, gathering her shawl about her. "I simply went for a little ride in a coach to clear my head. Now I'm tired."

Grandmama made to go to her, but Saber motioned for her to remain still. "We were about to search all of London for you," he told Ella, his heart still thundering. "And I will have an answer from you now. Where have you been?"

Ella looked at him. "I am not your child. Or your possession. When I'm ready—if I'm ever ready—we'll talk." Her gaze moved to the others. "Without an audience."

Chapter Twenty-four

Her bed was empty.

Saber knew panic as intense as any he'd ever known.

The casements were open. Wide open. A tree limb scratched the panes and he heard leaves rustle.

An intruder could have climbed that tree.

He started for the window.

"I'm here, Saber."

He halted and buried his face in his hands. "My God, Ella. I thought . . . Praise be, you're safe."

She sat on the window seat, all but hidden by a drapery. "There's nothing to be concerned about. You should be sleeping." She appeared to wear only a shift.

"I watched your room until your maid left."

"Please don't concern yourself with me further."

"Ella—"

"I've thought about this a great deal. I have pressed you and I have been wrong. Forget everything that has passed between us."

He went to her, braced a hand each side of her on the windowsill, and kissed the top of her head. "We must talk to each other. Really talk." She wore something white.

"Such an unusual man."

"Unusual? How so?"

She touched his jaw fleetingly. "Perhaps not unusual in your family. Men who talk to women. Men who care what women have to say. Little wonder you bend our hearts to your will."

Saber smoothed her hair. "I can only speak for myself. Your words are the words I hear when I'm alone." The words he wished were all he heard when he was alone.

"I believe you. But I also believe you have wanted nothing more than you want to be free, Saber. You never asked me to follow you around, to pester you with my foolish demands."

"What has happened?" he asked, very softly. "What happened this evening? Where did . . . ? Crabley and Rose spoke of a carriage. Where did it take you?"

"Nowhere!" Her dark hair streamed over her shoulders. She sat, curled into a ball. "Leave me, please. For your own good, just *leave*."

Saber stroked her hair again. "No."

She sighed. "I will not enter into one of your infuriating word battles, Saber. I wish to be alone. Please go away."

"No."

"This is my bedchamber. It isn't appropriate for you to be here."

"Rubbish. If you truly wish to be rid of me, you'll have to do much better. I never intend to leave you alone again. I have just decided. From now on I shall never allow you from my sight."

"That's ridiculous!" She swiveled sideways on the seat and turned her face toward the windows.

"We're going to be married. Husbands and wives are often

inseparable. Side by side at every moment. There's nothing ridiculous about that."

"Every person requires some privacy."

"I shall do my best to become invisible from time to time. Perhaps a certain ghost could give me lessons."

"Perhaps." She thought a moment before saying, "You certainly cannot be with me when I dress."

He almost laughed, but coughed instead. "I think I could manage to endure that."

"Well, not when I bathe."

When she bathed? Saber found it necessary to sit beside her. "That would be a great trial, but I'd manage that too."

"It would be impossible for you to make certain I didn't leave while *you* were bathing."

Mmm. The lady didn't know her power to distract a man. "An interesting dilemma. I shall simply have to take you into my baths with me."

"Oh! Oh, Saber, you are outrageous. Go away."

"No."

"I shall call for . . ."

"For whom? I believe I am the man in charge here."

She fell silent.

Saber waited, listening, watching. When she didn't move, he touched her cold hands, slowly ran his fingers up her bare arms, bent until he covered and surrounded her. And then he rocked.

He heard her swallow, and swallow again—heard the sound of a choked sob, felt her body quake.

"We cannot be together," she told him, her voice muffled. "Not ever. I am . . . I am what I am. Nothing can change that. I thought it possible to start an entirely new life, but I was wrong. Please, Saber, for the sake of our friendship, return to your bed now. As soon as, as—as soon as Papa returns, I shall beg him to take me away to Scotland. Then all I can do is pray."

Saber grew still. "All you can do is pray?" He raised his head. "Will you tell me what happened to you this evening?"

"No."

Saber stood up. "Very well. You have decided to be strong and bear this—whatever it is—alone. How noble—and how foolish. I shall simply have to take command. You have been left in my care, and I must care for you."

She didn't move, didn't look up at him.

Just as well. Saber took off his coat, wrapped it around her, and picked her up.

"Saber!"

He'd shocked her, he noted with satisfaction. A good beginning. At least she'd been forced to react.

"Put me down at once." She wriggled—to no avail, except to press a breast into his hand, and to cause him to grip her bottom more firmly through insubstantial cotton. "Saber! Put me down now! I am tired of men forcing their wills on me."

"Really," he said grimly. He would soon find a way to make her tell him what she meant by that. "These rooms are cold and I do not care for them. Mine are much more to my liking. We shall go there."

"You cannot take me to your rooms! Put me *down*."

He strode to the door. "You found nothing wrong in entering my rooms in Burlington Gardens, miss. My bed also, if memory serves. And now you will be silent or the entire house will be awakened."

Ella squirmed and waved her feet. "Good! I shall awaken them and bring them to my rescue."

"By all means bring them." Meanwhile, he would enjoy the twisting of her supple body against his. "I'll explain that you are in danger and must be watched over. I'll tell them that your rooms are too easily accessed from outside."

"Saber, what are you thinking of? You know you cannot—"

"I know I can, and I will." As he opened the door, he lowered his voice. "You told me you wanted no more secrets between us. There shall be none. You said you wished to lie with me all night. So you shall. Every night—starting now."

"Saber—"

"Hush. I want to take you where there will be no interruptions. Will you trust me, Ella?"

"What you propose is madness. The entire household will hear of it. The entire *ton* will hear of it."

She was fragrant, smooth, innocently sensual. *Innocent!* Yes, he could no longer convince himself otherwise. "There will be no talk," he told her.

"What of Bigun? And Rose?"

Saber laughed, a laugh that sounded as lacking in amusement as he felt. "Bigun and Rose have been told they will see nothing, and speak of nothing unless I tell them they may. They are both in a less than enviable position of late."

"Great-Grandmama was responsible for—"

"Grandmama is the Dowager Duchess of Franchot. She feels her own guilt at her part in what happened. For the rest, she has apparently been our ally from the outset. That will not change." He laughed again. "In fact, I pity anyone who gets in my way in this. I'm sure you haven't forgotten the sword in Grandmama's cane."

Ella chuckled too. "She is my inspiration."

"A grim thought. Will you let me guide you—at least for the present?"

Her arms, stealing slowly around his neck, were his answer.

He carried her into the hall and up three flights of stairs. The rooms he had chosen were in a separate wing high above the gardens and stables, at the back of the house. Some long-ago Franchot male had made those rooms his very private sanctum.

Saber produced a key to unlock the door that closed off the entire area. Once inside, he locked it again. The first room he reached was his bedchamber. "I'll make you comfortable in here and light the lamps."

"I am not a child, Saber. And I'm not a weak, foolish woman."

He threw back the counterpane and sheet, removed his coat from her shoulders, and settled her in the middle of his bed. "You aren't a child, or a weak, foolish woman. But you have suffered at someone's hands. That shall not occur again. I will not allow it."

"You cannot control the world."

"I can control my part of it. You are a part of my part of the world." He looked down upon her. She lay on her side, her knees drawn up to her chest beneath a thin, white gauze shift. Her hair spread like black silk upon white sheets. She kept her eyes tightly closed. "I do not wish to control you, Ella, only to look after you."

"So you think you can lock me away here forever? That will keep me safe?"

He laughed without mirth. "It would certainly offer you a measure of protection, but what a waste. No, beloved, we shall bring the secrets into the light between us, and then we shall see."

She was silent.

He covered her.

Saber lighted a small lamp on a marquetry teapoy near the fireplace. A few added coals and a puff or two of the bellows brought the fire to crackling life.

A glance at Ella showed she had not moved. Her breathing was soft and regular.

Exhaustion. Amazingly, she had already fallen into an exhausted sleep. By the heavens, he would find out who was responsible for whatever had been done to her this night. They should be punished.

He loosened his cuffs and rolled up his sleeves. His stock joined his jacket and he undid the neck of his shirt. For now he would let her sleep. When she awoke, they would talk.

Saber moved a chair where he could see her clearly, and sat down.

A speedy marriage and then they would remove to the country. Not to Shillingdown, which was too easily accessed, but to some remote place he would secure. Perhaps in Ella's beloved Scotland.

She turned onto her back and tossed aside the covers.

Frowning, he rose and went to cover her again.

While he stood over her, her arms rose, stretched above her head.

Saber drew back. He flexed his hands and made fists. He might be damaged, but he was, nevertheless, a man. Only a man. And he wanted this woman.

With gritted teeth, he left the room, crossed the hall to the study. With the door open, even if someone were to gain entrance to this part of the house, they could not enter the bedchamber unnoticed.

He lighted a lamp and seated himself at the extraordinary Italian rococo desk he'd found abandoned there. He would set about some business that shouldn't wait, and try not to think of the girl who lay so near, so vulnerable . . .

He'd been right. Anyone who came or went from the bedchamber would be visible from the desk in the study.

On bare feet that made no sound, Ella crossed to the study. "What are you doing?" She stood on the threshold of the room, the light behind making her shift transparent. "I felt you leave."

"I thought you were asleep."

"I was pretending."

"Why?"

She rested her weight on one leg. "Because I wanted to see what you would do."

He could not look away.

"I wanted you to come to me, and hold me."

"I"—he let his gaze travel over her—"I didn't trust myself to hold you, Ella."

"Why?"

He threw down his pen. "So full of questions. Don't you understand that I want you? I want you as a man wants a woman. I have already taken too many liberties, taken too much of you that was not mine to take."

Ella put her hands behind her back and strolled slowly toward him. "Surely anything I choose to give you is yours?"

He spread his hands flat on the desk. Did she know what she did? They had spoken of having no secrets, yet there were so many between them.

"I choose to give myself to you, Saber. If the liberties you speak of are those things we have shared, then please take them again. It is all we shall have."

Saber frowned. He gripped the arms of his chair. "I will find out what happened last evening, you know."

"It doesn't matter. In a way, it's appropriate. There are things we must accept because they cannot be changed. I was reminded of things in my life that cannot be changed—nothing more."

"Please tell me what has troubled you so, Ella."

"Who are you writing to?"

He glanced at the desk, at the paper he'd drawn out. "To Struan. To tell him I wish to marry you quickly. At once, in fact."

"So that you can save me?"

Save her? "Come here. Come where I can . . . touch you."

Ella came, hesitantly at first, but she came. Once at his side, she faced him with her back to the desk.

The soft fabric of her shift settled on her breasts, her belly, her thighs. She might as well have been naked. He could not have been more aroused.

Her nipples hardened beneath his gaze.

She pushed back her hair and he saw that her hands shook.

"There is nothing practiced about you, my love."

"Practiced? What do you mean?"

He shook his head. "Nothing. Just a passing thought." He must lead her carefully, gently. What he felt in her was beyond price—natural purity, and faith, faith in him.

"I feel . . . I feel wobbly! Isn't that silly?" She fumbled behind her for support.

Saber gripped her waist, smiled at her startled shriek, and lifted her to sit on the desk. "There. Oh, yes, I like you there. I believe I shall save my letter writing until later." He brought one of her feet to rest on his thigh, followed the slight bones from her toes to her ankles with a forefinger, trailed a path behind her calf to the back of her knee.

Ella jumped, and leaned to brace herself on his shoulders. "That tickles. And I know I shouldn't allow you to touch me so."

"How the lady does change her mind about such things," he told her. His heartbeat grew faster. "She wants to be touched. She doesn't want to be touched."

"I want to be touched."

He looked into her eyes. Muscles in his jaw tensed. His body ached with his need for her, and with the effort it took to restrain that need.

"What do you mean, Ella? You want to be touched?"

She reached for his hand and took it to her breast. "You have made me feel things I didn't know existed."

Slowly, she spread his fingers, pressed his palm to her budding flesh, and sighed as her eyes squeezed shut.

"I have remembered this," she told him. "Over and over, I remembered your hands upon me. But I know there is much more. I had thought to find Mama's book and read what I must know."

"You do not need Justine's book," he said. Blood pounded in his ears. His gut contracted. Other parts of him did anything but contract.

Saber held her thighs and leaned to press his lips to her throat.

She raised her chin.

Each inch of her skin inflamed him more, each inch that he explored with his mouth, with the tip of his tongue.

She tasted sweet, smelled of flowers, felt so soft.

Saber tilted his head to kiss her collarbone, the little dip above, the top of her shoulder, the side of her neck. He heard her moan, and smiled. He wanted to know all of her, and he would.

"Saber."

"Mmm?" He found the fragile spot beneath an ear.

"Saber!"

"Mmm?"

The folds within her ear fascinated him. He blew there, lightly.

"Saber!"

"Yes, my love?" The hollow beneath her cheekbone invited close attention, and the tip of her chin, the corner of her mouth—and the other corner of her mouth.

"It is extraordinary."

"I know." To kiss her brow he had to rise a little from his seat. "All extraordinary. Every bit of you. Everything that I feel with you."

He felt her hands inside his shirt, curling over his shoulders, and smiled afresh. His Ella was a delight wrapped in gossamer and so ready to be unwrapped. He would delight in unfolding her all the way to her center.

Saber settled his mouth on hers and her sweetness overwhelmed him. He stood between her legs and framed her face in hands that were none too steady. For a long time he was content to brush their lips together. Her fingers found the scar on his shoulder and smoothed the puckered skin. He hesitated only an instant before giving her mouth his full attention again.

Her sweetness could draw him out of darkness.

Her trust could banish doubt.

Her acceptance of every part of him could send the rest of the world away.

He sank back to his chair, drawing her face down to his. Her eyes closed and her lips parted. Saber tasted the soft moistness of her, felt the sharp edges of her teeth, the hesitant touch of her tongue.

To possess this creature was all he asked of life. To possess and protect and keep her close. With Ella there was no pain, no screams, no hate, no fear.

Carefully, he moved his mouth across hers, turning her face with each caress of lips upon lips. He felt the firmer thrust of her tongue, and warm pleasure spread within him. Her fingers dug into his shoulders. If he let her go she would fall against him.

Restraint.

Bracing herself, panting, she raised her head and looked at him. Her dark eyes were almost black, black and slumberous, the lashes like thick lace that cast shadows into obsidian depths. Her parted lips were wet and showed the evidence of his kisses. She held the tip of her tongue between her teeth and sucked in a breath.

Tapes at the front of her shift were all but untied. With one finger, Saber hooked them entirely undone—one by one—until the front of the scanty gown gaped.

Saber swallowed. So close he need not move to touch them, her breasts were revealed. Pointed, pink-tipped, small, yet not too small to fill a large man's hands. And onward, downward, the rest of her body was small. Her rib cage beneath the firm jut of her breasts tapered to a waist he'd have little trouble spanning.

She pulled the shift aside and stroked her breast as if absorbed. "You put your mouth here," she told him, looking up, taking one of his hands from her face, holding it beneath the softly heavy flesh. "I'd like you to do that again."

His rod grew unbearably full. Obediently, willing his urges to wait, he touched his tongue to the tip of her nipple—and absorbed the scouring of her fingernails on his back, and her sudden pressure against his face.

"Ah, ah," he whispered. "Too quick, my love. That way too much is missed, perhaps lost." With his thumb, he circled the center of her breast. She made ineffectual grabs at him, and he laughed. "A moment longer, sweet. The waiting heightens pleasure." It also tested restraint.

"I want . . ."

"I know what you want. I also know what I want. Let me lead us both there." He watched her face, her eyes squeezed tightly shut, her lips drawn back from her teeth—and circled the nipple again, and again, drawing a little closer each time.

"Saber! It burns."

"A beautiful burning. I burn too."

She abandoned his hand to work at the buttons on his shirt. He sighed when it fell open, and longed to feel her tender flesh pressed to his. Ella raked the pads of her fingers through the hair on his chest.

Saber attended to her other breast and her eyes flew open. A flush had mounted her cheeks, and a similar rosy hue painted her pretty breasts. And around and around the nipple he passed his thumb.

"I . . . cannot bear it."

"You cannot bear not to bear it," he told her. "Neither can I. We shall often suffer together like this. Should you like that?"

"Yes," she said on a noisy breath. "Kiss . . . Take . . . Take . . . it . . . Saber."

Take it. A passionate female who would, unless he was much mistaken, be experiencing a taking of quite another nature shortly, one she had never known. He thinned his lips. How could he have doubted her innocence? And would it have mattered if she were not so?

No. No, he would trade his life and everything he had just to spend what time he could with her, like this.

Saber cupped her breasts while he kissed each of her tightly closed eyelids. He kissed her lips until she opened her mouth wide and kissed him back, fiercely demanding, echoing the cries of her body for release.

The path to her waist was silken. The wide opening of her shift allowed him to spread his hands on her belly, to slide his fingers around her bottom, to separate and lift her—and to absorb her gasp into his mouth. Saber breathed in her shocked excitement and smiled secretly.

Ella pushed his shirt from his shoulders.

Saber bent and took a nipple gently between his teeth.

Her fingers drove into his hair.

He flicked the tip of his tongue over the stiffly budded flesh.

Ella arched her back.

Holding her hips, willing his own restraint, he suckled, aware of his pounding pulse, of each dragging breath.

Perfection.

Passion laced with power.

He drew perfection into his mouth, held passionate power within his hands.

He was only a man.

Saber dropped to sit again. He pulled her feet, one each side of him, onto the seat of his chair—and he slipped her wisp of a gown up long, smoothly golden limbs. Bending his head, he kissed the inside of a slender thigh, laughed, and winced away from her pinching grip on his hair.

"Oh, Saber," she moaned. "What are you doing?"

He kissed and nuzzled his way up her other thigh, nipping at tender skin, holding her still when she would have jerked.

"Saber?"

"You don't approve?"

"It's . . . I . . . Ye-es. Oh!"

In one swift move, Saber brought her knees over his shoulders and buried his face in the dark hair between her thighs. The tender mound beneath thrust helplessly at him. His tongue found the hidden place, found and curled around and beneath, and in forays into her passage.

His rod leaped. Soon. He must join with her soon, or die of his own need.

"Saber!" she all but screamed.

His need could wait. Tiny tugs with teeth and lips convulsed her supple frame, drew her closer and closer until she gripped his head with her thighs, held his neck rather than fall to her back.

Her taste made him drunk. Sheer sexuality, sheer womanly essence. Over and over he lapped at the ignited bud, and when she convulsed, he almost failed to catch and hold her. Ripples passed along her muscles. Her cries were small and incoherent—and amazed.

Saber stood over Ella, staring down at her, his vision blurred. Her head hung back, her black hair brushing the elegant desk and spreading over the paper upon which he intended to ask for her hand.

The shift was an alluring rag, tattered, torn completely from one arm, held about the other elbow by threads, a flimsy drape at her hips.

He eased her up to sit on the edge of the desk and held her against his chest while he shed his shirt entirely.

Ella reached up to smooth his face, pulled him down until she could claim his mouth in a searing kiss that bore only a lingering trace of uncertainty.

And while she kissed him, she rubbed her breasts slowly, languorously back and forth over his chest.

Haste made him clumsy. He tore at his trousers and sighed with relief when he could push them down.

Framing her face, he made Ella look at him. "You are my beloved," he told her, clinging to the fragile remnants of his control. "You have said you love me."

"And I do," she murmured, her eyes beginning to drift shut again. "More than my life. Saber—"

"I love you more than my life, Ella. I care for nothing but you. I have asked you to be my wife. You said that was impossible. So I ask you again: Will you marry me?"

When she looked at him again, passion had rekindled in the depths of her eyes. "If you want me, I will marry you. I will do or be whatever you want of me. I am yours, Saber."

"This should not be happening until we are wed."

She smiled and nodded. "I am not a completely green girl."

"No." Despite his condition, he grinned. "Certainly you are no longer a green girl, and soon you may be even less green."

Her regard became sharper. She glanced downward and her harsh gasp let him know she could see all there was to see of his craving for her.

The expression on her face changed to one of wonder. She ran the back of her fingers down his belly—a trail of fire so hot—until they came to rest against his shaft. "This is not all it's for, is it?"

Saber frowned. "All?"

"This male part of you. It grows large and hard for a purpose other than to . . . to . . . Saber, I loved what you did to me. Is that appropriate?"

He *would* die soon. "So appropriate, Ella."

"You know how it felt?" She inclined her head, watching his lips.

"I think so."

"Have you ever felt something like it?"

"I could. A man and a woman. A husband and a wife join bodies and they both feel exquisite pleasure."

Her gaze rose to his eyes. "So green," she said. "Like the bottom of the sea, I should think. Your eyes—"

"Yes. . . . Ella, I should like to join my body with yours. Although I ought to wait, I'd like to do this now."

"Ah." She smoothed his shaft to its distended head, held it in one hand, and explored the contours with minute care. "And we join with this? Of course we do. Tell me how. In my heart we are already married."

"I will show you how." He kissed her gently on the lips, on each breast. "Watch me, Ella. I should like you to see."

Dutifully, she watched him guide the head of his penis to the opening into her body.

He touched slick folds, saw her dark curls upon his engorged flesh.

Ella's slight shifting made him glance up at her. She brought her hands to rest on his shoulders once more. Anxious questions filled her eyes. He flexed muscles in his jaw and kissed her until her tension yielded.

Staring into her eyes, he pressed inside her.

"Saber?" Her grip tightened.

He smiled reassurance—and met resistance. "Is there pain?" he asked. "Tell me, Ella."

Ella bowed her head to watch once more. "A little. It doesn't matter." Her breasts rose and fell, vibrated with her tremulous breathing.

"The pain will pass, my sweet." Saber thrust into Ella, firmly, but gently—drove deep, deep past a barrier he felt give way to him. Deeper to bury himself within her, to join with her.

"One," she said softly. "To make us one. Oh, I never . . . I never knew." Her hips shifted perilously close to the edge of the desk.

"Let me, my love," he told her. He wrapped her arms around his neck and held her hips. Taking her mouth, he darted his tongue inside—and delved. He pushed far into her mouth—and thrust far into her body, only to withdraw until he all but parted from her.

She urged him back, threaded her hands beneath his arms and pressed her fingers into his buttocks, pressed and pressed with each drive of his rod into the heaven that welcomed him.

The room, his body, hers, all melded, melting together. His thighs were rigid, straining. He pulled her legs around his hips and no longer controlled the dance that he had not designed, had not practiced, not known since first he looked upon this woman.

Love had inspired him. Need long denied had driven him. Instinct had reminded him.

They were new together.

His seed spilled in a hot rush and his cry rent his mind. It was right.

"I love you," he shouted. "It is right, Ella. We are right."

"Yes," she said, so quietly he scarcely heard. "Yes. We are right and I love you."

"We will marry. Tomorrow."

She giggled and fell with him to the chair. Astride his hips, she sat, her body still joined to his. "We cannot marry tomorrow. Such a thing would not be possible."

"Your family approves." He stroked her face, her neck, her shoulders. "I will get a special license and it shall be done. You will be mine."

"It can be done so quickly?"

"Yes."

"And then you will be mine."

"Always. I already am."

She wedged a knee each side of him and rose a little.

He laughed and pulled her back to sit on his lap. "I like you exactly where you are."

"And I like you exactly where you are. But can't we do that again?"

"That?"

"The joining thingie." She darted to nip one of his flat nipples. "Does that feel . . . Well, do you feel that as I do?"

He raised his hips, watched her sigh and open her mouth, and he said, "I feel it."

"But not as much as . . . as the thingie."

He chuckled aloud, and the vibration brought his teeth hard together. "No, not as much as the *thingie*."

Ella planted her hands flat on his chest, fixed him with a serious stare, and began to lift herself rhythmically up and down.

"Insatiable," he cried.

"Your fault," she responded, lifting and sitting again, lifting and sitting. "You are a magnificent teacher. You will make me an expert."

Saber's energy began to seep back into his muscles and nerves. The fresh quickening he felt made him shake his head. "I will make you an expert, my girl? An expert and a magician."

Her hips moved more rapidly, jarring her breasts until he could not bear to do other than fasten his mouth there again.

"A magician?" she said, gasping. "A magician?"

"Yes," he told her, the white-hot rush beginning again. "A magician who has no need of any book to teach her to perform magic."

Curled beside Saber in his big, comfortable bed, Ella settled a knee across his thigh and hugged him. "You should sleep." Outside the sky was thick and black. "We should both sleep."

Her head rested in the hollow of his shoulder and he played idly with a strand of her hair. "You will sleep soon enough. Are you happy?"

"You know I am." Happy, and wonderfully sore—and barely able to wait to experience him again. He was rough and smooth, supple, and so hard, strong yet gentle, warm—

"Before you do sleep, I think there are things we must discuss. We have a busy day before us. I should like to know exactly what I must deal with—including last night's episode when you left the house in that coach. Bigun explained Grandmama's scheme to get us together—and how the notes were passed to us. Crabley told me the coach arrived and he had no reason to doubt that I had sent it since he had not seen me all day. He didn't know I was here. Neither did Rose."

"Someone knew I was supposed to go to the theater with you." She didn't wish to discuss this. "Someone knew and passed the information to another party." The thought of that place, of Uncle Milo's calculating blue stare, turned her cold.

Saber pulled her on top of him and stroked the length of her spine and back, repeatedly. "I shall discover who both knew and decided to use the information. Where were you taken?"

She pressed her face into the hair on his chest, stretched her arms up and threaded her hands around his neck.

"Answer me, Ella." Saber rubbed her body, passing the heels of his hands over the sides of her breasts. "Where—"

"I was warned," she said, and it hurt to swallow.

Saber waited, continuing to stroke her skin beneath the sheet. She felt him against every inch of her.

He said, "Go on."

"Remember my mother's brother? Milo?"

"You spoke of him."

"Last night I saw him again."

His hands stilled.

"He arranged for me to visit him so that he could tell me what I must do."

"The devil he did. And by what right—"

"By right of family loyalty. According to him. He is in financial difficulty and requires my assistance."

"He asked you for money?"

Ella sighed. Saber's ministrations had begun to make her yearn for him. "He told me what I must do. And he threatened me with certain things if I failed to do as I was told."

Saber's hands grew still. "He threatened you?"

"With having my past revealed to everyone in the Polite

World. With telling any man whose attentions I encouraged that I am—that I came from nothing."

The only response she heard was the thud of Saber's heart beneath her cheek.

"I was taken to Mrs. Lushbottam's. That is the—It is a bad house, Saber, where women behave strangely. And men just as strangely. It is the house where I was—"

"I know which house it is. I cannot believe this."

She told him the rest, all of it, and afterward, when he was silent a long time, she said, "So you see, if you were to marry me, there would always be the danger of some retribution."

"You think I fear that?" He set her gently beside him and kissed her. "I have seen hell, my love. These cowards are nothing to me—nothing but carrion to be dispensed with. Sleep. With the dawn I shall see to the matter of the marriage. Later, I'll deal with your uncle."

Chapter Twenty-five

How much longer must he suffer the interference of others? Furious that he'd been unable to stop Precious Able from accompanying him, Pomeroy Wokingham assessed the women in each of Lushbottam's windows before ringing the bell. A short creature dressed in pale blue interested him vaguely. She avoided his eyes. He liked that. The ones who were too willing bored him.

"Pommy?" Precious sounded excited. She'd intercepted him as he'd attempted to leave the Grosvenor Street house unnoticed, and threatened to awaken his father unless Pomeroy took her with him. "Pommy, is this the . . . Well, is it?"

"Shut up. You'll find out what it is soon enough."

She bounced. "It *is*. Ooh, how delicious."

The door opened to reveal the contemptible Milo. Even at such a late hour the man still stretched his dry old lips in a smile too cheerful for Pomeroy's taste.

"Why, Mr. Wokingham." He narrowed his eyes when he looked at Precious, and Pomeroy saw the other man take her measure—accurately, no doubt. "And a lovely companion.

What a delightful surprise, my friends. You come on in here. In need of something to tide you over, are you, sir? Well, we'll just have—"

Pomeroy pushed past him, shutting the old fool up. "We'll just have to talk," he said.

"Surely I can interest you in a little entertainment first? We're about to begin. A very interesting group offering, I assure you. Fresh from Persia."

Pomeroy's cock stirred, but he reminded himself not to be diverted from his purpose here. Not entirely diverted. "I had something more private in mind." Business and pleasure—at the same time—could be so titillating. "The piece in the window should do, I'd think. Creature in blue. Blond. Get her and bring her to the sitting room."

"Pommy!" Precious whined. "I thought we were going—"

"And we are. Soon enough. Some of us are capable of attending to more than one matter at the same time. Milo, perhaps you also have something for my friend, Precious?"

"Pommy?"

He glowered her to silence.

Milo clasped his hands together and bowed. "I do believe I've got just the thing. Something very nice. Yes, just the right thing for a young lady of such quality. Of course, it'll have to be cash."

Pomeroy fixed the man with a cool stare. "Do not have the temerity to discuss money, you Philistine. That will come later, when we discuss other matters."

Affecting a mocking bow, Milo backed away.

Pomeroy swept into Milo's dismal sitting room with its mismatched chairs and divans and appallingly annoying rose motif. "You're in for a treat," he told Precious, enjoying the anticipation of seeing her rendered silent for once. "Lushbottam's is guaranteed to satisfy even the most energetic among us."

Precious's blue eyes darted nervously about the room. "Not very . . . Well, it isn't, is it?"

He ignored her and sat on a small couch while she continued to stand.

"What's going to happen, Pommy?"

Pomeroy smiled a little. "Hard to be sure—absolutely sure. Let's just say we'll leave with more to remember than when we came, shall we? Why not sit down? Try one of the divans—quite comfortable actually."

She didn't move.

"Here you are, then, Mr. Wokingham," Milo said as he pushed the woman in blue before him into the sitting room. "Our little Blossom. Reminds you of a blossom, doesn't she? Blooming all over, so to speak. I'll just go for the other I mentioned. Why don't you get acquainted while I'm gone?"

Blossom made Precious appear almost svelte.

"Come and sit by me, Blossom," Pomeroy said. He could have chosen better, but no matter, he'd make the best of this piece. After all, a little idle diversion was all he intended.

The woman was older than she'd appeared at first. Probably at least five and twenty. Pomeroy preferred his females young.

Blossom sat beside him, her eyes still lowered. A simple enough pretense at a demure nature, unless Pomeroy was much mistaken.

"She's fat," Precious announced.

Blossom's eyes flew open and no trace of shyness lingered in the malign glare she aimed at Precious.

"Hardly fat," Pomeroy said, amused. "Nicely covered, what, Blossom? Round in all the right places, hmm?"

She slanted a knowing look at him.

"Blue becomes you," Pomeroy said, enjoying the waves of jealousy emanating from Precious.

The thud of feet on carpet approached and Milo came into

the sitting room. At a loping, graceful pace, two tall men followed him and he closed the door behind them.

Pomeroy studied the muscular young bucks with interest. They had thick, black hair, slender, handsome faces, and large, dark eyes that darted between the other occupants of the room, then back to each other. The two appeared to communicate without speech. Their skin was the color of pale coffee and glistened—all the way to the loose, white trousers they wore. They were both naked to the waist.

"Well, now," Milo said, rubbing his hands and smiling as if he were about to preside over a tea party. "Shall we get started?" He seated himself behind his desk and propped his chin.

Blossom wriggled closer to Pomeroy. He was more interested in the two men. They concentrated on Precious. She dipped her head and looked up at them, swinging her full, peach-colored skirts from side to side in what Pomeroy had dubbed her "winsome girl" manner.

"It's been some time since we saw you, Mr. Wokingham," Milo said, inclining his head at the men. "Entertain the young lady," he told them. "Pretty heads are for enjoying pretty things. They're no place for business, and they can't manage both anyway."

One of Milo's trained performers promptly sank to his knees while the other hoisted Precious's skirts and sat her astride his partner's neck and shoulders. Squealing, she tried to cover her legs. Her efforts were useless.

Pomeroy laughed and slapped his knees. "Most entertainin', Milo. Most entertainin'."

"Is this to your liking, lady?" the man beneath Precious asked. "I am your slave."

"Ooh!" Precious squealed again. "Whatever next?"

Her "slave" rose to his feet, and she gripped his ears.

"Do not fear, lady, I will not drop you. Your pleasure is our only wish."

Precious clung and giggled, her face growing very flushed. The man wrapped his arms around her limbs and rocked her back and forth on his neck. "To pleasure you, lady," he said, showing strong, white teeth.

Pomeroy watched the expression on Precious's face change from confusion to mounting arousal. He shifted to readjust himself inside his trousers. "Innovative," he said to Milo. "A marvel how you acquire this supply of novelties. But we have a score to settle, my friend."

"Oh, Pommy!" Precious cried, her eyes popping wide. "Pommy! What's he doing to me?"

"He" was the second handsome "slave." Lifting Precious's skirts over her head, he bared her bottom and used his supple thumbs to massage the dimples at the base of her spine.

Precious squirmed and moaned. She let go with one hand to bat at her skirts, only to grab her human mount again when she almost lost her balance.

"Doesn't this please you, lady?" Thumbs asked. He pinched Precious's white bottom until she yelled, then reached beneath her to apply swift, rhythmic strokes. "Or this, lady?"

Pomeroy hitched at himself and said, "I'm here on my own behalf this time, Milo. One word to my father, and I'll see you in the gutter. I have decided to take matters into my own hands. Things will happen my way, and quickly. Do I make myself plain?"

"Plain as plain, Mr. Wokingham." Milo continued to smile. Even as Precious raised her bottom like a rider going over a jump, he continued to smile. Milo smiled when she panted, and when the stroking between her folds grew more insistent. When she bounced and grunted, Milo still smiled.

Pomeroy's breathing felt labored. He pushed an arm

around Blossom's shoulders. Her eyes darted from the spectacle in the middle of the room, to Pomeroy, and she passed her pointed tongue around full lips.

He looked from her lips to her breasts. A little enjoyment was the least he should allow himself, particularly since it would annoy Precious.

"What have we here, then, Blossom?" he asked, tugging a white muslin fichu from the neck of her pink gown. Plump breasts were revealed to the large upper rims of darkly rouged nipples. "Very nice, my dear," Pomeroy said, his concentration momentarily diverted.

Precious's whooping cries reached crescendo an instant before she was tipped, facedown, upon a sagging divan. Thumbs flipped her over, and the two men sank beside her. Precious, her eyes glazed, hooked a dark head beneath each arm and appeared dazed.

"Anyway," Pomeroy said, clumsily opening the front of Blossom's bodice. "As I said, Milo, there's a score to settle, and we both know what it is. I've already waited too long."

Two silver balls materialized from a pocket in one of the men's white trousers. He handed a ball to his companion and they took turns to insert them into Precious, whose mouth opened in silent but obviously delighted amazement. She tried to sit up.

"No, no, lady," the man who had produced the silver balls said soothingly. "Stay as you are. You will know joy as you have never known it."

Thumbs removed his trousers, revealing a rod big enough to make Pomeroy frown. Inserted swiftly in the wake of the balls, the effect of the giant shaft on Precious was beyond all. She screeched and grabbed, and bucked and begged. . . . She begged for more of whatever these perverted, deformed beasts gave her. *Whore*. As perverted as they were. His father should know of it. That would . . . No, he could not tell his father, or his own plans would be revealed.

With the final parting of Blossom's bodice, Pomeroy was confronted with enough to absorb him, at least partially, for some time.

With detached pride, Blossom watched him play with her provocatively prepared nipples. She rested her hands passively in her lap while he scooped her immense breasts into his hands.

"Quite a show, eh, Mr. Wokingham?" Milo asked. "Worth a bit, I can tell you."

"And they've earned a bit, no doubt," Pomeroy responded, pinching Blossom's nipples and waiting for a response that never came. Annoyed, he took one of her flaccid hands to his crotch. She squeezed him hard, but her expression still didn't change. "Is she simple-minded?" he asked.

"Not at all," Milo said, chuckling. "Some gentlemen like a placid one. She can be something else if you want her to be."

Pomeroy studied Blossom and decided a silent woman was exactly what he needed at the moment. Precious made enough noise for several women. "Just keep squeezing," he told Blossom, jiggling her swelling breasts. She felt it, all right. "Squeeze until I tell you what I want next."

Blossom squeezed.

"What I intend to get isn't going to be shared," he told Milo, rushing as he felt his control slipping. "Do you understand me? You know the problem I've coped with for years."

"Some gentlemen like to share." Milo glanced at Precious, who writhed, a clever male mouth attached to each breast. "Some ladies, too, I might add."

Pomeroy narrowed his eyes. "I have shared enough. I'm not a child anymore. This time *I* decide how my affairs shall be accomplished. The devil take my father and his *wedding* plans. I'm not interested in his selfish games. What I want, I want, and you know you've got to get it for me. And quickly." At least Precious was too "involved" to hear a word he said. Later he might need her help. He was more likely to get it as long as she didn't know he'd soon have no use for her.

"It may not be possible to do what you ask quickly."

"Get down there," Pomeroy ordered Blossom, shoving her to the floor between his knees. The scents of spent sex wafted on the room's stale air, and he wrinkled his nose. The sooner his business—all of his business—was completed here, the better. He tore his trousers undone and told Blossom, "Use your mouth, now. Use it well."

Milo said, "I have not been idle on your behalf, Mr. Wokingham."

"Your time is up," Pomeroy told him. "I have already given you too much latitude."

"Surely you don't expect me to work miracles."

Blossom used her mouth very well. Pomeroy shifted forward on the couch. "I expect you to make good on our bargain."

"But—"

"I'll give you until the end of the week to get me what I want." He found release and fell against the couch. "Until the end of the week to get me what I'm owed."

"Mr. Wokingham—"

"Today is Monday. On Saturday I'll be back, and I won't be satisfied with having *her* between my legs." He pointed at Blossom.

Chapter Twenty-six

The dowager duchess watched the proceedings as if she witnessed hasty marriages in her family's London home every day.

Saber observed the aged bishop, an old acquaintance of his grandmother's, give the specially prepared license the briefest of perusals. "You do testify to the willingness of the bride's parents to agree to the marriage, then, my lady?" he asked, his voice quavering.

"Do get on with it, Dullington," Grandmama said, leaning heavily on her cane. "Much longer and we'll both be dead. Won't matter who was willing then, will it?"

The bishop bowed, showing the top of hair as white as his skin, raised all but transparent palms to the heavens, and "got on with it."

Saber glanced at the woman beside him and whispered, "Ella?"

She peeked up at him, her expression deeply serious, and she frowned.

In other words, *silence at so weighty a moment.*

The ceremony drew rapidly toward a close.

Saber put an arm around Ella's shoulders and noted the bishop's disapproving sniff. She wore a simple dress of cream silk banded with inserts of lace and scattered with tiny pearls and crystals. Flowers fashioned from lace, and with pearls and crystals at their centers, nestled in her smoothly upswept hair. Her only jewelry was the ruby star that had been his first gift to her.

She held a single cream rose, taken from one of the bouquets he'd never instructed Devlin to stop sending.

Exotic elegance radiated from Saber's bride.

"It's my duty to instruct you in the . . . er . . ." the bishop's voice trailed off.

Saber raised an eyebrow and waited.

"It's my duty to instruct you in the duties of a husband and wife," Dullington said, and went on to do so, at length.

"You are my wife," Saber whispered. "Ella, you are Lady Avenall, my love."

Her smile trembled. "And you have acquired a great trial, my lord, a great burden. I will do my best to make that burden as light as possible."

He wanted to tell her the only burden would likely be hers.

"Mama and Papa should be here," Max said loudly, creating a shocked silence.

Saber turned to his new brother-in-law, but the young man wouldn't look at him.

"That's quite enough, Max," Grandmama said.

Max's expression became truculent. "Well, they should be. We should wait for them to get back and do this all over again."

"I hardly think—"

"He's overset," Blanche said, surprising the small gathered company by interrupting Saber. "Come along with me, Max.

We'll go and sample the wedding breakfast. We aren't required here."

"Most thoughtful, Mrs. Bastible," Bigun said. Resplendent entirely in gold for the occasion, he joined Blanche. "I'll accompany you."

Max stuffed his hands beneath the tails of his coat. "I'm only worried about you, Ellie. Will you look after her, Saber?"

Grandmama said, kindly enough, "Your sister is not being taken from you. She will continue to be your champion."

Saber cast a thoughtful glance at his grandparent. He must not forget how insecure this boy had been and how, even now, the specter of abandonment must never be far from his mind. "You will have another home now, Max," Saber said. "You may come to Ella and me whenever you choose."

Max nodded, a crimson blush on his cheeks. Flanked by Blanche and Bigun, he went quietly from the room.

Crabley, who had been a silent witness throughout, cleared his throat and said, "Well, congratulations to you, m'lord. I'd best get to that breakfast before our young friend demolishes it. We all know his, er, capacity."

The bishop completed his instructions as if there had been no interruption. Grandmama presented him with the fat envelope Saber had provided and smiles instantly wreathed the cleric's dour face.

"Do join us for the wedding feast," Grandmama said with a decided lack of enthusiasm. When he nodded acceptance and left the room with surprisingly light steps, she rolled her eyes.

"I collect you do not admire our holy friend," Saber said.

"Then you collect entirely wrong, Saber, my boy," his grandmother told him. "You would do well to show suitable respect to members of the clergy."

Roundly chastised, Saber grinned nevertheless and drew

his wife into his arms. "I bless the man," he said, resting a fingertip on Ella's lips. "Of course I do. He has declared that you will forever be mine, beloved."

The soft Cotswold hills. Fields of purple linseed, of yellow rape, of tender green, and freshly turned brown earth, a quilt made by men's hands and stitched together with woolly hedgerows.

The carriage bowled through late-afternoon sunshine. Ella leaned her forehead against the window and allowed blossoms in the grasses beside the road to become blurry. Long purple orchid and yellow pimpernel. Here and there, patches of sweet woodruff showed their first clusters of tiny white flowers. She must pick some, as was her custom each spring, to dry for their sweet scent and place between her linens.

Their linens.

No longer could she think of what was hers alone. She was Saber's wife and the things of his life were now hers, just as her life was his.

Ella looked at Saber. He sat across from her, his face turned toward the opposite windows. From this angle his scars were hidden, his face the face she'd first seen as a girl of fifteen—the same but older, and, today, deeply fatigued.

"You're tired," she said, breaking a silence that had lasted for what felt like hours.

He glanced at her. "I'm well enough."

"I didn't say you were ill. I said you were tired. You didn't sleep at all last night, did you?"

"You slept."

"Yes, I believe I did. At least for a while. Does that mean I wouldn't know if you happened to doze for a few minutes? That I wouldn't have noticed if you closed your eyes in the chair where you spent our wedding night?" The instant the words were spoken she longed to be able to whisk them back. "Forget I said that, please, Saber."

"You understand nothing." Once more the landscape claimed his attention.

Every inch of Ella's skin tingled at the sharpness of his retort. She scrunched down in her seat and held the collar of her cape around her neck.

Saber might have been made of stone—stone with dark slashes beneath his eyes and a white line about his thinned lips.

She could not bear this tension between them. "I had not been to Maidenhead before yesterday."

"No?"

"No. And I thought The Dog and Partridge a delightful place."

"You must have stayed in enough inns before."

"Yes. But not on my wedding night."

His eyes closed, and she knew she did not imagine his pained expression.

"I could hear them singing beneath the windows."

Saber kept his eyes shut.

"I suppose they come from all around. Those people. From the farms, perhaps. For good company. And the landlord keeps such beautiful gardens, it's no wonder the people sit outside and—"

"They go there to drink," he said, still shutting her out.

"You did not like The Dog and Partridge?"

"For God's sake!"

"Saber!" Ella felt the prickle of tears and blinked hard. He should not make her cry. "What have I done? What happened since—?"

"Stop it. Please, Ella, leave me be. The inn was more than pleasant. I have always been particularly fond of it, in fact. I've stayed there many times."

"Yet you did not care to share a bed with me there." She had spoken it aloud. Good. Starting the way one intended to continue was the thing. Openness. She remembered that much from Mama's observations on the manner in which men and women should live together.

Rather than respond, Saber rested an elbow on his knee and buried long fingers in his hair.

"This is unbearable," she said, wishing her voice were more steady. "Pay attention to me, my lord!"

His face came up slowly. "I beg your pardon?"

"Do not take that tone with me. I gave you every opportunity not to marry me. You chose to insist otherwise. Now I am your wife and you will just have to make the best of it." Ella raised her chin.

"You are the best of it, Ella."

He spoke so softly, she had to lean forward to make sure she heard.

"You are my wonderful girl. I do not deserve you, but for some reason, you love me."

"Of course I love you."

Ella felt too warm. She took off her hat and placed it on the seat beside her. Their marriage had been a mistake. Despite his declaration of love, Saber was already withdrawing from her. She held her bottom lip in her teeth and sniffed.

"Oh, I say." Saber shifted to sit beside her and took her hands in his. "I have saddened you. What am I to do to make you happy?"

"Stop sitting on my beautiful hat."

He shot up, forgot to duck, and banged his head on a luggage rack. "Damn!"

"Saber!" She retrieved her ruined hat.

He promptly sat down again, rubbing the top of his head. "Never mind that." He took the white chip creation with its yellow and green tartan ribbons, and threw it across the carriage. "You shall have hundreds of them if you want them. Thousands, if that will stop your tears."

"My tears have stopped," she told him, still sniffing.

"But you are miserable." He flopped against the squabs.

Sitting very straight, she swiveled toward him. "The night before our wedding was heaven. I thought I should die of so much joy. Every touch of yours was a miracle, and I cannot wait to—"

"Please, Ella."

"Oooh, you are making me so angry. Last night was the night of our wedding, am I correct?"

"You know you are."

"Yet you chose to sit in a chair looking out of our bedroom window at The Dog and Partridge, rather than rest with me. Rather than be a *husband* to me."

At first he stared at her steadily. Then he bowed his head and offered her his right hand.

Ella frowned. "What is it?"

"Hold my hand, sweet. I am embarrassed."

She frowned even deeper, but took his hand in hers.

"The Dog and Partridge is a public place, Ella."

"Yes."

"I am a very private man."

"Yes."

"You make this so difficult."

She gave an exasperated sigh. "I don't understand you."

"Is it so complicated?" Saber brought her fingers to his lips. "You are a passionate creature."

Ella became even warmer. "I thought that was in order between a husband and wife—according to you."

"It is. It is. But passion can cause . . . well, certain *noise*."

"Noise?"

"Yes, noise." He kissed each of her fingers, then held her hand to his breast. "I prefer that your cries of passion not be heard by strangers."

Ella stared at him. She snatched her hand away and said, "Oh. Oh, what a horrid thought."

"I knew you'd understand."

"I understand that you find my . . . my passionate cries so ugly they embarrass you!"

Before she could turn from him, Saber grabbed her by the waist and sat her on his lap. "I find your passionate cries incredible. Incredible, and incredibly arousing. I will not share any part of you with another, including your cries. And—in case this subject should arise again—I am a man who prefers to feel secure when he sleeps. I cannot feel secure in an inn where people come and go."

She kept her hands in her lap. "Our door was locked."

"I have it on good authority that such locks are not to be trusted. I could not bear to have you mortified by some drunken intruder."

"I should not care for that either," she told him. "Not at all."

"Exactly." Saber sat her on the seat once more and went about pulling shades over the carriage windows before replacing her on his lap. "There, now we have privacy."

Ella fiddled with the silk frog at the neck of her cape.

"Let me do that for you," Saber said, and quickly accomplished the task of undoing the fastening. He easily disposed of the cloak altogether.

"What are you doing?" Ella asked. She felt nervous, excited—shaky—all at once.

"A recreation is what it's called, I believe."

To her total disbelief, he ran a hand beneath her skirt, stroked the inside of her leg all the way to . . . "Saber!"

"You do say that rather often, don't you?" He parted her drawers and slipped inside. "Mmm. Evidently our minds are not too far distant from each other. I do believe you will enjoy this as much as I shall."

Ella tried to draw away. "You can't be serious. You will not come to my bed at an inn, yet you want . . . you suggest. Well, in a *coach*?"

"A very noisy coach. My coach. And with several hours ahead of us before we reach our destination."

Alarmed now, Ella made another attempt to leave his lap—with pleasantly disastrous results. "Even if we were to . . . If we were . . . It wouldn't take *hours*."

"Certainly it will. Slip your bodice down."

Ella felt her nipples harden. "Saber!"

"Saber!" he mimicked, laughing while he made it harder and harder for her to think at all. "Off with it, I say. Now, wife, if you don't mind."

She didn't mind. Her bodice and chemise were around her waist when the waves of ecstasy broke. She heard Saber croon her name, felt his mouth on her breasts—and his strong arm supporting her. But very soon she was astride his thighs and his trousers were undone and he entered her.

"In a coach!" she cried, dropping her head back.

Saber suckled a nipple and murmured, "Very nice in a coach. Perhaps we should ride in a coach every day. Several times a day."

"Saber!" Her breasts were afire, her entire body burned.

"Ella! Oh, yes, Ella. Oh, yes."

"It will not take hours," she panted. "Not even seconds."

"Each time? You're right, my love." He groaned, leaned back, shut his eyes tightly, and she felt the warm rush within her again. "You're right, Ella. Think how often we can do this in even a few hours."

Paneling taken from a Spanish galleon after the Armada covered walls in the large vestibule of Bretforten Manor. Ella stood beside an ebony demilune as dark as the intricately carved panels. She pulled off her gloves and tucked them into her reticule.

No one had greeted them upon their arrival. Saber had obtained keys to the manor in the tiny village of Bretforten, from the landlord of the Fleece Inn, and had himself helped Potts carry in the trunks.

Darkness had descended as they entered the village, and now a fine, steady rain fell.

Saber's boots clattered on stone flags as he came in with the final valises. "Potts will deal with the horses. He'll be comfortable enough over the stables."

She smoothed her hair self-consciously.

"Beautiful house," Saber remarked. "I'd forgotten."

"I thought you probably intended to take me to Shillingdown," Ella ventured. "After the wedding."

"I never said I would. And surely you must have known we were heading in quite another direction. Eventually I shall take you on a more appropriate wedding journey. But I think we shall be happy enough here for the present."

He headed for a staircase fashioned of wood as rich as the vestibule. "I'll get you settled and see what I can find to eat," he said, starting to climb.

Get her settled. "Saber?"

"Let me take these up. You might want to wander around a bit. Get your bearings."

She didn't want to wander around or get her bearings. Instead, she ran up the stairs behind Saber and followed him through well-furnished rooms to a pretty yellow bedroom where he set down his burdens.

"Who owns this house?"

"Old friends of Devlin's. That's why he could not be at our wedding. He came ahead to make arrangements."

She glanced over her shoulder. "Devlin? Shall we see him?"

Saber laughed. "Hardly. A man knows when to make himself scarce. The owners are away at the moment."

"I noticed. There are no servants, Saber."

"I shall do whatever your maid would do," he told her, looking anywhere but at her face. "A woman will come in each day to take care of our essential needs. We'll use very little of the house."

"How long are we to stay here?"

"I think you'll be comfortable in this room."

Ella layered her hands over her middle. "How long do you intend for us to remain here, Saber?" *She* would be comfortable in this room?

He busied himself throwing open draperies at two windows. "By daylight you'll be able to see a lake from here."

"It isn't daylight."

"No." After a pause, he closed the draperies once more. "We'll remain at Bretforten as long as seems appropriate."

"How will you decide what is appropriate?"

"I will decide." He turned to her. "Please allow me to make these decisions for us."

Yet again he had become distant, autocratic. "I am agreeable to your making such decisions," she told him quietly. "I merely asked what that decision might be, but no matter. I will wait until you're more comfortable treating me as an equal."

He made no response.

Ella studied the room. "I would have expected you to choose something more to your own taste than this. You favor more bold furnishings." Flower miniatures in gilt frames covered one of the silk-hung walls. Meissen figurines, ladies in wide crinoline skirts, shared every surface with porcelain flowers and small portraits in silver frames. Fashion dolls posed in outdated copies of gowns probably once featured in Ackerman's plates, and hundreds of shells, crowded the shelves of a narrow glass-fronted corner cabinet. The delicate, feminine furniture was all French.

Saber made no comment about the room. Instead he lifted a travel case onto the embroidered yellow counterpane and undid the straps.

"You're really going to wait upon me?" she asked him.

He opened the case and began a clumsy attempt at removing clothes from between layers of thin paper. "I told you I will do what a maid would do for you."

"I think I would rather get back in the coach."

Saber dropped a nightgown and it slid to the floor. "What?"

Ella strolled to stand beside him. She picked up the nightgown and replaced it in the trunk. "I said I should prefer to return to the coach. I like the coach. We can instruct Potts to keep driving until we tell him to stop."

"Ella—"

"Of course, we'd have to stop for fresh horses, and to let Potts eat and drink from time to time."

Saber removed the gown again, very deliberately, and spread it on the bed. "And what about our need to eat and drink, madam? Would we not get a little refreshment from time to time?" The old humor had stolen back into his voice.

"Not until we were too exhausted to continue with more satisfying activities." She looked up into his eyes. "I love making love to you, Saber."

He drew her to him and kissed her.

Chapter Twenty-seven

She knew he had left her—yet again.

Ella rolled over and pressed her hand into the cold pillow where his head had rested.

"Saber?" Pushing her hair from her eyes, she sat up and peered into the darkness.

This was the fifth night they'd spent at Bretforten Manor. The fifth night in which she and Saber had loved until Ella had fallen into a happy, drained sleep. The fifth night on which she'd awakened to find him gone.

Each morning he'd appeared, withdrawn and almost shy, to help her dress. Their days passed with Saber closed away in a small library, while Ella tried to make conversation with the pleasant but reticent Mrs. Gabbler, who very efficiently provided for her master and mistress's needs.

On the morning after they'd arrived, Ella tried to tell Saber how bereft she'd felt to find he'd deserted her bed. He'd told her, in very few words, that there were things best left unsaid.

Things must change.

"And there are things that *shall* be said, husband," she

told the empty room—and felt encouraged by the sound of her angry voice. "I shall say them, and you shall listen to them."

She climbed from the bed and pulled on the beautiful lace robe Great-Grandmama had given her. "Where are you, you rogue? How dare you be so wonderful, then be so perfectly horrid?"

Carrying a candle, Ella ventured from the room and started along the passageway that led toward the front of the house. "I am not afraid," she said loudly. "I have never been afraid of darkness, or being alone. Saber? Saber, where are you?"

Not even an echo responded.

"Very well, I shall simply have to hunt you down."

Ella hunted through one empty room after another. Most doors she opened revealed the draped shapes of furnishings; no room revealed any sign of Saber.

Her anger mounted. He had pledged to share his life with her, yet he'd chosen to exclude a very large part of that life. "But I'm going to claim it all, Saber," she muttered.

A fluttering fear turned her hands cold. Where *was* he? "Saber?" If he heard her, he'd answer, probably with a bellow of fury. "Saber, where are you?" she cried as roundly as her lungs would allow.

No sign of him anywhere.

A corridor she'd never taken before led to several rooms where the drapes had been removed from the furniture. One of the rooms was a bedchamber.

Ella entered slowly. Curtains at the windows were open wide, but no moon shone through the glass. The dying embers of a fire cast a faint, reddish glow.

She made out Saber's trunks and looked at once to the bed. With one hand at her throat, she approached on tiptoe.

Her breath escaped slowly. Tangled bedding had been

thrown back. On a chest beside the bed lay Saber's watch and chain—and something crumpled and pale.

Ella looked closely, and swallowed. One of the flowers she'd worn in her hair at their wedding. She hadn't known he'd taken it.

"Foolish man! All men are foolish! Silly creatures afraid of their own hearts." She picked up the flower and held it to her cheek. "Ooh, you will have to deal with the raw edge of your wife's temper, my good man."

Also on the chest sat a familiar brass box. Curiously, Ella lifted the lid, and remembered at once where she'd seen it before. Military buttons, all the same, lay inside. She took several into her palm. Why would a man bring such a thing on his wedding journey?

She snorted. Why would a man keep sneaking away from his new wife on his wedding journey? Lord Avenall was a puzzle.

And the biggest puzzle of all was his current location. She set down the flower and slid open a drawer in the chest. Raising the candle higher, Ella grimaced at the sight of three glowing emeralds in the handle of a wretched dagger.

Hateful dagger. Why would he take it everywhere he went?

The questions would go unanswered unless she asked them of him. To do so, she must find him. And she would.

She took up her search on the lower floor, shouting Saber's name as she went. The notion to arouse Potts came and went with equal speed. What must be done, she would do alone.

But she could not find her wretched husband!

Desperation raised every hair on her body. Her scalp prickled. Perspiration dampened her back. All that remained were the kitchens.

Aware of cold striking up from stone, Ella opened a door into the pantry—and a chill draft plucked at the hem of her robe and gown.

The candle blew out and she set it down. The door to the kitchen garden stood wide open.

"Rattle-brained man," she said, but her voice broke and her teeth chattered together. "Walking around in the wind and rain, no doubt. And in the dark."

Perhaps he'd heard something outside and gone to investigate.

Ella wiggled her toes inside insubstantial slippers. She should go back for some half-boots—and sturdy clothing.

He could not be far away. He might even be within her sight—once she looked outside. And he might be in trouble and need her help.

The rain remained fine, but fell more densely. A cold wind had picked up. Trees bent and whined beneath its force and the rain slanted sideways. Ella wiped at her eyes and ducked her head to peer in all directions.

"You are beyond all, Lord Avenall. Absolutely beyond all." She set off toward the abandoned apiary, along a path between rosebushes laden with blooms she'd admired by day. Tomorrow their petals would be strewn and ruined.

When she reached the churchyard that flanked the property, Ella retraced her footsteps before setting off across the lawns.

Every breath tore at her throat now.

She began to run. "Saber?" Where could he be? "Saber!" The wind threw her words back at her. The rain soaked her clothes and wound them about her.

He could have fallen into the lake!

Sobbing, hearing the rough rasp of her breathing, she headed for the water.

If she hadn't seen the glimmer of his white shirt, she'd likely have run on until she bumped into him.

Wet hair clung to her head and lay in sodden heaps over her shoulders. Gasping, she stopped. Her arms hung limp at her sides, and she fought to be calm. The buttons she'd forgotten to replace in their box cut into her palm.

The lake captured what light there was and Saber stood over that light, his cloak billowing behind him. Ella had caught sight of his shirtsleeve as he reached to gather the heavier garment around him.

She opened her mouth but could not bring herself to shout his name, even though he would surely hear her now.

"Saber," she whispered. "What troubles you, my love?"

He stared over the shifting surface of the lake, a tall, shadowy figure unbowed by wind and rain.

Ella crept closer until a thick rhododendron bush shielded her from him. She parted branches and watched.

Saber's profile showed dark against the lake's reflected light. She thought he swayed, but could not be certain.

He stared downward into the water.

Surely he didn't intend to . . .

Saber walked backward and she breathed again.

He walked backward until he reached a willow. He sank to the ground beneath swaying branches, and leaned against the trunk.

"Saber," she whispered again, her eyes filling with tears. He was troubled, deeply troubled, yet he would not share that trouble with her. He preferred to come out into the unkind night—alone—and suffer whatever devils attacked him.

She hovered, uncertain whether to go to him or return to the house and never let him know what she'd seen.

He moved, slowly, heavily. Slowly he fell to his side, then, heavily, he rolled to his back and lay with his arms outstretched.

"Oh," Ella murmured. "The very idea. Oh, this is the veriest . . . Oh, my goodness."

Bound by her wet nightclothes, she left the cover of the

rhododendron and trod over squelching turf toward her supine husband.

Her supine, *stupid* husband.

He gave no sign of hearing her approach. But the wind would have made that difficult.

He did not turn his head toward her, even when she stood inches from his hand.

His eyes were closed.

The front of his shirt, open to the waist, gaped.

Rain, fiercer and wilder now, beat his face and body. He did not as much as flinch.

Ella dropped to her knees on the muddy grass, knelt at his shoulder, and squinted closely at him.

His chest rose and fell steadily. His thick, dark lashes were wet, unmoving spikes. He slept, slept deeply. In the wind and the rain, beneath a dripping tree, beside a lake—in the earliest hours of the morning, Saber Avenall, Earl of Avenall, *slept*.

"Oh, Saber," she murmured, and bent over him. She rested her cheek on his bared shoulder.

"Get back!" he shouted, so suddenly, so savagely, she screamed.

She had no time to cry out again.

Saber shot an arm around her shoulders and swung her across his body. "Not again!" he yelled. "You shall not have more of them!"

Ella fought. She struggled to grasp his collar. "Saber! It's me, Ella!"

They rolled, over and over, toward the lake, and Ella grappled with him. She kicked and wound her legs around his hips. "Saber! Stop it!"

His fingers curled into the neck of her robe and gown, and he said, "It is my place," in a deep, harsh tone. "I will do what

I must do." He ripped her clothing apart, bared her breasts, bared her body from neck to hip.

Willow branches lashed across Saber's back and Ella's face. She flinched, and pummeled his shoulders. The wind and rain were a roaring scourge.

"You're hurting me!"

As abruptly as he'd attacked her, he grew still—utterly still. He said, "Oh, my God," very softly.

Pinned beneath him, Ella stared up into his face. His hair fell forward and his eyes glinted. "Saber, what is it? What's wrong with you?"

"Nothing," he told her, and the fury of the gathering storm edged the word. "Why are you here? Why are you creeping around after me?"

"Because . . ." Why *was* she here? Why *was* she creeping around after him? "I did not creep. I ran and shouted. I searched the whole house. When there was nowhere else inside to search, I came out here to look for you."

"Why?"

"Why?" She managed to push her hands above her head. Filling her fingers with his hair, she said, "I ran looking for you, through the house and out into the wind and rain, because I am married to a fool."

"I beg your pardon, madam?"

"Do not presume to beg anything of me, my lord. It is I who will demand. Not beg, but demand. What sends you from my bed the moment I am asleep?"

Saber gently freed her fingers from his hair. "It's usual for a man and his wife to sleep in separate bedrooms, my love."

She wriggled and bucked—to no avail. "Except when the man wishes to . . . to . . . Well, when he wishes to. Then, when he has done so, he sneaks away? Why should it be so?"

"Ella . . . There are things you don't understand."

"You *keep* telling me that. So why don't you explain?"

Saber shifted his weight from her and rested his head on a hand. "I've wanted to," he said, very low. "How I've wanted to."

So there was something. "Then tell me now. Let me help."

"I cannot be helped—only given protection."

"Protection?" Her mind refused to work. "What . . . ? Protection from what, Saber?"

"Those who would . . . Oh, Ella, I have wronged you."

The rain grew even heavier. Ella welcomed its cold bite upon her face. Their two soaked bodies drew heat, one from the other. She felt every inch of his solid muscles, every inch of his skin against hers. "You cannot have wronged me," she told him. "You have rescued me."

"There is so much I want to tell you, and I will," he said. "I shall ask much of you, Ella."

"And I will give much. I'll give you all that I am."

He kissed her then, a soft, fleeting kiss at first, a slipping of his lips across hers, a trail of salty tenderness. Then the kiss changed. His lips grew harder, more insistent as his tongue probed her mouth.

Ella's heart thumped rapidly. She pushed her hands over the wet hair on his chest, across smooth, damp skin at his sides and around to his back where she began, as she always did, to rub his scars with loving care.

"I need you," he said when their lips finally parted. "Now."

"You have me, Saber. You will always have me."

"You don't understand. I—"

"I *do* understand. When you explain yourself, I understand."

"Very well. I want to make love to you, Ella."

"Here?" They were all but awash upon a sea of muddy grass.

"Here," Saber said, and kissed her again. He found a stiffened nipple and pulled it gently. "Is it the rain that makes your flesh leap?" he asked.

Ella's reply was to force a way inside his trousers and encircle his most sensitive part. "Is it the rain that makes *your* flesh leap, my lord?" Her breasts ached, swelled.

"We both know what happens whenever we are together, Ella. I have only to look at you and I am lost."

"I have only to think of you and I am lost."

"I do not even . . . No." He gave a short laugh. "That way lies a long, annoying discussion, and I find I cannot waste time at the moment."

Ella tipped up her chin. She pulled his face down to hers and kissed him, a long, lingering, deep kiss. She showed him how well he had taught her to kiss.

"I once thought you had lain with other men."

Ella grew still.

"I thought that when you were at that house you were used by men. The thought haunted me."

"Is that why you did not claim me, even though you had promised you would?"

"In part. I am not proud to speak of it, Ella. But there must be no falsehood between us. At first I was angry, as angry that you had been used as I was for what I felt I'd lost. I was a fool."

He hunched his shoulders over her, just touching his chest to hers. The hair on his chest flirted with the tips of her nipples.

"Saber! Oh, Saber."

"Yes, my sweet." His hands went around her waist, beneath what was left of her gown and robe, and he turned them to their sides. Facing her, he stroked her bottom and dipped to take a nipple into his mouth.

"I want you," Ella said.

"The way I want you?"

"Always."

He shifted, dealt with his trousers, and pulled her leg over his hips. "Always and in whatever manner we can devise?"

"Yes," she sighed, amazed at the exquisite friction created by his slow, rain-wet penetration. He pulled her half over him and rocked his hips upward into hers.

Ella arched against him.

Saber used one hand to hold her bottom while he moved within her, and the other to play with her breasts. "There was never another woman for me once I'd met you," he told her.

Ella said, "I choose to forget how we wasted our love."

"Do you know what I'm telling you?" he asked.

Each thrust brought Ella closer to the sweet release she must have.

"After the night of our first meeting, I never took another woman to my bed. Throughout these years, I have waited for you, even while I thought we could not be together."

She searched his face. "I thought . . ." She trembled with her love for him. "I believed men always, well, that they always did."

He smiled and, as quickly, grimaced. "You have unleashed the waters that were held back, my lady. From this day forth, this man always *will*. Aah. In my heart, I married you one night, sitting at your side on a stone bench when you should have been in your bed. Aah, Ella."

Ella drew her leg more tightly around him. "So we came together new, my love."

"Who would believe such a thing," he murmured, and a great spasm drove his teeth together—and drove words from Ella's lips.

Saber held her to him. She crooned little, unintelligible words against his neck.

"I am a monster," he told her. "I should get you inside and dry before this damp is the death of us both."

"Hold me," she murmured.

He held her, tightly, and remained buried inside her.

He glanced away, and a spark of light off some object in the grass caught his eyes. Reaching, he pried the thing from the mud and turned it over in his hand.

A button. One of their buttons.

"No! Oh, God, no, no."

Ella raised her head to look at his face.

"Where did this come from?" He stared down at her. "You? You brought this here to torture me?" There could be no other explanation.

"I was looking for you—"

"Do not touch things that don't concern you." As he struggled to calm his breathing and his thundering heart, his rod quickened within her. "Don't! Do you understand me?" He began to lunge upward once more. He could scarcely breathe at all. The button seemed afire in his hand.

"I didn't mean . . . Oh, oh!"

"Don't!" He ground his teeth together and squeezed his eyes shut. Here, with her, joined to her, he could drive the memories away.

Voices reached him gradually. Shouting voices.

Ella pounded his shoulder with a fist and said his name over and over, each time more frantically.

"Over there!" a male voice cried. "By God, I'll kill him for this."

"Wait, Struan!"

Then they were upon them. A hard forearm snaked around Saber's neck, caught it in the bend of an elbow, and squeezed.

"Careful," another voice shouted. "Don't break his neck."

The next sound was Ella's scream.

"The man's mad." Dimly, Saber recognized Arran's voice. "Ravishing the girl like this. Poor child."

It was Calum who said, "Have a care, Struan. It's all right, Ella, my dear."

"Papa!" she cried. "Oh, Papa!"

Arran said, "She's all but naked. Give me a cloak to cover her, Devlin."

Consciousness faded. Saber clawed at the relentless arm around his neck but could find no purchase.

Devlin?

Chapter Twenty-eight

Great-Grandmama pounded the carpet between her feet with her cane. "I will not have my decisions questioned," she fumed. "This is an outrage. You have taken a woman from her husband."

"Your Grace," Uncle Arran said, standing before the old lady, an elegantly massive man who dwarfed her. "I assure you we have only done what was best for Ella."

"Best to take her from her husband?" She shook her head in the beribboned nightcap she still wore, having rushed from her bed the instant she heard of Ella's arrival with Struan, Arran, and Calum.

Embarrassment so deep it rendered Ella speechless made it difficult for her to meet the gaze of any of the men. "There is a mistake," she said softly. "A misunderstanding." It was a fact she had pleaded incessantly, and to no avail, since they'd taken her away from Saber.

They had waited only long enough for her to dress before leaving Bretforten—and leaving Saber, unconscious, in Devlin's care. Throughout the day they had ridden and, when darkness descended, found an inn for the night. Setting off again early this morning, they'd made it to London and come directly to Pall Mall.

"I did not want to leave Saber," she told Great-Grandmama. "They would not listen to me."

"Headstrong whippersnappers," Great-Grandmama announced. "What right did you have to take Ella from her husband? I gave the marriage my blessing. All that was required. They were married in the eyes of the church. And what God has joined, let no man—"

"This is not God's work," Papa said. Ella had never seen him so pale, or so angry. "The man is mad. He married my daughter to protect himself."

Ella's face snapped up. *Protect*. Saber had used that word.

"That's outrageous," the dowager said. "He married her because . . . he loves her, whatever that may mean. Where is he? Where is Saber? On his way here, no doubt. Should I prepare for a duel in me own boudoir?"

Uncle Calum said, "Devlin North's with him. Devlin understands the problem. Don't know what we'd have done without him."

"How so?" Ella asked, finding her voice at last.

Uncle Arran's green eyes sought her. "It's best that you leave these matters to men, Ella." He was so handsome—and so *overbearing*.

"I have asked a question," she said, planting her feet firmly apart. "What has Devlin North done that's so wonderful? Apart from helping you to separate me from my husband."

"I don't know how you can speak so," Uncle Calum said. His hair and eyes were so like mama's. Dark hair with flashes of red, and serious, dark amber-colored eyes. "We will not speak of the condition in which we found you, but it was an ugly thing."

"Papa," Ella implored. "Will you, at least, tell me the truth of things? It was Devlin North who secured Bretforten Manor for us. He has been Saber's friend, or so we thought."

Papa touched her arm lightly. "You have always been too beautiful for your own good, my child. But that is not your fault. Neither is it your fault if men long to possess you. You should be grateful that Devlin came to us in Scotland—in a great fright, I might add—to explain what was happening."

Ella felt as if she were carved from ice. "Would you please share his insights with me? His insights into what was happening?"

"You *know* what was happening. You are loyal to your husband—even though he has abused you, ruined you—and that is admirable. But you are aware of the circumstances in which we found you. Devlin had been afraid of just such a thing—that, and even more degrading behavior. He has been a friend to Saber for many years. He seeks to protect him and will do so now."

Protect again. "Protect him from what?"

The three powerful men in the room glanced uncomfortably at each other. "From himself," Uncle Calum told her. "Devlin came to inform us that Saber had engineered a marriage to you, but that Saber is caught in the web of some madness."

She made fists. "Saber is not mad!"

"Not always," Uncle Calum said, scrubbing at his unshaven jaw. "It comes and goes. But when it comes, he is very dangerous. And his condition only grows worse. One day Saber will have to be institutionalized. Devlin could scarcely bear to speak of this to us. He believes you know of Saber's condition but that you will try to hide that knowledge because you think you love him."

"I do love Saber! He has done nothing dreadful to me!"

Uncle Arran swung toward her. "When we found you, you were naked, your clothing torn from your body."

"Lord Stonehaven," Great-Grandmama said weakly. "I don't want to—"

"I am forced to say these things, madam," Uncle Arran said to Ella. "Your so-called husband attacked you in the middle of the night, outside, in a storm, no less. If we hadn't come upon you, God knows what might have happened. I shall always be grateful to Devlin North for what he did."

"And I shall always *hate* him," Ella said. "He is a viper who used a good man's trust to bring that man down. You do not know this, but Devlin North offered for me himself—in secret, inappropriately."

"I know." Papa slipped an arm around her shoulders. "He told me as much, and he told me the reason. He thought it his duty to save you from Saber."

Ella gaped.

"Now, now, don't think any more ill of Devlin. He was quick to add that he would consider himself a very lucky man to be your husband. And, in fact, he has offered to take you regardless after all this is resolved."

"Oh!" Ella whirled away and back. She had never known such frustration, such desperation. "And you believed all this?"

"Certainly," Uncle Calum said, but his face was deeply troubled. "Not that you should think Struan has any notion of marrying you off to someone in a hurry just to save your—"

"My *reputation?* Hah! My reputation is intact, thank you all. And you can hardly marry me again when I am already married."

Papa stood in front of her, blocking any view of the others. He ducked his head and looked seriously into her face. "You have been through too much, my child. Away to your bed.

And do not concern yourself with this. Marriage to a man who is not in his right mind should be a simple enough thing to void."

She shrugged away from him. "Saber is in his right mind, I tell you. And the marriage shall not be voided. I love him!"

"I know," Papa said, clearly embarrassed. "Please trust me to do what's best for you. What we know shall not leave this room, except for the necessary official business."

"And what of Saber? What will you do with my husband?"

"He is not your husband," Calum said, avoiding her eyes. "Your mama will arrive soon enough, and your aunts. We shall all help you through this dreadful thing. And we shall help Saber, too. Believe that we will."

They were immovable. Their minds were completely set on this, and Devlin North had been the one to plant the evil seeds against Saber.

Ella looked to Great-Grandmama, who shook her head slightly.

So there was to be no help there. "I think I'll do as you suggest, Papa," Ella said, making herself smile at him. "I'm very tired. I shall go to bed. Will one of you send Rose to me?"

She left them amid a chorus of sympathetic sounds. Summoning Rose had been a precaution. As soon as she'd allowed the maid to think her mistress was tucked up in bed, Ella would find a way to leave Pall Mall and set off for the Cotswolds and Saber. She would have to consider carefully how she would divert Devlin for long enough to allow her to release her husband.

Her stomach burned at the thought of her dear Saber locked away, yet she felt in her bones that the only way Devlin would contain him would be by force, and while Saber was unconscious.

The buttons. Ella stopped on the stairs and almost turned

back. Military buttons. When Saber had been suddenly awakened, he'd cried out, "You shall not have more of them," or something similar. Was he remembering some horrible battle in India? The death of some of his men, perhaps? She carried on. All of these things would be made clear to her and she would help Saber overcome whatever troubled him so deeply.

A fire burned brightly in her sitting room and in her bedroom. Rose was already present, her blue eyes anxious. "Are you all right, then, miss—I mean, my lady?" The girl tugged awkwardly at the cap she wore over her blond hair. "Just you tell me what I can do to 'elp, then."

Ella kept all emotion at bay. "I'll go to bed, thank you, Rose. I've had a tiring journey. Where's Max? Back at Oxford?"

Rose rubbed her hands together. "Bigun went back to Lord Avenall's house. And Mr. Crabley's—"

"I did not ask about the staff." One finger at a time, Ella pulled off her gloves. "I repeat, has Max returned to Oxford?"

Rose's face turned a mottled shade of pink. "That's what everyone's supposed to think," she said.

Ella dropped her gloves on a table. "But he hasn't gone back to school? Is that what you're saying, Rose?"

"Aye." The girl's throat clicked as she swallowed. "I 'aven't known what t'do. I was going to go to the dowager, only you arrived, so I thought I'd . . . Well, I thought I should talk to you about it—like 'e told me. Only, I was afraid."

Ella hadn't eaten in far too long. Weakness overcame her and she sat down in the nearest chair. "Do you know where my brother is, Rose?"

The maid wrung her hands. Her young face worked.

"Rose? Please do not keep this from me."

"He was supposed to have gone by coach. I know 'e didn't. I saw him go to the stables and I followed. I begged 'im to talk to the dowager, but 'e wouldn't listen to the likes of me."

Ella rubbed at her eyes.

"You don't feel well, do you, my lady?" Rose said. "Mayhap you're already increasin'."

Ella looked at her askance. She knew what the word meant. "I hope I am," she said stoutly. "Yes, that would be the finest thing I could imagine. Now, Max left on horseback. Perhaps he decided to ride back to school."

"No, my lady. He only went a short while since. Right after you was returned with their lordships and the duke. Oh, I asked him not to do it. And I asked him not to make me a part of it. He said he'd made sure I saw him go to the stables because he knew I'd follow and there was something he wanted me to do for him."

Another of Max's intrigues. Irritation tweaked Ella's nerves. She waited for Rose to draw the courage to finish her story.

"Max wanted me to come to you and tell you he's had to go to the 'ouse you'll know of. He made me promise not to speak to anyone but you. Could cause his death if I did, so he told me, my lady. I 'aven't told a soul, and I won't. Oh, I'm so worried about Master Max."

Ella pushed to her feet. "Lushy's," she whispered.

"Beg pardon, my lady?"

"Nothing. Was there anything more? Did Max tell you anything else?"

"Just that you was to follow him to the 'ouse you'll know of. He said you mustn't let anyone else know where you're going, but you'd better get there before it's too late."

An alley flanked the tall wall surrounding the gardens at Pall Mall. Dawn's purple blush was upon the city. The smells were of roses in the gardens, and bread baking in the kitchens of great houses, and, faintly, the downdraft of smoke.

Saber paced, and chafed the rope burns on his wrists. Bigun followed him, reversing direction each time Saber reversed direction.

"Where the blazes is Crabley? What's taking so long?"

"He'll come just as quickly as possible, my lord. Crabley is a most reliable fellow."

Saber grunted and continued his tramping. If Crabley and Bigun had not arrived at Bretforten—apparently as a result of a message Bigun received from Margot—Saber would still be tied to a chair in a locked room.

He looked at his watch. "Half an hour! What can be taking half an hour?"

"I should think there are many possible explanations for the length of time—"

"Yes, Bigun," Saber interrupted. "I'm sure there are. But I want my wife and I want her now."

"Mr. North will likely be on his way soon, my lord. We hit him hard, but he's a strong man. Have we considered how to deal with him when he comes?"

"He will not come," Saber said, and hoped he was right. "If he does, I shall kill him. I promised him as much before you arrived."

Bigun looked away.

"No," Saber said, "what you're thinking is correct. I shall likely not kill him since I have sworn never to . . . I shall not kill him but he will wish he were dead. But Devlin is no fool. He will take his chance to put as much distance as possible between us."

"I think I hear someone coming," Bigun said. This morning his red silk tunic and white trousers appeared decidedly misused.

"Good." Saber faced the gate into the gardens. "Ella is the

answer to my—my condition. She can heal me, I know that now."

The gate opened and Crabley stepped into the alley. He closed the gate carefully behind him. His round, black eyes popped with anxiety. "The news isn't good," he said. "I had to be careful or they might have followed me out here."

"Where's Ella? Why didn't you bring her with you? Have they confined her somewhere?"

Crabley held up short-fingered hands. His mouth stretched wide, then formed a little O before he said, "I spoke with Rose. The girl's beside herself, but I convinced her to reveal what she knows. She hasn't told another soul. Afraid to."

Saber grabbed the butler's lapel and drew him near. "Tell me—"

"My lord!" Bigun said, working to pry Saber's fingers from Crabley's coat. "Mr. Crabley is most helpful. Do not abuse him, if you please."

Saber released Crabley as abruptly as he'd taken hold of him. "Yes, yes. Forgive me."

"You're anxious, my lord," Crabley said, brushing at his crumpled lapel. "Rose is very afraid. Seems she's the only one with certain knowledge. We'll have to go quickly, or we may be too late."

"Go where?" Saber and Bigun asked in unison.

"To a certain house?" Crabley raised his eyebrows questioningly. "Rose said Max told her to get Miss Ella—her ladyship—to follow him to a house they both know of. Whatever that means. Evidently the young man told Rose his life might be forfeit if she revealed his destination to anyone but Lady Avenall. And his life would be forfeit for certain if Lady Avenall didn't follow him there at once."

This time Ella was shown not into the rose sitting room at Lushbottam's, but into a larger room on the second floor. The motif here was grapes. Plum-colored grapes. Wax bunches cascaded from shell-shaped bowls supported by naked female forms. More bunches blossomed over painted tiles around the fireplace and crept with startling brilliance over the wallpaper.

The front door had opened before Ella had time to knock, and Milo had drawn her inside. His excitement showed in the unnatural height of his color, and in the clamminess of his fingers on her wrist.

He'd guided her up to this dreadful room and closed her in. She'd heard a key turn in the lock.

An hour or more had passed since then, with no sound from the passageway. The room was windowless, but lamps burned on tables beside a four-poster bed draped in almost the same plum color as the wax grapes. Heaps of pillows scattered the floor, and a chaise of pale mauve trimmed with gold-tasseled braid stood before the fireplace.

Ella tried the doorknob. She'd done so several times and knew it would not turn, but she could not help herself.

Footsteps sounded.

She withdrew to the farthest corner of the room and watched the door. Her stomach chased her heart into her throat.

The key turned in the lock.

Ella drew her cloak more firmly about her. She would ask to see Max at once, then demand to be allowed to leave.

Milo came into the room. He smiled, but Ella noted that his hovering hands trembled.

"As I've already said," she told him. "I've come for Max. Bring him to me at once."

"Of course," Milo said, glancing nervously over his shoulder. "He's coming right now. Come on, Max. Your sister wants to see you."

Milo stood aside and Max appeared. He came toward Ella with a plea in his eyes that sent her running to take him in her arms. "What is it?" she whispered, hugging him. "What's happened to you?"

"Do as he asks," Max told her. "He says that if you will, nothing bad will happen to either of us."

Ella held his arms and stood back. She should have used her best judgment and told someone where she was going. "Why are you here, Max?"

He bowed his head. "I was a fool. The night when I told you I'd been trying to get into White's"—he glanced at her—"I came here, not to White's. I came here because I wanted to know. I wanted to know if I could find out anything about . . . I wanted to know who I am. Who I really am."

"Oh, Max." She should have known he would come to this point. "You are yourself. Just as I am myself. Mother died and—"

"But I knew Milo hadn't," Max said, rushing now. "So I came to see if I could find out where he was. And he was glad to see me. Very glad. He told me . . . Oh, Ella, I've brought you terrible trouble. I'm sorry."

She shook him gently and looked at Milo, who remained near the door. "I'm sure Milo encouraged you to come here out of family affection," she said, sure of no such thing. "But we must return home now, before we are missed."

"I played into his hands. I made it easier for him. He wanted to get you here again, and he used me."

Goose bumps popped out on Ella's arms. "Milo won't do anything to harm us."

"Yes, he will!" Max jerked away from her. "He told me he wasn't my uncle. He said he was mother's lover, not her brother, and that I was his son. I believed him. I wanted to believe him."

Ella shook her head. "No, Max, no. You should have told me. I could have—"

"I know it isn't true." Misery weighted down the boy's

shoulders. "He admits as much now he's got what he wants. He will use us to control each other."

"That's enough," Milo snapped. "I didn't have to let you see him, Ella. Now you have, you know I have not harmed him. Yet. You will do as you're told, missy, and we'll get along well enough."

"We're leaving," Ella said, not feeling as brave as she sounded. "Kindly step aside."

"Is that any way to speak to your old uncle?"

"We never want to see or hear of you again. Make no attempt to contact us further, do you understand?"

"I've heard enough of your lip, miss," Milo said. "Out with you, boy. And don't try anything or your sister'll be the one to suffer."

Max stood beside Ella. "I'll not leave her to you."

"If you don't leave her to me," Milo said, all silk now. "If you don't, I'll have you dragged away and she'll be whipped by someone who'll enjoy the job."

Ella smothered a cry. "Go, Max. Please. I can take care of myself—and you. Just go for now."

He hovered.

"Go, Max!" Ella said. "Please."

With dragging steps, he did as she asked.

Milo waited until Max disappeared from sight and turned excited eyes on Ella. "Now we can get on with it. You'll do just as you're told, missy, unless you want that whipping. And don't think I wouldn't take pleasure in it—and in seeing that little nuisance of a brother of yours squirm too. Your mother shouldn't have spent herself trying to care for the two of you when I needed her. Now it's time for you to make good on what I lost."

Ella held herself rigidly straight. "I am a married woman. My husband will come to my rescue."

Milo snickered. "From what I hear, that isn't very likely.

Anyway, I hear your visitors arriving. Do as you're told. They've paid me well for what they want from you and the blunt's already spent."

Precious Able rustled into the room. A malicious smirk held none of the "friendship" she'd begged of Ella.

Chapter Twenty-nine

"I always knew you were a slut." Pink and white as a party meringue, Precious approached Ella with mincing steps. Her taffeta skirts swayed, and her extravagant evening hat bobbed. She clasped her hands behind her back. Her embarrassingly displayed breasts rose and fell with each rapid breath.

Confusion overwhelmed Ella. "Did you come to help me?"

Precious giggled. "Of course I did, Ella-the-whore. I've come to help you stop pretending to be something you're not. The *ton* knows all about you, but they're too afraid of the Rossmaras and the Franchots to tell you what they think of you. I'm not. I'll tell you to your face. Think of it. You being all high and mighty, when all you are is the *adopted* daughter of a viscount! Did you think no one would find out you used to be a whore?"

"No." Ella couldn't seem to think properly. "No, it's not true."

Precious brought her hands in front of her. "*Yes*, it is. And you still are. There are some things you can't stop being."

Staring at what Precious held, Ella stepped backward. A gown of flimsy red chiffon trailed from Precious's fingers.

Ella looked at Milo. "Why is she here? Why is she trying to frighten me?"

"Just do as you're told, missy," Milo said. "Remember that snot-nosed brother of yours, and do as you're told."

"You've got to put this on." Precious held out the gown and Ella thought the other woman's face registered something else behind the malice. "Go on. Take off your clothes and put this on."

"No." Ella shook her head and sat on the chaise. "You're ill, Precious. You must be. How can you be involved in all this?"

"Take off your clothes!"

Ella wrapped her cloak firmly about her.

A stinging slap to her cheek shocked Ella. Shocked and hurt her. She drew away from Precious, who now loomed over her, ugly patches of red staining her face.

Precious raised her hand again.

This time Ella was quicker. She ducked aside and grasped Precious's wrist at the same time.

Precious struggled furiously. Words Ella had never heard streamed from the girl's mouth.

Using both hands, Ella twisted Precious's substantial wrist. Precious grappled and screeched. "Let me go, whore! Let me go! Ooh, you're hurting me!" Under the weight of three ostrich plumes, her elaborate beaded evening hat tipped forward. She dropped the red dress.

"That'll do, Ella," Milo said.

She glanced at him and saw with revulsion that he found the scuffle enjoyable. "I'm a married woman. My husband will punish you for this."

Swiping at the ostrich plumes, Precious struggled ineffectually against Ella's strong hands. "You thought you were going to be a lady." She spat in Ella's face. "Well, a lady is as a lady does, and you're no lady. And your fancy marriage is over anyway."

"How . . ." Ella couldn't let go to wipe away Precious's spittle. "That's not true. Saber and I have been married a week now."

"You mean you've been rutting for a week," Precious said. "I know all about it. The marriage is going to be annulled. I don't know why anyone wants you . . . Get Pommy!" she shrieked suddenly.

Ella's limbs wobbled. "Pommy? Do you mean Pomeroy Wokingham?"

"Of course I do. Get him, old man! Get him now. Tell him he can put the red dress on his whore himself. I'm tired of helping him with this. He's got me." She glowered at Ella through the feathers. "I'm all he needs, but he's got you in his blood. So we're just going to get you out and be done with it."

She had to be strong. Ella applied another twist to Precious's arm and produced the expected scream. The girl was physically soft and weak. Ella had spent most of her life fending for herself, and even in the years at Kirkcaldy, she'd roamed the estate, more often on horseback or working beside a tenant wife than sipping tea.

Pomeroy Wokingham arrived. His thin mouth drooped petulantly. "You can get out now, scab," he told Milo. "And don't come back unless I tell you to."

"But the money—"

"I've already paid, fool. Get out."

"But—"

A hard kick, with the toe of a boot, connected with Milo's knee. He crumpled against the wall.

"Don't come back," Pomeroy yelled. "Go on! Go on!"

Whimpering, Milo shuffled away.

"Oh, Pommy," Precious cried. Ella let her go and she rushed, arms opened wide, toward Pomeroy Wokingham.

"Oh, Pommy, she's vicious. She twisted my wrist and spat at me. Imagine. She *spat* at me!"

Ella didn't bother to argue. There would be no point. Any more than there would be a point in asking what Lord Wokingham's fiancée was doing here—and in the company of Lord Wokingham's son.

"She spat, hey?" Pomeroy said with a smile that resembled a snarl. He shook free of Precious's embrace. "Good. Glad to hear she's got plenty of spirit. More fun that way."

"But Pommy!"

Pomeroy spared Precious a look. His eyes passed over her body but returned to her breasts. "They are your best asset," he said, obviously assuming no more explanation was necessary. He used a foot to shut the door. "Yes, your best asset. Why cover them at all, my dear?"

Before Precious could respond, and while Ella cringed, Pomeroy Wokingham tore open what there was of Precious's bodice, revealing her big breasts balanced atop a very uncomfortable-looking corset contraption. Stiffened buckram cups presented their jiggling, brown-tipped offerings rather like milk-jellies decorated with large spoonfuls of damson jam.

Precious batted coyly at Pomeroy but made no effort to cover herself. Rather, she put her hands on her hips and strutted before Ella. "She's scrawny, Pommy," she said. "Not like me. We could do it right here, if you like. In front of her. Come on, Pommy, I'm ready for you. I'm always ready fc you."

"In time," Pomeroy said, with eyes only for Ella. "Pick up the gown," he told her.

Sickened, she pressed her lips together and didn't move.

"Oh, we're going to be difficult," Pomeroy remarked. He crossed his arms and checked his fingernails. "I like that. So much more of a challenge. Things that come too easily can become boring." This time he did give Precious his attention. He tucked two fingers into her corset, between her breasts, and hauled her to him. Very deliberately, he squeezed each of her breasts hard, and laughed when she moaned with pain.

"Don't," Ella said. "Don't. You're hurting her."

"You shut up!" Precious told her. "And do as you're told. I'll help you, Pommy. You know I'll always help you."

His response was to pinch the silly girl's nipples viciously.

Ella turned away.

From the corner of her eye, she saw Pomeroy move toward her. "I've changed my mind, Precious. Get out."

"Pommy!"

"Get out!"

"But you promised. You said I could be here."

"Well, you can't. To keep you quiet, I pretended I'd let you stay—I was afraid you'd bring Father here at a run." He sneered at Precious. "Won't be able to do that now, will you? He'd only have to take one look at you to know what you've been up to with me. Just do as you're told and I may not tell Father what a little slut you really are. Now, stay out of my way. I've waited a long time to get what's mine, and I'm not sharing it—with anyone."

It. He referred to her as "it." Ella tried to be calm, tried to gauge her chances of making it to the door without being stopped.

No chance at all.

"Pommy, I don't want—"

"I don't care what you want, you stupid jade. I've shared everything for too long. Get out into the passageway and make sure no one comes in here."

Still half-naked and sniveling now, Precious did as she was told.

Leaning forward from the waist, Pomeroy approached Ella until he could poke his vile face into hers. "At last," he said.

"We're going to be alone, my gypsy. After so many years of waiting, you're going to do what I paid for."

Years! She avoided his pale, flat eyes. Only inches from hers, they gleamed almost opalescent.

"I won't look, you know," he said.

Ella didn't move. What was he talking about?

"Not until you're ready for me. Wouldn't want to spoil it."

With Precious gone, the odds for an escape were slightly better.

Pomeroy thrust the chiffon gown at Ella. "Go over there and change. Behind the bed curtains." He smiled, and trailed the back of a finger along her jaw. "So beautiful. You're going to dance for me, my beautiful gypsy."

She would not allow herself to flinch away from him. Instead she forced a little smile.

Pomeroy's smile widened. "That's the way. Be good to Pomeroy. He's earned it after all these years of waiting."

Again he referred to waiting a long time for something, something to do with her.

"Go along," he said, his tone singsong. "Go and do what Pomeroy tells you. I'll make things nice for us while I wait."

Panic dried Ella's mouth. She couldn't make her feet move.

Pomeroy gave her a little push. "Go along, now. Take everything off, mind you. I want you just the way you were when I first saw you."

Ella froze.

"Aha!" He capered, grinning and rubbing his hands together. "Now you know, don't you?"

"No," she managed to whisper. "No, I don't know anything. I don't know what you're talking about. When Saber—"

"Don't speak his name to me!" The grin died. Pomeroy's eyes narrowed. "That's all over. A little mistake I'll forget if you're a very good girl."

Ella threw the chiffon gown aside. "I shall certainly speak my husband's name. I'll speak it as often as I please."

Pomeroy's features twisted. He bared his stained teeth and advanced on her. "You have no husband. You're mine. I bought you."

Her heart missed beats. She grasped one of the bedposts.

"That's right. I bought you in this very house. Mine was the highest bid, but Hunsingore stole you. For what? That's what I'd like to know. You don't think I believe he just wanted to *save* you, do you?"

This man had been there—on that horrible night. "Papa," she said faintly. "He is the kindest of men. He took me—and he took Max—because he is generous. Just as Mama is generous and Uncle Arran and Aunt Grace. And Uncle Calum and Aunt Pippa. You know nothing of such people."

"Because they're better than I?" His face drew together in a fearsome glare. "They are no better than I. They merely hide behind their elevated titles and reputations. But I am beating them all tonight. When I have finished with you, they will be glad to get rid of you."

"Saber . . ." She could not finish her thought, or make more words.

"Lord Avenall is a madman. But I should thank him for that. Had he not been so, then your beloved relatives would not have done me the favor of returning you to London—and your dim-witted brother could not have been persuaded to trap you into coming here."

"Let me go."

"Never. Never again. This is to be our little ceremony of joining. Afterward I will take you away."

Ella rallied. She drew herself up. "It is you who are mad. How can you imagine that my husband will not look for me?"

Pomeroy took off his coat and set it on the chaise. The black and orange striped waistcoat he wore showed off the narrowness of his chest and shoulders. "I have it on the best authority—your brother's comments to the old man—that Lord Avenall is safely under lock and key. Enough of this! Do not spoil something so special. I do not wish to have to undress you myself."

When she didn't move, he picked up the gown and threw it onto the bed. "Put it on. I shall deal with the lights."

He went about lighting red candles he produced from a box on the mantel. All other lamps he extinguished, until a crimson glow washed the awful purple room.

When he'd finished, he looked at Ella as if she were a bad child. "Come, come now—"

"I shall do nothing you ask of me," she said clearly. "Nothing. Anything you take from me will be taken, Mr. Wokingham. I shall give you nothing."

He dithered, walking closer, and backing away again—then making half-circles in front of her, watching her all the while.

Ella felt cold, but clearheaded. He could do terrible things to her body, take her body, but he could not touch her mind. He could not put his fingers upon her heart or her soul. In those places her hatred for him would be strong. In those places she would guard her love for Saber no matter what happened to either of them.

"You break my patience!" Pomeroy darted at her. He snared the collar of her cloak and the clasp opened. As he pulled the garment away, she spun around, then steadied herself on the bedpost once more.

A surge of energy dulled Ella's fear. "You will never get what you want," she told Pomeroy. "Never. You tried to buy a child here in this house, but it didn't work. You want me now, but it still will not work."

He lunged.

Ella darted aside, and Pomeroy's head slammed into the bedpost where she had been.

"Bitch!" He flung himself around. A wide cut had opened on his brow and blood began to seep toward his right eye. "You'll suffer for that."

She saw the fire poker.

Pomeroy noted the direction of her glance and rushed to cut her off.

Ella all but threw herself toward the fire. Her hands closed on the wooden handle of the tool.

Pomeroy's hands closed on top of Ella's.

They fell and rolled, over and over. The stench of Pomeroy's drink-laced breath brought Ella's stomach roiling into her throat. She gritted her teeth and fought him.

With strength she'd never known she possessed, she clung to the poker.

Pomeroy took one hand away and dragged up her skirts. "You want it this way? Good enough, madam. Good enough." She felt his clammy fingers tearing at her drawers.

With all the power she could muster, Ella heaved, thrust a knee free, and struck at whatever part of him she could reach.

Pomeroy screamed. Tears bubbled in his eyes. His mouth opened wide, and he howled.

Pleased with her success, Ella repeated the blow with her knee.

Like a cornered animal, he lashed out, crying and screaming all the while. He blubbered, and while he did so, he destroyed every part of Ella's clothing he could snatch.

She willed her mind free of her body's struggle, and applied her knee yet again.

He struck her face. And he jerked, drew his knees up to his chest, and gasped. A table crashed on top of them, then splintered against the hearth tiles.

His next blow was to her shoulder. He pounded the fine

bones there with as much force as he could summon. Ella heard the impact, and felt her arm grow numb. Their two hands, one of hers, one of his, still held the poker.

"That is all," he told her through his teeth. He sat astride her and pounded the back of the hand that held the poker against the floor. Again and again he pounded, until, at last, she could hold on no longer.

"So be it," she said, tasting her own tears, her own blood. "But I give you nothing. And you are no gentleman."

With the poker upraised, he laughed as if at some great triumph.

"Yes," she told him. "What a man you are. You have beaten a woman in combat."

"And to the winner falls the spoils," he chortled, before Ella felt a draft of air fan her bared legs.

"Pomeroy!" a new voice bellowed.

"Get out," Pomeroy said, blood trickling in rivulets over his face now. "Shut the door, dammit. This is nothing to do with you."

Whoever he spoke to entered the room roaring unintelligibly.

"Pommy, you've got to stop and let him help." Precious sounded truly frightened. "He's very angry, Pommy. Oh, do stop. We mustn't be—"

"Shut *up,*" Pomeroy said, his words hissing through his lips. "Go away, Father. And take that bitch with you."

Lord Wokingham. Ella squirmed beneath her attacker. She could not bear him touching her. Surely his father would stop this disgusting assault.

"We agreed," Lord Wokingham said. "We were to have our little wedding ceremony for Precious and me. Then we would put the gown on Ella and you could marry her, so to speak. I've looked forward to it. But what do I find? I find me own fiancée half naked out there, while you're in here being selfish."

"But I did send for you, Woky," Precious said through hiccuping sobs. "I did send the coach, didn't I?"

Pomeroy reared up, the poker brandished aloft. "I don't need either of you."

Before Ella could draw a breath to scream, the Honorable Pomeroy Wokingham smashed a poker into his father's head, and raised the implement to strike again.

Holding the tattered parts of her gown together, Ella scrambled to her feet.

The older Wokingham's spindly legs buckled. An expression of piteous shock widened his eyes. Flesh lay open to shining white skull bone. Blood gushed from a huge wound and from the man's nose.

"Woky!" Precious cried at last.

Pomeroy struck again, slashing at his parent's face and ear this time. But blood already poured from the man's mouth, and his eyes had grown flat and unseeing.

Slowly, without another sound, he fell backward, his legs folded unnaturally beneath his heavy body.

Voices in the passageway reached Ella. She couldn't hear what they said, didn't try. Lord Wokingham lay dead before her, dead at the hands of his own son, who now turned his attention to Precious Able.

"No," Ella whispered. "Leave her alone."

"I cannot imagine why you insist upon bringing me up here," another woman's voice announced from the passage. "I have no wish to prolong our acquaintance, Mr. Milo."

The voice stopped Pomeroy from swinging at Precious. She promptly swooned into a heap on the carpet.

The sight of Countess Perruche, arguing with Milo, was a final unreal stroke. Spent, Ella slid to sit on the floor. She reached her cloak and pulled it around her.

As she came into the room, the countess looked over her shoulder at Milo. "I paid you well and you did a poor job of things. But all is well now."

"So glad," Milo said, a cunning twist to his lips. "I made sure the pieces of chiffon were delivered. And the letter. And then I had a piece of luck with the boy coming to me."

"Boy?"

"Max. Her brother. He came, and that helped. I was able to give Ella the message about how you'd let everyone know about her life here at Lushy's if she didn't do like she was told."

"I have no interest in that," Margot said. "Fortunately Lord Avenall will never have reason to think I manipulated what had to be. I could not risk losing his patronage. Now I shall not have to. I am to become his helpmate. There will be an annulment. Mr. North can have the girl. I shall care for Lord Avenall—and his money."

Milo laughed. "A nice arrangement."

"I'm here to make sure you understand that you are never to mention our acquaintance . . ." She saw Lord Wokingham's body, and Precious still in a faint, then Pomeroy with the poker in his hands. *"Mon Dieu!"* She did not notice Ella.

"Oh, my," Milo said conversationally. "These domestic spats can get so unpleasant, can't they?"

"This is nothing to me," Margot said, turning away.

She turned away and walked into Saber.

"Hold her," he told Bigun, who followed him. "Don't let the *countess* go. Oh, Ella." He waved for her to retreat. "Get back, my love. It's all right. I'll deal with this fiend."

Pomeroy had no chance to raise his poker before Saber attacked. He caught the other man by the front of his shirt and drew him up until he could stare coldly down at him.

Before Ella's horrified eyes, Pomeroy contrived to change his grip on the poker he still held. Slipping his hand down the shaft, he grasped it just above the pointed end. He drew his hand as far away from Saber's back as possible.

"No!" Ella cried, flinging herself forward and clutching Pomeroy's wrist just as it would have sent the filthy metal point gouging into Saber's flesh.

He released the weapon. Ella fell to the floor and the poker clattered away.

Saber spun around and bent over her.

"Pomeroy!" Ella shouted. "He's getting away."

"He won't get far," Saber told her, gently gathering her to him. "Crabley's outside the front door with a pistol, and instructions to use it."

"I want to be with you," she told Saber. "I never want to be parted from you again."

He frowned as he touched her face where Pomeroy had hit her. "You never will be. Not as long as I live. My God! What's that?"

Clattering and thudding sounded from below—and gurgling screams.

"Gawd aw'mighty," Milo said, raising his voice. He still maintained his position half in and half out of the room. "Look at the mess in here. Who's going to pay for it? that's what I'd like to know. And listen to that racket. What does an old man have to do to get some peace?"

The thunderous crashing and screaming ceased soon enough.

"Bring her," Saber told Bigun, referring to Margot. He glanced at Precious, who had struggled to her feet. "Get yourself to my house in Burlington Gardens. We'll send you back to your parents—with an explanation of your behavior. They can decide your fate."

Precious blubbered afresh.

"I came here to help Ella," Margot said, slapping ineffectually at Bigun. "Tell him, Ella. I came to help you."

Holding Ella against him, Saber walked slowly past Margot and into the passageway. As they approached the stairs, Ella buried her face in his chest. "They did not mean to do you any harm," she said, referring to Papa, Uncle Arran, and Uncle Calum. "They were told you were mad and they thought they were saving me from you."

"I have Devlin North to thank for that. Margot sent Crabley and Bigun after me, but only to make the pretense of helping me. Devlin was to do away with both of them. She and Devlin misjudged Bigun particularly. He has fought in ways they cannot even imagine. And Crabley is a man I would trust at my back."

"Is it over now?" Ella asked him.

"We have more to overcome. But I believe we can do it. That night—by the lake at Bretforten—you broke through something I had thought could never change."

"You are not mad," Ella told him.

"No," he agreed. "I am not mad. But I need to deal with those things I have hidden for so long."

Ella kissed him quickly as they continued walking.

Saber started to speak, but tried instead to stop Ella from seeing the scene at the bottom of the stairs.

"Oh, no, no!" Precious Able screamed. She ran past them and down the steps. Her hat trailed by a pin and her gown was in tatters.

Ella pulled herself from Saber's arms and looked after the other woman.

At the foot of the stairs, Precious fell to her knees beside the unmoving and grotesquely distorted form of Pomeroy Wokingham.

Crabley stood over the pair. He looked up at Ella and Saber and spread his arms. "There you are, Lord Avenall. Lady Avenall." He pointed to Pomeroy. "They do say more people die of falls than anything else, don't they? People should learn not to be in such a hurry, particularly coming downstairs."

"Is he dead?" Saber asked.

Crabley's face worked through a series of frowns and grimaces before he pulled a pistol from the waistband of his breeches. He studied the weapon with evident disappointment. "I don't think he'd be any deader if I shot him now, my lord."

Epilogue

Castle Kirkcaldy, Scotland, Late Summer, 1828

"Ye dinna *so*, Max Rossmara," Kirsty Mercer said, planting her thin hands on her hips. "And me da says it's pleasin' t'the devil when ye tell stories."

Max rolled from his back to his stomach and squinted up at the ten-year-old who stood before him. "If I say I fought a dozen men in London, then I fought a dozen men in London, Miss Kirsty Mercer." The little blond girl, daughter of Robert and Gael Mercer, whose families had been tenants on Rossmara lands for generations, had known Max from his first days at Kirkcaldy.

Bright afternoon sunlight shone through the child's long curls. She shook them back and planted her feet apart. "Ye've grown uppity, Master Max. I suppose ye're too good for the likes o' me now."

"Come, come, now, baby," Max said, catching Kirsty's wrist and urging her to sit on the dry grass in front of him. "You're my favorite Scottish kelpie. Always will be."

She applied a forefinger to his nose and brought her eyes so close to his that hers crossed, and he laughed. "Dinna laugh at me," she said, giggling herself. "At least say ye dinna kill anybody in that foreign place. Me ma says a man who kills isna' a man unless he'd die fer the want o' the killin'."

"Aye," Max said, beginning to slip into the brogue he'd once deliberately adopted. "Well, since it's you I'm talking to, and since I know you'll like me no matter what, I'll tell the truth."

He rested his chin on his folded hands. Life was good at Kirkcaldy. After what he'd almost done to Ella, he didn't deserve to be here with the rest of the family, but he was grateful they refused to let him leave them. Uncle Calum had helped the most. He'd told Max how he'd risked everything to be sure who he was—and how much he regretted never having met his father. If Uncle Calum could admit a few mistakes, why should Max do less?

Kirsty maneuvered onto her tummy, stretched out, and copied Max's pose. She'd mimicked everything he did from the day he'd first been taken to visit her parents' cottage. He'd only been a child of eleven then, rather than a man of sixteen.

"So tell me, then, " Kirsty said. "The truth, Max."

"I didn't kill anyone."

"And ye dinna fight a dozen men?"

He closed one eye and looked into her blue ones with the other. "No," he said without intending to. "No, I didn't fight a dozen men. I didn't even fight one."

"Hmm." Her hair shone. She plucked at yellow blades of grass. "I like ye, Max Rossmara."

"You're passable yourself, Kirsty Mercer."

"Hmm." She wrinkled her nose. "Ella . . . Lady Avenall's even more beautiful than when she wasna' Lord Avenall's wife."

"Ella's beautiful," Max said, and felt the twist of self-disgust that had become his frequent companion. "And good. And brave. Saber's not so bad, either."

"He's bonnie," Kirsty said. "Ye've a verra bonnie family. My da and ma say as much a' the time."

"They're right," Max agreed. "Bonnie and honorable."

"And kind," Kirsty said, never taking her gaze from him. "Ye're all kind. I love ye all. Even the old one who makes me scairt."

"The dowager?" Max tweaked her chin and smiled. "She's the best. And we all love ye, too." He glanced around. Uncle Arran and Aunt Grace sat with their children under the wide branches of an oak at the foot of the rise where Max and Kirsty lay. Uncle Calum and Aunt Pippa walked, arm-in-arm, down steps from a terrace beneath one of the castle towers. Papa and Mama were on their way from the lodge to join the rest of the family for a picnic.

When he'd last seen Great-Grandmama, she'd been arguing with Blanche Bastible about a bonnet.

Who knew where Ella and Saber were, except they were together? They were always together.

"Elizabeth grows tall," Grace, Marchioness of Stonehaven, said. "I believe she will escape the curse of being as short as her mother." The company of her husband and children never failed to fill her with peace and joy.

Arran put a powerful arm around her shoulders and pulled her against his shoulder. He leaned against the oak. "If Elizabeth resembles her mother in any manner, she is favored," he told Grace. "She has your fair hair."

"And your green eyes, my lord."

"We are fortunate in our three children. But, above all, I am blessed in you."

She kissed his cheek. "I painted you again yesterday."

"Oh, no!" He drew away from her and pretended to curl up as if in pain. "No, no, say it isn't true!"

"Arran Rossmara, you are a beast!" She pummeled his broad back and the children came, running and shrieking at the prospect of a family romp. "Behave yourself, Arran. Calum and Pippa are walking in this direction. And the others will be here soon enough."

He caught her around the waist and swept her to her back on the grass. Elizabeth, Niall, and two-year-old James entered the fray.

"I don't suppose we shall see Ella and Saber too soon," Arran said, his green eyes flashing as they did when he looked at her and thought of private times. "They have more sense."

"More sense? I painted you and you laughed at me. I shall not be easily diverted."

"I shall look forward to seeing your latest *representational* painting of me. Do I bear the customary gold adornment?"

Grace smiled. "You do indeed."

"Well," Arran said. "Since you insist upon painting me naked, and in paying particular homage to what you must consider to be my best feature, one hopes you have done it justice."

Grace contrived to steal a covert squeeze of the "feature" he mentioned.

Arran bared his teeth. "Have a care, my sweet, or you will embarrass us both. On second thoughts, don't have a care. Be carefree."

"As you say," Grace agreed. "But I've just discovered something that must be set straight at once."

"And what might that be?" He gathered her in one arm and sat up. With his other arm, he surrounded their three small children.

"Hello, Calum!" Grace called. "Hello, Pippa. Come and join us." To Arran she whispered, "I shall have to retouch the painting. I've obviously grossly underestimated your *best feature.*"

He laughed aloud. "We'd best collect ourselves. The clan is about to come together."

"Where *are* Ella and Saber?" Grace said.

"They'll be along," Arran told her. "With eyes only for each other. And wherever they are, you can be sure they're together."

Calum, Duke of Franchot, drew his duchess to a halt some way distant from Arran, Grace, and their children. "We should let the boys catch up, Pippa." At three and two, William and Charles were fiercely independent and liked to make their own way. They had negotiated the flights of stone steps to the lawns but were diverted by something to which William pointed.

"Oh, *bother*," Pippa said. "Look at him. Falling into a flower bed already. That child cannot curb his curiosity for a moment."

"I seem to recall that his mother has always been adventurous." Pippa had never hesitated to embark on lone journeys through their estates in Cornwall. He held her arm more tightly beneath his. "But I don't think your venturesome nature is what I like best about you."

She folded her hands on his forearm and swung away. "My coquettishness? That's it, isn't it? You love the way I flirt." When she laughed, her deep-blue eyes sparkled and he was once again enraptured by the dramatic contrast to her dark hair. "Calum? Isn't that what you like best about me?"

Overwhelmed by his feelings for her, he drew her close and rested his chin atop her head. "If that was what I liked best, there would be precious little else to like."

"I like everything about you, Calum. I always have."

"You once didn't like my temper."

"You needed your temper—and your fearlessness. I know that now."

Calum studied Pippa's face. "What I love most about you is your gentleness. Your gentleness has made me a gentler man, a more thoughtful man."

"Only a strong man dares to be gentle," she said, smiling at him.

He glanced past her. "Struan and Justine have arrived. Ah, how good it is to be gathered together here."

"Mmm. I wonder where Ella and Saber are?"

"Who knows." Turning her toward Arran and Grace beneath the great oak, he steered her onward once again. "Although we do know they're together. They're always together."

Her only mistake had been to wait, to wait even the short time she had waited before traveling to Scotland—and to Struan. Lady Justine, Viscountess Hunsingore, laughed, and steadied herself as the carriage drew to a halt.

"And what amuses you so, my dear?" her darkly handsome husband asked. "When you chuckle like that, I wonder if you have some secret you have kept from me."

She looked at him from beneath thick lashes. "Oh, I do. A great secret."

Struan leaped to the ground, caught her by the waist, and lifted her from the carriage they used to travel between the castle and the hunting lodge where they made their home. He reached back inside to pick up tiny Sarah and to help two-year-old Edward to the driveway.

"I shall not press you for your secrets, Justine. I have learned the folly of imposing my will—trying to impose my will upon yours."

"Such a clever man I married," she told him. "Because you are so clever, I'll share the reason for my laughter. It's because I'm happier than I ever thought possible. And I laughed at myself for being such a goose."

"A goose?" He looked at her sharply.

She inclined her head. "For ever allowing you to leave Cornwall without me—after we first met. And then for not following you to Scotland immediately."

Struan remembered the night when she'd arrived, declaring that she had come simply to "help" him. How quickly that had changed. "But you did follow," he said. "I choose to thank God for that. Otherwise, I should have been forced to hunt you down myself. So much more of a chore."

This time they laughed together, and turned together at the sound of a hard little cough. The dowager, with Blanche at her shoulder, stood a short distance away.

"Grandmama!" Justine said. "What an—incredible bonnet." More gray than black, the brocade creation all but trembled with the weight of jet and crystal beads suspended beneath the brim.

The dowager raised her head, causing the dangling decorations to bobble. "There, Blanche. I was right. Justine has always had the most marvelous taste in all things, and *she* thinks this bonnet suitable."

Justine turned away in time to hide her smile. "It looks as if we shall be the last to arrive," she said when she could control her voice. "They're all over there under Grace's oak."

Struan adjusted his grip on Sarah and let Edward run toward the lawns. "Not Saber and Ella."

"No. No, you're right. They will come—when they remember." She shook her head. "How those two do live for one another."

"For and through one another," he agreed. "And how grateful we are for that. They are inseparable."

Saber and Ella stood at a window in Revelation, the tower that had been Arran's bachelor quarters, but which he now shared with Grace.

"I love Scotland," Ella said.

Saber hid a smile. "I'm surprised to hear you say as much."

"You know—" Ella pursed her lips and poked his ribs. "You fun me, Saber. I suppose you mean that I 'say as much' far too often."

"There is nothing you say that I would not listen to as often as you wish to say it," he told her, pleased with his own charming repartee. "I love Scotland too. How could I not love it when it means so much to you?"

"You, sir," she said, narrowing her eyes and pointing at him, "are a silver-tongued rogue."

"Only with you, my love, only with you."

She turned to look through the windows. "We should join the others."

"Surely we have time—"

"No," she broke in tartly. "We do *not* have time. You, husband, are insatiable."

"And what a trial that must be for you."

She threw her arms around his neck and kissed him. Ella kissed him until he feared they might be forced to delay going outside.

When he slipped his hands from her waist to her bottom and pulled her against him, she placed her fists firmly on his shoulders and arched away. "In case you forget the event, my lord, we are barely out of our bed—again."

"Haven't forgotten," he said, nuzzling her neck, licking the hollow above her collarbone—and the soft rise of her breasts. "Unforgettable."

"In that case—"

"Repeatable."

"I beg your pardon?"

"Unforgettably repeatable."

"Saber, we have to—"

"Repeatably unforgettable."

"Repeatably isn't a word." Giggling, she fell against him. "We are supposedly taking a stroll to collect ourselves before presenting our faces to the others. I suggest we continue—and quickly."

"We could do the other quickly."

"You are *impossible*."

"Thingie," Saber said, chuckling deep in his throat. "A quick thingie?"

"You horror! I've made a monster of you."

Saber grew still. He framed her face and checked every beloved feature. "You took a monster and made him human, marvelously human. You made me believe in myself again. You made me seek the light when I would have sunk deeper and deeper into the darkness. I truly believed I was doomed to madness."

Her expression grew serious. "Only by confronting the darkness could we hope to take away its sting, Saber."

"I wish I could completely chase away the specters."

"Perhaps they will disappear one day. Meanwhile, you have me at your side to help you. And the episodes grow fewer and fewer."

His smile spread from the inside. Saber felt its warmth engulf him, and saw Ella's eyes glow with reflected pleasure. "We went through hell, you and I," he told her.

"And we escaped," she said. "I try not to think of the past—particularly not—"

"Not of what happened to you at Lushbottam's? When you were a child, or when our enemies were unmasked?" They had made a pact never to avoid the events that had all but destroyed them both. "We have the future to look to now, Ella."

"It will wait." Ella caught his hand and pulled him. When he held his ground, she scowled and yanked harder. "The past is over but not forgotten. The future is to be anticipated and planned for. It is the present in which we live, my love."

"Hmm. And in the present our company is expected elsewhere?"

"Indeed. So, if you will allow me to lead you, my love?"

Reluctantly, grinning at the effort she expended, Saber did allow his wife to urge him, step by step, toward their appointment with the family.

When they emerged from the tower into the sunshine, he whirled Ella back into his arms and kissed her soundly. "A pact, beloved," he said. "Can we make a pact?"

"Name it. They are all watching."

"And enjoying every moment. Our pact shall be: Together, forever."

Ella grew still. She raised her eyes to his. "Forever together, beloved."